# YOUNG PATTULLO

BY THE SAME AUTHOR:

*Novels*
MARK LAMBERT'S SUPPER
THE GUARDIANS
A USE OF RICHES
THE MAN WHO WON THE POOLS
THE LAST TRESILIANS
AN ACRE OF GRASS
THE AYLWINS
VANDERLYN'S KINGDOM
AVERY'S MISSION
A PALACE OF ART
MUNGO'S DREAM
THE GAUDY

*Short Stories*
THE MAN WHO WROTE DETECTIVE
STORIES
CUCUMBER SANDWICHES

# J. I. M. Stewart

# YOUNG PATTULLO

A Novel

LONDON
VICTOR GOLLANCZ LTD
1975

ISBN 0 575 01940 9

*Printed in Great Britain by*
*The Camelot Press Ltd, Southampton*

A Staircase in Surrey

\*   \*

YOUNG PATTULLO

# I

For my generation, or rather for my age-group in the narrow sense of the call-up, sudden death remained to the end of the war at a substantial remove. Short of random annihilation from the sky (of which there was little in Edinburgh), we were assured of life until enlisted, and almost assured of it through the further months required for our training in one form of combat or another. We were still in the enjoyment of at least the tail-end of this security when, quite suddenly, it was all over. The bell had sounded, the winning glove been raised in air, and the contenders were back in their corners being mopped up.

For us it had been a spectator sport; we had simply kept our seats. But boys who had been little more than a year ahead of us, with whom we had played in the same eleven or fifteen and whose successors we had become as prefects and the like, had endured the counting of their remaining days in missions, knowing what the statistics said. When we realized we had got off we professed not to believe it. Badly as modern history was taught us, we said, we had picked up too much of it to be taken in. Vast convulsions don't abruptly cease at the sounding of a gong. After a great war come nasty little ones all over the globe. If we weren't booked for curtains above Normandy or Berlin we could still be sure of some lethal occasion in swamps or jungles or arctic snows. Somewhere the Japanese would go on fighting and fighting and fighting, or somewhere else the British government would decide to support a white army against a red one—or, failing that, a red one against a white.

These were persuasions bred of guilt at having escaped rather than of clear thought. Seventeen and eighteen, or even seventeen and nineteen, are virtually the same age. So, like

Achilles, we had been hiding among women while great things were going on, and we'd have felt better had they continued long enough to allow us a brief whiff of them. But although fighting did persist in one corner of the globe or another, very few of us indeed were to be drawn into it. What lay ahead was post-war National Service, which meant being rapidly turned into imitation officers on some god-forsaken Perthshire moor or—more exotically—at Oswestry or Mons. And even this, if we passed the right examinations and got into the right university, we might have the choice of deferring until after we had taken a degree.

Such was my situation when I unexpectedly won my scholarship. In any circumstances the prospect of Oxford might have alarmed me, and the few days I spent there writing my papers and being interviewed revealed in addition one exacerbating consequence of being an artist's son. My father had chosen the college at which I was to compete entirely on the score of its visual appeal, after a perambulation of the city in which he had turned down even Magdalen as architecturally not quite up to the mark. So I found myself scribbling furiously amid surroundings which showed to my provincial sense as oppressively august, and as quite without that hint of the modestly domestic which I detected during my more or less furtive prowlings, each afternoon, through the quadrangles of Oriel, Jesus, St Edmund Hall, and similar foundations of what might be called the middling sort. I had been tumbled, I told myself, into a haunt of the most shattering privilege, like a beggar upon whom some trick is played in a folk-tale. My fellow-postulants at the long tables in the college's lofty hall were the sons of dukes and earls to a man. Or, rather, to a boy, since the notion that we were men didn't occur to me.

So convinced was I of this that I found myself taking comfort from what my brother Ninian termed the Glencorry connection. It was an ignoble resource. One has to be true to one's order, and my order was my father's. It was because he was a painter that I was going to be a playwright. Whereas the

Glencorrys were—next after our Pattullo uncle, the minister in Aberdeenshire—the principal figures of fun in Ninian's and my own family zoo. It was pitiful that I should seek to derive confidence from Uncle Rory simply because he wrote letters to *The Scotsman* (on the iniquities of hydro-electric schemes and anything else that might make sense of the Highlands) signed *Roderick Glencorry of Glencorry*—to which he would have liked to add, had convention permitted, *twenty-second of that Ilk*, intimating thereby that the Glencorrys had sat tight through several centuries on the same tumps of heather.

When I became conscious of this frailty (for I was still concocting answers to a paper ambitiously entitled 'Outlines of English Literary History') I shoved into an answer, whether appositely or not, a couplet of Dryden's which says something about *a successive title, long and dark, Drawn from the mouldy rolls of Noah's Ark*. I can't be certain that it wasn't this display of erudition that won the heart of my future tutor, Albert Talbert, and resulted in my being informed by telegram a few days later that I had become the college's next John Ruskin Scholar.

It was with a duke's or earl's son—or at least with a boy from a school catering for such people—that I had some conversation during the days in which this faintly absurd examination was going on. His name was Stumpe, which didn't sound particularly ducal but at least was as old as John Aubrey. (For I must record that, at that time, I had acquired a respectable amount of totally random reading: something which conceivably emerged as meritorious in one grappling with the Outlines of English Literary History in three hours by the clock.)

Stumpe explained to me, during the drinking—cautiously, on my own part—of a pint of beer in the bar of the Mitre Hotel, that for us it was pretty well an open award or nothing: this because of all those bloody men back from the war. I hadn't thought about that aspect of the competition, and Stumpe had to amplify. There were several categories of such people, and the college was bound to find room for them ahead of us. Some had been in residence for a year or more before being whisked away to fight, and now the fortunate survivors among them would be coming back. Others, known for some reason as cadets, had been sent up to Oxford as an obscure temporary expedient, and with little regard paid to either their intellectual or their social eligibility; the unmassacred among these would also be returning. A third lot—about whom Stumpe seemed a shade less censorious—would be as new to Oxford as ourselves, having done no more than secure places in the college before being called up. The whole crowd were bound to be as bumptious as hell. But at least they wouldn't stand for being treated as kids—not after years of having got drunk when they pleased and sleeping with no end of women as well. So there was bound to be a general loosening up, and those of us who did get in straight from school would benefit from sundry resulting freedoms.

I listened to Stumpe respectfully, and even ventured to express my appreciation of his society through the offer of a second pint of beer. To my relief he declined this, pointing out that it would be embarrassing if, during the afternoon paper, we had several times to ask leave to go to the loo. (I was hearing this word, I believe, for the first time.) We might meet again that evening, he suggested, and go round a few pubs. He would probably bring along a couple of friends.

The proposal was quite agreeable to me. With each paper I wrote it seemed that my chances of establishing any permanent connection with Oxford were becoming steadily slimmer, and if as a result of some drastic introduction to intemperate courses I performed yet more feebly on the following day— well, it wasn't going to matter a bit. But I might as well study the natives during my brief English foray, and Stumpe was sufficiently unfamiliar to me to represent quite promising material for a page in my journal. I had recently taken to keeping a diary thus entitled—inspired, I imagine, by the marathon performance of Arnold Bennett a decade or so before. Stumpe's friends might yield something as well.

The proposed conviviality didn't, however, happen. As we went in to dinner in hall Stumpe drifted past me unregarding and sat down at a remote table. Afterwards he just vanished. I was disappointed by this—the more so since the boy I sat beside didn't utter a word to me throughout the meal. I comforted myself by observing that he appeared to be of an uncommunicative temperament in general, for in reply to a question addressed to him by somebody on his other hand he uttered the one word 'Downside' with freezing curtness, and remained completely silent thereafter. He struck me as most disagreeable, and I even blamed him for sending me back to my room in a gloomy mood of my own.

The room itself was gloomy, being situated on the ground floor of Rattenbury. This is the Victorian part of the college, and a guidebook had told me (as my own sensibilities would have done) that it is inferior in aesthetic pretension to the other buildings. I now managed to manufacture a grievance out of this. It was because I was judged of inferior pretension myself that I had been thrust into so bleak and ill-proportioned an apartment, through the inadequate windows of which the summer dusk could be viewed only between the interstices of much pseudo-mediaeval wrought-iron, rather as if I had been incarcerated like Bonivard, or Faustus's unfortunate girl-friend in the opera. The room felt, for some reason, quite as damp and chilly as I imagined the castle of Chillon to be; its lighting was crepuscular; and I was facing it after a meal which had been meagre and unappetizing beyond even the standards of that time. Here, at least, there wasn't much that was august in evidence. The scanty furniture included numerous empty bookshelves, a Medici print of a droopy Corot tree, and a large fly-blown lampshade in tattered pink silk. On a table covered with an ink-stained serge cloth lay my open notebooks: a sprawl of puerile appraisals of Milton and Fielding and Hardy. It was beyond me to take another glance at them. I sat down and sombrely considered what Stumpe had said.

His notion of a licentious returned soldiery behind whose

bayonets, as it were, we might ourselves advance upon emancipated pleasures didn't stir my imagination at all. I believed that if I did fluke a place at Oxford I should there work very hard indeed—a conviction stemming from the view (later to be considerably modified) that the study of literature at a university is the best preparation for becoming a writer. But much more important than this was the fact that I was in love.

I was—to use the word my mother would have liked—'romantically' in love: to the extent, indeed, of having existed for some months in that state of enchantment sheerly through the eye which Romeo was obliged to endure for several minutes before engaging Juliet in the extemporaneous composition of a sonnet. I had not yet so much as spoken to the beautiful Janet Finlay. Indeed, since I simply sat in front of her in church, and since she there seemed wholly indisposed either to join in the hymns or audibly to repeat the Lord's Prayer, I couldn't have sworn that she was not both deaf and dumb. Such intense states of feeling, bred entirely in the imagination, and in their inception floating free of any specific erotic design, can appear merely bizarre in retrospect. But this one was potent with me, so that Stumpe's remark about sleeping with no end of women passed me by as foolishness—as it might not have done some years later.

What chiefly depressed me in recalling Stumpe's remarks was the suggestion of a barrier, in age and experience and interests, between myself and a majority of the people with whom—if I had unexpected luck—I should be living at Oxford. At school, although not myself much of a games-player, I had tended to make my friends among the athletically inclined. This was partly because they were nicer to look at than the stars of the Classical Sixth. But it was partly because I owned an undisciplined mind, and disliked more industrious and successful boys whom, in my conceit, I judged to be no cleverer than I was. So I was consciously rather short of mental stimulus, and had just lately been reckoning (not altogether erroneously) that in an Oxford college heterodox characters like myself would be rather thicker on the ground. And now I couldn't imagine that men three or four years senior to me —and back from anything so tremendous as a war—would be disposed to pay me the slightest attention. This was to turn out a misconception in itself. Moreover it ignored the possibility that the knowledgeable Stumpe, although broadly right about his facts, had got the proportions of the coming set-up wrong. Actually, the intake of schoolboys was going to be quite large. I might have guessed as much had I reflected on how many of them had been encouraged to have a go at the current set of examinations.

As it was, I spent half-an-hour sunk in despondency. I was still despondent when I heard a knock on my door. That anybody should thus civilly apply for admission to my presence was disconcerting in itself. Nobody ever knocked at a door of mine—except occasionally my Uncle Rory during my summer holidays at Corry, when he had taken it into his head, at some hideously early hour, that I ought to be out and scouring the heather in the interest of my health. On these occasions I would reply from beneath the bed-clothes—and often, I am afraid, as sulkily as was at all prudent in the light of my uncle's exigent standard of the manners proper in the young. But now I called out confidently enough. It was Stumpe who entered the room.

'Oh, hullo,' Stumpe said. 'Do you mind if I come in? Or are you mugging up for tomorrow?'

'No, of course not.' As I said this I felt rather ashamed of my open notebooks. 'Do sit down.'

'Oh, good. Missed you in hall.'

'Yes. I'm afraid there's nothing to drink in this room.' I offered the apology out of some vague sense of the canons of academic hospitality. 'Not even the end of a tin of cocoa, as far as I can see.'

'I've had a drink, thanks. I went over to the Bulldog with a Colleger. He was a bit of a bore.'

'I see.' I wondered whether a Colleger was Stumpe's equivalent to a star of the Classical Sixth. 'Clever of you to run me to earth.'

'One of the porters knew.'

'They seem a knowing crowd.'

'Lord, yes. Never forget a face, and so on. Recognize your crumbling features after thirty years. Like royals and the idle classes generally.'

There was a short silence, in which I felt I had shown an inadequate sense of the sophisticated character of Stumpe's last observation.

'It wasn't much of a dinner,' I said.

'Not fit for the cat. I say, what an awful room.'

'Yes, isn't it?'

'I expect I'll get rooms in Surrey Quad if they'll resign themselves to putting up with me at all. My grandfather had rooms there. My father never came up. He says he hadn't the right sort of brain. Did yours?' As he asked this question, Stumpe gave me an appraising glance.

'No. I had an uncle at New College, although I can't think he had the right sort of brain either. Surrey looks rather splendid.'

'Yes. It was built by Christopher Wren, just like St Paul's.' Stumpe offered this staggeringly erroneous information with complete confidence. 'But they say, as a matter of fact, that the baths are better over here in Rattenbury.'

'That's something.'

I felt our conversation wasn't going too well, being disjointed to the point of awkwardness. But Stumpe seemed quite contented. He wasn't a fool—he was, in fact, going to win some sort of exhibition—and I think his thus dropping in on me was respectably motivated by genuine intellectual curiosity. Perhaps his grandfather had told him that at Oxford he should cultivate the advantage of rubbing up against all sorts. His next question lent support to this conjecture.

'I say—are you at some sort of day-school?'

'We're most of us day-boys.'

'And are there girls?'

'No—no girls.' Quite unjustifiably, I took this further demand for information as designedly insolent. 'I suppose there are girls at your school?' I asked.

'Of course there aren't.' This time, Stumpe really stared.

'Funny. I've always thought of it as one of those co-educational places.'

I was pleased with this, and expected it to produce indignation. Some loose association of ideas, however, had prompted Stumpe's mind to move elsewhere—as now transpired in a startling manner.

'I say,' he said, 'have you ever had a woman?'

'No, I haven't.'

This brisk admission produced another—and this time interesting—silence. Stumpe had, so to speak, moved into the round. Years afterwards, I would sometimes recall the occasion —this when a character whom I was labouring to create would suddenly behave *out* of character, and have to be reassessed as a result. At the moment I couldn't have said at all meaningfully that Stumpe was behaving out of character, since his character was something about which I knew nothing at all. I did have a sense, however, that in so abruptly raising an intimate matter he was at least acting out of type and out of turn. Whether this was indeed so I don't really know to this day. English school-boys may be less reticent than Scottish ones. On the whole, I judge that certain stresses of adolescence had endowed Stumpe with an interesting measure of eccentricity, at least in a temporary way.

'It's a worry,' Stumpe said. 'I mean, when to begin—and *how* to begin. One might leave it too long, and never get into the way of it at all. It's awfully risky holding out against nature, wouldn't you say? There's some word for what can happen—atropos or something.'

'I suppose Atropos might take a disabling snip at you with her shears, and altogether spoil your matrimonial chances. But atrophy's the word you want.'

15

'That's right—atrophy.' Stumpe was unresentful of my didactic tone. 'A mental sort of atrophy rather than a physical perhaps. A man *can* run off the rails, you know. It's a bit alarming. I can tell you I have some damned odd fantasies when it comes to quiet half-hours with sex. Flage, and all that. Do you?'

Stumpe had produced a word unknown to me, rhyming with 'badge'. It must have been straight from the mint, but I sufficiently got the idea to be inwardly scandalized. Not in our closest moments could Ninian and I have conducted such a conversation with each other, and I didn't know that it is characteristically with total strangers that obsessed persons are liable to take such plunges. But I felt I mustn't put up the shutters on Stumpe, nor indeed did I want to. If not impressive he was at least serious. Most of the sex-talk I heard at school was smut, and to be responded to with sniggers. So I answered Stumpe's last question and several more. Within a quarter of an hour a curious effect of warmth and intimacy had established itself between us. One part of my head knew that it bore a factitious character. Still, there was no vice in it.

'I have a cousin who believes that an actress is the thing,' Stumpe said. 'Actresses have the temperament. Of course, it would have to be an unimportant one—for a start, I mean.'

'You might work your way up.'

Stumpe laughed loudly at this—a reaction which, for a moment, surprised me.

'But I have another cousin,' he went on, 'who says that actresses are an Edwardian idea, and that it can be pretty well any girl one meets at a dance. But—do you know?—I somehow don't fancy that. It doesn't seem quite the thing. And she might be a virgin, after all—which would be a frightful responsibility.'

'But mayn't some actresses—young ones, of course—be virgins too?'

'That's perfectly true.' Stumpe now looked at me admiringly. 'As a matter of fact, there's a chap in my house whose father

16

owns several theatres. And he says that quite a lot of actresses are pure.'

Stumpe had uttered this last word awkwardly. It was clearly a sacred one, hazily associated with close female relatives, and it produced a shift in our talk. I found this a relief, since by way of playing fair I had passingly offered a number of confidences a good deal against the grain.

'Are there any theatres in Scotland?' Stumpe asked.

As a transitional passage this displayed enviable conversational virtuosity compensating for its revelation of a not too well-stocked mind. The theatre was already in my blood, and it was at some length that I put Stumpe right. He bore it very well. He was willing to learn. This made it odd that he was emerging from a famous school so lavishly furnished with ignorance. But no doubt there were whole regions of discourse, wholly unknown to me, in which he was well clued up.

We returned to the subject of Oxford entrance, and he once more produced his phrase about bloody men back from the war. It almost looked as if there was another obsession here. I didn't myself know quite what to think about men back from the war. Some of them could be called bloody, I supposed, in the sense in which the term is applicable to the sergeant at the beginning of *Macbeth*. There would have been times when they staggered to their feet after a shell-burst and found themselves smothered in the stuff. That surely entitled them to be regarded as heroes. Yet I recognized this as a conventional and tribal idea which didn't, for good or ill, find much of an echo in my heart. We had at school a shocking institution known as a punishment run. It was supposed to be an enlightened and humane substitute for a beating—although in fact it could include quite a whack of that from bigger boys strategically located *en route*. In any case, you arrived back from it pretty shagged, so that your fellows awkwardly avoided your eye. Ninian when a prefect had once taken a token swipe at me on such an occasion, and for a time it had rankled between us. I now discovered that I saw men back from the war as in a similar whipped and hounded category. They had been given a gruelling time. And what it had done for their dispositions was anybody's guess.

Stumpe wouldn't agree about the gruelling time. He saw most repatriated warriors in a light that was to become fashionable in novels about ten years later. They had sat on their arses in offices, intriguing against each other in any way they could, and been intermittently dined and wined by uncles and aunts high enough up to be immune against the rationing and so on imposed upon the vulgar herd. And now they were going to be all round us in the college—supposing, once more, that we got in. They might even be accorded preferential treatment in such vital matters as being given rooms in Surrey.

'Have you by any chance had a brother up here?' Stumpe asked. The question, which came abruptly, had brought him oddly to his feet.

I told him that I hadn't. Ninian—although I didn't add this —had achieved the glory of shaping to be in the Royal Marines Commandos, and there was certainly to have been no arse-sitting in that. But the gong had gone. Ninian was already back in Edinburgh, studying law.

'Have you?' I asked.

'Yes. My brother Charles.'

'Will he be coming up again?'

'No, he won't.' Stumpe had reached the door, and his hand was on the knob. 'He was killed at Salerno, as a matter of fact. They blew his head off. Do you know? I think I'll try a bath. Good night.'

I tried a bath myself. If the baths in Rattenbury were really superior to those in Surrey, then the baths in Surrey must be museum pieces of no common sort. But the war had at least accustomed me to a maximum of five inches of hot water, and here the stuff was in unexpectedly abundant supply. The boy who had snapped out 'Downside' so disobligingly was having a bath too. Nude and steaming, we stared at each other without acknowledgement through doors that had come off their hinges. If I didn't myself utter, it was because I had already decided he was an uncivil character I wouldn't care for.

But first impressions can be fallacious. In the following October, when Stumpe and I had both come into residence, we occasionally addressed a word or two to one another in the quad—perhaps with a shade of embarrassment, although I can recall nothing of the sort. Later we made do with a passing nod. Finally—and with the true undergraduate ability simply to rub out false starts—we ceased to bother even with this. But the boy from Downside was Tony Mumford, who was to become my best friend.

## II

Dᴜʀɪɴɢ ᴛʜᴇ ʟᴀᴛᴛᴇʀ part of that summer I was despatched to Corry Hall on a longer holiday than usual. Unlike my parents and my Edinburgh acquaintance in general, Uncle Rory and Aunt Charlotte saw nothing remarkable in my being booked for Oxford. My uncle merely judged it—on grounds which were for some time obscure to me—anomalous that I should be going to the college of my father's picturesquely arbitrary choice. A place at New College, he maintained, would have represented the correct ordering of the matter. He appeared to have forgotten—if, indeed, he had ever noticed—that Oxford undergraduates are divided into scholars and commoners, and that a boy who has gained an open award at a particular college is obliged to take up residence in it. His sense of the situation appeared to be that I was still free to choose. Arrived at the railway station, I had only to direct a taxi-driver to take me to whatever college I liked, and so settle the matter. It lay with me to say 'New College', be driven down the tortuous lane leading to the obscure portal of that magnificent foundation, and there ask to be shown into the presence of its Warden—whereupon the details of my sojourn would at once be determined.

This vision of current academic life was my first intimation that, since my last visit, Uncle Rory had been going increasingly dotty. But an element of reason always lurks in madness, and presently I worked it out. My uncle (as I had told Stumpe) had himself been at New College. This was because, at the time, his elder brother, the heir of the Glencorrys, was still alive. New College was the proper college for younger sons—and so, by an extension of the hereditary principle, for scions in a general way. My own destined college was for eldest sons.

So what my father had contrived was subversive of the settled order of things, and to be regarded as a legacy of the indiscretion which had prompted my mother to marry a person whose origins were totally obscure.

Thus baldly stated, these facts do my uncle an injustice. So far as I can tell, he had never, since the day he first acknowledged his sister's marriage, treated my father other than with respect. He would probably have observed the same propriety had my mother married a grocer or a plumber. But there also harboured in him, I believe, a dim sense that something called Art held a licensed place in what I was soon to hear lecturers call the Great Chain of Being, and that it was proper that its practitioners should be accorded moderate notice by their betters. Confronted by the colour-print after Corot in that dismal Rattenbury room, he would have been unable to pronounce with confidence that it was not an original oil-painting by Poussin or Rubens. But had somebody driven Poussin or Rubens up to Corry and introduced him as a well-regarded artist, my uncle would not have hesitated in putting his hand to the decanter with his best sherry.

There could be no doubt that he was turning a little odd. Corry Hall is a largish nineteenth-century mansion by David Bryce. Contrived in the Scottish baronial style, and for some reason smothered in whitewash from basement to roof, it is reputed to hold encapsulated within itself a structure known as Duff's Tower and dating from the year 1264. Both Ninian and I had put in many hours hunting for this antiquity, and as our skill in trigonometry and solid geometry grew we became increasingly confident that nowhere in the building could there be an area of more than some three square feet which we were unable to account for. Duff's Tower had thus to be regarded as no longer other than notional—a conclusion we refrained from communicating to our uncle, fearing that he might be considerably upset. For Duff's Tower—or rather its date—was important to him. Corry Hall is like a miniaturized version of Blair Castle, which is also the work of Bryce. But Cumming's

Tower in that more exalted dwelling is supposed to date only from 1269, and upon this flimsy chronological structure Uncle Rory based the contention that the Glencorrys were of a higher antiquity than the Murrays, and indeed than the antecedent Stewart line of the earls of Atholl themselves.

I don't think that my uncle would ever have spoken with positive disrespect of a Duke of Atholl, any more than he would of my father, or—for that matter—of the fishwife for insulting whom he had once so famously caned Ninian. But whenever he uttered the name 'James Atholl' (which was apparently the correct manner in which to refer to a duke with whom one familiarly passed the time of day) his tone suggested that, whatever the present man might be like, the further back you went among the Murrays the more dubious a crowd did you find yourself rubbing shoulders with.

Pursuing this virtually dynastic contention, Uncle Rory had recently taken up genealogical and historical studies for the pursuit of which neither his abilities nor his acquirements equipped him. He was, it might be crudely said, as uninformed as his wife and even less intelligent. But this is again unfair to my uncle, considered simply as a human being. To my aunt, although I suppose she was a harmless woman, I never kindled; there was nothing about her that could be identified and held on to as hinting either character or personality; my uncle might have rummaged her at random out of a gigantic deep-freeze labelled *Upper-class Englishwomen: Standard Model*. It is true that Uncle Rory himself might also be viewed as a stereotype, but he was a more sympathetic figure than Aunt Charlotte. The mental stock-in-trade of the one was as limited and frequently absurd as that of the other. Uncle Rory, however, had a beguiling extravagance which was denied his wife.

These are not conclusions that have come to me only in maturity. In their essentials, my earliest holidays at Corry revealed them to me. In particular, I think I was always aware of the touch of sacred strangeness in Uncle Rory. The Glencorrys may be guessed to have a history of mental instability,

22

for the family legends are full of ghosts, of 'callings', of the second sight, which are probably mythologized equivalents of intermittent neurotic vagary. The liability emerged in my mother. It was because she was nervously unwell that my present stay at Corry was planned to last throughout September.

Later in that month—my uncle told me shortly after my arrival—the duke would be 'putting on his show' at the Highland Gathering at Blair Atholl. The expression, which if not disrespectful was at least sardonic, referred to the duke's custom of opening this annual athletic occasion by marching on to the field at the head of the Atholl Highlanders. For a reason to which I shall come, we ourselves failed to attend the Gathering, so I don't know whether this feudal manifestation actually took place. It was certainly a regular occurrence at a slightly earlier time, and it may still happen today. Chronology was not my uncle's strong point. He had the utmost difficulty in remembering just what stretch of years is indicated by such a term as 'the seventeenth century'. It is an uncertainty conceivable in the mind of a cultivated Italian when studying British history, but disabling in a Scottish laird developing antiquarian interests.

I have heard that dukes as a class each individually possess some privilege permitted to no other subject of the crown. According to the Glencorry (which is the style under which Uncle Rory liked to hear himself referred to) James Atholl's unique distinction was that of being permitted to retain a standing army, and the regiment which followed him on parade beneath the windows of Blair Castle was precisely that. Whether this was indeed the case, I again don't know. I am writing of long ago; the twentieth century had not yet reached its middle term; even so, it seems probable that no practical significance even then continued to attach to the matter. But it held great significance for my uncle. His researches inclined him to the view that this ducal prerogative stemmed from the circumstance that the Murrays of Tullibardine had at one time been sovereigns of the Isle of Man. But the history of the Menavian islands is of a complexity equalled only by its obscurity, and Uncle Rory had somehow arrived at the conclusion that forebears of his own had been prepotent there round about the time of King Gorse. From this he moved on to the persuasion that King Gorse (or perhaps King Orry—if, indeed, Kings Gorse and Orry were not identical) was a character from whom he was himself lineally descended. At this point I suppose it would have been possible for the uncharitable to declare that my uncle was already far gone in lunacy. He managed to go a little further simply by persuading himself that he was thereby entitled to a standing army too. He was putting in quite a lot of time designing a uniform for it. I have recorded elsewhere that he disapproved of what he called the invention of the kilt; and for this reason his men were to appear in galligaskins. They would have looked rather like a Papal Guard.

All this was as harmless as the ploys of another uncle, famous in *Tristram Shandy*. And with the Glencorry the hobby-horse was ridden more intermittently than by Uncle Toby. The obsession merely came on him from time to time. What Aunt Charlotte made of it I don't know. She had been brought up in a stockbroker belt in the Home Counties, and had not subsequently armed herself with much knowledge of Scottish history. The only field in which she might have been declared possessed of any historiographical expertness was that of the Wimbledon championships; what she didn't know about Suzanne Lenglen and similar monarchs of the tennis-court wasn't worth knowing. She would have been inclined, I feel, to judge her husband by what she could pick up of his neighbours' opinion of him. But Corry Hall scarcely enjoyed a neighbourhood in the English sense, whether of a town or county order. And the people who did come around, if not precisely like Uncle Rory, were at least more like Uncle Rory than like Aunt Charlotte. It is probable that they kept to themselves any unfavourable impression of the Glencorry's developing interests. They were nearly all kinsmen of his, in one degree or another.

My aunt's isolated situation, together with conservative persuasions less imaginative than my uncle's, had exerted a considerable influence on the upbringing of my two cousins, Anna and Ruth. Had Aunt Charlotte lived in South Kensington she might have tumbled to the fact that at least some trafficking with the spirit of the time was requisite in a mother concerned that her daughters should be adequately 'in the swim'— launched, that is, on a current likely to land a girl expeditiously on the shores of reputable matrimony. 'Nobody could be more broad-minded than I am,' she was fond of saying. 'I am entirely in favour of occasional tournaments in which we could actually *play* against the professionals. The cricketers do so, as everybody knows, and no harm has come of it. Only I will not tolerate modern ideas at Corry. It is fortunate that your uncle entirely agrees with me.' At this Uncle Rory would nod composedly, no doubt thinking that the kilt or the generating of electrical energy was being referred to. Actually, 'modern ideas' was a potent and comprehensive, if unexamined, concept. It included much dogma in the field of education, with the consequence that the virgin character of my cousins' minds was perpetually fascinating to me. The daughters of the surgeons and advocates, architects and accountants and professors, with whom Ninian and I were acquainted in Edinburgh, were commonly able to give us points on such matters as the aorist and the optative; and Janet Finlay, seldom for long out of my thoughts at that time, commanded more correct if less fluent French than my father. Anna and Ruth, who had been sent to some exclusive boarding-school in England, were innocent even of such 'accomplishments' as the Misses Pinkerton may be supposed to have laid on for Amelia Sedley and Becky Sharp in their academy on Chiswick Mall. They could neither sketch picturesque ruins nor play the piano. They certainly didn't understand the use of the globes.

25

These deficiencies need not have been crippling in themselves. My cousins had their natural place in a society not given to intellectual or artistic pursuits. But they were both senior to me by several years, and had been entitled to regard themselves as grown-up while the war was still going on. They could have driven staff cars, or learnt to shove model fighters and bombers about a table, or made themselves useful in any one among a number of auxiliary capacities. They would have gained a good deal of independence as a result, but there would have been involved assumptions about the company young women may properly keep—with whom they can go where, and when—acceptance of which would have meant that modern ideas were creeping in. What they did do my wartime holidays never revealed. What they did now was to lead a narrow and baffled life at home, cut off even from others of their own sort who were returning to not very different courses. They walked dogs, visited old women in the surrounding clachans, occasionally trailed out after men on a shoot, and discontentedly assisted in counting the number of creatures shot.

'Have the girls been out and around yet?' was a question which Uncle Rory never failed to ask at least once in the course of the day. It seemed to represent the full range of his curiosity about them, and he seldom showed any consciousness that their needs might exceed, or differ from, those to be postulated of a couple of well-bred spaniels. (Ninian said that Anna and Ruth had been inoculated in their youth against distemper, and that their discipline had been humanely achieved by means of taps on the nose with a rolled newspaper.) My aunt would reply, 'Anna is helping the minister to distribute *Life and Work*' or 'Ruth said she might walk to the head of the glen', and that would dismiss the matter. In fact, my cousins on the whole disliked outdoor activities, and spent much time in their rooms, or in obscure and chilly corners of the house, idly turning over *The Field* and *Scottish Country Life*, or engaged in the desultory reading of illicitly procured and mildly libidinous romances.

In my earlier times at Corry I had barely distinguished between them. Both were handsome rather heavy girls, who seldom had anything noteworthy to say; and if I didn't pay much attention to them they hardly ever paid any to me. I was too young to be of much interest—a fact which continued to hold true now that they were grown-up and I was nearly so. Perhaps because I had no sisters, I was inclined to extend over these girl cousins a species of sexual tabu, and this for long precluded what might otherwise have been a feasible fooling around. We seldom even romped together. Or at least I never romped with Ruth, who was the nearer to me in age. She was a solid sort of girl who never became, even to the most accidental touch of my hands, a sexual object at all. It turned out a little differently with Anna.

Most of my wanderings around Corry were solitary; its moors remain in my mind as the terrain of those thinking or dreaming walks in the course of which, I imagine, many more talented young men than myself have portentously brooded over their destiny. But through several summers I used to go, or be taken, on occasional tramps in my elder cousin's company. I would have a rucksack, heavy because of the enormous bottle of repellent mineral water with which Mountjoy, my uncle's factotum, insisted on providing us. Anna would have a shooting-stick. We might, or might not, be accompanied by suitable dogs. To my uncle or aunt we presented a wholesome and socially acceptable spectacle as we marched off from the house.

We had nothing to say to each other, and a casual spectator might have concluded that my only utility to the young lady lay in carrying the expedition's supplies. This would have been an error. Our engagement—Anna's and my own—usually took place either just before or just after our picnic. It was a crudely ritualized affair, and very uninventive. Commonly, we would affect a dispute over some casual object—an interesting chunk of granite or a bird's feather. This would lead into an episode of flight, pursuit, tackle, tumble, and full-scale wrestling-match. Anna—although, to her mother's sorrow, not athletically inclined—was a well-developed and powerful wench; I myself was not yet full-grown; commonly I had my work cut out to subdue her. It was stiff muscular effort and undeniably exciting. I can recall at this moment the strangeness of the mingled smell of my cousin and the heather. The contest ended when Anna's body—prone or supine—and all her limbs were firmly pinioned beneath my own. She would then say sharply, as to a troublesome child, 'Duncan, that's enough!' and I would release her and roll away, panting.

This phase in our relationship eventually petered out. I had learnt something about sensuality—and particularly that female sensuality had in my cousin Anna a notable exponent; in relation to her, in fact, I had an intuition of trouble ahead. If it was I who eventually called off these expeditions (which I take to be the possibly shameful truth) it was not from any primitive fear of incest: the tabu-element was not all that strong. Nor was it, I am afraid, the issue of moral feeling; rather it was controlled by quite shallow social awareness. Observation—the result of other walks taken elsewhere—had persuaded me that behaviour of this particular sort was a characteristically plebeian, as well as adolescent, method of securing sexual enjoyment. But what really browned me off was that conclusion to the affair whereby I was abruptly demoted from masterful youth to reproved small boy. So it was at about the time that the down on my cheek was yielding to stubble that this cock-teasing on my cousin's part came to an end. It left me not much affected—but, if anything, resentful rather than beholden. When at length at Corry an incredible event occurred I suffered the proper feelings in a more than proper degree. I was, in fact, shattered. At the same time I cannot be certain that I was left without an unamiable flicker of a thought to the effect that Anna had got what she was booked for.

These sexual episodes had been the more unedifying as

belonging to a period when I had no honest use for feminine society. I was still much taken up with a romantic attachment to a snub-nosed younger boy called Tommy Watt. Indeed, my passion for Tommy—round whose shoulders I never so much as put an arm—outlasted my tumblings with Anna, and came to an end only with his accidental death. The succeeding year or eighteen months, which brought me to the verge of going up to the university, must have been, developmentally, the most crowded of my life. In this last pre-Oxford holiday at Corry I was a different youth from what I had been hitherto. The fact was important only to myself. Nobody noticed it.

I was surprised that Anna didn't; that she seemed unaware of that subtler chemical change which turns boy into man not merely under a bathing-slip (I used to swim in a pool in the Corry, something which would have been regarded as indecorous in my cousins) but under his hat as well. (I had again brought my school cap, now finally to be abandoned, to Corry; something was still needed to doff to the tenants' and labourers' wives, and I should have felt a fool in a deerstalker borrowed from my uncle.) Anna appeared hardly aware of my presence at all. It would be misleading to describe her as withdrawn, since the term implies a cogitative habit behind a mask of passivity. But she would glance at me almost without recognition, and the conversation upon which her parents insisted at table seemed particularly a burden to her. It struck me that she too might be undergoing some process of maturation. What my father—whose French tended to the demotic at times—might have called her *nichons* were gaining in prominence.

That Ruth had known about her sister's employment of me in earlier years remains conjectural. If she had, she must have felt some prompting to challenge her own power of exciting me in the same way. She would have liked to know that she had at least the trick of it, to be exercised at will. But she never —it secretly annoyed me that she never—showed the slightest awareness of me as a physical presence. On the other hand, Ruth did now talk to me quite a lot, both during the dull

29

family meals and occasionally in tête-à-tête. She was more intelligent than Anna, even if equally uninformed, and she had seen that although I was too young, ineligible, and consanguineous for the purposes of matrimony, there was at least something to be said for me as a window on the outer world. Perhaps she was conscious of ignominy in being constrained to use a schoolboy in this way, and was compensating for such a feeling whenever, as frequently happened, her address to me took on a jeering tone. But this was commonly in private. To anything of the kind my uncle, however smothered in galligaskins, was remarkably sensitive. Whereas Aunt Charlotte would talk a good deal about persons being well-bred or ill-bred, Uncle Rory regarded such remarks as in themselves a token of dubious breeding, and would never himself utter them. But he was alert to actual bad manners. There was an occasion upon which he dismissed his grown-up younger daughter from table because she had mimicked the flat vowels that I would import into phrases like 'a vast castle'. It would have been the vowels that Aunt Charlotte frowned on.

Ruth's interest stepped up sharply when I mentioned (on the strength of Stumpe's conversation) that in college I was to be surrounded by young men a good deal older than myself. The notion of a large undergraduate *milieu* of returned warriors of her own age struck her imagination at once. So much was this so that she produced a box of chocolates—they were still hard to come by—and seemed to propose extended talk on the strength of them.

'Shall you become friends with them, Dunkie,' she asked, 'or will they be stand-offish and treat you as a kid?' Everybody at Corry knew my family name, but only Ruth employed it— no doubt because it was a diminutive to which it was easy to lend a mocking inflexion.

'As you treat me? Probably I'll be a kid. Almost a fag. Or a batman. They'll most of them have had batmen, I expect.'

'But at Oxford there are men called scouts who do that sort

of thing.' Ruth had taken my suggestion seriously. 'Why are they called scouts?'

'Origin unknown. I've researched. The dictionary says so. I met one when I was taking the scholarship examination. He was on the fatherly side.'

'The fatherly side.' Ruth repeated this as if it were a remark the fatuousness of which could be brought out by satirical echo. It was a habit the more insufferable for being completely random. 'Have another chocolate,' she added, recollecting that she was chatting me up. 'The square ones are good.' Ruth had an eye on the round ones for herself. She liked soft centres.

'No, thank you,' I said with formality. 'I ought to be getting in training. I think I'm going to row.'

'To row?' She looked at me momentarily round-eyed. 'In the Varsity Boat Race?'

'Of course not. Just row.'

'I know—in Eights. Daddy has told me about Eights Week. It's one of the few times when there are any girls around. It must be a bit dull, living in a university where there are no women.'

'There are quite a lot of women. Five colleges full of them, as a matter of fact.'

'I don't think so.' Ruth spoke with imbecile assurance. 'Mummy says there are just some people called Oxford Home Students. Eccentric girls with long teeth, who live in the houses of the dons.'

'I believe it was like that at one time.' The foggy time-lag which pervaded Corry Hall quite frequently inspissated itself like this.

'At one time,' Ruth mimicked, as if scoring a very strong point. 'So what happens—Daddy says—is that men bring up their sisters and so on for Eights Week, and for Commem Balls and things, and introduce them to their own set.'

'To their own set,' I echoed. This attempt to take a leaf out of Ruth's book made no impact, and I ought not to have been prompted to mockery of my cousin, since a strain of pathos surely attended the wistful vision she was conjuring up. 'Perhaps you'll come some time,' I said awkwardly. 'If there really is any sort of fun going on.'

'That's jolly decent of you, Dunkie. I don't suppose Daddy and Mummy would mind. Daddy says you have become a very reliable young man.'

'Does he really?' It seemed impossible to produce a response any less feeble than this to such information. Ruth's shift from silly condescension to an equally silly notion that I was now somebody to be courted disconcerted me a good deal. And I disliked the Daddy and Mummy business; it didn't befit my cousin's—as I felt them to be—advanced years, and it had a bogus feel to it into the bargain. Daddy and Mummy were the jaws of an impasse she hadn't a notion of how to get out of —although she would have been ready to scream if that would have been any good. I saw no solution for her myself. Not even in coming up to Oxford and meeting some bloody men back from the war.

Nevertheless I had entered into a commitment of honour to entertain at Oxford a female relative of inconvenient age. I had no idea how one did this, or whether one did it at all, and I was unsustained by any feeling of honest attachment to my cousin. The situation was depressing, and as a consequence I went in search of Mountjoy, who had become a resource of mine when I was feeling glum at Corry.

Mountjoy welcomed my visits to his quarters, although it was in an undemonstrative and even slightly wary way. His scrutiny was sharp but rather the reverse of lingering—a characteristic that puzzled me until I contrived to see in it a proper instinct of respect for my more elevated social station. Certainly I felt that he was keenly aware of me, so that I was puzzled again by what seemed his reluctance to acknowledge that my years now rendered implausible any fondness whatever for a fizzy drink called Kola. He had been at Corry ever since I could remember, perhaps as little more than a garden-boy at first. Although his present employment was unambiguous, he was a man of some mystery both in my own and (I gradually gathered) the general view. It was known that he had been born in Paris, and believed that his illegitimacy—which was taken for a fact—had been of a romantic, or indeed exalted, order. He was handsome in a manner scarcely suggesting ascetic courses; one would have said at once that he was a man of ability; and I myself, studying his nose and mouth, was of the opinion that, appropriately bewigged, he would have been indistinguishable from the second Charles. (I felt I owned a certain authority here, my father's stand-by employment as a portrait painter having at one time induced me to make a study of regal iconography.) It seemed to me quite on the cards that Mountjoy was the offspring of some more or less legitimate pretender to the throne of the United Kingdom. Speculation of this kind had been encouraged in me, I remember, by a reading of *The Adventures of Harry Richmond*.

Socially regarded, the personable young Mountjoy was elusive. He wasn't half-gentry, and he wasn't a fallen gentleman —or any of the other anomalies of which one is accustomed to read in fiction. The most surprising thing about him was that he should be at Corry at all, since it would surely be quite against my uncle's instinct to harbour there anybody with this sort of equivocal aura hanging about him. Reflecting on this, I had come to wonder whether Mountjoy might not be a by-blow (another term out of novels) of the Glencorrys them-selves, and one a sense of duty to whom Uncle Rory had elected to discharge by maintaining on the estate at a superior level of menial employment. I was insufficiently experienced to appreciate the unlikelihood of this conjecture.

'Difficult times at Corry,' Mountjoy said. He was studying a map in order to work out the best disposition of a new system of snow screens. As such things must cost money, I took him to be referring to financial exigencies. I had lately ceased to take it for granted that a Glencorry of Glencorry must neces-sarily be opulent—even if, from time to time, he appeared to judge it perfectly feasible to set up with a standing army. In fact I was now suspecting that the wolves might not be too far from the door.

'I am sure you manage everything very well, Mr Mountjoy,' I said politely. With the exception of Uncle Rory himself, everybody at Corry was required to address the quite youthful factor in this way.

'That's as may be, Mr Duncan.' Mountjoy himself was equally correct. I had still been 'Master Duncan' on my last visit; approaching undergraduatedom had promoted me. 'But difficult times. A household of womenfolk, Mr Duncan, is a tricksy thing.'

This glimpse of the sweep of Mountjoy's thought surprised me, as did an unguarded hint of animus in his voice. For a moment I felt I ought to disapprove, and then I reflected that here again was perhaps no more than reasonable promotion. The Glencorrys who were to inherit Corry lived in Canada. Nobody ever saw them, or much heard of them. Ninian and I were the only relations to visit the place regularly, and we tended to be thought of among my uncle's people as the young lairds. It was, so to speak, a purely honorary position, since nobody was so ignorant as to suppose us in any direct line of inheritance. We enjoyed prestige, all the same. If Mountjoy judged me, in the light of this and of my established adulthood, a proper person with whom to hold confidential talk, it wasn't for me to snub him too quickly.

'The young ladies are restless,' Mountjoy said. 'And who's to blame them? It's a dull life for them, as you and I know. I wouldn't care to blame her ladyship, I need hardly say.'

Whether my aunt had any title to this manner of address, I don't know. I should suppose not. It didn't appear, however, to be something my uncle had thought up when in his King Gorse vein; it was vaguely prescriptive among what might be called his retainers. How being a Somebody of that Ilk places one in point of titles of honour I have never found out. Perhaps it was left a muddle at the time when the Chiefs were deprived of their hereditary jurisdiction. At the moment, however, it was my job to back up my honoured hostess. King Duncan had done as much even for Lady Macbeth, although he can hardly have been unaware that she was a menacing woman.

'I should call my aunt,' I said, 'an extremely conscientious person.'

'You're right there, Mr Duncan. But she has never quite taken to the way of life here, if you ask me. And not greatly to the folks around either. It doesn't help the young mistresses —nor does some of the laird's high thinking, right as he no doubt is about it.'

'Probably not.' Now I might really have shut up Mountjoy, had it not suddenly come to me that he was a genuinely worried man. This appeared in his idiom. He didn't commonly employ the kind of modified folk-syntax he was now using, and there was something defensive in it. 'It would certainly be better,' I said, 'if Anna and Ruth occasionally got away for a bit.'

'It would that. The Glencorrys have imaginations, Mr Duncan. You have your own share, if I may say so, and I'm thinking it will take you some way yet.'

'Oh, do you think so?'

'That I do.' Mountjoy must have possessed considerable acuteness to know that I should be flattered by this, although I suppose that my juvenile ambitions as a writer may somehow have got round to him. 'But it's a thing can lead more ways than one,' he continued. 'Hasn't it led the laird to some uncommonly curious genealogy?'

'I suppose it has.' I was conscious that Mountjoy had here contrastingly chosen a manner of speech which deliberately touched in the mysteriousness of his hinterland. 'But it's perfectly harmless,' I said firmly, 'and entirely honourable as well.'

'Of course it is.' Mountjoy glanced at me in a kind of convention of approval. He might have been (although I didn't quite believe it) in the enjoyment of the correct feudal attitudes, and reflecting that this was how a young Glencorry ought to speak up. His next words, however, were on an egalitarian note. 'But it may be a hereditary liability that takes other people in other ways. Those girls, for example. They might get fancying I don't know what.'

'Mr Mountjoy, just what are you talking about?'

The adult severity I managed to import into this question pleased me. It seemed to please Mountjoy too. He wasn't going to be rebuked but was quite ready to be challenged—which was the more interesting because challenge was precisely what I'd sometimes felt his intent but fleeting glance to shy away from. It struck me again what a good-looking young man he was. Stripped to bathe in the Corry, as I had once seen him, he was good-looking all over. He must, I thought sagely, be extremely attractive to women. Already there were bound to have been plenty of women in his life, and I wondered why he wasn't married. Perhaps he had decided against 'settling down', and still went in for a succession of mistresses. But just how that could be squared with holding down the job of factor on such a pervasively depopulated estate as Glencorry wasn't at all clear.

'Well, Mr Duncan, I'm saying in the first place that those young women haven't enough to bite on. I believe we're agreed as to that. But I'm also saying that, supposing anything out of the way happened, we might have to think twice about what to make of it.' Mountjoy paused on this, but I remained silent. I judged his remarks to be unsatisfactory, and felt them to be occasioned by some irrational alarm which I couldn't at all get hold of.

'And not believe the first thing we were told,' Mountjoy said.

I continued silent, still aware of something I lacked the experience to interpret, and displeased that it was my cousins who were being held to lurk in the background of it. Perhaps the explanation was simply that Mountjoy's social indeterminateness didn't go all that deep, and was in fact clearing itself up. He was essentially a servant—which is, of course, something a factor needn't necessarily be. He was subject to the alarms of a dependent who may be turfed out at any time, and whose instinct is to safeguard his own position when there is a hazard of somebody else making off with the spoons. In his present case, the spoons were represented by one of my cousins, or conceivably by both of them. It was as simple as that, and this enigmatical conversation was for the record.

Even so, I was getting angry. I'd like to think that—bringing, as it were, the young laird's boots into play—I'd at least have kicked something more explicit out of the man if there hadn't at this moment come a diversion. It was Mountjoy who spotted it. He was a quick-witted person.

His business room (Uncle Rory had one of his own elsewhere) was perched over an archway at the back of the house which led to a detached line of disused stables. There still hung about it a smell of leather and embrocation and saddle soap, although there was no longer a horse between it and the horizon. It was hung with estate maps, and with obsolete calendars and almanacs which appeared to be the offerings of hopeful agricultural merchants long gone out of business. On a shelf put up for the purpose there was ranged a line of tarnished silver cups, and of silver medals embossed with improbably rectangular cattle, trophies which had lost interest for my uncle since his antiquarian pursuits had taken charge, but which he judged it proper that Mountjoy should be permitted to display. The room was in fact a monument to a Corry no longer viable. Its elevated situation offered, through cobwebby windows, a considerable vista of heather—*one sullen power*, as Dr Johnson had remarked, *of useless vegetation*.

'There's Colonel Morrison,' Mountjoy said, 'coming over the brae.'

Colonel Morrison was my uncle's chief—indeed almost his sole—crony. He lived in a somewhat solitary situation in the next glen, and dropped in from time to time—with the aim, I used to think, of recruiting himself on malt whisky for the return journey. Not, indeed, that one could imagine Colonel Morrison affected by liquor. He was that kind of middle-aged bachelor who keeps his figure and his form, and is never visible except in the clipped, brushed and braced condition which calls forth the term 'spruce' and stops just short of the conception of the elegant. Like my uncle and aunt, he was unfailingly courteous, but differed from them in seeming to regard gaiety as a social duty as well.

Mountjoy's eyesight was good; he had detected the approaching colonel a quarter of a mile away. The colonel of course had no means of knowing himself to be observed, and there was no need to take any immediate step to welcome him. But my young nature was suggestible; when at Corry Hall the Glencorry connection commonly had its way with me; I felt I must step out to meet our visitor. Moreover, I'd had enough of Mountjoy for the moment, or at least I felt a need to think him over before advancing our peculiar conversation further. So I said good-morning to him and set out. I had a further motive in the fact that a stroll with Colonel Morrison was never likely to be boring. The oddest thing about him was his possession of a considerable amount of reading. I supposed his premature leaving the army to have been due to some physical disability the existence of which was accompanied by no outward sign. Intellectual restlessness might also have been a factor. Possibly some family tradition had tumbled him into what he had come to feel the wrong career. He never went about without a pair of field-glasses slung over his shoulder. There was something symbolic or emblematical about them: they signalled a man always wanting to get things a little clearer than they were. Perhaps he felt one could never be certain there was no threat on the horizon—a wariness proper in a military man. He lived with a housekeeper and a couple of menservants in a snug but reclusive way.

The field-glasses were trained on me now. Having identified me, Colonel Morrison gave a wave and quickened his pace— an amiable action which I reciprocated. Peewits were making a great to-do overhead. They might have been applauding the pleasing spectacle of an elderly man and a young one thus hastening cordially to a meeting.

'Good-morning, Duncan,' Colonel Morrison called out briskly, and he shook hands with me when I came up. 'Well settled in again, I hope?' He glanced at me rather—I thought—as at a recruit on parade, and then gave a temperately approving nod.

'Yes, thank you, sir. But I'm feeling rather unsettled in a general way. Facing the unknown, you know.'

'Ah, the Varsity.' The colonel articulated this word as if aware of its archaic character, or of the continued propriety of its use only by a non-Varsity man. 'I was delighted to hear you have decided to go to Oxford. A wise decision, Duncan. I congratulate you.'

'Thank you very much. But it has been my father's idea, really.'

'Then your father's a sensible man. And he might well be what he is—the finest painter we have, to my mind—without in the least being *that*.' Colonel Morrison paused on this deft praise, rather as if to give me an opportunity to take note of it. 'You didn't, I suppose, have a shot at a scholarship while you were about it?'

'Well, yes—I did.' I paused in turn—perhaps suspecting that the colonel, in his dextrous pursuit of the agreeable, was feigning ignorance of something he had in fact heard about. 'As a matter of fact, I've fluked one.'

'Admirable! But you are chargeable with self-consciousness, my dear lad, if you apply such a foolish expression to your achievement. Acknowledge your own abilities soberly as you go along, Duncan. It's a good rule in life.'

We were now stepping out together, and I made no attempt to reply to the colonel's last remark. He was fond of delivering himself of preceptual wisdom in this way, and had the knack of doing so with a marked lightness of air.

'By jove, yes!' he went on. 'A scholarship at Oxford or

Cambridge is a great thing. A baton in the knapsack, eh?'
Colonel Morrison put a hand on my shoulder—but lightly and
diffidently—to steady himself across a minute beck. 'Or like
going straight to Staff College from your mother's milk.'

'My headmaster says it's a first step to modest distinction or
keen disappointment, and that only time will show which. He
probably has the experienced professional view, sir.'

'Not a bit of it. I declare him to be a dreary man. What do
you propose to do with yourself afterwards?'

'Aunt Charlotte thinks I ought to become a parson.'

'Well, I'm blessed! A minister, eh?'

'Not exactly that. She calls it taking Holy Orders. So I'd
have to be turned into an episcopalian first. It gets you further,
she says. You can become a bishop.'

'Sad nonsense, Duncan.' Colonel Morrison laughed softly;
he enjoyed sharing with me a little cautious irony at my aunt's
expense. 'But the dear lady is a Sassenach, after all. Come, now
—what's your own notion of the thing?'

'I want to write plays.'

'Excellent! Must be far more fun than novels. Think of all
the stodgy padding Tolstoy and fellows like that have to put
in. Money in the theatre, too. Take that entertaining old rascal
Bernard Shaw. Made a fortune that way. No need at all for him
to have gone on and married an heiress. Although a nice
woman, mark you. Or take Willie Maugham. Not always
wholly agreeable, perhaps, but as clever as paint. And with
plays running in half the theatres of London. Buy himself a
steam yacht any day.'

'It wouldn't be my idea to make masses of money out of
plays.'

'Of course not. Artist and all that, eh? But no harm in its
coming along incidentally. Shakespeare, for example. Ended up
with the best house in town.'

I almost expected to hear the colonel add something like,
'I always used to enjoy dropping in at New Place when passing
through Stratford.' He found a naïve pleasure, surprising in so

urbane a man, in this particular region of name-dropping. It is conceivable, of course, that at some period of his life he had enjoyed a distinguished literary acquaintance, but he had never produced hard evidence of anything of the kind. Persons of military or political or social consequence, of whom he must have known a fair number, never entered his conversation.

'I shan't fail your first first-night, Duncan,' he continued amiably. 'Meanwhile, you can tell me about what's going on in the theatre now. For I hope you're making a substantial stay at Corry?'

'Well, yes. Aunt Charlotte has invited me till the end of the month.'

'Good. Good.' As Colonel Morrison said this, he slowed his pace and came to a halt. The front door of the house was before us, and it would have been natural to mount the steps and enter. My companion, however, glanced around him. 'We'll just take a turn in the garden,' he said. 'Interested to see how Elizabeth of Glamis is getting on. Not having much success with Floribunda myself.'

I guessed that Elizabeth of Glamis must be a rose, although I don't think we actually got round to spotting her. Colonel Morrison appeared preoccupied. I caught him glancing at me curiously and in a manner which didn't strike me as at all his habit.

'Glad you're making a decent stay,' he said. A lack of conviction in his tone surprised me. I knew he liked me, or at least liked any fresh and lively talk I could put up, so it could scarcely be that he felt me to be a nuisance about the district. 'You've grown a bit since you were here last,' he said, crisply but inconsequently. I supposed the remark to be true, but wasn't sure whether it was gratifying. A young man, as distinct from a boy, likes to think that his inches are accomplished. 'In fact,' Colonel Morrison concluded, 'you've become a distinctly attractive youth.'

My surprise increased. The colonel had his fondness for the agreeable, but to offer a personal remark like this on a note of

41

flattery wasn't at all his style. Nor had he sounded such a note. On the contrary, he had spoken with something like gloom.

'What are the girls doing, these days?' he asked casually.

'I don't really know. They're a bit elusive, really. Ruth talks to me from time to time, but I never seem to get much out of Anna.'

'Humph.'

'What do you mean—humph?' I asked laughing. I knew that the colonel liked me to challenge him in this direct way. At the same time, my curiosity had quickened. I had an instinct that, for the second time within an hour, my cousins were going to turn up in an enigmatical context.

'I have a notion, Duncan, that you were seeing rather more of Anna a year or two ago.'

I found that—very shockingly—my eyes were on Colonel Morrison's field-glasses. The notion they conveyed sent the blood hotly to my face. It was of course inconceivable that the colonel should indulge the instinct of the *voyeur*, nor would the territory of his habitual perambulations have afforded him much scope if he had. But what those binoculars might on some specific occasion inadvertently have focused on was anybody's guess. My circulation continued to behave badly.

'Anna and I,' I heard myself say firmly, 'used to fool around a bit, as a matter of fact. But we were both younger then.'

'Anna wasn't all that younger. Duncan, I think she's rather a tricky lass.'

Mountjoy's word had been 'tricksy'. The coincidence of these two phrases came on me with forceful effect.

'Old friend, Duncan. Fond of your uncle and aunt. Interested in you for years.'

'Yes, sir.'

'Mind your Ps and Qs, if I were you. *Verb. sap.*—eh?'

I felt more than a moment's interest in the colonel's thus adopting the role of the gruff and embarrassed military man. I was reminded, too, of one or two previous occasions upon which he had spoken to me with some seriousness on the hazards attending the sexual side of our natures. He may have judged my father and uncle to be equally unlikely to do much in the way of timely warning, and it occurred to me that commanding officers might sometimes think it incumbent upon them to address their subalterns confidentially upon such topics. It had been undeniable that a certain morbidity had marked these admonishments; the danger to one's health which attended—as the colonel expressed it—'going with a woman' was prominent in his thought. But I had accepted his counsel in good part, not feeling that he was poking around or getting any illicit change out of his topic. And this present talk was essentially on different ground. Colonel Morrison must fear that my cousin Anna might at any minute set about seducing me in earnest, and that this wouldn't be at all the thing.

'Look,' I said. 'I can honestly tell you that Anna hasn't the slightest interest in me. Even less than Ruth. As a matter of fact I've felt—ever since getting here this time—that she's more remote than usual. Of course I realize I don't know much about these things. But I can assure you it's all in the clear—absolutely.' I paused for a moment, a fresh thought striking me. 'Sir—has Mountjoy been talking to you about me?'

'Mountjoy? My dear Duncan!' Colonel Morrison smiled at me whimsically, but I realized I was being made aware (as I sometimes was made aware at Corry) that I didn't quite know the ropes. 'I have a word with Mountjoy from time to time. He's a capital chap, and invaluable to your uncle. But I'd hardly touch on intimate matters with him.'

'No, of course not.' I was suitably abashed. 'It was just something came into my head.'

'Then enough said.' Colonel Morrison contrived a glance of modified gaiety, and turned to make his way out of the garden. I thought he was going to give over, but he proved to have something more to say. 'Anna dropped into tea with me only yesterday, as a matter of fact. Quite a tramp for her. Nice of her. Lonely old chap, and so on. Something you do yourself, Duncan, from time to time. Appreciate it.'

'I always enjoy coming over, sir.'

'Good, good. Stayed quite a long time. Mrs Ogilvie did us a very good tea, I'm bound to say.' Mrs Ogilvie was the colonel's housekeeper and, in a certain degree, companion; as the linchpin of his comfortable establishment, she was held by him in high esteem. He didn't much care for a wider female society. By the surrounding gentry he was generally believed to have been something of a lady-killer in his youth, but to have suffered some experience which had induced a marked and no doubt meritorious retreat upon celibate life. 'Yes, a capital tea,' he now continued. 'You know those drop-scones of Mrs Ogilvie's, eh? And always had a kindness for both the girls. She chatted with Anna. Hardly out of the room, as a matter of fact.'

I felt I had scarcely ever heard more amazing words. They had the effect of illuminating, moreover, my recent confabulation with Mountjoy. The one man was as scared of Anna—or of what Anna's imagination might get round to—as was the other; and this conversation, too, had been for the record. Nor was that quite all. Blowing about, I felt, had been something yet more surprising: a kind of generalized irrational panic before the mere female animal.

I hoped Uncle Rory wasn't going to prove subject to this malaise. Certainly he wasn't immediately infected. Colonel Morrison joined him, drank his whisky, smoked a companionable pipe, and walked away—leaving his neighbour wholly unperturbed. Life at Corry Hall showed every sign of going on precisely as before.

It was during the succeeding few days, I remember, that I read *Anna Karenina*. Perhaps the name had exercised some unconscious pull. I wasn't made much aware of the padding which, in the colonel's view, was a marked feature of Tolstoy's writing. Being in love, I found much of the novel unbearably moving, even though I was aware of it as traversing areas of feeling about which I knew very little.

I wasn't merely in love with Janet Finlay; in a few brief

weeks before being banished to Corry Hall I had rocketed from mute adoration of her to the status of an articulate and, as I saw it, masterful suitor. But this didn't prevent me from now thinking about Anna a good deal. I approached the suddenly perplexed subject cautiously, even persuading myself that it was Tolstoy's novel which was leading me to ponder on the nature of sexual desire in women. Since Anna remained, however, so very much the immediate instance, her image was soon accompanying me monotonously on my solitary walks.

All my discoveries at that time were mixed up with the discovery of words, and Anna appeared to become clearer in my head when I remembered a recent accession to my hoard. This was *nymphomania*. My *Shorter Oxford Dictionary* (which was in two huge volumes) marked the word as 'alien or not naturalized'; my *Pocket Oxford Dictionary* (from which I was tardily learning to spell) was of slightly later date, and printed the word without any such qualification in its *Addenda*. I was fond of this category of incoming words, and had a good command of them. So I now imagined myself as going home and exclaiming to Ninian, 'I say—a frightful thing about Anna Glencorry! She's gone completely nympho.' (I supposed that the contraction would have been my own contribution to the growth of language.) I felt that I had now solved the enigma of my cousins. An elderly bachelor like Colonel Morrison might well be nervous about perfectly normal women. But a husky young man like Mountjoy was another matter. His apprehensions of a dangerous involvement with his employer's daughter could only be occasioned by conduct thoroughly out of the way. Anna had been tearing off her clothes and screaming in his presence. Something like that.

There was also, of course, hysteria, which wasn't quite the same thing. My mother was hysterical at times, but I was quite sure she wasn't nymphomaniac. Yet *hysteria* came from a Greek word meaning 'womb', and Ninian had solemnly warned me that in a fit of hysteria a normally respectable girl could baselessly accuse one of the most frightful sexual excesses. Like many high-powered lawyers in the making, Ninian had began by interesting himself in the criminal and sensational side of legal practice.

So I carried these semantic ruminations with me around the glens. An obvious question emerged. Could I have been astray in assuring Colonel Morrison that Anna nowadays didn't take the slightest interest in me? Wasn't it the colonel who was right in endeavouring to alert me to her as a menace? And it *would* be a menace. Although when I lay awake at night imagining that the door might softly open and Anna slip into my room the fantasy was sufficiently exciting to make my head swim, I knew perfectly well that such an episode would be at once a disaster and a fiasco. There was nothing unnatural in this. It just so happened that my emotional orientation at that time had suddenly become such that anything of the kind was bound to strike me as horribly degrading, and in consequence to turn out humiliatingly anaphrodisiac. I felt rather ashamed of my own puritanical nature as thus revealed. I thought of the robust behaviour of Tom Jones and of similar eventually irreproachable lovers not in an interim immune to what came casually along. It was no good. I decided to lock my bedroom door. When I discovered that the lock was without a key it is true that some spark of renewed anticipation momentarily lit up in me. But nothing like a conflagration followed.

Then all this proved to be nonsense.

'I'm going to have a baby.'

Anna made the announcement to her parents, her sister and myself one day in the middle of lunch. We all stared at her dumbfounded. She had spoken much as if saying, 'I'm going to be sick', and the impression was enhanced by her then at once getting up and hurrying from the room. Ruth burst into tears, but refrained from following her. Aunt Charlotte didn't follow her either; she turned pale, crumbled bread, and said, 'Elspeth must be told that Anna is unwell.' (Elspeth was the aged and creaking parlourmaid, who was fortunately occupied in fetching ground-rice pudding from the kitchen.) Uncle Rory, too, hadn't moved. I caught him looking at me inquiringly, as if he judged me to be the person present who was most likely to have kept his wits. Probably he was uncertain that he hadn't suffered some aberration of hearing or even of the imagination, and wanted to ensure against making an ass of himself. I had jumped to my feet and was heading for the door. Anna's words had been in a sense quite vague to me; I scarcely had their bearings at all; in my mind there was even the confused thought that somebody might have had the decency to tell me that my cousin was married. Yet this didn't cloud my knowledge that she was in the sort of fix that makes some immediate gesture of solidarity important. But my aunt's voice stopped me.

'Duncan, sit down. It is kind of you, but sit down at once.'

I did as I was told. That it should occur to Aunt Charlotte at such a moment to offer me an approbatory word astonished me and gave her authority.

'But will she be all right?' I asked. I was already seeing the situation more clearly, and was morbidly envisioning my cousin as climbing to one of the bogus battlements of Corry Hall and pitching herself over its crenellations.

'She will be as right as is at all suitable. What must not happen is that she should be encouraged to make scenes—to make a further scene. Ruth, stop crying at once.'

I passed Ruth my handkerchief, and acknowledged to myself that, if in a hard way, Aunt Charlotte was doing rather well. It was perfectly true that, whatever the dimensions of Anna's misfortune, she had revealed its general existence to us in a self-dramatizing or exhibitionistic fashion. I was shocked to find myself suspecting (what indeed proved to be true) that she was going to make the most of the thing.

Yet any thought of this sort occupied only one side of my head. In the other a sense of the matter was building up that was to produce a minor dramatic manifestation of its own.

47

But that lay a little ahead. At the moment I was wondering how Uncle Rory would make himself felt in the affair. When outraged by Ninian's incivility to the fishwife he had made himself felt in the most literal sense, and it seemed to me probable that he would at once seek out his daughter's seducer, this time armed with a horse-whip. But Uncle Rory made no immediate move, and the thought of Ninian brought other considerations to my mind. Ninian had been precocious in his love-affairs, and numerous treatises on sexual psychology, to which I had gained access with some difficulty at the prompting of this situation, had persuaded me that I was well-informed in the field. I wondered whether Uncle Rory knew nearly as much about it as I did. He might well be totally innocent of the ways of the modern world. Did he know, for instance, that nowadays young people quite often slept with one another in an experimental spirit, and were sometimes careless or clumsy at it, with the result that they had hastily to get married? It looked, after all, as if such was Anna's case.

But if this came to me from life something else now came to me from literature. I had lately read a tremendous little play by Yeats called *Purgatory*, the most accessible theme of which appeared to be the dismal consequences certain to succeed upon a high-born lady's going to bed with a drunken groom. Anna would pass very well as a high-born lady; she had King Gorse behind her, after all. (I was rather fond of King Gorse. If he was my uncle's ancestor he was thereby my own as well.) Was it conceivable that Anna had found a drunken groom? At this point I naturally thought of Mountjoy.

Mountjoy wasn't exactly a groom—nor, so far as my knowledge went, was he of an intemperate habit. Still, he was, so to speak, within the bracket. And wasn't it precisely out of it that he had been trying to wriggle during our strange conversation? The unscrupulous young Mountjoy was going to deny his paternity. At a pinch, he would blame Anna's condition on somebody else.

My phase of irrational horror before the situation must

have begun at this point. It signalled its arrival in terms of another recent accession to the word-hoard: '*sleeping around*'. This was taking the place of terms like 'promiscuous' and 'loose-living' in colloquial speech. And now I thought of Colonel Morrison. Just *what* I thought I can't imagine. But I had a nightmarish vision of Anna roaming the moors in darkness.

Perhaps I had started her off. *We* had roamed the moors, with the result that things had happened to me known hitherto only in wet dreams. If Anna had a more inflammable imagination than I had it was possible that she had just never looked back. I was confronting this squarely when I realized that lunch was over, and that I had actually consumed a plateful of the ground-rice pudding, helped down by cold stewed prunes. The inflexibility of life at Corry had asserted itself. We parted without further word. My uncle, in fact, hadn't spoken at all. But something in his mere movement as he left the room told me that he was a bewildered man.

I wondered what to do. To seek out Anna herself would be intrusive—in addition to which it must be supposed that she would be closeted with one or both of her parents. Perhaps I could do something to cheer up Ruth. But I had no idea of what Ruth knew, and I therefore had a fear that, if I sought her out, she might suppose me to be fishing for information. My other thought was that I should follow my uncle; that there existed an almost ritual need that, at least for a few minutes, the men of the family should be in consultation together. I had received from Uncle Rory, in the very moment of revelation, that frankly appealing glance. But it was for Uncle Rory to take an initiative here. Moreover, a nephew doesn't belong to a family in the narrow sense. Struck by this, it now occurred to me that the correct procedure would be to pack up and leave Corry forthwith. A gleam of sense, however, told me that, as an entirely junior person, I couldn't properly take an initiative here either.

So I moved into the least frequented room in the house. This was the library: an ungenial apartment of considerable size and one actually containing a great many books—nearly all of them for some reason kept under lock and key in glazed bookcases. It was now quite familiar to me, since I had recently taken the momentous step of letting it be publicly known (even at Corry) that my idea of a normal day included a couple of hours' 'work', and that by 'work' I meant writing. At Corry the library was my chosen spot for this. I remember that I liked to have several dogs with me during these sessions. A picture of Sir Walter Scott in similar surroundings at Abbotsford was probably at the back of my mind.

I certainly couldn't 'work' at present, but I might be able to read. Because I had lately taken to planning literacy in a big way, *War and Peace* was to follow *Anna Karenina*, and both books were lying on a window-seat now. I was about to start on the new one when I recalled the opening of the old. I picked up *Anna Karenina* and read the brief paragraph again:

> All happy families resemble one another, each unhappy family is unhappy in its own way.

Did such categories mean much? I remembered that, long ago, Anna and Ruth and I had occasionally lightened the tedium of Corry evenings by playing the primitive card-game called 'Happy Families', and this recollection suddenly submerged me in morbid feelings about lost innocence.

This spurious nostalgia wore off, and gave place to something which was at least genuine. There came to me a sense of what, in its nakedness and absoluteness, had been done to Anna's body, and of what was happening within the mysterious darkness of her body now. Day after day in that darkness, a child was growing towards the light. The thought roused in me more than the simple awe natural to such a contemplation. I had feelings of revulsion and horror as well. These I was helpless to understand, or at least to understand fully, but perhaps I was not wrong in telling myself that the possibility of the child's being harshly and unregardingly fathered, or even not fathered at all, affected me deeply. Yet no romantic sentiment attached to Anna herself in my mind. I remembered her rather too beefy body, wriggling stupidly and shamefully beneath my own, with a dispassionate distaste which appeared unrelated to any sort of strong emotion at all. Perhaps I somewhere felt guilty, all the same; felt guilty not on account of those trivial, sticky, clothes-encumbered episodes in the heather, but rather on account of all the blind itch and impatient lust which I was coming to realize men brought to sex —to 'having sex', as I was one day to hear my juniors habitually express it.

I must have spent quite some time with these growing-pains that afternoon, since I became abruptly aware of my uncle entering the library with the words, 'I have asked Elspeth to bring us tea'. There was nothing unprecedented about this. Some such occasion took place nowadays whenever either Ninian or myself stayed at Corry. And it wasn't that Uncle Rory thought it proper to hold, in this private manner, an inquisition into our affairs. He was concerned for our manners and bearing, and also—to the extent his understanding reached —over the problems of our careers. But, unlike Aunt Charlotte, he was too punctilious to have regarded explicit reference to such matters on his part as in order unless undertaken at the suggestion of our parents. And such a use for Uncle Rory would certainly never have entered our parents' heads.

I had come to suspect that my uncle, although so much given to notions of lineage and primogeniture, would have been quite content to see the Canadian Glencorrys swallowed by an earthquake, and my brother in consequence become, by favour of the Lord Lyon King of Arms or some such person, heir to the Chiefship. Uncle Rory was fonder of Ninian than of myself —intuitively aware, I think, of the man of public consequence in the making. I had once found myself reflecting, with an odd jealousy, that if it had been I who was rude to the fishwife I should probably have been less intimately corrected; that the walloping had established something. Nevertheless Ninian was *not* the heir; we were both simply nephews out on a female line; we were treated on a strict equality, one effect of which was my periodic admission to these tea-table conferences.

What Uncle Rory would discuss—or rather make rambling remarks about—was an assortment of small current problems connected with the administration of the estate. They were effectively matters in Mountjoy's control, and the play of my uncle's own sagacity over them was so unimpressive that one ended up fervently hoping that Mountjoy was an honest man. As I now watched Elspeth bring in the tea—with more ceremony than if it had been into my aunt's drawing-room— and my uncle standing with no more than his familiar air of worried abstraction before the empty fire-place, I wondered whether his sense of a proper drill was such that nothing un-customary was going to pass between us now. But this was to stumble in my always slightly uncertain sense of Uncle Rory's mind. He waited only for Elspeth to close the door, and then spoke at once.

'Duncan—here's the full devil of the thing. She won't tell.'

'Won't tell?'

I produced this stupid echo partly out of mere surprise at hearing Uncle Rory mention the devil at all. I had never heard anything like an imprecation on his lips before.

'Who the fellow is. She won't say.'

As often with me, I had a moment of clarity before confusion set in. If Anna was going in for a nameless-shame line, then Anna was being even more of a nuisance than need be. In a queer sense I had no sympathy for her, although at the same time I was probably as aghast at what had befallen her as her father was.

'It will come out by stages,' I said firmly. 'Anna must be in a state of terrible shock. Telling us all like that, instead of first going quietly to my aunt, shows that. She just mustn't be rushed.'

'I suppose you're right.' Uncle Rory appeared grateful for this steadying speech from a male kinsman, and I indulged myself, I hope briefly, in the irrelevant vanity of feeling grown-up. 'Only,' Uncle Rory went on, 'it's a kind of thing in which there's no time to lose.'

I saw that this was the theme of the shot-gun marriage. It brought into my head (and the further irrelevance shows how unaware I was of what was really going on inside me) a place in *Man and Superman* where somebody says something like 'The scoundrel must be found and forced to marry her'.

'At least you can give her till tomorrow,' I said. 'Perhaps she'll tell Ruth. Or perhaps Ruth knows.'

'*You* don't know?'

This pulled me up. For a moment I wasn't even sure what its implication was. But Uncle Rory—at least for the present—immediately cleared up any ambiguity.

'I don't mean her necessarily telling you, Duncan. I know she keeps herself to herself—even from someone as close in age to her as you are. But you notice things. Undoubtedly you notice things. Mountjoy says it will get you somewhere one day.'

'I haven't noticed anything at all, Uncle Rory.' This, in a strict sense, was true. I had been told things, rather than noticed them—and by both Mountjoy and Colonel Morrison. I was possibly going to be in a delicate position.

'There's that young fellow Petrie over at Garth,' Uncle Rory said. 'Back from the war, and said to be a loose fish enough. But he's in the Blues, you know. Surely he wouldn't risk it? My daughter isn't a chorus-girl or a superior tart. They'd turn him out.'

I held my peace, since here was territory on which I had nothing to offer.

'Or there's the Macwherry. I've never trusted that crowd. Bogus family, if ever there was one. No man for a girl to go out with on a dark night.'

'But has Anna done that with Mr Macwherry?'

'No, no—only a thought.' Uncle Rory shook his head, and I again saw how bewildered he was. He had hit, however, upon what he appeared to regard as a fruitful line of speculation, and he went on for some time with a review of the surrounding male gentry as possible seducers of his daughter. Grooms and gillies didn't seem to strike him as an alternative field. Remarking this made me think of Mountjoy again. What exactly had Mountjoy said? He had begun with something about a strain of imagination in the family. But that had been only a way of getting round to the insinuation that my cousins might at any time fall into a kind of morbid romancing which a recipient would do well to think twice about. There could be no doubt as to what had been specifically in his mind; it was that one of the girls, presumably Anna, might start romancing about a love-affair with him. And Colonel Morrison, as if by a mysterious infection, had been under the same anxiety—in addition to which he had been afraid that Anna might also get going on me. They were both envisaging, presumably on the basis of at least some personal experience, the unleashing of a thoroughly pathological exhibition at Corry.

This line of thought gave me an idea.

'Uncle Rory,' I said, 'don't you think it's possible that Anna is making the whole thing up?'

'Making it up?' My uncle was in his turn reduced to idle repetition. 'Making what up?'

'That there's a baby. I've been remembering something that I've been——' I broke off, realizing that it would be discreet to steer clear of Colonel Morrison and Mountjoy, whose anxieties ought to have been advanced—if to anyone—to my uncle and not to myself. 'I've remembered something I've read. Hysterical women sometimes imagine themselves to be pregnant. Quite baselessly. Even virgins do. And produce apparent physical signs of the thing.' I didn't pause to be surprised by this freedom in my own speech. 'Perhaps Anna's case is like that.'

'Good God!' Disconcertingly, Uncle Rory clutched his head and gave a sudden moan of despair. 'Then she's mad?'

'No, no. It's not madness, exactly—if that *is* it, I mean. Or only a temporary kind.' I was unnerved by the effect my brilliant suggestion had created. It seemed for the moment as if the thought of lunacy in the family was more terrible to the Glencorry than would be any number of illegitimate children. Thinking to bring comfort, I had in fact opened up an abyss.

But this extremity braced my uncle. He was rather a meagre man, sandy and wispy, and the old-fashioned Norfolk jacket and knickerbockers he habitually wore for most of the day often seemed to emphasize the fact.

He now drew himself up so sternly that he was wholly impressive.

'Duncan,' he demanded, 'do you believe that? That there's no baby?'

'No, sir—I don't think I do.' I was abashed and feeble. I somehow knew very well that there was a baby.

'Then don't alarm me with such ideas, my dear boy. Nor your aunt. Not that your aunt would be troubled by idle talk of imbecility. She could have no doubt as to Anna's condition. She tells me that she now recalls having been aware of certain intimate signs. We need not be specific, Duncan. Nor, indeed, know about such things.'

'No, Uncle Rory.'

My uncle's portentous reticence can scarcely—it is now clear to me—have referred to anything of the slightest evidential consequence. My aunt, seeing the truth perfectly well, had simply said something to shortcircuit his first bewildered incredulity. But upon myself this vague conjuration of physiology had a different and disproportionate effect. I felt once more a kind of horror before the dark mystery of pro-creation. And this in turn triggered off a further feeling. Set down before my recently acquired typewriter, I should have converted it into an essay on birth, copulation and death as the brute bases of existence, only to be humanized by rites and ceremonies and fidelities and tremendous vows. As it was, I simply felt a dismayed sense that Anna looked due to be distinctly short-changed in her current transaction with Great Creating Nature. And meanwhile my uncle, whose head was unencumbered by such abstractions, had asked a question.

'But why, Duncan? Why should she?'

'It's a natural urge, I suppose.' I was at a loss. 'Everybody feels it—except eunuchs, and people like that.'

'No, no. I mean, why should she refuse to say?'

'Oh, I see. But really, Uncle Rory, I don't know.'

'Haven't you any ideas?'

'Well, yes.' I suppose I couldn't bear to be judged barren of ideas, for I rapidly cast round in my mind. 'It's possible that Anna has . . . has had the misfortune to . . . well, to fall in love with a married man.' I found myself surprised at the prim way in which I felt it necessary to express this possibility. 'And then it has happened—the baby, I mean. And she wants to protect his honour, or not break up his marriage, or something of that sort.'

'That *is* a possibility.' Uncle Rory looked as if he wanted to be impressed by it. 'Yes. The Macwerry's a married man. Not young Petrie, though. But Admiral Farquhar is. And Thompson and Lumley and Lavington and D'Arcy-Drelincourt.' As before, my uncle resourcefully lengthened out his list of postulants, his face progressively brightening the while. Then he stopped abruptly, and was once more in sombre mood. 'No,' he said. 'It won't do, Duncan. The wrong tack.' He shook his head in a manner that rather touchingly suggested a sober realism. 'Not like Anna, when you come to think about it. If you ask me, it's simply that she doesn't know.'

'Doesn't know!' Not unreasonably, I stared at Uncle Rory aghast.

'That's it. I remember a fellow in my regiment—a bit of a bounder, who ought never to have got in—used to make a joke about a circular saw.' My uncle paused for a moment on this obscure reminiscence, and I continued merely to goggle at him. The distresses of the day might have been described as stirring him up a bit (as, indeed, they were stirring up me). After all, he must know more about life than was suggested by the manner of it that he imposed upon Corry Hall. And perhaps he knew more about his daughters than I did. 'Yes,' he went on. 'She can't name the right man—or not with any certainty. And what may follow after that? Naming the wrong one, if you ask me. And pretty well at random. Like bobbing for apples at Hallowe'en.' He paused again on this—as he well might, since it was the first simile upon which I had ever heard him venture. 'And—good God, Duncan!—I've been badgering the girl. When the fact is, she must be shut up.'

'Shut up!'

'Kept quiet. Bundled out of the country. Lord knows what. Don't you see? She may name anybody at any time. Dear old Jim Morrison, for instance. Or even a wholesome young fellow like Mountjoy. Then the fat would be in the fire! Solemn talk about it in their confounded Kirk Session, or whatever they call it. You can't *do* that sort of thing here.'

'Uncle Rory, I'll marry her.'

'You'll *what*?' My uncle, in his turn helplessly gaped.

'I'll marry Anna. I'm old enough. And first cousins are allowed to. It will solve the thing.'

There was a silence—during which I saw my uncle putting the simplest of interpretations on my wild and whirling words. The ravisher of his daughter stood, revealed and repentant, before him. But, although dotty, he wasn't a fool, and in a moment the absurdity of my impulse came to him.

'Pull yourself together, boy,' he said gently. 'Thank you. But pull yourself together.'

The oddity of my behaviour—if such a weird vagary can be called behaviour—has never fully explained itself to me. As I have to keep on repeating, I was in love. Boyishly but deeply, I was just that. I don't believe that, in any normal social context, the appearance before me of the most beautiful girl in Europe would for a moment have shaken my romantic fidelity to Janet. Yet what I had said I had meant. It is conceivable that the phrase 'bundled out of the country' had done it. There hadn't been much of rite or ceremony about that. The thing is embarrassing to look back on now, almost half a lifetime later. It presents me as a kinsman, a Christian gentleman, a loyal adherent to the Glencorry connection. It presents me as the lord knows what.

At least such heroics are a bubble to be pricked, or a balloon to be gently deflated. My aunt was rather less gentle than my uncle. When my curious proposition was communicated to her (for it didn't occur to Uncle Rory to keep it to himself) she must have concluded that I had become too deranged to remain as an acceptable guest at Corry Hall. I was inclined to agree with her—in addition to which I had a strong enough motive for wanting to be back in Edinburgh. And the following morning's post brought a letter from my father. My mother was very much better. She was still singing rather loudly about the house, but there was nothing out of the way in that. I had better come home when I wanted to. I did want to. I wanted to very much. So the abbreviating—or, rather, truncating— of my annual holiday was decorously arranged, and I found myself back in my native town with some weeks in hand before going up to Oxford.

Janet had returned from visiting her uncles and aunts and cousins in Skye: unknown and distant people of whom I was extremely jealous, but of whom I tried to approve both on general egalitarian principles and on the score of having had a crofter grandfather myself. Reunited, however, Janet and I went in for the pleasures of the town as conceived by the more intellectually inclined of the *haute bourgeoisie* therein—frequenting museums, picture galleries and concert halls, and talking much and rather at random about books. Janet, although falling upon this with an odd avidity, termed it ironically our topping-up with culture. It was, she said enigmatically, one way of life, and we might as well have a stab at it. Janet Finlay was beginning, in fact, to have her elusive moments—like the girl in Barrie's sentimental play who is going to be called away by the fairies.

It was to be quite a long time before I heard anything at all about what had happened to Anna Glencorry.

# III

M<small>Y</small> <small>UNCLE</small> <small>SPOKE</small> of 'the two universities' as he might have spoken of 'the two sexes'. That Oxford and Cambridge played their prescriptive roles with any supporting cast, however dim, would scarcely have occurred to him. He had lived for the greater part of his life in Scotland. Niched somewhere in his head must have been a bare knowledge of the existence of universities at St Andrews, Glasgow, Aberdeen, and Edinburgh. But that the first three of these had been in business since the fifteenth century and that the fourth was a going concern within the lifetime of Shakespeare was probably information with which the particular slant of his antiquarian studies had failed to acquaint him. It was at Oxford that I myself was to become conscious of the astonishing historical blankness which may be entertained by persons themselves of ancient lineage. I might have picked up a hint of it from Uncle Rory, had it ever come to me to reflect on the matter.

I had not been brought up to think or speak in Uncle Rory's way. More of my schoolfellows went to the University of Edinburgh than to Oxford and Cambridge together. My father, long after his reputation as a painter had become as much continental as native, continued to regard as our family's main claim to distinction the circumstance that his brother the minister had 'been through' college in our native city, and had there 'sat under' some particularly eminent professor of divinity. Nevertheless—as I have explained—it was a certain whimsicality on my father's part that despatched me across the Border.

I can think of two groups of people who may be spoken of as having 'gone up' to Oxford not once but twice. It occasionally happens that men who have spent no more than three or four undergraduate years there, and who have subsequently followed paths having little or no connection with academic life, return to the university in later middle age. They may be civil servants or ambassadors or bankers, trading-in the tail-end of their professional careers for the dignified leisure that attends upon being head of a college. Or they may be of more modest station, engaged in some activity hitherto not favoured by the learned but now through a shift of fashion declared worthy of scholastic regard, and therefore to be taught or professed by new men recruited for the purpose. This was to be me; after many years during which university people of any sort rarely came my way, I was to go back and try to turn myself into a teacher. The feel of the thing proved to be much that of 'going up' again. I was to be conscious, for example, of old bewilderments. Was it drama that I was expected to teach, or was it dramatic history? Nobody appeared to know. Long ago, my tutor Talbert had been vague like this about the examinations for which he was supposed to be preparing me.

The other twice-born people I think of are those forebodingly revealed to me by my abortive acquaintance Stumpe: young men who had come to Oxford straight from school and were now, only a few years later, coming there again straight from war. Their wars had, no doubt, been as diverse as their schools, but broadly speaking they shared a common experience, so it was natural to regard them as a group. In my first undergraduate weeks in college I used to think about them a lot. I felt surprised that they were not more readily identifiable than they were; not to be spotted in the quad simply by a martial bearing or something of the kind. A number of them were married, but it nearly always took time to discover this. Their general unobtrusiveness (so remote from Stumpe's prediction) was puzzling then, although it is comprehensible in retrospect. There is a poem in which Matthew Arnold tells a girl (to an effect of undesigned comedy) that a sea rolls between them: their different pasts. The young men returned from the war were determined to have nothing to do with such a sea; their idea was simply to get back to square one and muck in again.

It can't have been all that difficult, since Oxford itself goes in for continuities fairly massively. Yet there were at least superficial ways in which the place had changed more during their short absence than it subsequently did during my very much longer one. Merely consider breakfast, lunch, and tea. When, as an undergraduate, I wanted tea I got it for myself or in a common room, and for breakfast and lunch (or, of course, for dinner) I went into hall. But for boys who had entered the college in, say, 1938, the first two of these meals were carried to their rooms, across rainy quads and up stone staircases, by menservants (most of them already elderly) who had also kindled coal fires, emptied slops, and conjured up hot water by the quart or gallon. The lunch might be anything from bread and cheese and beer to an elaborate entertainment designed to gratify their most sophisticated acquaintances. There was a separate and smaller tribe of youths, more or less of their own age, who on demand would appear in the afternoon bearing tea and muffins, and who at other times cleaned their bicycles and mended punctures. It would be tedious to enlarge on this sort of thing.

That all disappeared overnight, it seems, pretty well as the first sirens sounded. As in Shakespeare's play, *with a quaint device, the banquet vanished*: only here the magic was that not of Prospero's wand but of Hitler's Panzers. Any revival of such dispositions during my undergraduate years always had about it an air of anachronism, indeed of social anomaly; and I was thus of the very first generation to belong wholly to the period of what was to be called the social revolution. When I returned to Oxford in middle age this immediate post-war change had simply established itself a little more distinctly. Pupils—for I was to have pupils—who a generation before would have entertained me with the air of inhabiting a Stately Home now did so in their digs and off their own bat, with much competent scurrying in and out of make-shift kitchens which were probably bathrooms as well. In point of hygiene there may have been something to be desired, but there can be no doubt of the larger wholesomeness of the change.

I had friends, sons and grandsons of former members of the college, who were inclined to take on the character of *laudatores temporis acti*. Tony—Tony Mumford, whose rooms were across the landing from my own on our staircase in Surrey—was the most intelligent of these. Senior boys at English public schools, he said, enjoyed various powers and privileges—but they weren't dispensed, for example, from trooping in to communal feeding three times a day. So the new Oxford system, in this seemingly trivial matter, didn't provide them with the sharp contrast which had obtained under the old. A contented sense of having attained adulthood had resulted from having somebody like a decrepit private footman staggering up your own staircase with your very own bacon and eggs. Such tangible tokens of being grown-up kept people quiet—conned them, in fact. It was like putting ten-year-old brats in long trousers; their vanity was gratified and they did what they were told. The dons had always run things that way; they regarded you as Other Ranks and dolloped out a corresponding discipline—but got away with it by calling you 'Mr Pattullo' or 'Mr Mumford', arranging to have sundry plebs scurrying round calling you 'sir', and generally laying on the hollow appearance of independence. It would take dynamite really to change their ways. Potentially, however, there was dynamite in the simple physiological fact of earlier maturation. People were now going to grow up earlier because they were better fed—the lower classes in particular. And there were going to be economic and political factors too. Our children—Tony's and my own— would find themselves coming legally of age at seventeen or eighteen: military service, earlier pay-packets in the wake of an expanding economy, a general loosening up of old family structures would make that inevitable. (Tony, the most frivolous of youths, had an uncanny nose for such things; I sometimes marvel that I didn't then spot in him the successful politician in the making.) So life in a college like this would become more and more a schizophrenic affair. It would no longer be possible to run such places as, in essence, bloody convents. Which made it stupid not to go on running them as, superficially, tolerably decent hotels.

I don't know that I was impressed by Tony's arguments, but from the first I was a good deal impressed by Tony. But for him, I don't think Oxford would have sold itself to me as completely, or at least as quickly, as it did. I was becoming aware of one thing and another as evoking in me an occasional complexity of response which might be professionally useful one day, but which had its simple origin in the fact of my parents' belonging severally to distinct classes of society. If this endowed me with a certain detachment, that was a free bonus contingent upon my birth, and unrelated to any merit or effort of my own. Tony's set-up was different. Although I learnt little about his people and their background throughout the few years of our first intimacy, it was obvious that what lay behind him were entrenched prejudices and assumptions of a formidably integrated sort. So all the odd reservations and ironies which—at least as a young man—he was able to bring to play upon the new world in which I found myself had to be chalked up, it seemed to me, to the credit of his own will and intellect. It was essentially, perhaps, a matter of brains. Long afterwards, I was to decide that what chiefly distinguished Tony from his son Ivo was the fact that Tony was intelligent and Ivo was not, and my disposition to support Ivo through his graceless university career was prompted by the feeling that an intellectually limited and over-privileged boy is peculiarly at risk if brought up within the shadow of a heavy-weight father prowling the corridors of power. But this is to run far ahead. At the moment, Tony and I are both still in our nonage. And I am a more serious youth than he has any intention of admitting himself to be.

In fact our acquaintance began in the moment when I put out a hand to stop Tony throwing an empty champagne bottle through a window. He was as astonished as he was indignant.

'You bloody awful man,' he said, 'who the hell are you?'

'Pattullo. You're too tight to recognize your nearest neighbour.'

'Bugger my neighbour!' Having dropped the bottle, Tony paused to grope for it in the semi-darkness of Surrey. 'You needn't be in a hurry, young Pattullo, to come arsing round asserting your rotten neighbourliness. I didn't arrange it, did I? Answer me that.' Tony found the bottle, and there was a crash of broken glass. It added little to more extensive effects of the same sort going on in Surrey at the time.

'It's you that's being in a hurry, you ass. Take a look at your pals. They're thinking just that. How long have you been around, for Christ's sake? Not long enough for them to welcome you as the life and soul of their silly riot. Another five minutes, and you'll find yourself in that fountain.'

I must have turned on this intervention, and been inspired to the robust idiom in which I couched it, by nothing more worthy than the instinct to put on a bold front when thoroughly frightened. There could be no doubt about the riot—or at least the effect of riot—erupting around us. I don't suppose that more than half-a-dozen youths were involved. But in addition to window-breaking they were expert in the noises of the hunting-field—and these, being unfamiliar to me, were alarming. Having read about such frolics in fiction was not proving an adequate armour when confronted with the fact.

Tony—upon whom I had stumbled casually in this situation —made a movement which I interpreted as preparation for a swipe at me. But this wasn't so. The grass around us was littered with bottles; they glinted, dull green and gilt, like the dangerous projectiles they were. I wondered where on earth, after five years of war, so much champagne could have come from. Tony had his eye on another window and was feeling for further ammunition—which was, after all, the only honest response to my expostulation. But there was a clink of glass, and I heard him exclaim,

'I say! I think you may be right. I've heard a word or two from them I don't quite like. And—do you know?—here's a full one! Some silly sod's brought out a full one. Come on, young Pattullo.'

In another moment we had slipped unobtrusively away from the group of revellers. Although I found being addressed as 'young Pattullo' highly offensive, I registered a first feeling of respect for Tony Mumford. A man who, when very drunk, could take a hint, size up a false situation, and promptly extricate himself from its probable consequences (to wit, immersion in three feet of cold and fishy water) was a companion not to be despised. We found our corner of Surrey, and climbed the staircase.

'Come in,' Tony said, throwing open his door. 'What's your bloody name?'

'I've told you. And you keep on repeating it. Pattullo.'

'You don't think I'm going to drink champagne with a man while calling him by a daft name like that?'

'You can damn-well leave my name alone.'

'But it *is* daft. So's mine. Mumford. Mumble, mum, bum, bumf. No good at all. Shame of my ancestors.'

'All right. Duncan.'

'Tony. Find a chair and I'll find glasses. Champers shouldn't ever be drunk in those things shaped like saucers. Vulgar invention of Edward the Pox-maker, I've been told. Deep glass, narrow at the top—that's what's proper. Keeps in the bubbles. Can find a couple of swizzle-sticks too, as a matter of fact. Had them off an aunt. Have you any swizzle-sticks—aunts, I mean? Useful creatures at times.'

I stated the number of my aunts, and wondered what Aunt Charlotte would make of Tony Mumford. He was much closer to her world, I suspected, than to Uncle Rory's. On the other hand, she strongly disapproved of inebriety, and I had a suspicion that she regarded my father as a drunkard. If she

66

apprehended that I was in danger of going the same way, she would deprecate this fresh association. Tony was opening the bottle with an expertness plainly bred of habit, but at the same time distinguishably with an effort after maximum effect. The cork accordingly flew across the room, and landed with a smack dangerously close to a large oil-painting which hung over the mantelpiece. In a dim light I could distinguish only that this appeared to owe its inspiration to classical antiquity. It surprised me that an undergraduate should travel around with such an object. In the corresponding position in my own room across the landing I had hung, after some hesitation, what was at the time my most prized possession, a water-colour study for what had become one of my father's most celebrated paintings, the *Young Picts watching the arrival of Saint Columba*. I reflected with satisfaction that, as compared with Tony Mumford, I was certainly the owner of the artistically superior article.

The champagne was already frothing into the first glass when I found myself almost saying, 'But the bottle isn't yours, is it?' This legalistic ineptitude, urged upon me by the moral stance to which I had been brought up, I fortunately refrained from uttering—if only because the answer was already plain to me. Tony had stolen the bottle as definitely as if he had strolled through a wine-shop and slipped it into a brief-case. It wasn't even as if he had belonged to the gang fooling around in the quad. He had simply butted in on them in an over-confident fashion—and had been induced by me to come away (I now saw) only when he had spotted the chance of liberating this quite costly means of refreshment.

'Stolen sweets are best,' Tony said contentedly. He had considerable power of reading one's thoughts. 'A remark first made in some shockingly bawdy context, I don't doubt. But, of course, the point about champers is that it ought *not* to be sweet. I'm afraid this may be. But let's try. Your health, Master Duncan Pattullo.'

'Your health, Master Antony Mumford.' I couldn't say less

than this. Indeed, I had sufficient sense to regard the moment as a serious one. At the same time, being of fanciful mind, I wondered whether some sombre symbolism attended my thus drinking a first Oxford toast in purloined *Moët et Chandon*. The bottle added, I noticed, the words *Première Cuvée*, which certainly meant 'first tubful'. I wondered just how champagne was made in tubs. 'Did they bring you up on champagne at Downside?' I asked.

'No—on cider. Monks and people put in a great deal of time making cider. How do you know I was at Downside? I don't know where *you* were—nor care, either.'

'It was the only word you condescended to utter to somebody who tried to make civil conversation to you in hall. When we were up for the scholarship examination, I mean.'

'I was diffident, Duncan. Shy. Overawed.'

'You were nothing of the kind. I thought you most disagreeable, as a matter of fact.'

'Then you had the advantage of me. I didn't think about you at all.'

'Of course you didn't. You weren't aware of me.'

'On the contrary, Duncan, I rated you the prettiest boy in the circus. That's why I didn't *think* about you. I just didn't dare to.'

This was a kind of badinage new to me. I remembered that Tony Mumford and I had also stared at each other in stony nudity in a subterraneous bath-place in Rattenbury. It had surely been quite without any disposition to admire one another's charms. His last remark was a matter of requiting one home truth with another. Tony *had* been disagreeable. (He was going to continue so, towards anybody he disliked or was merely indifferent to, for some time. But I was to watch him disciplining himself in point of this disadvantageous habit. By the time he went down he was being charming to everyone; could have been described, in fact, as well on his way.) But if Tony could justly be called disagreeable, it was no doubt equally true that 'pretty boy' represented an accurate description of me. I was slim and fair and looked even younger than I was; and it was from my mother that my features came to me. For some years I was going to find these harmless circumstances embarrassing.

Acknowledging that a certain immediate frankness had established itself between us, I decided that Tony Mumford and I were going to get on quite well.

'I wouldn't call it *too* sweet,' I said judicially. Champagne had not, in fact, often come my way.

'Not too bad. Mustn't look a gift horse in the mouth. Nice that it's a whole bottle. Last us for the outside of an hour in a lingering way. Particularly with the swizzle-sticks.'

Tony got up and wandered round the room. His movements —and, indeed, his articulation—obliged me to conclude that he wasn't drunk at all. This puzzled me. I had yet to learn that he was one of those extraordinary people who can emerge from, and then again subside beneath, the effects of liquor at will. It is an enviable endowment, rather like that of an absolute command over sleeping and waking, and one probably particularly useful in political life.

'Here they are,' Tony said with casual pride. 'Thought I'd unpacked them. Essential for the second glass.'

I made a note that I was being officiously counselled not to commit the solecism of using a swizzle-stick too soon. The contraption itself was familiar to me, Ninian once having brought one home from the twenty-firster of an older friend. But that had been a wooden affair like a pencil with a stumpy star-fish at the end; there had been room for everybody to sign his name on it. The instruments which Tony had had off an aunt were made of silver and on the principle of the umbrella; you pushed a ring along a shank and there bobbed out at one end a miniaturized version of such a thing blown inside-out and stripped of its fabric. The ribs were of fine silver wire, and tipped with tiny blobbles that looked shockingly like gold.

'Elegant,' I said, and was conscious of rather overdoing the sarcastic note.

'Yes, aren't they? Quite exquisitely vulgar. I'll tell you what. We'll stow them away after this, and you shall have them for a wedding-present. Commemorating our first uncouth meeting, you know.'

'I think I'd rather have a crate of champagne—which would cost about the same money. Pink, if you feel an extra touch of vulgarity to be the appropriate thing.'

'Well, well, well!' Tony fiddled with his swizzle-stick as a man might do with a watch-chain, and treated me to a relaxed and friendly stare. 'It looks as if we can drop those sophisticated remarks. So what? I suppose we could talk smut or cricket or rugger, or inquire into the existence of God. Be under-graduates, in fact. We've taken it on.'

'Do you get a lot about God at a Catholic school?'

'Nothing out of the way. It's not exactly an optional extra —but nothing out of the way. Reasonable bunch of men. Civilized, in fact. I expect you get quite as much God in your Caledonian conventicles. Would you describe yourself as having been religiously brought up?'

'Not particularly.' I was at sea as to whether Tony's question was seriously intended, and decided to give it the benefit of the doubt. 'Conventionally, rather. My father's an artist, and I don't suppose he believes in the Incarnation, and things of that sort. But he thinks it's proper to do a certain amount of going to church. It's partly because he has a great respect for a brother of his who's a minister—a clergyman. And it's partly because he was brought up in a simple home of what's called the God-fearing sort.'

'Yes—I see.' Tony looked at me thoughtfully. 'Did your mother have the same sort of upbringing?'

'Not exactly.' I said no more. I was becoming aware of Tony Mumford as being, at least in some respects, a singularly acute youth.

'Your father's Lachlan Pattullo?'

'That's right.' I felt a start of pleased surprise. 'You know his work?'

'Not precisely that.' For the first time, Tony had hesitated. 'As a matter of fact, I've been looking chaps up. You know that list of freshmen they give us? I've run through it with *Who's Who*, spotting the papas. Came on yours in that way. I'm not very hot on modern painting. Of course I'm sure I'd know his work if I was.'

I suppose that astonishment held me silent. This action of Tony's was beyond my mental range. Even odder was the fact that, after only a moment's hanging fire, he had confessed to it. This, I can see now, was our definitive moment. Tony and I were to be other than mere neighbours. He had, so to speak, shown me the works.

'It says,' Tony went on easily, 'that he's going to be top man up there next year. That right?'

'Well, yes—in a formal way. President of something. It doesn't mean he'll paint any better.' I said this kindly but firmly. Confronted by a young tycoon and silver swizzle-sticks, it was incumbent upon an artist's son to show the flag.

'Savvy,' Tony said with a grin. 'In fact—and in the same lingo—*touché*. Still, in the matter of commissions and all that it will make a bit of a difference?'

'It will make Difference Number One.' I found Tony's sticking to his own standards attractive. 'Difference Number Two will be when the appropriate people recognize the quality of what he turns out. A good many of them are in Paris and Rome and New York.'

'Double savvy. And proper respect and all that, my whole-some child. My father's a banker during the week and a country gent at week-ends. Takes all sorts, you know.'

'Takes all sorts?'

'To make a world.'

'I suppose so.'

Having said this, I was silent again, and drank stolen champagne. Something faintly self-congratulatory and even smug was creeping into our colloquy. I distrusted it. I was aware—not quite for the first time—of having arrived in a

71

place immensely armoured in assurance, in inherited confidence. I wondered whether it was going to be of much use to me.

'I say!' Tony said. 'They're not half stepping it up.'

This was indisputable. In Surrey there was now a notable hullabaloo. It drew Tony. A good part of him wanted to be out in it—which was why he had made that indiscreetly premature effort with an empty bottle. I took satisfaction in having yanked him out of that.

The racket astounded me. I couldn't think where all these young savages had come from. Stumpe was conceivably one of them, but Stumpe hadn't struck me as likely to be particularly rowdy. Nor had anybody else. I had even reflected that there seemed to be less *joie de vivre* and *élan* around than might have been predicated on the evidence of popular romances of university life. People went about in a noticeably subdued and decorous fashion. But that was by day. This was night.

'Do you suppose it's a regular thing?' I asked.

'Can't be. Much too expensive. It's just a dining club letting off steam. Mayn't even happen again this term.'

'I suppose that's why nobody comes out and stops it.'

'Perhaps.' Tony seemed to find this speculation naïve. 'Would you care to have to try? The Provost himself would be a little hunted hare at the first view-halloo.'

'It certainly sounds like that.' I realized that it was the suggestion of hot pursuit rather than mere uproar that was so spine-chilling. 'Are those horns being properly sounded, or are they just blowing away at random?'

'Haven't a clue. Not one of your fox-hunting men.'

'I don't feel a fox would content them at all—let alone a hare. I think they're absolutely yelling for blood. The real thing. Do you think there's somebody around who's a bit unpopular?'

'Oh, most unlikely.' Tony replied casually—but I don't think he was quite at ease, any more than I was. 'They may scrag one another now and then. But all in jest. The young barbarians at play.'

Immediately beneath us, glass crashed, shivered, showered, tinkled in a big way. A wild cheer went up as from a whole army—this, I suppose, because the surrounding quad acted like a sounding-board or echo-chamber. Then there was a moment-ary lull. It was only because of this that we heard a knock on Tony's door. I reacted by spilling some champagne on my trousers. I was in a thoroughly jittery condition. But Tony appeared unperturbed by this sinister nocturnal summons, and called to come in.

'Oh, excuse me!' The head of a young man of our own age had appeared in the doorway. It had appeared rather near the lintel, and somehow conveyed an immediate suggestion of belonging to what my father would have called a ganglin body —loose-limbed and awkward. The young man wore large circular spectacles in a steel frame—the sort of thing, I thought, that at school goes *en suite* with cage-like dental contrivances designed to corner vagrant teeth. 'I'm extremely sorry,' the young man said, and glanced from one to the other of us in a fashion so vaguely oblique as to convey no convincing im-pression that he distinguished either Tony or myself. He was trying to decide who was the owner of the room. 'My name's Mogridge. I'm downstairs. You may have noticed my name above the door. Mogridge.'

'Yes—I have.' I produced this reply myself, since Tony appeared unprepared to utter. 'You're directly under me, as a matter of fact. I'm over the way from Mumford here. I'm Pattullo.'

'Oh, how do you do?' Mogridge had now come into the room. He was diffident but not embarrassed, and offered us a tentative smile.

'How do you do?' Tony said belatedly. 'Do sit down. Have some champagne.'

'Thank you—but I won't barge in.' Mogridge was quite clear about the character of the invitation held out to him. 'I just wanted to say I hoped I haven't been disturbing you.'

73

'Disturbing us?' Tony stared at Mogridge blankly, as he well might. The lull outside was over, and the field in full cry again. 'Tonight, you mean?'

'Yes—with my 'cello. I'm afraid I've been playing it rather late. That affair with rules they've given us says not after eleven. Nothing noisy after eleven. But it's my cadenzas, you see. I can't satisfy myself, and it's awfully tempting to go on till one gets better.'

'Yes, of course,' Tony said. 'We all have the instinct to improve. I have it myself. I got a prize for effort, as a matter of fact, at my private school. Sorry to boast.'

'For effort?' It appeared that the 'cellist was impervious to sarcasm. 'I don't think there were prizes for effort at my prepper. And not at Marlborough, either. But the music was pretty good there. Does either of you have an instrument?'

'We both have,' Tony said. 'The same instrument, it turns out to be. Wouldn't you call that an extraordinary coincidence? And here it is.' Tony raised his swizzle-stick in air and shook it. A tiny sound—almost, as it happened, to be termed musical —issued from it as the little gold blobbles collided. 'Do you know it? It's called the Chinese chinks.'

'There's something called the Chinese block in a full orchestra. It doesn't give a definite note, I believe. It's Temple blocks that do that. Temple blocks give a definite note. Although they're nothing but chunks of wood with holes bored in them.' Mogridge offered these instructive remarks at leisure. If he was aware he was being made fun of, he didn't betray the fact. 'But I must be off,' he went on. 'I promise to put away the 'cello for the night, so you shan't be disturbed again. I just felt I must apologize for being thoughtless. Good night.'

'Oh, do stop for a few minutes.' Tony, although rather going in for bad manners, appeared readily won over by good. 'And have a glass of this stuff to initiate our acquaintance.'

'Thank you very much.' Mogridge dropped into a chair without fuss. I saw that he was experimenting with a moustache. But it was not this, or not this alone, that lent him an air of faint anachronism. Something else—and I don't think it was his clothes either—already rendered that suggestion of throwback to an earlier period (Edwardian or even late Victorian) which was to be so pronounced in him a quarter of a century later. At the moment, I wondered whether this was a subjective impression of my own; whether, for example, Mogridge just happened to correspond in appearance to somebody in an old illustrated edition of *Tom Brown's School Days* or perhaps *Eric, or Little by Little*. I was struck, at the same time, by some peculiarity of his vision. When disposed to hold you in full focus he would move his head to the left and appear to concentrate on a spot a couple of feet wide of your right shoulder. The effect was that of somebody about to attempt a place-kick in a stiff breeze. I was to conclude later that a large part of Gavin Mogridge's appearance of extreme vagueness was due to this ocular peculiarity. When you did catch his gaze direct you were likely to be aware that it was penetrating beyond the average.

'It's Saint-Saëns's Concerto,' Mogridge was saying as he accepted champagne. 'The solo parts in the first movement. A bit tricky, really.' He paused. 'A bit tricky, the first movement of Saint-Saëns's Concerto. Oh, thank you very much.' He had been offered Tony's Chinese chinks, now again become a swizzle-stick. 'Amusing things, these. Rather amusing, swizzle-sticks. I want to get on to Elgar's Concerto, as a matter of fact. To play the finale of that with full orchestra would be quite something. But I don't deny I've some way to go. I've some way to go to Elgar. Have to face it.'

'But not tonight.' Tony repressed a yawn. I believe he judged himself to have turned on his best behaviour, as became a host, but there was an obstinate glint of mockery in his eye. 'About those cadenzas, by the way. You haven't been aware of a certain amount of crescendo going on at the same time? A spot of allegro pomposo, as it were.' Tony paused on this, apparently pleased with it. It was to be his line to mingle a cheerfully philistine note with random exhibitions of know-ledgeableness in one field and another. But Mogridge looked (if Mogridge could be said to look) quite blank. 'Out in the quad, you know. Listen.'

'Oh, those chaps! Yes, I suppose there is a bit of a din. They've been drinking, I'd say. Wouldn't you say they'd been drinking? That's it.'

'Doesn't it terrify you?' I asked.

'Terrify me?' There was an entire blankness in Mogridge's response. 'Does it terrify *you*, Pattullo?'

'It absolutely takes the pants off me.' I felt this frankness was due to myself. 'And I'd feel particularly vulnerable, if I was on the ground floor like you.'

'You could sport your oak, I suppose. But sporting your oak is said not to be quite the thing. It's felt not to be on, sporting your oak.'

For some minutes the din had been less shattering—the mob, I imagine, having moved into Howard. But now it was coming back again. This was the most alarming effect yet. It was impossible not to believe that a score of rowing hearties and rugger toughs were making a bee-line for us, solely intent upon the destruction of Messrs Mumford, Mogridge and Pattullo—three quiet youths rationally conversing in an upper chamber.

'I expect it's just some of the men out of the Forces,' Mogridge said comfortably. 'They feel they're due a bit of fun—and quite right too. A lot of them had a pretty dull war. But not everybody. Not everybody had too dull a time. I was talking to a chap last night. When only a subaltern he had to navigate a whole brigade across the Western Desert, just with a compass and by the stars. It must have been quite something, that.'

'Almost,' Tony said, 'like playing that Elgar finale against a whole orchestra.'

'Just like that!' Mysteriously for a moment, our visitor was a man transformed. 'But I must be off,' he said, standing up. 'Yes, I must certainly go to bed.' He turned to me. 'I don't think there's really the slightest risk of anybody coming up here and mucking around. But if any of them do, just stamp hard on the floor, Pattullo, and I'll run up and lend a hand. Thanks awfully for the champagne, Mumford. You must have a tiptop wine merchant. Good night.'

'Well, if you must go,' Tony said, and stood up. 'Of course, I expect you're accustomed to this sort of racket—at least in the middle distance. For you live in Cambridge, don't you? Isn't it there that your father's a professor?'

'Yes, it is.' Mogridge had paused at the door, decidedly surprised. 'How did you know?'

'I've heard of him, naturally.' Tony produced this quite unblushingly. 'Good night, old boy. Nice of you to have looked in.'

We listened to Mogridge's footsteps fading. Tony shared out the last of the champagne. I stood up and wandered round the room. The big picture over the mantelpiece proved to portray a group of Roman ladies in the languorous enjoyment of gracious living amid a vista of marble halls. Their attire, if obviously sheddable, was decorously unshed; their attitudes, on the other hand, were such that any one of them might have been posing as Leda contentedly awaiting the embrace of the next swan.

'Good God, Tony!' I said. 'A thing like that just isn't good for your health.'

'It's a Victorian effort, as you can see. Astonishing what that prudish age would take in a pictorial way. Anything to activate the little swizzle-stick, one might say.' Tony was obviously proud of this dubious artistic possession. 'You're welcome to drop in on my wenches at any time.'

I record this as being the first of innumerable salacious exchanges, all equally imbecile, which Tony's painting was to prompt. No small circumstance during my first weeks in college surprises me more in the recollection than the facility I discovered in myself for bawdy talk. At school I had been a shade inhibited in such matters. And my father's fellow-artists, although I believe them to have been highly inventive in the field, commonly refrained from it when Ninian or myself was in their company, a thing which happened frequently enough. Some of the witticisms which the Lord Chamberlain was occasionally to insist on my excising from my plays must have had their origin in this entirely salubrious aspect of my under-graduate years.

'I don't think Mogridge would approve of it,' I said of the picture, as I wandered away to inspect Tony's books. 'But whether he saw it or not, one just couldn't tell. Still, you've made quite a pal of him, haven't you? Two new pals in one evening, and both through knowing all about their distin-guished fathers on the strength of a reference-book. You'll go far. Will Mogridge? What did you think of him?'

'One of the last Romantics, if you ask me. Perhaps one of the last *great* Romantics.' Tony was lounging back in his chair. 'I'm a classical man myself.'

I was discovering that Tony Mumford owned quite a large number of classical texts. I wondered how much he frequented them. That he had made a perceptive if extravagantly couched remark about our late visitor didn't enter my head. It was something he wasn't going to make a habit of. Gavin Mogridge fairly quickly came to bore Tony.

'Listen!' Tony said, and sat up.

What I had to listen to was sudden near-silence. A moment before, the uproar in Surrey had been unabated. Now it had simply stopped, as if turned off at a tap. One heard instead footsteps, a few opening and closing doors, young and well-modulated voices calling out casual good-nights. These muted and respectable sounds were certainly being produced by the Dionysiac rout still vocal minutes' earlier. Oddly, this was the most unnerving part of the show. It was as if the wild beasts that had been let loose about the college had discovered some treacherous magic which enabled them to cloak themselves in human form. I might be passing the time of day with them in the quad next morning, or sitting next to one in a lecture. And if wild beasts can turn human at will, it is evident that humans are liable to turn wild beasts at a drop of the most casual handkerchief.

'Revels ended,' Tony said sleepily. He was immune from any such thought as I had been entertaining. 'Better jettison the incriminating evidence, don't you think?' He walked over to a window, threw up the sash, and hurled the empty champagne bottle far into the darkness of the quad. I listened, horrified, for the crash of its breaking against stone, or for whatever sound would result from its impact on somebody's skull. There was only a faint thud. The bottle must have landed on grass at the far side of Surrey. 'Just another contribution to the quad-men's haul in the morning,' Tony said. 'I expect they flog them to rag-and-bone merchants. The simpler classes of society, you know, favour them for turning into table-lamps.'

'I'm going to bed,' I said, '—like that chap Mogridge.' Tony's action had shaken me. I moved to the door, and with my hand on it reflected that it was only on a basis of candour that Tony Mumford and I were likely to have much of a joint future. 'That was a bloody silly thing to do,' I added. 'Good night.'

'Good night, young Pattullo.' Standing in front of his masterpiece of Victorian *volupté*, Tony grinned at me—carefree and totally unoffended. 'I appoint you my wee Scottish guardian angel. Good night, sweet laddie, good night.' He stretched his arms luxuriously. There was already something slightly heavy about him, and I was to recall him in this pose many years later.

'Oh, I'm so sorry!'

I had to say this, because I had almost knocked somebody down. The staircase and landing were in near-darkness, since the lighting had been switched nocturnally to the merest glimmer. I didn't so much see the figure I had bumped against as merely sense him. I put out a hand and found it gripping a trembling arm.

79

'I say,' I said, 'are you all right?'

'Yes. Yes, thank you.' The voice was trembling as well. 'Are you Mr Mumford?'

'No. My name's Pattullo. Mr Mumford'—I managed to re-iterate this appellation with a civility which both my father and Uncle Rory would equally have approved—'is through there. Behind me, I mean. I've just left him. Are you looking for him?'

'Oh, no—not at all!' The suggestion appeared further to perturb the agitated person beside me. 'I'm Mr Bedworth. I'm Bedworth. Cyril Bedworth.' The young man was concerned to get this right. 'You won't have heard of me. I'm at the top. Of the staircase, that is.'

'Yes, I know.' It was true I hadn't exactly heard of Bedworth, but I had noticed his name on the letter-rack downstairs. 'They're pretty stingy with the lighting, aren't they? Like the black-out again.'

'Yes, aren't they?' Bedworth was finding a certain relief in speech. 'And in the quads, too. I thought it was all right, you see. They seemed all to have gone away.'

'Those ghastly rowdies, you mean?'

'Yes—them.' Bedworth, whose mind seemed to be moving rather slowly, caught the suggestion that we were on the same side of a fence. 'So I came out——'

'Out?'

'Of a doorway. It was quite dark in it, and I thought I'd be all right. Things went quiet at last—suddenly, in fact—so I thought the coast was clear. Then something seemed to whiz past my head.'

'I expect you imagined that. Natural, when all that rumpus had been going on.'

'I actually felt it in my hair. Or I thought I did. But I suppose you're right.'

'I'm sure I am.' The thought that Tony Mumford might have brained this timid person didn't greatly entertain me. 'But look,' I went on, 'I'm just going back to my rooms.

Won't you come in for a minute?' I was about to add, 'I've got some whisky there'—but felt that, at least if prematurely disclosed, the information might be other than reassuring. 'We ought to have got to know each other by this time.'

'Yes—we should.' Although Bedworth jerked this out, it was with conviction. There came to me—dimly, and for a moment—the perception that he had clear views about the place. I didn't get far with this. I was too occupied with my big-brother turn. Perhaps I had a faint sense that Tony Mumford had been patronizing me—or would have been benevolently so doing if I'd let him. I'd have a go at Bedworth now.

But I am aware, as I write this, that it isn't really true. My actual impulse towards Bedworth that night must have been more respectable. He was confronted with a new environment stranger to him by several vital degrees than it was to me. At the same time, I felt myself to be much a *spectator ab extra*, and I was very determined not to underplay the part. (Indeed, what was intellectually mature in me—which wasn't much— whispered of the advantages to an artist of resisting facile assimilations.) So I felt a tolerably honest wish to support this new acquaintance. Accordingly, I opened the door of my room, flicked on the light, and pretty well shoved Bedworth inside.

Having entered, he just stood. There wasn't for the moment, of course, much else he could do, but he somehow managed to do it awkwardly. He must have been chronically aware of his outward man as unimpressive, since his figure was weedy and his complexion spotty. I saw that he was wearing his scholar's gown—doubtless under some antique persuasion that this was enjoined upon him after dark by the discipline of the university.

'Do sit down,' I said. 'And won't you take off your gown?' I detected this as sounding too polite. 'And why are you wear- ing it, for heaven's sake? I'm told you have to for lectures still. And when you go to your tutor, until he turns chummy and tells you not to. And, to the end of your honoured days as Provost, Bedworth, you'll never be allowed a dinner without

81

it. But that's it. It's not meant for impressing shopkeepers, or instead of a duffel-coat or an umbrella.'

'Oh, I see.' Bedworth acted obediently and spoke absently. He was still half-listening for renewed threats of violence from the quad. Then he looked about him. 'The rooms down here have very high ceilings,' he said disparagingly. 'And extremely large windows. I shouldn't wonder if they're rather cold in winter.'

'Probably they are.' I was getting out the whisky. 'Aren't yours the same?'

'No. They have the character of attics. The bedroom is rather small. But the study is quite commodious—only one has to be careful not to bump one's head. I think they will prove to be quite warm when it turns chilly.'

'I'm sure they will. Have some whisky.' I saw that Bedworth was looking extremely surprised. 'It's just,' I added hastily, 'that my father gave me a couple of bottles to bring up with me. Adulthood, and all that. And he wants me not to drink gin.'

'I've nothing against alcohol,' Bedworth said guardedly. For a moment he appeared to ponder what followed from this, and he then accepted carefully the very small amount of my precious Glenlivet that I had poured for him.

'It will do you good,' I said. 'You must have had a nasty time, hiding in that doorway. Did you find it terrifying?'

'The rag?' Bedworth queried cautiously.

'Yes, the rag.'

'It was a little discomposing. You didn't yourself——'

'Christ, I was in a blue funk, Bedworth. I was saying to Tony Mumford that it pretty well took the pants off me. I nigh beshat myself, as our older writers say.'

This facetious pedantry (to which I was no doubt assisted by the stolen champagne) quite pleased Bedworth. He smiled for the first time—a smile wary, or at least shy. He then sipped his whisky, and looked momentarily so disconcerted that I burst out laughing. It was abominably rude, and all I felt I could do was to jolly the thing along.

'I say,' I asked robustly, 'surely I'm not the first person about the place to offer you a drink?'

'Mr Talbert gave me a sherry.' Bedworth paused on this. 'Talbert,' he said, 'gave me a glass of sherry. But you offer me a whisky. It's interesting, isn't it?'

I was entirely at sea. We had not yet all been taught, by appropriately well-born professors, what hidden chasms divide U and non-U speech. Bedworth must have been something of a pioneer.

'I think I'm right,' he went on—obviously seriously involved with his problem. 'One can't say "Give me a sherry", as I did a moment ago. That's a solecism. But one *can* say "Give me a whisky". You know, there must be the same exquisitely fine distinctions in French—and even perhaps in German. Think of setting out to master them! It's absolutely fascinating.'

'I suppose so.'

'I think of doing my research on something of that kind. Are you going to do research—after taking Finals, I mean?'

'After taking Schools,' I said maliciously.

'Yes, of course.' Bedworth was unresentful. I knew he would never speak of Finals again. 'The B.Litt., for instance. Have you thought of that? I've been looking up the regulations. And after that there's the D.Phil.'

I professed myself innocent of these ambitions, and even not too interested in them as animating other people. Bedworth, nevertheless, continued to discuss them for some time. He even accepted, in the course of his exposition, the second dram that I was sufficiently punctilious to offer him. All this occasioned a certain revulsion—or at least mild reversal—of feeling. Within seconds of grabbing him by the arm in the semi-darkness of the landing I had established him in my head as a wholly sympathetic character, a latterday Chaucerian Clerk of Oxenford, spending his grant exclusively on books, and much given to praying for the Minister of Education, whose bounty it was that enabled him to scoleye. What he had revealed about the exiguous head-room allowed him by the college augmented this impression. Now I was telling myself that he was a boring little man, a keelie out of a snot-school, concerned only with the mechanics of finding himself a dreary career as a pedagogue. Fortunately these unbeautiful feelings (which were never again going to visit me at all starkly in relation to Bedworth) didn't affect my manners, such as they were. I don't believe it was even with particular ostentation that I rammed the cork into the whisky-bottle half-an-hour later. And Bedworth seemed to retire to his upper regions contentedly enough.

I found myself lying awake for some time, endeavouring to check up on his philology. I thought I could hear Colonel Morrison saying, 'Mrs Ogilvie, be a good soul, and pour me a whisky'. I was sure I could hear my uncle's 'Elspeth, please bring some sherry'. I certainly couldn't hear my aunt saying, 'I'll have a sherry'. But then I couldn't hear her saying, 'I'll have a glass of sherry', either. Yet that might be only because she disapproved of drink entirely. I began to invent a scene in a play (a play rather in the manner of Colonel Morrison's friend, Willie Maugham) in which two men in dinner-jackets stood in front of a sideboard. One said to the other, 'I say, old chap, will you have a sherry?' and was thereby exposed as an unspeakable outsider. When I had achieved this potential contribution to English dramaturgy I went to sleep.

# IV

BECAUSE I WAS to be twice-born to Oxford in the manner I have described, my memories necessarily involve themselves with two generations of undergraduates. They differed in various ways. Nicolas Junkin of Cokeville Grammar School, whom I was to find occupying my old rooms in Surrey when I turned up for that college Gaudy which was so unexpectedly to feed a middle-aged playwright back into Oxford life— Nicolas Junkin and my own contemporary Cyril Bedworth came from very similar backgrounds. This didn't, of course, prevent their differing in character. But of equal significance was a difference in their relationship to the college which was a consequence of that full generation lying between them.

The balance of the place had shifted. The deeper causes of this lay in social history and the drift of social legislation, but the immediate cause was simply a change in academic standards. When I came up after the war the conditions of entry—although I didn't know it—had remained almost unchanged since the start of the century. The university's requirements in the way of learned accomplishments were minimal to the point of the absurd, and once a boy had satisfied these it was open to any college to approve of him and take him on. This didn't mean that the colleges were not in stiff competition with one another to secure able and industrious youths. They were. It did mean that most of them took for granted the validity of the proposition that a body of undergraduates ought to be a mixed lot; that some should read and some should row; and moreover that Uncle Rory's 'two universities' owned a particular responsibility to educate, if remotely educatable, those boys whom inherited wealth or tradition was particularly likely to promote to positions of public responsibility later on. In a college like my own, these persuasions and contentions produced, class-wise, a very marked effect.

A good many years before Junkin's time, however, the university—suddenly conscious, one has to suppose, of presiding over an unacceptably archaic scene—effected a cautious change of policy. A new matriculation standard was imposed: one falling not inordinately short of that required by the provincial universities. This sounds pusillanimous, but was quite sensible. The pitifully thick, the incorrigibly idle, even the pronouncedly inane: these, however socially acceptable, were now, except through error or chicanery, ruled out. But, as before, once the university tests of schoolboy attainment were satisfied, the colleges could do as they pleased. If still disposed to entertain a tenderness for the loitering heirs of city directors they retained a qualified liberty to do so. At the same time, they continued free to pay not too much attention to the marks and grades and ratings arrived at in huge public examinations. Their own traditional entrance tests went on as before, and they were thus able to engage in an activity dear to the heart of dons: that of distinguishing the gleam of future promise through the fog of present immaturity. This last exercise was not, I imagine, unproductive of fiasco. But it brought to Oxford occasional prizable eccentrics who would have stood little chance elsewhere.

There was nothing dramatic in the impact of these changes upon the college. The kind of young men, for instance, who so perturbed Bedworth and myself by their zeal in breaking windows were still well represented in Junkin's time—Junkin's neighbour, Ivo Mumford, having some claim to be among them. They were merely thinner on the ground. There were now as many Junkins as Mumfords, and their attitudes and tone became, accordingly, a more substantial part of the scene. I believe that—perhaps particularly during the 1960's—undergraduate feeling as a whole evolved a good deal under the influence of this growing number of young men who possessed, among other things, a more adult grip than their fellows on the economic facts of life. Thus Ivo received a handsome allowance from his father, and when he had exhausted it he simply ran down to Otby and collected a large tip from his grandfather. When Nick Junkin was broke he got a vacation job on a building site. On the whole the public school boys (although scarcely Ivo himself) responded to the challenge of this sort of independence. They were soon on the building sites themselves.

Intellectual independence is another matter, and here I come back to Bedworth and Junkin as presenting a contrast referable in some degree to that quarter of a century lying between them. Bedworth was from the first a young man of intellectual habit, but it was a habit with a conformist bent. He was anxious to assimilate himself to what he conceived of as the academic spirit of the place. Hence his precocious interest in the B.Litt. and D.Phil. and his seemingly absurd persuasion that there was matter of learned substance in how a man asked for whisky or sherry. In fact, his instinct was not altogether at fault, and a line is probably traceable from these first researches into social nicety to that highly respectable monograph of his critical maturity, *Proust and Powell*. Cyril Bedworth was all set, one might have said, to become a conventional don, piously revering a *status quo* and devoting a good deal of doggedness to defending it. He was to turn out to be something rather different.

Junkin as an undergraduate lived more apart from academic things. Our first meeting—on that eventful Gaudy night— would reveal that he had been in the college for a year without picking up the slightest notion of how the place was run. The stamp which Oxford was setting on him (and I don't doubt it was considerable) appeared in no immediate particular. It had not, for instance, affected his speech, which remained that of his own region, enriched by a close study of the more demotic texts of Harold Pinter. ('Flake off', he had said that night to Tin Pin, the forsaken mistress of a friend of his referred to as 'that swine Julian'.) In their own way, Junkin's interests were as distractingly extra-curricular as were Ivo Mumford's, although he contrived in spasms to work a good deal harder at his books. The last fact is within my knowledge because he eventually became my pupil for a time. In this relation he was willing to show an occasional awareness (usually solicitous in tone) that I was more than twice his age. But his vision of society was distinctly unhierarchical, and he was quite without the youthful Bedworth's disposition to treat his seniors with an anxious deference.

The relationship of teachers and taught makes a large theme. It is supposed to change radically between school and university, and I think it probable that—in Junkin's time as in my own—freshmen were inclined to arrive in college with substantial expectations of a transformed social status vis-à-vis their elders. Here is the moment of growing up; restraints are to be removed and the forms of discipline altered; it is reasonable to suppose that along with this will go a more frequent and intimate commerce between old and young. I doubt whether I myself entertained this hope with more than average fervour, but early in my first term I was harangued on its fallaciousness by a man called Buntingford. Buntingford was a junior don who had been turned on in an effort to combat my scant ability to cope with Latin unseen translation. For some reason I was expected to 'do' Latin for a term before getting on with the job for which the late John Ruskin (or some unknown admirer of his) was presumably paying me.

'Good God,' Buntingford cried out despairingly as I entered his room for the second or third time. 'It's young Pattullo again!' Tony's 'Young Pattullo' had somehow caught on; Buntingford, who probably didn't know of Tony's existence, had gathered that it was the amiable way to address me.

'Yes—it's me, I'm afraid.'

'It's quite absurd, you know.' Buntingford pointed to my effort at elucidating a chunk of Tacitus. It was lying inside his fender, as if only some stiff exercise of self-control on his part had preserved it from the flames. 'That you should be required to address yourself to such mysteries! The result is like the gibbering of apes. But, no—I mustn't exaggerate. Like the gibbering of Hottentots.'

'You mean I've no chance of passing the exam?' My voice must have betrayed genuine dismay.

'Oh, no—you'll pass the exam.' Buntingford appeared surprised. 'You see, there will be an English heading to the thing, just to give you a clue. Something like "An Unpredictable Element in the Movement of Public Opinion". Or perhaps "Marcellus Offers Reasons for Rejecting the Proposals of Prudentius Clemens". You must just offer a short prose meditation suggested by the theme. Make it a tolerable bit of writing. You write, as a matter of fact, quite well.' Buntingford paused, and picked up my exercise. He seemed needlessly pleased with himself. He was a very new tutor, and I judged him to be in process of working out a technique for more or less simultaneously insulting, amusing, and flattering the young. 'All the same,' he said, 'I suppose we'd better go through your effort. Do you think?'

'It would be awfully helpful, sir. If it's not too much of a bore, this is.'

On this note of civil accommodation, we worked through my piece. Buntingford then tossed it aside.

'Beta-query-minus,' he said unexpectedly. 'You'll be perfectly all right. Come along for another couple of goes near the end of term, if you want to. Have some madeira. Can't stand those gallons and gallons of ghastly sherry.' We had some madeira, in an atmosphere of proper relaxation. 'Has it come to you,' he asked, 'how much, in this place, you're going to look up unfed?'

'A hungry sheep? No, it hasn't. And am I?'

'Well, young Pattullo, just consider. Here's me, for example, politely showing you the door.'

'Isn't that because I'm not one of your real pupils?'

'You have a point there. But it's my point too. I have about a dozen chaps at any one time, addressing themselves in a long-term way to *real* Latin and Greek. See?'

'Yes—of course.'

'I work quite hard with them, and do the proper fatherly stuff as well, when required. Bills, antagonistic parents, girl-trouble, phobias and despairs—the lot. But that's just with my own little bunch—stray exceptions apart. Perhaps you'll get the same hand-out during the next three years from Talbert and Timbermill. I don't know. But hardly anybody else will have a word with you. So you see how different dons are from school-masters.'

'I thought that about apes and Hottentots quite school-masterish.'

'Have some more madeira.' Buntingford showed not the slightest displeasure at what I now see to have been rather an impertinent remark. 'And consider any decent school, such as your own. It's an odd fact, by the way, that hardly anybody comes up to this intellectually undistinguished college except from markedly good schools. And you won't think that when I say good I mean posh. Will you?'

'Not if you tell me not to.'

'Very well. Cast your mind far, far back, young Pattullo, and remember what it was like. You wander from form-room to form-room, being taught half-a-dozen different things by half-a-dozen different people during the week. Right?'

'Right.'

'They all know Pattullo from Mackonochie, and Mackonochie from Pattullo. Most of them chat you up a bit when they run into you. Some of them entertain you from time to time. Wives and daughters, and all that. Tea-parties when you're youngsters; wine and cheese in your final year. Not an awful lot of it, but a general feeling of informed interest blows around. Right again?'

'Well, yes—allowing for some regional differences.'

'Let's not allow for them. Let's take a guess at your own school. Old fashioned and arid, curriculum-wise. But outside that: sailing, forestry jobs, a beginning to rock climbing in the Cairngorms, skiing ditto, parties going abroad every holidays. Masters with the know-how on hand—and rather interesting people, some of them. Agreed?'

'Yes—I have to buy all that.'

'Very well. And you haven't done much inquiring around you here if you imagine there's a lot of that sort of thing on tap.'

'I suppose there isn't. But isn't it a matter of our no longer being exactly kids? Being on our own, and so forth?'

'Fair enough, so far as it goes. But the main point's patent. Dons just aren't interested in the young at large to the extent that schoolmasters are. Listen, Pattullo! I may be talking dogmatic balls. But accept it for the moment as true. How would you account for it?'

This seemed a reasonable challenge. I felt that Buntingford, who had devoted just ten minutes to the state of my latinity, was laying on a copy-book tutorial after all. These widely-ranging discussions are frequently referred to in nostalgic reminiscences of university life.

'I suppose they're cleverer,' I said. 'Dons, I mean. Or, at least, they're more interested in abstractions and intellectual issues and things. And also'—I added this hopefully—'in research.'

'What in God's name is that?'

'Making knowledge, as opposed to just transmitting it.' I felt Buntingford's interruption to have been a shade oafish. 'It probably becomes extremely absorbing—and it's also likely to be a way out, so far as undergraduates are concerned. Too tough or technical or recondite for them—so it doesn't really constitute a substantial common interest. I can see all that. Still, they have plenty of time on their hands—haven't they? One can be aware of *that* without much inquiring around. They're not kept at routine jobs to anything like the extent schoolmasters are. And they have those enormous vacations thrown in. No, I haven't really found an answer. There must be something else. Perhaps some sheerly temperamental difference.'

'Perhaps so. Dons are shy. I'm extremely shy and retiring myself. You must have noticed it.'

'Yes, sir. But I'm doing my best to coax you to talk.'

'Young Pattullo is an infant satirist, a mocker in the making. But think! I do feel you've overlooked something. That specialization.'

'Like six subjects—or at least three or four—at school, and really just one here for years on end? Yes, I see.'

'Enormously important. Mind you, specialization doesn't much insulate don from don; they get chattering away to each other, all right. Nor undergraduate from undergraduate; you'll find your closer acquaintance won't more than half of them be reading English. But it does affect the get-together business between old and young. It's as I was saying in my own case. A tutor does his stint with his own pupils, and that's it. I don't suppose it matters all that. Interesting phenomenon, all the same.'

'Do you think things have changed much?' I asked. 'I know your own memory can't go back all that far.' This was fair enough, since Buntingford could not have been more than four or five years older than myself. 'But from what you've heard about before the Kaiser's war, or about just between the wars.'

'Less and less celibacy around, for one thing. Or at least I rather feel so, although I don't think I've ever seen any statistics. Curious, if it's true. One doubts whether the proportion of males not much drawn to the eternal womanly alters from period to period. Obscure subject. Then money—less of that going, without a doubt. Your old-style college fellow tended to have something quite comfy of his own. Surprising number still do, for that matter. More and more of us near the bread-line, all the same. Nosing round for honest subsidiary employments. Writing reviews for sixpenny papers. This new highbrow programme on the radio: out-relief for dons, that's going to be.' Buntingford put away the madeira, which I took as a sign that my tutorial was coming to a close. 'I'll tell you another thing. It's something that wouldn't occur to an undergraduate. These places—Oxford colleges, that is—get all cluttered up administering themselves. They have what are called Governing Bodies—meaning nearly everybody you'd call the dons. Endless debate on matters utterly frivolous from anything that could be called an academic point of view. How much we can discreetly pay the chef, and whether motor-cars should be allowed in the Great Quadrangle, and who should be empowered to say what where about bugger-all. Desperate stuff, and people get hooked on it. Like a drug. Time-consuming isn't the word. Still, not a headache of yours.'

I concurred in this. Buntingford's last remarks had failed to claim much of my attention. I had something else in mind.

'Do I gather,' I asked, 'that when I've finished doing these bits and pieces this term I'll just be with Mr Talbert all the time?'

'That's right—or Talbert and Timbermill. You won't have met Timbermill yet?'

'No, I haven't.'

'Well, I imagine that will be it.' Buntingford grinned at me maliciously. 'A weekly hour with each of them for the rest of your days.'

'Shall I bore them terribly?'

'I shouldn't like to guess.' Buntingford's grin broadened. He must have approved of my putting my question that way round. 'Time will show,' he said. 'Well, thank you very much.'

In one of Galsworthy's novels there is an elderly character who regularly complains that nobody ever tells him anything. It was to be my own feeling, I remember, when I eventually returned to live in the college. The fellows, now my colleagues, were attentive and conversable, but were so anxious to avoid anything in which there might be detected an instructive note that it was almost impossible to extract information from them. In this they were observing, in their own fashion, a courtesy as rigid as Uncle Rory's: a codified and somewhat patrician attitude endemic to the place, and existing there in a mysterious independence of the social complexion of a majority of the individuals composing what would elsewhere have been called the staff.

To some extent, at least, this convention obtained in the reception of new arrivals of the most junior sort as well. My earliest undergraduate days in college were full of mysteries and perplexities which it appeared to be nobody's business to resolve. Perhaps the assumption here was that one had been told all that it was necessary to know by a grandfather who had become familiar with the minutiae of undergraduate life while himself resident in the college sometime in the 1880's. Until I had Tony Mumford to appeal to I had to spend quite a lot of time and ingenuity in working things out on the mere basis of one casual hint or another. Occasionally I got my answers badly wrong. This was certainly so in the matter of Timbermill.

At the time of my encounter with Buntingford I was already being taught by Albert Talbert. This expression is not, indeed, the first that would occur to me by way of indicating what went on in Talbert's tutorials. I doubt whether it existed at all in undergraduate currency. 'I'm going to Talbert this term', and not 'I'm being taught by Talbert this term', would have been my natural way of speaking. Dons, however, were, and are, quite clear that they 'teach'.

'Dr Timbermill,' Talbert said huskily at the end of one of our contemplative sessions, 'would like to see you tomorrow morning at eleven o'clock. I am very glad indeed that he finds it convenient to take you for your work in Anglo-Saxon. Various possibilities have been in my mind. But nobody could better meet your needs than Dr Timbermill. Eleven o'clock.'

'Thank you very much, sir.' There was no chance of not being impressed by Talbert when he said this sort of thing. I knew by now that he intermittently entertained mistaken notions about my identity, and would in consequence make obscure plans to prepare me for some totally irrelevant examination. But he was certainly a most eminent scholar; I

94

had checked up on this and there could be no doubt of it; and he thus so completely embodied the archetypal conception of the absent-minded professor that it was difficult not to feel him as having, magically and alarmingly, scrambled into three-dimensional reality from the surface of a comic strip. He had given me this information about Dr Timbermill with a gravity suggesting the considered resolution of a problem of the greatest complexity and significance. Thus—I was made to feel—had Talbert, brooding long upon the destinies of Pattullo, maturely pronounced that it should be. But was it Pattullo who was really in his head? Was it Pattullo that Dr Timbermill veritably wanted to see? Had Buntingford not happened to mention the name of Timbermill in the way he had, I should have had no assurance upon this point at all.

On the following morning I put on my scholar's gown—a garment still inducing both self-consciousness and self-satisfaction—and went in search of Timbermill. I had no idea in what part of the college he would be found, and a list I had been given headed 'Gentlemen in Residence' held no mention of him. So I made my way to the porter on duty at the main gate; there was a team of these bowler-hatted men, and all were known to be equally omniscient. But the porter had never heard of Dr Timbermill. In a kindly enough way, he was even a little dismissive of my inquiry; he seemed to regard me as seeking knowledge about a mere outer darkness beyond the walls of the college. It was still only a quarter to eleven, so I didn't panic. I remembered another address-list—quite a fat directory, with the whole university included—which was to be found in the Junior Common Room. So I made my way there, and consulted it. I think I had a lurking fear that Timbermill—so apt for my learned purposes and progress—didn't really exist. Perhaps he had died ten or fifteen years before. Perhaps Talbert was imagining him.

The directory was reassuring. '*J. B. Timbermill*'—it read—'*M.A., D.Litt., F.B.A. (Balliol, New College, Merton.), 20 Linton Road. Tel. 54320.*' I wrote all this down before I saw how perplexing it was. The elusive Timbermill seemed to share himself out between three colleges, none of them my own. Balliol, Merton, and New College were all within five minutes on my bicycle. Ought I to scurry frantically round the lot? Or should I ring up 54320, offer many apologies, and beg for instructions? Thus in doubt, I became aware of the presence in the J.C.R. of a second-year man whom I knew to be a pupil of Talbert's. There was not, as at school, held to be any absolute impropriety in taking the initiative in addressing someone unknown and senior to oneself. A mild aura of indecorum hung over such an act, all the same. How did I begin? I couldn't very well say 'I beg your pardon', or 'Excuse me': these were impossible formalities in such a place. On the other hand, 'I say!' seemed on the breezy and familiar side. There wasn't any time to be lost. I opted for 'I say!'—uttered, if possible, in a tone suggestive of humility and diffidence.

'I say, can you tell me where to find a don called Timbermill? Talbert says I've to go and see him about Old English.'

'Oh, yes. One or two of our crowd are occasionally farmed out to him. He's an old creature somewhere up in North Oxford.' The man I had nerved myself to address was perfectly amiable, and I was rather pleased with 'our crowd' as including the two of us. 'Farmed out', on the other hand, had an odd ring. I suppose it was the first time the expression had come my way. It was vaguely suggestive of sinister things happening to babies.

'Would Linton Road be in North Oxford?'

'Yes. And that's where the chap is. I remember now.'

'He does his tutes at home?' This, for some reason, struck me as strange and irregular.

'I'm sure he does. I think I've been told he never goes out.'

'You mean he's some kind of invalid?' As I asked this I was looking at my watch.

'I don't think so. Or not exactly. Just a nut-case, I imagine.'

'Thank you very much. How long on a bike?'

'Ten minutes with luck. On the right, off the Banbury Road. I say, are you Pattullo?'

'Yes.'

'My name's Badgery. I'm your predecessor on that Ruskin ticket. Do come in and have a drink one evening.'

'Thanks—I will.' Although properly gratified, I was making for the quad and its subterranean bicycle-place. The big bell was striking eleven almost directly overhead.

I pedalled up St Old's like mad. When you're in a hurry it's quite a hill. Carfax was a chaos. The traffic was less dense but more haphazard than it was to be in a later period. So far as bicycles went, a final battle was on. The university still claimed to command the streets with them. Particularly, as now, on the stroke of the hour, undergraduates hurtling from tutorial to lecture or lecture to tutorial wove in and out as they pleased, ignoring new traffic-lights, and jerking cars and buses to a halt. You stuck out an arm and in the same instant executed a right-angled turn. It was a fight against increasing odds, including a progressively firm police-force. As it happened, I encountered this last phenomenon now.

Somebody had told me that, if confronted by a red light and the eye of a bobby at the same time, I had only to jump off my bike, shoulder it, and march confidently ahead. Pedestrians didn't have to heed the lights unless they pleased. So that was that. I put this doctrine into practice at the George Street corner, with the result that I found myself arguing with a young constable. He seemed no older than I was. I had been told that the police kept as aloof as they could from all under-graduate goings-on, and I wondered whether I was making history. My line was to offer various learned remarks about the law. His turned out to be an appeal to common sense; he was just pointing something out for my own good and safety. Unless I was prepared to tell him he was wasting the time of an important person, this cut the ground from beneath my feet. So I apologized and rode on. Of course, time *had* been wasted. It was already eleven-ten.

St Giles', which is as broad as a meadow and ought to have been easy going, turned out a disaster. At the far end of it there were more policemen, some of them on motor-bikes. There was also a file of very grand cars, and into one of these was stepping an old gentleman in fancy dress. He might have been Father Christmas on his way to take up his duties in a department store. In fact he was the Judge of Assize, emerging from his Lodging on the way to court—which was why there was also a line of trumpeters, at this very moment trumpeting like mad. Meanwhile, the stoppage was complete. It was clearly the idea to hold the populace in awe by making as much bother as possible out of getting the old person safely sat on his bench at the other end of Oxford. A detour was my only resource. I executed it with decision, but unfortunately at the expense of losing my sense of direction. It was eleven-twenty by my watch by the time I was back on the Banbury Road.

By this time I was really worried. I imagined Timbermill (D.Litt., F.B.A.) pacing furiously up and down a massive library while waiting for D. Pattullo (nothing at all). It didn't strike me that turning up half-an-hour late for an appointment on which I had been inadequately posted couldn't be the end of the world. All sense of proportion had deserted me. I began to feel as if I was in one of those anxiety-dreams in which an endless sequence of obscure impediments attends upon some vital journey, and in which (in my own experience, at least) the tension can mount to a totally irrelevant sexual climax. I wondered, as I pedalled, whether an awful humiliation of the sort wasn't actually going to befall me now. When my back tyre suddenly punctured with a small pop I positively had to take a grip on myself.

Could I go on riding? Within yards, that proved to be impracticable, for the road was in need of repair and the wheel would have buckled in no time. Ought I to abandon the bike and run? This would certainly be the quickest course, and I'd have adopted it if there hadn't been a number of people around: it was confusedly in my mind that such behaviour would be judged bizarre or laughable, and I feebly shrank from that. I therefore continued at a rapid panting sort of walk, shoving the bike along in the gutter beside me. Eventually I found myself in Linton Road.

There wasn't, I saw with relief, all that of it. There were large, solid, rather ugly villas well set-back on either side, and at the far end the road left off before the drive of what was presumably a dwelling of yet more substantial pretension. Near me as I paused to look for house-numbers a small group of children had chalked out a species of pitch on the pavement, and were playing a street game such as one associates with the humbler inhabitants of great cities; the accent in which they called the score to one another, however, was uncompromisingly upper-class. Several older people were also in evidence. I glanced at them as I hurried forward again, thinking that I might inquire of one of them about Dr Timbermill. My scrutiny revealed that their seniority was, in fact, extreme. That they were residents in this superior suburban quarter was evident from the circumstance that they were without exception pottering in or out of doors and garden gates—most of them with the help of multipedal devices designed to promote the locomotion of the infirm. I might have been outside an old folks' home, but for the fact that these octogenarians and non-agenarians plainly belonged to the same superior *rentier* class as the infants playing hop-scotch or whatever it was.

I hadn't come to Linton Road, however, in the interest of sociological observation. It seemed to me quite a weird locality for tutorials to be conducted in, and I was strongly persuaded that I was the victim of some ludicrous misapprehension. Nevertheless, I had better inquire. Approaching me now, as it happened, was an aged figure, at once tottering and commanding, and wearing what was then known as an Anthony Eden hat. I put him down as a retired colonial governor or Indian civil servant (in which I was probably quite right, since I had in fact penetrated within an enclave of such persons) and judged that he might still sufficiently command some of his faculties to be able to answer a simple question.

'Excuse me,' I said—breathlessly and perhaps imperatively. 'Can you tell me where a Dr Timbermill lives?'

'The last house on the right, sir.' The aged figure, as he produced this reply, gravely saluted me. As I had never been addressed as 'sir' by an octogenarian before, nor had a hat doffed to me in such circumstances, I was considerably abashed, mumbled my thanks, and hastened on. At least I had made it at last. My goal was no more than twenty-five yards away: an enormous and brutally hideous house, standing in the middle of an untidy garden. I hurried forward, and had just propped my useless bicycle against the kerb when my attention was arrested by a new and untoward appearance. The carriage-drive before which Linton Road terminated was no longer empty. Rather oddly, a cow was ambling down it. This cow was closely followed by a second cow, and the second by a third. In fact there was a compacted mass of the creatures. As I stared at them in astonishment, they ceased to amble and charged.

Perhaps it is over-dramatic to speak of such harmless and udder-encumbered brutes as charging—nor does 'stampede' seem an appropriate word. But at least the effect was disconcerting. The beasts' heads were lowered in a menacing way; they slavered, as if emotionally disturbed; I formed the view that several were specifically eyeing me with a malign intention. It would be prudent to nip into Dr Timbermill's garden and close the gate behind me.

'Turn them, boy, turn them! Don't stand there like a fool —turn them!'

There could be no doubt that these words were addressed to me. The voice was a woman's—a cow-wife's, it had to be supposed—and rose from an invisible source behind her errant charges. I judged the terms in which I had been addressed to be disobliging, and I had no impulse whatever to put on any species of rodeo-turn. I'd much rather have confronted even the infuriated (as I had come to think of him) Timbermill. Moreover, I now caught a glimpse of the cow-wife. She was of diminutive stature, suggesting some wretched peasant stock, who might well be left to the consequences of her own in-competence by a John Ruskin Scholar going about his learned occasions. But of course I was too well brought-up for such considerations to avail with me—and in the cow-wife's tone, moreover, there sounded a sort of Glencorry echo which brought me literally to my toes. I believe I thought confusedly of Ninian's fishwife. I found myself—with every appearance of an undaunted bearing—hurling myself upon the serried mass before me.

'Coop, coop! Coop, coop, coop!' This hullabaloo came from the cow-wife—injudiciously, it appeared to me, since it could only serve further to alarm the brutes and drive them forward. I had no choice but to produce my own counter-demonstration.

'Coop, coop, coop, coop!' I shouted. The result of this was striking. The cows felt it was up to them. Without intermitting their progress, they began to bellow—or if not to bellow to ululate or moo. I waved my arms. I yelled at the top of my voice, like whoever it is in Shakespeare who outroars the horned herd. (And this herd *was* horned; that unnecessary armament had not yet been bred out of dairy cattle.)

My intrepidity (if it was that) was rewarded. The enemy wavered, broke, turned, bolted—dividing before the cow-wife like a rushing stream on either side of a very small rock. Or the enemy did this with one exception. A single cow had slipped past me, and was galumphing off in the direction of the traffic on the Banbury Road.

'After her, boy, after her!'

There could now be no doubt about the cow-wife. She was even more upper-class than everybody else in this weird corner of the globe—belonged, in fact, to what Nick Junkin was to be fond of calling the cream of the cream. I am afraid it was my sense of this that made me continue abjectly to obey her. I went hurtling after the escaped cow, my gown billowing behind me. It was clear that an outflanking movement was essential. I must overtake the creature—on the farther pave-ment, so as not to increase her pace—and shoo her back before we were submerged together in a thundering cavalcade of lorries and buses.

I was fleetingly aware of the polite children as continuing their plebeian diversion undisturbed, and of the aged mille-pedes arresting their already almost imperceptible progress to observe my efforts with mild interest and approbation. It appeared probable that I had become involved in what was quite a familiar spectacle in Linton Road.

Linton Road is intersected by Northmoor Road, and this circumstance proved inimical to the simplicity of my design. The cow, when I had successfully headed it and turned it towards home, executed a brilliant swerve into this alternative thoroughfare and lolloped off more or less in the direction of the English Channel. I went pounding after it. I found myself overtaking a casually conducted crocodile of schoolgirls; one of them, who appeared to be in charge, was as senior as my own Edinburgh love, Janet Finlay; and this, as a mere fleeting perception, sent a small stab to my heart. But at least I was once more gaining on the cow. And the file of girls, although amused, comported themselves with decorum.

The cow now made a mistake. Arrived at the bottom of Northmoor Road, it turned not right and towards uncharted liberty but left and thus round the block, so that what would presently confront it over its right horn would be its own front gate. This route, however, produced the further harassment of confronting me with a second juvenile audience. This time it was boys: a score or more of small boys wandering round the purlieus of what appeared to be a large preparatory school. Becoming aware of the chase, these actively disposed little creatures naturally joined in it. They brought imagination to it at once—cracking imaginary whips, whirling imaginary lassos, and urging each other on with a remarkable diversity of blood-curdling cries. Whether cows possess a homing-instinct I don't know, but the present cow did now seem to have formed clear notions on where to go. Within a further minute, it had vanished through the gates from which it had issued. So had all the other cows. The cow-wife, however, remained. At the sight of her, the rout of small boys scattered and fled with cries of dismay. I'd have liked to bolt myself, but felt it due to the dignity of my years to stand my ground. Recalling the terms in which I had previously been addressed, I expected to be robustly reproved for having so botched the business. The cow-wife (to continue thus absurdly to denominate her) was about four feet high, but appeared yet shorter through being bowed with age. There was something unnerving about her, all the same.

'I am so extremely grateful to you. It has been most kind.' The cow-wife, although dressed entirely as a cow-wife ought to be, had spoken much in the manner of a duchess at a ball —thanking a mere earl, perhaps, for picking up her fan or her handkerchief. She now glanced at my gown. 'May I ask,' she said, 'your name, and the college you come from?'

I gave this information.

'How very interesting! All my brothers were there—except Charles, who was clever and had for some reason to go to Balliol. I hope you will come to tea, as several of the young men are free to do. Sundays, as you no doubt know. So kind! I am so grateful!'

At this, the cow-wife withdrew up her drive—at the end of which I could just glimpse among trees a gloomy-looking mansion of no antiquity. I recalled the near-desperation of my position. Could I face Timbermill more than three-quarters of an hour after I had been due to present myself? Was it not very possible that he had been viewing through a window of his curiously unappealing villa the entire course of this farcical episode, and concluding it to be a pretty poor specimen of what Bedworth archaically called a rag? I was now in a most untidy state. There was even a rent in my gown. I must have caught it on a railing during the pursuit, but I could almost have believed it to be a consequence of the sort of thing that happens in a bull-ring. What if Timbermill judged me to be improperly attired for academic conference, and ordered me ignominiously from his presence?

By this time I was pushing open the garden gate again, since I knew perfectly well that I had to go through with it. Once on the path, I became aware of a young man emerging from a shed and wheeling a bicycle. He was obviously an undergraduate. He might conceivably be one of Timbermill's pupils. I had a shot at addressing him.

'Excuse me—am I right that a don called Timbermill lives here?'

'Top floor.' The young man looked at me curiously. I wasn't only dusty and dishevelled; I was still, although I hadn't realized it, blotched, puffing, and blowing. 'Have you been in a fight, or something?' I didn't think the young man believed this to be a tenable hypothesis. He was merely being funny, and I resented what I now decided to be a glance of vulgar amusement.

'As a matter of fact,' I said crossly, 'I've been chasing a bloody cow.'

'Oh, that! Old Mrs Triplett's brutes. Always getting out of hand. They're a pedigree herd or something. The servants' staircase for you, by the way.' The young man laughed loudly, as if conscious of having achieved a notable stroke of wit. 'No offence, man. They've mucked around with the house, you know, and made a perfect slum of it. Only the backstairs now go right up to the top. Timbermill is pretty well all right at the moment, I believe. But you'll soon find out. Seeing you.' With this highly conventional expression, the young man jumped on his bike and rode out of my life.

Reflecting that front doors are not for backstairs folk, I walked round the house in search of some modest means of ingress. Until it reached a variously pitched roof, the whole structure was severely cube-like in suggestion, as if a Brobdingnagian child had put it together out of building-blocks. The walls were sheathed in the grey and gritty integument known to builders as pebble-and-dash; in patches here and there, however, this had come away and been replaced—in a spirit even more utilitarian than that animating the building at large—with plain plaster or cement. I had previously made one or two tentative excursions to North Oxford (which I understood to be inhabited almost exclusively by married dons), and had been chiefly struck by a domestic architecture much in the Gothic taste, and owning a close affinity with Rattenbury Quad. As a John Ruskin Scholar, I had a duty (it might have been maintained) to acquaint myself with these curious Venetian importations to the Thames valley. But now I was perhaps a quarter of a mile farther from the centre of the city than on any previous foray, and as a consequence had moved from one era to another so far as aesthetic matters were concerned. The historical sense was no doubt still active among the learned persons inhabiting these outer environs of the sacred town, but the play of economic forces now forbad them to lend it expression through mason's work borrowed from the Palazzo Rezzonico or the Ca' d'Oro.

Such reflections (if I really entertained them) can only have been a delaying tactic. I had by now built up Timbermill in my head as in a state of insensate fury at the non-appearance of Pattullo, and it would have been nice to persuade myself that I was sufficiently unperturbed to pursue speculative courses. But the moment of truth had come. I found myself confronting a side-door, badly in need of paint. Affixed to it by a drawing-pin, the head of which had long ago rusted away, was a discoloured scrap of pasteboard on which a scrawled 'Timbermill' could just be deciphered in an ink gone brown with age. Since there was no means at this point of making my presence known, I opened the door and walked into what proved to be a proliferation of coal-cellars, larders, sculleries and laundries, all as forlorn and untenanted as if they had been excavated in some dead city in the heart of Yucatán. Rising from a stone-flagged area at the end of all this was a staircase of meagre proportions, up which it would not be at all easy to carry coal-scuttles or trays. It was certainly what I had been directed to. I climbed. There were three successive landings, each with a single door which had been bricked up. These must once have provided access to the main bedroom floors of the house. Then the staircase narrowed yet further, presumably because this terminal flight had led only to attics intended for such scant repose as was allotted to maid-servants long ago. Yet it couldn't, of course, be all that long ago, since the whole place was of a hypertrophied jerry-built sort of the between-wars period. So it wasn't, at least, heavy with memories of the doing to death of generations of menials. Even this part of Oxford had fairly soon began a slither into a modern world. As a consequence—and as the undergraduate with the bicycle had intimated to me—the house had been hacked into the semblance of a block of flats. Dr Timbermill (F.B.A. and whatever) appeared to occupy a modest if elevated station in it. I wondered what on earth would happen to him in the event of fire.

There was a final door, this time a practicable one, and again a discoloured card with the name of my appointed tutor. Was I really going to make this pilgrimage every week of every term for three years on end? The thought was dispiriting. Presumably I'd accumulate considerable expertness in coping with Mrs Triplett's vagrant herd. I looked for a bell, but there wasn't one—nor a knocker either. I tried a diffident rap with my knuckles. No response succeeded upon this application, and there was nothing for it but to try the door and, if it opened, walk in. I did so, expecting to find myself in some sort of small lobby or passage. It wasn't so.

What must have been almost the entire area beneath the low-pitched roof of the house had been gutted to make a single enormous chamber. There was a central space which would have accommodated several billiard-tables without one's much noticing them, and from this there ramified, yawning and cavernous, a number of tunnel-like extensions burrowing deep into the eaves. Since something was required to support the ceiling and tiles overhead, isolated wooden posts rose here and there from the floor to strategic points among the rafters. A stage designer, obliged to conjure up beyond a vast proscenium arch a plausible representation of Hjalmar Ekdal's attic studio in *The Wild Duck*, might have gone for a very similar effect. Only here, instead of the miscellaneous clutter of a nineteenth-century photographer, there were simply thousands and thousands of books.

The books, of course, were entirely as expected. I dimly wondered (this because I was becoming at that time con-scientiously Eng. Lit. minded) whether something like this had been Dr Johnson's set-up in Gough Square. In fact the bizarre place surprised me less than had the habitat of my other tutor-to-be, Albert Talbert. Talbert, for reasons which over a great many years I was never to discover, inhabited in college a very small square room containing almost nothing except a small square table, two hard chairs, and a small empty bookcase. If stumped for a date (which he seldom was), Talbert would turn to this bookcase, appear perplexed, and murmur at his huskiest and weightiest that it had been for some time in his mind to shelve in it what he called 'a succinct reference library'. I was in a real library now. In this particular, at least, I had not been at fault in imagining the surroundings of the infuriated Timbermill.

'Nothing today, thank you.'

The voice had spoken from the near darkness of one of the tunnels. I was myself in near darkness too, and I supposed that this explained the words which had come to me. They might reasonably have been addressed to a baker's boy or a milkman. I found them discouraging, all the same.

'Sir,' I said, 'I'm extremely sorry to be so late.'

'Not at all, my good fellow. I haven't been incommoded in the slightest degree. There are empties, no doubt, but still, I believe, an untouched crate of bottled ale. Only I should be most grateful if, next week, you would bring a dozen of mead. It isn't really mead. That distinction, I fear, cannot be granted it. But it serves. It serves.'

The tenebrous character of this attic region had been in part the creation of my own mind. I could now see Timbermill perfectly well. He was sitting at a desk (which did need a reading-lamp) at the far end of the room. His figure was indistinct, but a shaft of sunshine, striking through what must have been some small skylight, was at play upon his hair. It was silvery hair, and of the sort so fine-spun as to be virtually weightless, and thus to float above the scalp like a halo or penumbra. Because of this appearance, I decided at once that Timbermill had reached extreme old age. I was never quite to shake off this persuasion. In fact, he could have been no more than five years older than Talbert, and thus not much more than thirty years older than myself.

At the moment, however, I was less held by any visual impression than by an auditory one. Our conversation, so far, had held merely the mild madness which I was coming to associate with first encounters with dons. Timbermill's misapprehension was precisely of the kind that Talbert might have entertained, and in addition to this he rendered much the same effect of learned absence of mind, of swimming into awareness of you across a sundering flood of recondite concern.

There was nevertheless a difference between the impression the two men gave. I had already come to know where Talbert appeared from when with an effort he heaved himself ashore to cope conscientiously (according to his lights) with one more pupil. He had been weighing a comma here or a turned letter there in some Elizabethan text photographed or projected upon an interior screen in the depth of his mind. Questions of taste, of the superior poetic propriety of one reading over another, might have some peripheral significance for what was in hand. But essentially Talbert inhabited in his abstraction a logical and rational world in which one shoved around ponderable counters until one got one's answer right. Timbermill's inner world, on the other hand, quickly became enigmatical. The queerness of this lodging, and Badgery's casually intimated persuasion that its occupant never ventured out of it, suggested that I was simply in the presence of a university eccentric of the kind that emancipated undergraduates sometimes drop into first novels. But it wasn't clear to me that Timbermill was in fact a real-life equivalent of this species. If he had been, I was persuaded I'd have had some sense, right at the start, of how he ticked—of the line he took in establishing himself that way. As it was, he puzzled me, and this largely on the score of his voice. It was nervous in the old sense of the word: sinewy and vigorous, indeed *staccato*. Even the business about ale and mead had come out like that. At the same time, and contradictorily, there was much more sensibility behind his barking at me than I'd yet heard from anybody at Oxford. It was no good, however, standing dumbly before him and confusedly speculating. For a start, I had the simple job of establishing my identity. I advanced into the room, so that he could at least see me as academically habited.

'My name's Pattullo,' I said. 'Mr Talbert has sent me to see you about Old English.'

Timbermill received this with a short explosive laugh, which for a moment I thought to be directed against some futility in my visit; then I realized that it acknowledged and dismissed the error under which he had addressed me so far.

'About *what*?' he said.

'Old English, sir.'

'Anglo-Saxon, please!' This too came explosively. 'Would you call Latin Old Italian?'

'No, sir.' Being much confounded, I felt I had to keep my end up. 'But I suppose it is, in a way.'

'It's nothing of the kind. Did Mr Talbert call it Old English?'

'I don't think he did. I think he called it Anglo-Saxon too.'

'Then well and good. But we must report to one another accurately, you know. It's our business. Otherwise we get nowhere. Do you understand me?'

'Yes, sir.'

'I believe you do.' Timbermill said this as if he were convinced of something thoroughly surprising. 'Sit down.'

I sat down—hurriedly, and on what I took to be a chair, but which turned out to be a stack of bound journals. All this was very intimidating. But there was no effect—as the words set down on a page must suggest—of anything like bullying about it. Timbermill was seriously concerned to establish a relationship with me. And, once recalled to his present surroundings, he was entirely on the spot. I knew at once that, unlike Talbert, he would never suppose on one day that I was Jones and on the next that I was Merryweather or Montgomery.

'Duncan Pattullo,' he said. He hadn't referred to a note.

'Yes, sir.' I was tremendously impressed.

'Talbert says your father is the eminent painter. He hasn't got it wrong? He does get things wrong, God bless him.'

'Mr Talbert is right this time, sir.'

'Young Picts, eh?'

'Yes, sir.'

'And Saint Columba. A most distinguished performance. You must do as well, Duncan. I shall call you Duncan.' Disconcertingly, the explosive laugh came again. 'But in a kind of long ship of the Saga Age.'

'Sir?' I knew that historical accuracy wasn't my father's strong point. But Timbermill had thrown in something handsome and acknowledging about him, so I didn't need to be offended.

'Dear old Columba—God bless his memory as He blessed his mission—in the sort of contraption popularly supposed to have been favoured by vikings. Eh?'

'I suppose so, sir.' I hesitated, and added venturesomely, 'I'm one of the young Picts, as a matter of fact.'

'Ah! So you have your niche already, Duncan. A precocious corner in the Temple of Fame. Where have you read about a Temple of Fame?'

'In Chaucer, sir.' I wondered whether I was overdoing the Sir business. At least it came naturally to me.

'You've come up unusually young, haven't you?'

'I don't think so. Just a little short of the average, I'm told. Among the freshmen straight from school, I mean.'

'You look round about your sixteenth birthday to me.'

I ought to have been annoyed by this—not the less because I knew it was a justifiable impression. I used absolutely to long, at that time, to be a little less slim and pink and white. A generation later—in Nick Junkin's generation—I'd have endeavoured to tackle this problem by growing a downy beard.

'I do beg your pardon.' Timbermill said this so rapidly and jerkily that the effect of unforced courtesy the words conveyed was remarkable. He was apologizing for the offence he hadn't, in fact, given. 'That toil of growing up. Eh, Duncan?'

It was at this moment that the Yeats joke was born. I must have carried it straight back to college from this curious encounter—perhaps to murmur pityingly to a flamboyant Tony Mumford of the distress of boyhood changing into man. Certainly by the end of term the whole little group of us—my intimates, as Arnold Lempriere would have expressed it—were fooling around with the poet much as the doomed battery fools around with Jane Austen in Kipling's story. But my present reaction was simply to be startled. Albert Talbert would have heard of Yeats, but have regarded him as a person active only after the history of English literature had come to a close. I'd have taken it naïvely for granted that a man like Timbermill, who had presumably become a Fellow of the British Academy on the score of large traffickings with *Beowulf* and similar deliverances of hoary eld, must be even more unsullied by modernity.

'What books have you bought?' Timbermill asked briskly.

'For Old—for Anglo-Saxon? None, so far.'

'Then here you are.' Timbermill reached into an extremely disordered pile of papers, and without any effect of rummaging pulled out a duplicated sheet. 'Get along to Blackwell's now. And Fridays at eleven, please. From next week. You and I aren't supposed to get together until Hilary Term. But an early start will do you no harm. There's a grammar to learn. Begin learning it.'

This was adequately dismissive, and I scrambled gingerly off my perch, which had been giving hints of proposing to disintegrate under me. Timbermill got to his feet too—an act of politeness that revealed itself as having the further aim of taking a keen look at me in a clear light. The effect on me was notable; it was like turning a street corner and running straight into the Ancient Mariner. I told myself I hadn't met quite that sort of glitter before. I even felt—perhaps because the interview had been stretching while it lasted—that there was an element of the preternatural about it, and that I might be in the presence of a mage or wizard in disguise. Even the room seemed to change as I made my way across it to the door. The posts which in a prosaic and utilitarian way held up the roof might have been dead timber in some sacred grove which a magic stronger than its own had blasted; the tunnel-like openings beneath the eaves and gables of the big house were as glades and ridings in a forest haunted by trolls and norns. This nonsense would scarcely have come to me, I imagine, had I not supposed—accurately enough—that Germanic mythology must be very much Timbermill's sort of thing. Long afterwards, I was to think that there had been something precognitive at work in me during these moments.

Timbermill opened the door to show me out—something which Talbert would have done only if not quite sure whether he had been teaching one of his own male pupils or a girl from Lady Margaret Hall. For a second he laid a hand lightly on my arm.

'Your college,' he said, 'has a most notable history. It also happens to be prolific in young idiots. Have a thought to that. Good-bye.'

I made my way down the narrow staircase and out into Linton Road. I glanced round cautiously, but there weren't any cows. There was only my bicycle, with that tiresome flat tyre. I wondered whether I was going to get any lunch, for it didn't occur to me that I could do other than visit Mr Basil Blackwell's book shop straight away in quest of Sweet's *Anglo-Saxon Reader* and related works. At the corner of Northmoor Road I ran into the old gentleman with the Anthony Eden hat. He seemed to have progressed by several yards since our previous encounter. He addressed me more familiarly this time—almost as if we were established acquaintances.

'Find him all right?'

'Yes, thank you, I did. But I was fearfully late.'

'Remarkable man, I believe. Not that we see much of him.'

'I'm going to see him quite a lot,' I said. And I went on my way, the bicycle bumping beside me in the gutter. I wondered whether, as Buntingford had hinted, I was really destined to be bored by Dr Timbermill. His suburban retreat, at least, already had a charm for me. I was sorry when I left it for the bustle of the Banbury Road traffic.

# V

Tony Mumford ran a car. He might have been said, indeed, to keep a car, much as a man keeps a mistress. Clandestine arrangements were necessary, and Tony's vehicle had its love-nest in the woodshed of a compliant old lady—retired, I think, from service in the Mumford family—some way down the Abingdon Road. Freshmen were not supposed to possess cars. Their seniors were permitted them, but the vehicles had to be segregated in authorized garages which might have been regarded as a species of *maisons de tolérance*. After dark, moreover, they were required to display little green lamps, and thus acquired the air of mobile establishments of the same sort. But such associations were in the main without substance. I have read that an astonishingly high proportion of the citizens of the United States lose their virginity in automobiles, but I doubt whether they were thus much employed among us—perhaps because most of them were rather on the small side for anything of the sort. People used their cars for such blameless purposes as dashing up to theatres in London, or running out to golf-courses and point-to-points by day, and by night to such hotels in the surrounding countryside as were reputed to offer a superior cuisine to young gourmets. It was when Tony discovered I could play golf that he divulged to me the fact of his having this sort of pleasurable resource under, as it were, his protection.

Whether he was at risk of being subjected to any proctorial severity because of his irregularly maintained possession is doubtful. As cars became, in those immediate post-war years, easier to acquire, the regulations about them probably broke down or crumbled away in the comfortable fashion characteristic of Oxford life. For one thing, the returned soldiery (contrary to the expectations of Stumpe) proved to be more often matrimonially than licentiously inclined, and mechanical transport cannot reasonably be denied to a man, however pronounced his academic juniority, who has a wife who needs to go shopping.

My immediate acquaintances were nearly all young celibates. Tony, I believe, was as innocent of active heterosexual experience as (again) Stumpe, but free from Stumpe's anxieties concerning the risks of holding out too long against nature in this regard. He may conceivably have been in what was my own state at the time: that of an adolescent lover whose imagination is in a phase of total ascendancy over the more immediate demands of the flesh. It wasn't a state, I am sure, about which I allowed Tony the slightest hint in myself, so the possibility of his having been practising a similar reticence himself can't be ruled out. I judge this, however, to be improbable. Tony's attitude to sex was consistently ribald. The picture over his fireplace, being a 'conversation piece' in the curious modern sense of an object generating agreeable talk, was a kind of advertisement of what you had to expect of him. He exhibited, moreover, remarkable powers of indecent invention, and commonly with enough wit thrown in to prevent his performances being indictable as mere smut. It took me months to catch up with him in this particular social accomplishment.

But if his motor-car was his sole mistress, he showed himself capable, at least on one occasion, of exploiting the fact in the interest of libertinism of an advanced sort. Nobody could call unresourceful in the quest of amusement a man who proposes to employ his mistress for the seduction of an innocent companion. Tony employed Rosinante in just this way. Rosinante was his name for the car: rather a grand car, but one disinfected of pretentiousness by being of marked and ramshackle antiquity. His victim was Cyril Bedworth.

I don't think we'd much have made fun of Bedworth if we

hadn't rather liked him, and if we regarded him as fair game it was because, being a serious man, he was staggered by the amount of frivolity he found around him. He was also a man of firm character—an underlying fact which his general inconsiderableness of appearance, and the timidity with which he so clearly had to wrestle, were quite sufficient to conceal at first from our callow regard. He knew that his seriousness was right and our frivolity wrong. His remarks were frequently censorious. His exceptional poverty (which we were also slow to tumble to, and which must have been the consequence of a more than customary stinginess on the part of some grant-dispensing authority) didn't help.

I used to have much more conversation with Bedworth than Tony had, but this was chiefly because I treated him as a handy crib at the time when my efforts at Latin were receiving only the decidedly casual assistance of Buntingford. Bedworth could construe Latin fluently, and I might bang on his garret door half-a-dozen times in a morning for this purpose without appearing to tax his patience in the least. If this at all struck me as remarkable, I doubtless told myself that Bedworth enjoyed an opportunity for showing off. He certainly showed himself the master of whatever simple Latin text it was that I had become involved with. On the other hand he had done no Greek at school and I had; indeed, Greek, which I had liked, wasn't in quite as bad a way with me as Latin, which I hadn't. So Bedworth and I would usually have a kind of return match. He would ask me the etymologies of obviously Greek words, and I would tell him that something was clinical if it happened at a bedside, and that cynics and cynosures both had to do with dogs. It never occurred to me that Bedworth could get this sort of information as expeditiously and more reliably from a dictionary, and that in establishing the fiction of an equal give-and-take between us he was acting out of considerable delicacy of feeling.

It is true that Bedworth could also be very boring, and even rather irritatingly self-righteous. He felt I needed organizing (which was true) and that I'd benefit from taking this or that leaf out of his own book. He had a wall decorated with an array of charts and time-tables and work-schedules which he kept up to date with various coloured pencils from day to day, and he was tiresomely quick to detect any tendency of my mind to wander from them as he urged upon me the merits of his system. In addition to this pedagogic trait, he frequently betrayed embarrassing symptoms of social unease. He would have agreed with Timbermill that our college was peculiarly prolific in young idiots. His own word was 'socialites', which he occasionally varied with 'butterflies' or (here, perhaps, with a humorous intention) 'effete sprigs of aristocracy'. He was a proud man, and moreover he admired all the right things, courage among them. Hiding in a doorway during that nocturnal tumult in Surrey had been entirely rational, but I believe he had found it traumatic, all the same. I had been, as I have recorded, thoroughly frightened myself. But I had announced the fact blithely at the time, and couldn't now recall my condition to any effect of humiliation. Nevertheless, I probably rated myself as a vastly more sensitive person than Cyril Bedworth.

I don't think that Tony regarded our top-floor neighbour with other than a tolerant eye, but what he said about him was apt to be disparaging. 'Kind of chip-on-the-shoulder type,' he would say. 'Inferiority complex, and so forth. Can't think what you see in him, running up and down his staircase all day. Or, rather, I blush before the evident truth. Oh thou my lovely boy. That's it.' Maintaining that the spotty Bedworth roused irregular desires in half the college was one of Tony's favourite extravagances.

In fact, the truth lay rather the other way on. I discovered this some time before Rosinante enters the story, and I became much more interested in Bedworth as a result. Before the spectacle upon which he peered down from his chart-bestrewn eyrie he was of a divided mind. The young idiots *were* young idiots, and he would shake his head over them in what was often an insufferably holier-than-thou way. But it was a head in which there lay concealed a spark of what must have been at first wholly reluctant admiration at least for aspects of the life into which he had tumbled. Not that 'tumbled' is quite right. It was I who had tumbled into Oxford—first tripped up, as it were, by a vagary of my father's, and then on the strength of a flair for scribbling in which no merit inhered. Bedworth —there could be no doubt of it—had sweated at the job when he was a kid. He was an obscure Jude, born into a slightly more liberal age than Hardy's hero; a career had been open to his talents, and he would certainly carry on, unseduced, as he had begun. But that spark was there. At times it glowed perceptibly enough. It almost—if the thing can be expressed without patronage this way—kindled his imagination. So many happy youths, so wide and fair a congregation: Bedworth at Oxford, like the equally solemn Wordsworth at Cambridge, was not quite capable of surveying them with an undelighted heart. The comparison, however, is delusive. Cyril Bedworth wasn't going to be a poet.

I could have been sure of this, but not of any more positive direction in which his secret and unacknowledged enlargement of feeling might lead him. I was in less doubt about myself. My surrender to Oxford was almost entire. Unlike Bedworth, I had no sharp ambivalences to cope with. I didn't believe that industry was virtuous and frivolity to be deprecated; even although owning a certain seriousness, I didn't believe in this; so frivolity gained for me no additional relish from being associated with guilt. Retrospection has revealed to me that I was sometimes home-sick. But I approved of the place extravagantly and, again unlike Bedworth, was willing to announce the fact—although I was careful to add that this made me doubt whether I was right in the head. Yet I knew no marriage was being consummated, and that when my three years were up out I'd go. Albert Talbert's embarrassing persuasion, frequently to be expressed many years later, that as an undergraduate I had indulged what he was pleased to call 'the mad thought of a fellowship' was a flight of fancy which I can't, to this day, recall without annoyance.

I don't quite know why it should have been of Tony and me that Bedworth first allowed himself more or less overtly to approve. It may have happened simply because we were among his nearest neighbours, and were seldom other than polite to him, even if it was sometimes in a teasing way. But I think, too, he was attracted to us as, so to speak, a well-balanced package. I hadn't a scrap of his scholarship—and as a consequence of this was a good deal more widely read than he was. I thus ranked as an improving association. (Tony claimed to have spied on a kind of diary of Bedworth's which had contained the entry: *7.30–8.50 p.m. Talked to D. Pattullo in hall about major works of Dostoevsky.* The marathon conversation certainly did take place.) Tony, on the other hand, must have represented for Bedworth something unholy and glamorous: the very flower of the care-free and insouciant *jeunesse dorée* of the college, as confident in their total ownership of their surroundings now as they had formerly been of their childhood's ponies or their infancy's rattles. The spectacle of Tony and myself as what Tony, with an affectation of the old-fashioned, called chums was somehow gratifying to Bedworth.

He would occasionally cast on us a disapproving regard, all the same. Had he not done so one morning half-way through our first Hilary Term the Rosinante episode would simply not have taken place. We had clattered down the staircase, Tony and I, with our golf-clubs clanking in their bags, and had overtaken Bedworth in the quad. He was gowned as he commonly was, and carried an armful of books, together with an elaborate contrivance for unfolding on a desk and taking notes. He was bound for a lecture, and pained that we were not.

'Morning, Cyril,' Tony called out—cheerily, but with a glint in his eye. '*Wohin der Weg*, my tender Juvenal?' Tony was increasingly fond of showing off to the learned in this random way.

'Oh, good morning . . . Tony.' We had disciplined Bedworth in this matter of Christian names, but they still made him rather nervous, all the same. 'Good morning, Duncan,' he added, with rather more confidence. 'It's Bisson on *Phèdre*.' He looked at me reproachfully. 'He's said to be frightfully good.'

'*O ciel! Oenone est morte, et Phèdre veut mourir!*' I exclaimed despairingly. We enjoyed deluging Bedworth with crackpot erudition.

'It is the first mild day of March,' Tony shouted. 'Why not with speed put on your woodland dress?'

'Oh, but I don't think——' Surprisingly, Bedworth ceased to look censorious, and gave us his rare shy smile. Tony sparkling like this was something he was by now beginning helplessly to fall for. It represented an irresistible confluence of charms. 'And bring no book?' he asked, heroically playing up.

'Just that.' Tony actually took Bedworth by the arm. 'Come on! You do play golf?'

'Oh, no!' But Bedworth's helplessness grew. 'I have an uncle who does,' he added, rather wildly.

'Then you know it's extremely easy. Do come. We're getting out my car.'

'Your car?' Bedworth was scandalized.

'Yes. Doesn't your uncle have a car?' Tony could manage things like this without insolence. 'Do come with us. It will be tremendous fun.'

I think I had the decency to feel uneasy. In moments like this it was impossible to disentangle Tony's genuine good-nature from his propensity to extract amusement from malice.

'We've got lots of clubs,' Tony said, and actually made the words sound sensible and persuasive. 'You won't need your gown, of course. But we can leave it in the woodshed. It's not a bad place for gowns—even scholars' ones.'

And thus, it may be said, the fall of Cyril Bedworth was accomplished. We marched across the Great Quadrangle, making the clubs clank as noisily as possible. An elderly don watched us with undisguised benevolence. My uneasiness didn't abate. Bedworth was experiencing happiness, and it wasn't really his thing. He continued in this unwonted state even when we had dumped or perched him on Rosinante's dicky-seat. This was a feature of the car which peculiarly evidenced its archaic character; one felt it to be descended from something on which it had once been appropriate to accommodate a lackey or a small black page. It didn't occur to me that it would be more graceful to take up this modest station myself. Bedworth had to clutch the two golf bags. We drove ostentatiously through Oxford in our illicit conveyance.

On the golf course at Frilford Tony became a model of good conduct. He was a better player than I was, despite my nationality, but I had proved good enough to give him a decent game. This morning, however, that went by the board. Tony's sole concern was to teach Bedworth the rudiments as effectively as he knew how. The fairways were almost deserted, and this helped a lot. But the salient fact of the situation was that Bedworth proved a surprisingly apt pupil. Commonly when one begins to play golf one finds that, more often than not, club and ball simply don't connect; one's swipes meet empty air. Quite soon, with Bedworth, this wasn't often happening. He commanded notable concentration, and moreover was making a tremendous effort of the will. I can see him now, standing in a bunker and working out in his head a provisional theory of how to employ a niblick to chip his ball back to the turf. Tony was as intent as he was, and had utterly banished the notion that he was contriving comedy. It came to me, with a sense of the largest relief, that the occasion was a success. I don't exactly mean by this that Bedworth was enjoying himself. What was going on in him was happiness still, which is a different condition. Unfortunately it didn't last.

There was, as I have said, no crowd. The nearest players were two or three holes in advance of us, and I was vaguely aware of them as suggesting a married couple in middle life. Our own progress was inevitably of a pottering sort. So it seemed certain that the people in front would draw yet further ahead. Behind us, I could see nobody at all.

On most golf courses, however, one comes once or twice upon a couple of holes, not necessarily consecutive, running in parallel. Traffic-wise, the effect is much that of what was then beginning to be called a dual carriageway. You are advancing in one direction while just across a strip of no man's land somebody else may be advancing on the other. Just such an accident of the terrain had suddenly brought the married couple much nearer to us. I glanced at them fleetingly, and was conscious of a faint sense of identification before I returned my attention to Bedworth. His drive had been commendably straight, but not exactly notable for length; the ball lay on promisingly smooth turf in the middle of the fairway. Tony decided to instruct him in the use of a brassy, a club which he had not attempted to employ hitherto. Bedworth examined it very carefully.

The driver and the brassy are the most difficult clubs for the beginner to control. The basic idea of each is the gaining of length, and he is thus tempted to put sheer beef into his stroke to the neglect of anything else. Bedworth did this, essaying so violent a swing that I expected nothing to happen at all. But this was not the case. The ball sustained a very marked impact indeed, but had at the same time been badly sliced. A fraction of a second after I perceived this our ears were assailed by a howl of agony.

What had happened was patent, for the man in the other fairway was hopping about on one leg and clutching his other ankle in both hands. The posture of the woman somehow suggested less solicitude for her husband than indignation against whoever had assaulted him. It occurred to me that it would be extremely bizarre if the person whom the innocent Bedworth had inadvertently winged turned out to be a don. Then I realized the truth.

'Tony,' I said, 'it's the Provost.'

'My God, so it is!' Tony glanced swiftly at the hapless Bedworth, upon whom recognition of his enormity was dawning with what was perhaps a merciful slowness. 'Hell's bells!' Tony went on—but not at all despairingly. 'Stay put, both of you. One's enough. I'll fix it.' He strode off rapidly in the direction of the injured player, who was now consulting his dignity by managing to stand on two feet again. I myself did as Tony had ordered me. He believed he could control the situation much better on his own than with Bedworth and myself producing a chorus of apologetic gabble. He was probably right. And I didn't have the slightest doubt that he was going to claim to have been the Provost's assailant himself.

I tried rapidly to estimate the awfulness of our situation. It seemed quite probable that neither the Provost nor Mrs Pococke would know any of us from Adam. The time hadn't come when Tony and I were to be summoned to regular tea-drinkings in the Lodging. We had been to one large sherry-party there, and at the end of our first term joined a file of youths making a formal valedictory bow to the Provost in hall. There was no reason to suppose that Cyril Bedworth's case was any different. And Tony could present adequate apologetic and solicitous remarks without any need to identify himself. So perhaps it wasn't too bad.

And I had by now been sufficiently drawn into Tony Mumford's world to feel that it couldn't in any case be as bad as it was funny. I was still, indeed, very much a schoolboy. It was hard not to think of the Provost as a headmaster, and of ourselves as three truants about to be summarily dealt with— although in point of fact (at least while Rosinante remained safely out of sight) we were spending the morning as we were perfectly entitled to do, and as scores of other undergraduates were certainly doing at this moment. But, confusing as the situation was, my memory tells me that it chiefly amused me. Had the Provost, tumbling to our identity, rusticated us on the spot, there would at least have been a story to tell which would vastly have entertained my father; and to be banished from Oxford for the remainder of the term would be infuriating but not precisely tragic. Unfortunately Bedworth was all too plainly in a different case. His regrettable complexion had taken on a bluish tinge, rather as if the sky had literally fallen on him. He possessed, so to speak, no relevant context within which to place what had occurred, had no notion of the scale of it, was without even an approximate clue as to how the Head of an Oxford college behaves when reduced to yelping aloud on a golf course. I believe he saw his career as possibly in ruins. But this didn't prevent him—after a moment's sheer paralysis, indeed—from acting. I became aware that he was going after Tony at a run. There was no means of stopping him, and perhaps it would have been impertinent to try. All I could do was to run too.

We came up with Tony when he was demonstrably making a tiptop job of his apologies. Mrs Pococke was, I thought, being a bit tart; it was her line that a radically inexpert player ought not to be loosed on a golf course at all. But the Provost, although still in pain, was all forbearance and urbanity. Previous glimpses of him more or less from afar ought to have told me that this would be so. 'Edward Pococke,' my kinsman Lempriere was to say to me one day, 'believes the grandeur of life to consist in its decorum.' And decorum certainly was having an outing now. It controlled the restrained but considered gestures with which the Provost acknowledged the propriety of Tony's anxious concern while at the same time deprecating any excess in it. Tony, as I had suspected was his intention, had taken on the guilt of the deed. I was amazed to see that he was actually carrying a brassy.

All this was a little troubled by the arrival of Bedworth and myself—particularly Bedworth. He had pushed in on an impulse deserving to be called noble, and it was sad that he cut so unfortunate a figure as a result. His own apologies, in addition to perplexingly falsifying what Tony had been representing, carried a lamentable suggestion of abject disarray.

His accent had cracked up. The Provost, remarking this, turned extra gracious to Bedworth. He might have been all the Heads of Oxford colleges that ever had been, making up for all the snubs they had delivered to all the Jude Fawleys since the beginning of time. But was the Provost—I suddenly asked myself—now looking at all three of us curiously? At least I realized why Tony had wanted to go on his embassy alone. The Provost—or his wife, for that matter—was less likely to recognize a single junior member of his flock than he was three of them in a bunch. The instant perception of this not unsubtle psychological fact was a good deal to the credit of Tony's intelligence.

The episode was nearly over. The Provost had taken two or three steps to and fro, by way of showing himself—as the football commentators say—'restored'. For each of us he could be observed preparing a kindly and dismissive smile. He began with Bedworth—and on Bedworth his gaze momentarily paused. Again for the briefest space, his eyebrows elevated themselves. I looked at Bedworth myself. Bedworth—and neither Tony nor I had noticed it—was wearing a college tie.

Our civil farewells were concluded. It had been a fair cop. I had a feeling that the Provost hadn't even been amused. He was a man easy to make fun of, but he had a certain largeness, all the same. That he had been clobbered by youths from his own, and not another, college didn't strike him as in the least an exacerbating circumstance, and if he felt that we ought to have been at our books he knew that the circumstances of the case didn't admit of his saying so, or of his docketing the fact in his mind in any way.

It was Tony who was furious, and before we had got back to our abandoned golf bags, before I could spot the danger and squash it, a certain amount of damage was done. And it wasn't really forgiveable. There was nothing to prompt it except Tony's wounded conceit that his masterly handling of the situation had been mucked up after all.

'You bloody little fool!' he said savagely to Bedworth. 'What are you going about in a damned silly thing like that for?'

Bedworth's hand went to his throat. He was completely bewildered, but at the same time desperately hurt. I ought to say that there was no positive solecism in wearing a college tie. It was a discreet affair of little golden croziers on a dark blue ground. I believe it also came in other colour-schemes for those who had gained distinction in one or another athletic pursuit. In these choicer forms it was positively prized. Even the bedrock version was considered harmless enough. It tended to be favoured by dons who had drifted in on us from obscurer colleges. There were those undergraduates who maintained that in certain circumstances an actual propriety attended its exhibition. If you had occasion to wear a London suit, for example, when travelling abroad. Still, Tony Mumford wouldn't have worn a college tie. He would have classed it with ash trays and biscuit tins bearing the college arms.

Such canons were obsolete, I think, when I returned to Nick Junkin's Oxford. But this wasn't Nick's Oxford; it was Tony's Oxford still. I had a furious wish to step behind Tony and plant a golf shoe accurately where it would hurt. Bedworth's humiliation was vivid to me. The tie represented a first movement of his imagination towards an idea of the college such as he had probably never entertained when sweating his way towards Oxford through the upper forms of an indifferent school. Moreover the money laid out on the thing must have given him anxious thoughts. Now he was being contemptuously told he'd got it wrong.

I was to be glad I hadn't assaulted Tony. (A kick on the arse is one boy's ultimate insult to another, after all: worse, somehow, than any humiliation a prefect can inflict.) By that evening his remorse was extreme. For a time, indeed, his sense of guilt made him more insufferable than I'd ever known him before. He groped towards hideous and patronizing schemes of atonement. He told me, for example, he'd take the poor devil out to a square meal. He ended, I believe, by bursting into Bedworth's attic round about midnight and apologizing in what I haven't any doubt was very proper form. After that, and strangely, we became quite a trio for a time. But this, of course, didn't last. Cyril Bedworth came to bore Tony, just as Gavin Mogridge did.

# VI

THEY WERE BOTH—Bedworth and Mogridge—rather quiet men. I'd have been quiet myself, I suppose, had not Tony and one or two others elected me into their company—in which case these blithe spirits would have thought of me dismissively as 'dim' or 'grey', and I'd have had a worthier academic career than in fact I achieved.

Mogridge's quietude was, of course, modified by his 'cello. It drew me into his rooms from time to time, although more in a spirit of disinterested curiosity than of musical appreciation. I couldn't be unaware of the instrument, since I heard it as I passed his door and also as I sat at my desk or lay in bed. The strains, the auditory effects (for it is hard to describe the total phenomenon) came up the chimney as well as through the floorboards and open windows. Many people round about the college must have been suffering similarly, although more frequently from pianos than from stringed instruments or wood-winds. The unassuming men hired upright pianos (cottage pianos, they were sometimes called) from shops in the town. Others were capable of arriving with grand pianos in their baggage. Of these I imagine that many had parents constrained to live in houses rather smaller than hitherto, and the monsters had been carried off from areas of relegation in furniture depositories or summer-houses or garden sheds. Their decrepitude was often detectable as soon as a chord was sounded. They may also have suffered in transit—and particularly its final stages. Few Oxford staircases are well-adapted to the humping up and down of out-size Bechsteins and the like.

Mogridge's 'cello, on the other hand, was almost certainly in sound working order, since his ambitions were professional rather than merely amateur. This made more perplexing, and even distressing, the fact that the sounds emitted seldom seemed (even to my unsophisticated ear) quite right. But what positively worried me were certain mysterious concomitants of the performance. It was almost necessary to believe that something depraved was going on—although it was still in the womb of time that there slumbered that alarming fictional character whose quiet half-hours with sex (as Stumpe expressed it) took place to the accompaniment of Beethoven on a record-player. Mostly it was a matter of grunts and a disturbed respiration, but these manifestations were occasionally punctuated by short, sharp cries of agony. It was as if Mogridge had the Provost cornered in his room, and was intermittently turning from a bow to a brassy.

It proved a mystery not particularly hard to solve. Mogridge would not have cared for an audience in a general way, but seemed prepared to make an exception in my case—I imagine for no better reason than that I was an artist's son, and that it was an artist he himself desperately wanted to be. He knew that I was friendly rather than critical, since I had explained to him how years of attending the performances of the Scottish Symphony Orchestra along with my mother enabled me to identify numerous musical compositions while leaving me at a merely primitive level of analysis and appreciation. So I used to sit on Mogridge's sofa from time to time and watch what was going on. It was more interesting and even agreeable than just having to listen from upstairs.

The *maestri* (and *maestre*) whom I had been accustomed to observe from a middling distance in Edinburgh's Usher Hall had been detectably quite hard at work. There had been, for example, a magnificent Hungarian girl who could plainly have wielded a sledge-hammer or a wood-cutter's axe at need, but who didn't extract astounding things from her 'cello without marked physical effort, so that I sometimes wondered whether this would have been doubled had her instrument happened to be a double-bass. The total effect was graceful and commanding nevertheless. Mogridge lacked these attributes so far. He copiously perspired, and at close quarters the grunts and gasps forced from him suggested an expenditure of the sort of energy required of one not yet habituated to the operation of a chain-saw or a pneumatic drill. It was his breathing-technique that constituted the crux of the matter—as much, it seemed to me, as if he had dedicated himself to the trumpet or the loud bassoon. His entire muscular system, moreover, was in a state of high tension from first to last, and it was this that explained those sudden cries—equally interpretable as of agony or love's ecstasy—which had arrested me from above. Mogridge, as he played, was subject to violent cramps. I had no knowledge that this was a hazard which most executants on fiddles of one sort or another have to be trained to overcome, so I judged the circumstance more bizarre than in fact it was. But at least I sympathized. At school I had been liable to sporadic and inept athletic ambitions, had gone privily into 'training' for one event or another, and would eventually succeed in jumping over eleven hurdles at the expense of thereafter rolling in anguish on the grass as a consequence of what had happened to my calves. It was thus that I arrived at the perception that Mogridge's case was one of fundamental ineptitude too, and that he might crudely be declared to be fiddling up the wrong tree.

'Why have you come up to Oxford at all?' I asked one day, during a pause in which Mogridge was massaging his fingers. 'If you just want to play that thing, I mean. Oughtn't you to be in Vienna, or somewhere like that?'

'It would be better, I agree.' Mogridge, like most English schoolboys of his sort, was habituated to a dispassionate casual candour, and didn't resent it in the least. 'A conservatoire would suit my book better. It's the right place to study music, a conservatoire. Because it's what it's for, don't you see?'

'Yes, I do see.'

'But you know what parents are. Parents are—well, you know what parents are, Duncan, don't you? Only perhaps you don't.'

'Why shouldn't I know what parents are?' The suggestion that I might be in some state of ignorance in this regard offended me.

'Well, I mean you might be an orphan. You mightn't *have* parents. One oughtn't really to take it for granted—not when one's getting to know a man. The assumption might be painful —if his people had lately been killed in an accident, or even put in gaol, or something like that.'

'Well, I have parents, as you perfectly well know. They're alive and kicking, and they haven't even been put inside. And it was my father who took it into his head to dump me in this place.'

'But, Duncan, hadn't you been thinking of it yourself?'

'Well, yes I had, as a matter of fact.' I was getting accustomed to the sagacity of Mogridge peeping out from time to time. 'But it was my father who brought it off.'

'It seems just right for one with your literary interests.'

'I suppose so.' It hadn't occurred to me that I had been going around revealing anything describable in this way. 'But, Gavin, isn't there a lot of quite decent music in Oxford?'

'Oh, yes—there's *that*. But it isn't Vienna or Paris or Rome, all the same. Rome and Paris and Vienna are quite different. But, you see, I haven't got to the point at which I can seriously think of a musical career. Or rather, at which my parents can seriously think of it. They feel that I ought to have something else to fall back on. It's reasonable enough. It's not as if we had money. My father, as you know, is just an ordinary Cambridge professor, like everybody else.'

'But there must be all sorts of musical careers. You mayn't ever be a Suggia——'

'Oh, I couldn't be that, anyway, Duncan. She was a woman. Suggia wasn't a man.'

'Well, you know what I mean. You could have a very honourable career with your 'cello not quite at that level. Just in an orchestra, for instance. Isn't there always a clump of the things in an orchestra? Or playing in a tea-shop.' It wasn't easy to refrain from making fun of Mogridge. 'Or as a busker.'

'A busker, Duncan?' The term seemed unfamiliar to Mogridge.

'The sort of chap who entertains theatre queues.' Whenever I got to London much of my time was spent in such queues, and I felt I knew what I was talking about. 'Of course, it's violins, mostly. But I've noticed an old man with a 'cello, and he was proving very popular.'

'But—you see, Duncan—I'd rather never be heard of than not be among the greatest.'

This silenced me. I couldn't even—at the risk of obtruding literary interests—tell Mogridge that he had echoed certain words of John Keats. I recognized that I had got near to jeering, and that Mogridge knew I had, and that he didn't propose to be offended as a consequence. Cyril Bedworth under a similar assault would have been much hurt in mind. I wondered whether hidden beneath Mogridge's mild manner there lay some maniacal confidence in his own destiny which acted as a kind of waterproofing against any sort of cold douche. It came to me uncomfortably that his people in Cambridge were probably a pretty liberal and cultivated crowd, and that they hadn't vetoed a great conservatoire for their son without giving him a run for his money and consulting expert opinion. And music was like that. It wouldn't have been possible for my parents to send me for a time to a top teacher who would then have a very fair notion of what sort of playwright was latent in me. But Mogridge's promise must be more or less predictable.

It seemed necessary to speculate on what a failed 'cellist could do, particularly if temperamentally prompted to be among the greatest. On subsequent calls I used to glance around Mogridge's sitting-room in search of clues to any subsidiary interests he might possess and be in a position to develop in the quest for an alternative career. He had put up on his walls a number of photographs too small for such a decorative purpose but of excellent quality in themselves.

Some of them carried the familiar silhouette of Mount Everest —at that time, of course, unconquered—with ant-like creatures manipulating ice-axes and snow-ladders in the foreground. Others were close-ups—secured it was impossible to tell how —of men of like mind improbably clinging to horrific but unidentifiable precipices. Questioning, however, elicited the fact that mountaineering and rock-climbing were not among Mogridge's own activities; he explained to me, more abruptly than I recall his speaking on any other occasion, that the state of his vision would have precluded his ever being more than a pottering sort of climber.

If there was no line in his pictures, neither was there in any books he kept in evidence. One of these, indeed, was a Bible —an object in those days not much obtruded in undergraduates' rooms. But it was unsupported by anything further of a devotional or theological nature, so that its importance, if any, remained problematical. On the whole I judged it no more likely that Mogridge would enter Holy Orders than that I should do so myself (even although it was the career that Aunt Charlotte was in the habit of recommending to me). There was a short row of textbooks obviously bought on the advice of a tutor, and the other volumes on view had a similar air of having landed up with their owner without any very positive volition on his part. I could see things like *The Oxford Book of English Verse*, *The Essays of Elia*, *Romola*, *The Poems of Tennyson*, *Shakespeare* (just like that), *Birds of the Wayside and Woodland*, *Stories from Dante*, *The Seven Lamps of Architecture*— all heavy with the suggestion of edifying benefaction on the part of elderly relatives. There were no paperbacks, although these had become fairly common. All in all, one didn't get the impression of Gavin Mogridge as a restless and penetrating intelligence.

I found this unassuming set-up attractive, if only because I was a good deal involved with people who, like myself, were rather too much concerned to be clever. Even Bedworth was touched by something of the sort, although with him the effect aimed at didn't include the flippant. So Mogridge and I were quite thick for a time, and once or twice a week we would join up either in his rooms or mine and make tea. Mogridge was fond of toasting anything toastable in front of a gas-fire, and had considerable skill in doing so: an accomplishment which I have ever since regarded as a by-product of the English public-school system. It was as a result of this habit that I made an odd discovery.

'Duncan—will you get out a bigger plate from the cupboard?'

Mogridge had called this out urgently. He was engaged in producing anchovy toast—a delicacy which was enjoying what was perhaps a brief post-war revival—and the butter was getting out of hand. I jumped up obediently, made for a cupboard, and opened its door. It wasn't, however, the right cupboard. And it contained not crockery but books. I don't doubt that there was some subconscious prompting behind my mistake. It was almost the same action as I was to perform —and with an equally surprising result—in Ivo Mumford's room and in the presence of Ivo's father, Tony Mumford, Lord Marchpayne.

There was plenty of unoccupied shelf-room around, so I had to conclude at once that some reticence on Mogridge's part was responsible for his keeping a large number of books as he did. It was my first conjecture that they were improper books, and that he surprisingly owned a substantial collection of what would later be termed pornography, but which then appeared in booksellers' catalogues as *Erotica* or *Curiosa*. Had this been so, he would, I imagine, have been unique in the college. We were a generation quite without a sophisticated taste in such matters. The fact that Tony possessed a copy of *Justine* and that I had a *Fanny Hill* probably placed us among the major proprietors of anything of the sort. And they lay about casually for any of our acquaintance to have a go at who pleased.

A single glance at the actual contents of Mogridge's cupboard embarrassed me. I don't think I'd have been more so had the door opened on, say, a Teddy Bear, redolent of the fabulous Oxford of Evelyn Waugh. The first thing I saw was a batch of 'Biggles' books, stacked beside several of their Kaiser's War equivalents, written by a man called Percy F. Westerman. Then I saw—rapidly—*The Scarlet Pimpernel*, *The Riddle of the Sands*, *King Solomon's Mines*, *The Four Adventures of Richard Hannay*, *Revolt in the Desert*. There were dozens of books of that sort. The majority, which I didn't have time to scan, appeared designed for juvenile rather than adult readers.

'Wrong cupboard,' I said briskly, and closed the door and moved to the right one. The natural thing would have been to make fun of Mogridge's retarded condition in this unimportant matter of literary taste. But something told me not to, and I handed him in silence the largest plate I could find. He received it placidly and without comment, and certainly he didn't appear in the slightest degree discomposed. But then he never did. I concluded, weighing the matter up, that he had been too occupied with his cuisine to remark the observation I had made.

A certain loyalty to Mogridge was born in me out of this episode. When I had left him and climbed to my own landing I paused outside Tony's door, and then turned away and went into my own rooms. Provided, as I was, with an amusing story, it would have been the natural thing to barge in on Tony and treat him to a twopence-coloured account of it. The impulse to refrain must have risen from a dim notion, unclarified in my conscious mind, that I was myself rather more Mogridge's sort of person than I was Tony's. Tony had never confided to me what walk of life he intended to pursue. It was a subject (as was that of his family) about which he had an instinct to be cagey. But I was sure he and I should never, when the great world had received us, row in the same boat; his attraction for me was that of a temperament contrasting with my own. But when I thought of Mogridge's 'cello, certainly when I listened to it through the floorboards again, I was visited, perhaps for the first time, by some sense of the artist as one condemned to envy this man's art and that man's scope. If Shakespeare felt this strongly enough to tip it into a sonnet then so, presumably, did Ibsen and Tolstoi and Stendhal. It got you, in fact, even if you were no end of a big fish. It would certainly get you if you were among the minnows. I didn't think I was going to be, as Mogridge was, blankly wrong about myself. I'd learn to play, roughly speaking, according to the score. But I did know, already I intuitively knew, that I'd never make the damned instrument behave wholly as I wanted it to. Long afterwards I was sometimes to wonder whether, if I *had* like Mogridge been utterly wrong, Chance would at length have mended the error as brilliantly and arbitrarily as it did with him when he tumbled, roll of bumf in hand, out of that wrecked aeroplane in the company of a gaggle of bewildered professors of archaeology. In a sense, of course, he possessed from the start that other life. Those books cast longer shadows than I could see—or than anybody, for that matter, could have seen even when *Mochica* won its just but astonishing acclaim. I myself didn't possess, metaphorically speaking, any secret books in a cupboard. So I was really, as I plugged away at a tragedy modelled on Eugene O'Neill or heaven knows whom, more at risk than Mogridge was when the relevant bits of Saint-Saëns's Concerto wouldn't emerge from his big fiddle even quite in tune.

## VII

SINCE THEY WERE all—Tony Mumford, Cyril Bedworth, Gavin Mogridge—on my own staircase and in my own year, they had been my natural associates at the start. There were other men on the staircase as well. Opposite Mogridge on the ground floor was an elderly don called Tindale, familiarly known to us as the White Rabbit. He did have a scurrying air. Although he said 'Good morning' if he met you in the doorway it was in a manner suggesting that intimacy would be carried too far were he put in a position obliging him to say 'Good afternoon' later in the day. Tindale possessed several rooms, including (unfairly, as we thought) a bathroom and loo private to his own necessities. Tony and I came next, and above us were two men in their second year. Their names were Kettle and Fish, so it was to be supposed that some waggish bursar or dean was responsible for their present propinquity. There is always an initial difficulty in taking seriously persons with absurd names, particularly if they come in tandem. Kettle and Fish, however, had to be taken seriously, as will appear. It was naturally some time before they felt it proper much to acknowledge the existence of a new set of juniors. Above them, and almost concealed behind the balustrade of Surrey, lived Bedworth; his low-hutched chambers sprawled over the whole area, and were in consequence (as he had assured me on our first encounter) commodious enough. In various corners and cubby-holes they tended to disappear beneath the leads, so their effect was of a miniaturized version of Dr Timbermill's quarters in Linton Road. Bedworth didn't, it is true, run to thousands of books. He had a surprising number, all the same. I was myself just ceasing at that time, and not to my advantage, to be distinctly a poor man's son, and I recognized on

Bedworth's shelves what I was to recognize in the Headington abode of the Talberts: certain assumptions in choosing between this and that familiar in my own home. The purchase of each of Bedworth's books, it was to be supposed, had been a matter of the same anxious financial consideration as must have attended his sole known excursion into vanity in the unlucky matter of the college tie.

It seemed to be quite in order to take very little interest in women. Anybody who did so pertinaciously and to patently practical effect (like that P. P. Killiecrankie who later became a prebendary) was rather looked down on. This surprised me. My brother Ninian had possessed several girls when no older than I was now. My own case was different. While still sexually inexperienced I had formed with Janet Finlay a boy-and-girl relationship which I thought of as holding the seeds of maturity. I owned no notion that hurrying time never permits without risk a pause or intermission in the ripening of love, and in my ignorance or conceit I must be said to have banked Janet while absorbed in other enterprises. The bank was to be robbed, and it served me right. But my condition meanwhile had the effect of making me only a detached spectator of this aspect, or non-aspect, of college life.

The only girl who appeared regularly on the staircase belonged, strangely enough, to the White Rabbit. She turned up on two afternoons a week, vanished into Tindale's rooms, and the oak banged to behind her. The circumstance at least provided us with the material of ribaldry. Bedworth, who knew all about the learned occasions and interests of our senior members, explained to us that Tindale was writing a book on the Pelagian Heresy; that he had reached a critical stage in his research turning on the action of Pope Zosimus in A.D. 418; and that the young person was simply steering him through it with a typewriter. Detective-work did, it was true, track her down to some sort of secretarial agency in the town, but we were far from feeling that this proved much. We formed the habit of terming any known womanizer (such as Killiecrankie) a Pelagian.

Freshmen on their arrival were provided with a book of rules and regulations which nobody would own to having taken the trouble to peruse. I had myself at least turned over its pages. Approximately every second paragraph began with the word 'Gentlemen' and went on to particularize one or another thing that gentlemen might or might not do. They were, for example, not permitted to have ladies in their rooms after 11 p.m. This astonished me not because of either the earliness or the lateness of the hour, but simply as being on the record at all. These sanctioned visitors, if they existed except notionally, were uncommonly unobtrusive. Apart from the residual returned-warrior element, the undergraduates among whom I found myself were schoolboys lately or all but lately liberated from weirdly monastic educational establishments, and they were still nervous and cautious about the whole thing. They contacted girls in lecture-rooms (indeed, frequently attended such places merely for that purpose) and took them out for walks or to cinemas and tea-shops. But positively having them around the college obtruded an element of publicity and commitment they appeared to think twice about. The exception took the form of occasional big parties, as if there were a general sense of safety as lying in numbers. The dimensions of the sexual revolution which had come about by Junkin's time were to be among the more striking impressions of my middle years. But young manhood, and womanhood too, will out, and in my own time a main consequence of all this lingering reluctance frankly to grow up was that when adult sex did strike it tended to strike hard. Much harder, certainly, than when girl-trouble turned as much a matter of everyday as broken limbs brought back from winter sports in Switzerland.

I became friends with Martin Fish as the result of an episode which, if it held a certain muted drama in itself, didn't seem to presage disaster. One wouldn't have thought of Fish as disaster-prone. He was an Australian, which is a circumstance observable as giving a man, whether agreeably or not, a birth-right of toughness. I felt this in Fish from the start, although in him the quality was superficially obscured by an overlay of English manners, apparently acquired in a very Anglophil and expensive boarding-school in his native country. So he was a kind of half-foreigner, much as I was myself. The fact hadn't established any bond between us; his circle of acquaintance was already formed, and we got along on what I used to think of as pausing terms. When we ran up against each other, that is to say, we didn't make do with a mere nod or couple of words (as in the terminal stage of my relations with Stumpe) but would engage in what an anthropologist from an alien culture would probably have supposed to be a short ritual dance. It consisted of circling one another idly in a swaying and balancing act to the accompaniment of a brief exchange of remarks and inquiries about nothing very much, and the general idea was that of moderately pressing occasions of one's own at play against a civil reluctance to part. We were probably both aware of it as a convention we had picked up from others more advanced than ourselves in the amenities and graces that English undergraduates evolve. And Fish had his genuine occasions at all times; he was a controlled and purposeful man, although not like Bedworth obsessively so, and was making his way with decision towards whatever goals he had set himself during his Oxford years. I thought of him as probably destined to own hundreds of thousands of sheep and a good deal of furniture of authentic antiquity. He was, in short, a sympathetic character in his way, and with a good deal of the impressive magic of adulthood already attaching to him. But it is deplorably true that the battle is not always to the strong nor yet favour to men of skill. Time and chance happeneth to them all.

Although I was in love with Oxford I still didn't greatly enjoy leaving home, and this feeling extended at least to the beginning of my first summer term. I knew that here was another chunk of the happiest days of my life starting up, but that I had left part of myself elsewhere, all the same. I was naturally more subject to this reaction than were boys who had been regularly packed off to boarding-school three times a year from the age of nine. (It must certainly have been in the first few days of this term or the preceding one that I had scratched in a secret place a kilted Rupert Bear saying, bubble-wise, 'Ye maun thole it, Dunkie'.) So every now and then I would go off in a consciously brooding manner by myself. I had, indeed, something real to brood about. Janet had been in Skye, as was increasingly habitual with her, almost throughout the holidays, and our few meetings were unsatisfactory. I was aware that I hadn't, so to speak, been pulling my weight in our relationship; that I was younger than I ought to be, and that Oxford, although absorbing, wasn't improving the position; even that between Janet and myself there was developing a block, a no-go situation, which I didn't understand a bit.

These feelings, then, took me off by myself—perhaps not more than two or three times all told—in the first week of a May which to my northern sense already held all summer in its grasp. I decided to go on the river. Being alone on the Cherwell in a punt or canoe would picturesquely enhance my solitude, whether in my own regard or that of anybody who cared to observe me. Attending upon Timbermill in Linton Road had brought to my notice a boat-house scarcely a hundred yards from his hideous dwelling where craft could be hired with less bustle and difficulty than at Magdalen Bridge or elsewhere further down the river. I went out to this place on my bike after a twelve o'clock lecture, munched a sandwich in a tea-garden attached to it, and hired a canoe. I was offended when the man who pushed me off asked me whether I could swim, although he could only have been obeying some standard instruction. Swimming was among my more respectable athletic accomplishments. This proved to be just as well.

The Cherwell is a stream about which idylls have been composed. Its waters sparkle, are crystalline, turn to a tumble of golden guineas as sunlight strikes through the willow-trees. Lush meadows line its either bank. Kine are to be observed peacefully pasturing, and the little clouds in the blue sky above are like well-tubbed sheep. On this afternoon in late spring I was giving these appearances a fair chance, and here and there the authentic Arcadian note was evident. On the whole, however, I found myself afloat on a sluggish and muddy river, lined with trees perfunctorily pollarded and so untidily overhanging the water as to threaten one's head if one paddled, or equally vital parts if one was out with a punt. There were occasional bathing-places of varying degrees of pretension, but it was the same opaque stuff that ran through each and it didn't look all that inviting. The miscellaneous debris floating slowly down stream ranged from chocolate-papers and ice-cream cartons to the fractured limbs of quite sizeable trees. Some of these last had got themselves stuck in the muddy bottom and presented alarming snags if you weren't watching out.

It was too soon after lunch for anyone to be around, on shore or afloat. Solitude made me fanciful, and I caught myself imagining that I was exploring the upper reaches of a tropical river. Here and there the main stream was joined by gloomy tributaries so canopied by black poplars as to seem as subterranean as Acheron. Savages performing obscene rituals in a krall would have been quite in order. But in fact nobody was visible.

I told myself it was Mogridge who presumably went in for day-dreams of communing with Umslopogaas or She who must be Obeyed, and that juvenile fantasy with me was a thing of the past. All that I was honestly feeling about the Cherwell was its small likeness to the Corry or the Tummel. And this couldn't be called its fault; it hadn't invited me on any false pretences to repose upon its bosom. I decided to make the best of it, and struck out more vigorously with my paddle—an implement over which I had achieved just enough control to keep myself on a straight course. It was quite hard work, all the same, and by the time I reached Water Eaton I decided that I'd gone far enough up-stream for the day. Water Eaton is a house standing a little back from the river—which, at least at that time, seemed to be the only channel of communication it bothered to maintain with the outer world. It was old, seemingly untenanted, and as unpretentious as an ancient and spacious dwelling is ever likely to be. I found that I approved of it. It was the natural terminus to my outing, much as a glimpse of the college tower had been the end of my father's tour of Oxford in quest of a place of education for me. I edged up to the bank, scrambled ashore, and secured the canoe to an exposed willow-root. The river curved here, the bank was eroded in places, and the water seemed surprisingly deep.

There was short dry grass a few yards back, and a smell of clover in the air. The sun shone confidently in a clear sky, so that I judged the afternoon to be not so much warm as hot; invisible insects supported me in this view by producing a kind of midsummer hum. I sat down facing the river and with my back against a tree, and dutifully brought out a book. (The book was probably one the study of which had been enjoined upon me by Timbermill and not Talbert. I had become attached to Talbert, but only Timbermill was getting any work out of me.) I hadn't opened it before I heard voices from the river.

'I could, you know. I'm sure I could!'

These words came to me, quite clearly, from what was still an invisible source. It was a woman who had spoken, and something indefinable in her tone rather than what she had said, made me wait with some curiosity for what was going to appear. There had been a man's voice as well, and now it said something I couldn't distinguish. But I guessed what sort of craft was coming down stream, since in addition to the slow plash of blades there was the cluck of oars in rowlocks. It must be a rowing-boat, and quite a small one.

'Don't be so absurd! Of course I can.'

The voices had sunk to a murmur before the man replied in this way to something I hadn't caught, and I couldn't tell whether he was amused or annoyed. I did suddenly know, however, who was speaking. That faintly antipodean accent belonged to my neighbour Martin Fish. In another moment he was in view. At least his back was, since he was at the oars of a tiny dinghy, sculling lazily. Facing him in the stern, and facing me, was a girl of about his own age. I had a glimpse of her as very pretty, and as in some state of what was no doubt attractive animation. This impression sharpened into a sense that she was putting on a turn. I could see that she was meant to be steering but was in fact doing nothing about it. As I continued to watch, Fish glanced over his left shoulder as he rowed—a precaution he must frequently have to take when with so regardless a companion. As I have noted, all sorts of inconvenient objects hang around in the Cherwell, anxious to cause trouble.

'Shall I find out?' the girl asked.

This time, Fish made no reply, but turned back to regard her (I thought) doubtfully or fixedly. Were he to follow this up by looking to his right, he and I would be at once at gaze. I reacted to the perception by humping myself hastily away from the tree against which I had been leaning, stretching myself prone on the grass, and burying my nose in my book. From the river my appearance thus presented nothing more identifiable than the soles of a pair of shoes and a foreshortened view of grey flannel bags. This unsociable conduct was not occasioned by any suspicion that something awkward had blown up between Fish and his companion in the dinghy, which he wouldn't thank an acquaintance like myself for taking a dekko at. It was the simple fact of his being out with a girl that made me shy, producing a recrudescence of the mere schoolboy in me. For had one of my form-mates, only a year before, encountered me walking along Princes Street with Janet, he would have been as likely to avert his gaze as take

144

his cap off. On the other hand, my evasive action conformed to the then ruling Oxford *mores* as I have described them. If a man tagged around with a girl, you let it be his own affair.

I heard the dinghy go past at an unhurried pace. Fish and the young woman had stopped talking, perhaps as having noticed my sprawled form within earshot. I stayed put for a couple of minutes, since Fish would now be facing me if I turned round and sat up, with the result that we should have to hail each other after all. When I did scramble upright the dinghy had disappeared round the next bend down stream. From that direction there now came fresh sounds which I took to have a different origin. People were shouting and splashing in a way that suggested the likely appearance, coming up river, of a rowdy party skylarking in a punt. But this impression lasted only for a moment. There weren't all that many people involved, and the sounds didn't, on reconsideration, in the least suggest jollity. I jumped to my feet, and raced off in their direction.

The first thing I saw was the dinghy. It had capsized, and was floating keel-upwards down the river. Fish and his girl were bobbing about in mid-stream. The spectacle ought to have been instantly alarming, but seconds went by during which I was merely amused. Although it was so early in the summer term, I had already seen two or three punting tiros tumble over their poles into the water, and the incidents occasioning nothing more than unfeeling laughter from friends. Moreover, as one could punt up the Cherwell, it seemed improbable that it was anywhere more than five or six feet deep, and it certainly didn't go in for the sort of current that would sweep one helplessly before it. I didn't however enjoy a sense of diversion for long, and I was kicking off my shoes even as the first sense of sudden sharp crisis rose in me. The girl's clothes were still holding her up rather than dragging her down; she might have been charitably described, moreover, as swimming. I didn't feel all that interest in her. This was because I was looking at Fish, and Fish—momentarily—was looking at me. We were staring straight at one another—this was the dominant and horrid fact—and there was blind fear on Fish's face. He cried out, he gurgled, he managed the imbecile gesture of waving his arms in air. And then he just disappeared. Whether or not he was actually out of his depth, he was contriving to drown expeditiously before my eyes. There could be no question of the priorities involved, and they weren't of a chivalric order. This remained true even although the girl's difficulties seemed likely to increase with an uncomfortable speed.

'Float, blast you!' I shouted at her furiously, and went after the muddy business of rescuing Martin Fish. It wasn't very difficult, and he may be said to have behaved well. I had him on the bank quite quickly, and was in a position to haul out the girl before she had got too far in the direction of the North Sea.

We then had the resource of collaring, righting, and bailing out the dinghy. I say 'resource' because the aftermath of the affair threatened to reek of embarrassment. There was the awkward business, for a start, of my being a hero. I hadn't undergone the slightest risk—unless one were to imagine, in an access of melodrama, a demented Martin Fish clutching my throat and dragging me down to a watery grave. Still, there had to be gratitude and expressions of esteem. Then, again, the relationship of Fish and his lady must be supposed modified by the incident. For the present, however, it was in an unknown direction and unpredictable degree. I'd have formed a clearer idea about this had I been able to arrive at the slightest notion of what had been going on. It isn't easy to overturn a dinghy on the placid waters of the Cherwell. My first guess was that the craft had been hopelessly wormed, and that either Fish or Martine (which, curiously, turned out to be the girl's name) had put a foot through the bottom of it. Had this been so, only a little panicking and grabbing might have turned it turtle. But when we got it right way up again it proved perfectly sound.

Then there were the snatches of conversation I'd overheard.

'I could, you know. I'm sure I could!' That seemed an easy one; Martine had been proposing to do something silly. But then, after brief exchanges I hadn't made out, Fish had said, 'Don't be so absurd! Of course I can.' They hadn't, I felt, been making their respective claims about the same thing. Then, 'Shall I find out?' Martine had asked challengingly. And at that the couple had passed out of earshot.

The puzzle all too clearly connected itself with the fact that Fish couldn't swim. He couldn't swim a stroke. Plenty of husky men are in that condition. Fish was thoroughly husky. Beside him, I was a mere rabbit. And Fish was an Australian, one of a race whom travel-advertisements at that time accustomed us to think of as perpetually perched on surf-boards amid Pacific breakers—either this or drilling in life-saving teams dauntlessly prepared to do battle with shoals of sharks. Thinking over these matters, I formed the provisional view that, as a girl-friend, Martine called for firm handling.

At the moment, and in trying circumstances, she was being demonstratively nice to her humiliated lover. She was being nice to me too, but with a perplexing suggestion that something clandestine was necessary in thus including me in her regard. She seemed, in fact, a play-acting type. Of course misadventure, when it runs to a large element of the ludicrous, tends to produce false notes. And we were undoubtedly feeling silly. In our disgraced condition, muddy as well as wet, we had miles to go. With a sunny afternoon wearing on, the river was filling up. Nobody shouted at us, or even laughed, but we were undoubtedly the object of amused regard. It was something I didn't myself want to suffer further on a long walk from North Oxford back to college, and I remembered with some relief that the canoe might be dropped at a boating-station further down the river. I could have stripped myself of everything except a pair of unnoticeable pants, shot ahead, and been taken for a wholly unremarkable devotee of early sun-tan. I thought perhaps I ought to do this, rather than present myself (at least to my two companions) as the solicitous convoy of a pair of branded incompetents. I decided, however, to paddle gently behind the dinghy, near enough for an exchange of cheerful remarks. These proved edgy.

'I like my Fish best out of water,' Martine shouted at me with gaiety and over her shoulder. Fish, tugging at the oars with the concentration of a man who seeks to get something over, produced a smile not easy to interpret. I was confirmed in my impression that her idea of niceness was of a teasing sort. As a couple, Martin and Martine obscurely suggested the title of a mediaeval romance. Perhaps it was this quirk of nomenclature that had drawn them to one another in the first place. It seemed doubtful if they were exactly soul-mates now.

'What about Parson's Pleasure?' Fish called out suddenly. 'It's going to be a bit awkward for Martine.'

I realized, not without satisfaction, that this was so. The celebrated bathing place is no more than a short reach of the river, and is dedicated to the use of males, young and not so young, who favour swimming and sun-bathing unencumbered by garments of any sort. For this reason it exists behind a kind of stockade, and women boating up or down stream are required to disembark and by-pass it on foot. It did seem a little hard that Martine should be required to do this—thus exposing herself further to a public gaze—in her present dripping condition.

'I could go in,' I called back, 'and see if there's somebody to borrow a coat or something from.'

Martine, however, vetoed this on the score of inconvenience to myself and the possible lender. Suspecting that an exhibitionistic strain, or Godiva complex, was really at work, I didn't pursue my suggestion. As it was improbable that I'd know any of the available nudists, it would in fact have been an awkward commission. So Martine walked round Parson's Pleasure as she was, and took rather long about it. Perhaps she paused to explain herself to acquaintances. As a result of this, Fish and I, when we had got the dinghy and canoe over a contraption known as the rollers, had to manage a couple of minutes alone in one another's company. It ought to have been perfectly easy—a bit of a relief, indeed. Actually, we were slightly constrained.

'It has been a thing with me for a long time,' Fish said. 'In fact, since a kid.'

'Kind of regular hydrophobia?' I asked, and at once realized the ineptitude of a humorous note.

'They say these things are quite unaccountable. It ought to be because of a sailing accident or something when I was a boy. But it may equally well have to do with the water going out of the bath when I was a baby.'

'I suppose so.'

'In Australia, baths in the country are often rather primitive. The water just disappears through a hole in the floor. That could be more frightening than its just going down a pipe.' Fish frowned. He was perfectly aware that these speculations had an awkward ring. 'Anyway, I've never been able to get into the stuff at all. The sea, I mean, or a river or even a swimming pool. It could be pretty difficult at school. I had to pretend I had the wrong sort of skin.'

'It's just a specific thing?'

'Oh, yes—absolutely.' Fish had taken my meaning, and his response carried complete conviction. I knew that if I had to face a gang of toughs, or go under fire, Fish beside me would be not a liability but an asset. It would probably be me who'd be the funk. Unfortunately I couldn't make the point to him without impertinence, and had to wait for him to go on. 'As a matter of fact,' he said, 'it sometimes makes me a bit reckless at other ploys.'

'I can understand that.' I was suddenly liking Martin Fish. His last words had again been simple; they lacked the slightest suggestion of his seeking means to rehabilitate himself in my esteem. I had a feeling, too, that he'd like to tell me more, and that it would do no harm to encourage him. 'Look,' I said, 'I don't want to barge in. But has this happened partly because you told the girl you could?'

'What do you mean, Pattullo—*could*?'

'Could swim. You see, I happened to hear you tell her not to be absurd, and that of course you could. Coming from a boat, that sounded, somehow, a bit like swimming.'

'That's right.' Fish had turned pale as he glanced first at me, and then at Martine who was coming up with us. 'She'd somehow suspected I couldn't, and was making fun of me. I suppose I got upset, and told that bloody stupid lie. Christ, Pattullo—I was a silly bugger! She'd said something about being able to capsize the dinghy so as to find out. And then——' Fish broke off. 'Jump in, darling. You'll be in a hot bath in no time.'

Climbing into the dinghy, Martine rewarded this solicitude by stroking Fish's cheek. She was giving me a Mona Lisa smile as she did so.

During the next few days I thought a good deal about Fish and Martine, although I didn't expect to see much of them again. Their relationship bewildered me, and this made me feel that I could learn from it; that it promised more instruction in an interesting sphere than did, for example, those scandalous glimpses of P. P. Killiecrankie's amours with which Tony and I had on several occasions diverted ourselves. Anybody can sit back and imagine the beast with two backs. Fish's mysterious predicament—as I felt it to be—messengered itself obscurely from unknown territory. Nothing in my own experience helped me to understand what was going on. Unless, very remotely, it was my cousin Anna's amusing herself in the heather by first exciting me and then calling me humiliatingly to a halt. I took it for granted, however, that Fish and Martine had actually been sleeping together. This was because I perceived, intuitively rather than on the evidence so far, that Martine's hold over Fish was for the time being absolute. She could entertain herself as she pleased, and I supposed that this malign privilege belonged only to a mistress. Of course it doesn't, as I was later to realize. And in fact—although we were to become close companions for a time—I never did learn whether Fish and Martine had been lovers.

'Could you come in to tea this afternoon?' Fish suddenly asked me one day in the quad. 'Martine's coming, and she'd like to thank you properly for helping us out like that. I'd be awfully glad, Duncan, if you would.'

I wasn't sure I wanted to be thanked properly by Martine, but at the same time my curiosity was strong. I decided on a cautious acceptance.

'Yes, of course,' I said, '—and thanks awfully. I've got Talbert at five, but I'll come at four.' This lie (for I didn't, as Fish did, feel bad about casual lies) struck me as a cunning way of controlling a situation which might develop awkwardly.

Fish's room, when I arrived in it, proved predictably full of business-like books, and of equally business-like cricket bats and pads and tennis rackets. There was a painting of arid hills and ghostly eucalypts slightly recalling my father's manner, and there was another which, years later, I'd have known at once to be by Sidney Nolan. I judged these to be evidences of the substantial circumstances of the antipodean Fishes. It was the room of a most normal young man. I didn't know whether Martin Fish had come to Oxford straight from school, or from an Australian university, or from the war. I thought of him as older than myself by a good deal more than the academic year currently separating us. His effect of maturity, of having firmed up and become less labile than the rest of us, was to give its edge to the developing situation.

Martine was disposed on a window-seat, gazing out in an inappropriately romantic manner at the severely classical splendour of the library on the other side of Surrey. It was before girls at Oxford had been forced by male competition to adopt any bizarre note in their dress. It was also before the advent of tights, so there was apt to be a more abrupt sense of transition to arrangements one oughtn't to be goggling at than obtained at a later time. Whatever dress Martine was wearing, moreover, was of sheath-like effect and, somehow, damp-looking, as if she had once more just bobbed up out of the river. I was later to find she had thought this out.

Fish left the first greetings to Martine. It was as if he really expected her to make a speech. She did nothing of the kind. It was borne in on me that she had announced her intention of doing so merely out of an idly curious wish to see me again, and that Fish himself wouldn't have had any strong prompting to ask me to tea. This was depressing. And now that I was in the room and on display, Martine felt no obligation to speak to me at all. Except with speaking looks. I got them, and Fish got such conversation as she offered. This wasn't a comfortable division in itself. But Fish got something else. Martine had a technique of caresses which were not in the least affectionate or even merely sensual. They were taunting and lecherous. I had glimpsed this in the dinghy, when she had stroked Fish's cheek. Now, moving around in order to make the tea, she ran her fingers through his hair, touched his upper lip as if stroking a non-existent moustache, suddenly blew softly in his ear. Later, she sat down on the floor at his feet and passed a hand stealthily up the inner side of his thigh. The Killiecrankie spectacle apart (and that was so comically bawdy as somehow not to count), I had never witnessed anything of the kind—or only perhaps as a boy stumbling amid the sand dunes of Dunbar or North Berwick upon the love-play of remote plebeian persons. I could actually now watch in fascination just what was happening to Fish as this went on. Martine herself wasn't watching it. To a very uncomfortable effect, she was watching me.

Of curious interest as this behaviour was, and effectively though it acted on my own nervous system, my one wish was to see ten-to-five, or thereabout, turn up on Fish's clock. I was convinced that Martine's actual interest in me was pretty well a zero quantity, and that if she saw any employment for me at all, it was simply as a handy little whip with which to operate on Fish. I also judged that, at least for the moment, this wasn't coming off. It was very possible that Fish, who had decent feelings, would have preferred to be pawed in privacy. But these fond attentions were driving him too crazy for thought. And now I came on a cardinal point in the whole affair. Fish was blankly refusing to see what was to be seen. He was fatuously or obstinately blind to the whole nature and quality of Martine. If, for instance, he noticed her making those stupid eyes at me, he told himself that they simply took the place of that thank-you speech.

The tea-party didn't end without a further development of the *Belle Dame Sans Merci* theme. Fish had a record-player in his room, and Martine decided to turn on some music. So far as I could see, she chose a record at random, as if merely to provide a background for anything further it occurred to her to say. She did, in fact, go on talking sporadically to Fish. I don't remember about what, and perhaps I didn't even pick up much of the sense of it at the time. She was certainly trying to poke him up, to get some sort of response to challenge out of him, and the general effect was of murmured needling reference to matters which remained obscure to me. If Fish was worried, he didn't show it. Actually, I don't think he at all lucidly was; he was still besottedly regarding Martine as marvellous. I felt it to be a vision of her that might crack at any time; that he was exercising a taut will about the girl without, weirdly, allowing himself to become aware of the fact. He was doing some fondling himself, but it was mostly a chaste stroking of her head which there wasn't the slightest impropriety in my witnessing. I'd had enough, nevertheless, and I was just going to mumble something and clear out when Martine got to her feet and began to dance. The record-player was still grinding out noises which may have been perfectly acceptable in themselves, but which didn't seem apt for choreography.

We were witnessing an exercise in free expression, or something of that kind. Martine was miming rather than dancing, and I told myself she did it damned badly and was putting up a thoroughly pointless show. Girls at her sort of school were probably taught that it was artistic to pretend to be the waves of the sea or a lonely cloud or the last rose of summer. Then I suddenly saw that she was rowing a boat.

I must have stared at Martine in childish horror. She now had her hands above her head and was clawing wildly at air. Her features were contorted into a convention of panic which would have done credit to a fifth-rate Hollywood actress in a movie. And she did have that appearance of being dripping wet.

'Do you like it?' she demanded, and this time it was to me that she addressed herself. 'It's called the Australian Boat Song.'

I glanced at Fish. He was actually managing to smile at Martine gently, rather as one might smile at a child who has unwittingly committed some trifling *faux pas*.

'I don't quite see the point of it,' he said, and passed a hand over his eyes. 'I don't see it, darling.'

'Well, I do see it,' I said, and jumped to my feet. 'I say—what a bore—Talbert-time. Thanks a lot for the tea, Martin. Seeing you, Martine.' And at that I bolted from the room.

There must have been similar occasions at which I wasn't present, for Martine performed her job at leisure. It was presumably quite her thing. Working on the disintegration of Fish, she must have been looking ahead, and she even took to dropping in on me. I remained for a couple of weeks the only person who knew what was going on; and as she knew that I knew, it seems likely that I held a certain technical interest for her. I was very young and vulnerable—so could she line me up, even after I had been privileged to have a glimpse of the whip at play? But for circumstances necessarily unknown to her, it might have been a rational hope. As it was, I trembled at times, and when she disappeared I experienced a sense of physical frustration which surprised me.

At least she did disappear entirely, having no doubt been called away elsewhere. Nobody ever saw her again. I don't think even Fish himself did. Her activities being concluded to her satisfaction, and there being no more fun to be had, she simply walked out and forbad him to follow. Perhaps he didn't, or perhaps he did. He never told me. He may have written, telephoned, hung around likely places, sent flowers, stood staring at curtained windows and closed doors. Or perhaps, beaten, he simply took what had visited him. I don't know.

I was left with Fish. The whole staircase was left with Fish, for his condition became such as was not to be concealed. I used to go in and sit with him, since he himself just sat. It wasn't over his book, since he did no work at all. Quite as much as Bedworth, he must have been a model tutee. But now, not only did he write no essays, he cut his tutorials altogether. We had gathered that this was a hazardous thing to do. It mightn't be long before Fish was sent to the Provost and given a rocket —or admonished, which would be the Provost's own word. In which case he'd either have to mend his ways, or confess to the nature of his present disability, or risk being treated as merely contumacious. Any way on, it seemed a bit hard on Fish, who was so clearly an industrious and responsible character when in his senses.

I wasn't too sure about the uses of silent sympathy. It seemed a kind of giving in, an accepting of the pitch of the trouble at Fish's own estimate. If I had been required to act as a guard in a condemned cell, and was unprovided or unhandy with the comforts of religion, I'd no doubt have sat mum in the same way. So I did try to talk. And Fish would often manage a polite reply; it was somehow one of the more trying aspects of the situation that simple good manners appeared to be, to his own mind, about all he had left to cling to. But nothing I could say really reached him, all the same.

So it was necessary to seek help, and I started by consulting Tony. Everybody was aware that there was something wrong with Fish, but it was probably Tony alone who had noticed how much I was sitting in on him. Tony struck a practical note at once. His experience of even the most peripherally relevant sort was at least no more extensive than mine. (In fact, it was quite certainly a good deal less.) But Tony possessed what I lacked: a sense that he was born to handle things.

'Oh, that little bitch!' he said. 'Yes, I've seen her around. Needs her bottom smacked, if you ask me.'

'It's a bit too late for that. Besides, Fish isn't like you. He's a gent, not your best type of English public-school boy.'

'This is no time for joking,' Tony said, virtuously and un-expectedly. 'You're sure she's finally ditched him?'

'Certainly she has. She's getting on with her vampire act elsewhere. A Zuleika, or however she sees herself.'

'Then the man must shop around. It's the only thing in such cases.'

'How do you mean—shop around?'

'Go out and find another tart, of course.'

'I don't think Martine is a tart, exactly. More of a tail-twisting type. Pathological, really.'

'If the man's a masochist I suppose it narrows the field a bit. But he can still go shopping. He might put some sort of discreetly worded advertisement in *Isis*. Or in a news-agent's window. That's said often to bring remarkable results.'

'Who's being funny now?'

'All right. But you're probably being a bit morbid about the thing. A perfectly nice girl is almost sure to serve equally well. And if Fish is too glum to take an initiative, we must do the job ourselves. Find a wench, and damned well plant her on his mat.'

'Listen, Tony—do we know any girls? They've all been booked by the bigger boys—and they tuck them away out of sight. A freshman hasn't a chance. Even for himself, let alone as a pimp. So stop kidding.'

'I'm only trying to help.'

I realized that, in a way, this was true. Tony's suggestions seemed merely frivolous. But in practice, and while still only suspecting the facts of the case, he had been trying to help already. Fish never now managed breakfast in hall—something not remarkable in itself, since the meal was generally regarded as a pretty grisly one, frequently to be abjured by right-minded men. But he did generally turn up to lunch and dinner. At dinner our freedom of association was restricted as a consequence of the college's maintaining the archaic institution of a scholars' table. Fish was some sort of scholar—I suppose a Rhodes Scholar—and this meant that, of the people on our staircase, only Bedworth and I could dine beside him. But lunch was a free-for-all, and Tony had taken to sitting with Fish when he could. He was very capable of carrying on a cheerful and assured talk with seemingly no awareness that he wasn't getting much in return; capable of this and, it must fairly be said, of not overdoing the act. When I had—rashly, perhaps—told him all I knew, he didn't use the information to force Fish's confidence; in fact he probably didn't admit to any consciousness at all of Fish's depressed condition. Thoroughly ignorant of love and love's shipwrecks though he was, he probably did a better job than he would have done twenty-five years on, when he had presumably gone through other experiences and vicissitudes than those which were to gain him his seat in the Cabinet. A harsh judge would say, indeed, that Lord Marchpayne was the sort of man whose sensibilities, at least in some directions, coarsen with maturity.

It was otherwise with Cyril Bedworth. When I eventually became a fellow of the college, and found Bedworth about to take up the office of Senior Tutor, not much time was to pass before I realized that he was the man to whom to take any awkward thing. In many ways he remained awkward himself; you would have said that, in his mid-forties, he still had to fumble his way into personal relationships; he was even liable to produce touches of what might be called the old attic-varlet syndrome. But he had become rather a wise man as well as a wholly reliable one. He would have been thoroughly good about Fish. He wasn't that now. Almost as soon as I had consulted him in his turn, I began to feel some reason to wish I hadn't.

'I'll have a talk with him,' Bedworth said, having listened

to me carefully. 'It's true he's a second-year man. But then, Duncan, we are scholars, all three of us. That's an important point. It makes it more appropriate that I should speak to Fish than that Mumford—Tony, I mean—should. Or that man Mogridge downstairs. Yes, I'll have a serious talk with Fish. From the point of view of his work. I can appeal to the sense he ought to have of his responsibilities in view of the fact that he is on the foundation of the college.'

'I'm not sure that, technically, he is quite that.' It was in some dismay that I took refuge in this quibble.

'No matter. It has been judged proper that he should wear a scholar's gown. That is extremely important.'

'I've an idea it's what's called a senior-status gown.'

'No matter, Duncan. We mustn't be pedantic before a grave issue like this.' Bedworth spoke as if in serious reproof. 'Fish dines with us, and that, for me, settles the matter. I shall appeal to him, as I say.'

'Perhaps it's not exactly——'

'This young woman has no doubt behaved very badly, and I deeply sympathize with Fish. I shall tell him so. But he must set his face against unmanly repining. I shall urge that upon him. I shall mention the case of Keats.'

Bedworth, if chargeable in those days with a touch of self-importance, was a man of his word. That afternoon I saw him walking slowly round Long Field with Fish. He was doing all the talking—presumably expounding the view that a morbid obsession with Fanny Brawne, and not the severities of *Blackwood's* and the *Quarterly*, had been responsible for expediting Keats's decline into the grave. It seemed improbable that Fish's melancholy, or whatever it was to be termed, would be much alleviated by such considerations—if only because Fish, an absorbed mathematician when in his right mind, might well have only the dimmest notion of who Keats was. I didn't reflect that Fish's state was one in which any sincere concern, honestly expressed, would be at least in some degree comforting and supportive. I thought of Bedworth as perpetrating an assault upon his privacy, and felt that I was myself responsible for this through having gone busy-bodying around. But this didn't prevent my now hurrying off to Mogridge. He seemed to be my last resource, so far as the more responsible characters in my immediate circle were concerned.

'Does Fish have an instrument?' Mogridge asked at once. 'I've a notion I've heard music coming from up there. If so, we could possibly do something together. Anything that's distracting is good when it's distraction that's needed.'

'No doubt. But all he has is a gramophone, and I think it's just what may be called standard equipment. I've heard it only once. It was when this Martine woman turned it on in order to produce a particularly nasty gibe at him.'

'It sounds a bit low—employing music like that.' Mogridge was deeply shocked. 'I'd imagined I'd heard somebody playing a piano.'

'That's Clive Kettle, on the other side of the landing. He's sometimes playing his piano above my head while you're playing that thing of yours under my feet, as a matter of fact.'

'Oh, I see.' Mogridge was unaware of any element of irrelevant complaint in this. 'Kettle's another second-year man. He ought to know Fish quite well. Has it ever struck you, Duncan, that it's funny having a Kettle and a Fish like that?'

'It has crossed my mind.'

'Perhaps Kettle could be encouraged to have Fish in and play to him. Or perhaps Kettle and I could play to him together. I believe Fish is a mathematician. I think I've heard that maths is his thing. They're often musical, mathematicians. Einstein is said to be very fond of music. Do you know that Einstein lived in this college for a time? It would have been rather interesting to meet Einstein, don't you think?'

'Yes, I do.'

'But, of course, that's not the point at the moment. I see that.'

'Quite so, Gavin. It's you and me and Fish who live in the place at the moment.' I didn't feel at all impatient with

Mogridge. As not infrequently, I had a sense that his mind was working quite effectively behind all these sagacious remarks. 'The question is, what's to be done. The chap really is in a state. He simply broods on the thing all day. It's melancholia, or something like that. They'll have him in the Warneford, if he doesn't look out. Or if we don't look out.'

'Mental hospitals are said to be very advantageous sometimes. When it's a question of madness, I mean. Still, it's no doubt to be avoided, if possible.' Mogridge paused. 'If music's no good,' he said, 'the proper thing is foreign travel.'

'It's an idea.' I was impressed by this piece of traditional wisdom. 'But how the hell is Martin Fish going to do foreign travel? Here we are, not too far on in the summer term. And Fish is supposed to be working hard for Schools in a year's time.'

'I have a notion Fish is quite well off. I happened to go to lunch in the Lodging last term. Because of my father's being a professor at Cambridge, I rather think. This Fish was there. Mrs Pococke introduced us to each other in a formal way. She does some rather odd things—I suppose because the Pocockes are more or less new to the job. And she murmured to me something about pastoralists. In Australia, that means whacking great landowners. So Fish is probably in the mun. He could try Samarkand. Or Totonicapan. Or Titicaca. Or even the Friendly Islands.'

'The Friendly Islands sound just right. Or the Society Islands might do equally well.'

'Yes, of course, Duncan!' Mogridge kindled to my appreciation of these places. Not that, again, I wasn't impressed. He had made their names ring out in a startling fashion. As Tony had maintained, he was a great Romantic—perhaps as much so as Bedworth's John Keats. 'So you see,' Mogridge said, 'it boils down to jockeying him through the rest of this term, and then getting him out of the country. And you'd better go with him, if you ask me.'

'But I'm certainly not in the mun, Gavin!' I said this before

160

remembering that it wasn't true. Not long before, the Metropolitan Museum had bought a Lachlan Pattullo, and my father had promptly divided the considerable proceeds between Ninian and myself—disguising this characteristically impulsive action as a manœuvre prompted by deep financial cunning. So I was more prosperous than I had any title to be for some years ahead. 'In any case,' I added feebly, 'I've an idea of going abroad with Tony.'

'You'll have to change your plans,' Mogridge said placidly. 'Unless, of course, you have some strong family obligation. A parent who is very ill, or something of that sort. One has to put first things first, or there's a danger of getting them in the wrong order.'

'My parents are both perfectly well,' I said. 'I've told you so.'

'Yes, of course. You wouldn't be thinking of going away with Tony otherwise. So there's no difficulty there.'

'I've been thinking only of a fairly quick trip, Gavin. As a matter of fact there's a girl at home that I don't want to miss out on for too long.'

I was extremely surprised to hear myself telling Mogridge this. Girls at home—individual girls at home, as distinct from libidinously conjured up flocks of them—tended to be a tabu subject. Moreover it was my instinct to be very close indeed about Janet—and the more so of late, when I was becoming increasingly conscious of some unknown factor in our relationship. On this ground even Tony was no confidant of mine. Perhaps it was because I had possessed myself, quite accidentally, of the secret of those romantic books of Mogridge's that I thus—as it were in requital—divulged a secret of my own.

'That's important, of course.' Mogridge had received my communication with characteristic sobriety, but at the same time seemed prompted—even at the cost of irrelevance—to a confidence himself. 'It's a sort of thing I think about sometimes. It seems to me that anybody who wants to be an artist—if it's only to play the fiddle, Duncan—should think very carefully about love, and getting married, and that sort of thing. They can be tremendous distractions, don't you think? Particularly if one starts in when very young.'

'My father's a tolerably undistracted painter. And he fell in love and got married when very young indeed.'

'As young as you are now, Duncan?'

'Well, no—I suppose not quite.'

'Are you really in love, Duncan?'

'Yes. At least it feels like that.' Mogridge had asked his straight question so simply that I found myself answering without constraint.

'And the girl?'

'Well, I hope so. Perhaps this summer I can make sure.'

'Then that *is* a priority.'

'Only Janet'—I was even more surprised to hear myself uttering my beloved's very name—'will be away for quite some part of the holidays. So perhaps I *could* go off with Martin Fish.'

'I honestly think you must, Duncan. You see, you've taken the chap on.'

I nodded submissively. Mogridge's power of lending weight to the self-evident had never struck me so forcibly before.

# VIII

FISH WAS INDEED my affair to the extent that, if anything
was to be organized for him, I'd have to do the organizing.
I had been pitched into his disaster—or rather had kicked off
my shoes and dived into it—fortuitously, but I had to see him
through it nevertheless. The first essential seemed to be to get
some signal from Fish himself. I had been spending hours with
him, and had at least an inkling of how he was feeling. But of
what he thought I hadn't a clue. Was he doing anything that
could be called thinking at all? Baffling questions surrounded
his state. Did he, for instance, still have in his head a picture of
Martine which wasn't Martine in any objective regard? Or had
he gained an accurate but impotent sense of her as the little
slut she was? Did he know what she had done: exploited her
discovery of a ludicrous Achilles' heel in him to ditch him
contemptuously and with a slow-motion sadism when she had
become bored? Floundering ignominiously in the Cherwell,
he had in effect been put through a symbolic enactment of
impotence. There had been no doubt of his irrational terror;
it must have been like a clutch at his vitals. Perhaps one had to
put down the unmanned Fish as suffering the ravages of a
primitive castration complex.

These speculations, if extravagant, had their modish fascination; we were most of us depth-psychologists at that time.
They didn't prevent me from coming to the fairly sensible
conclusion that Fish must be got to talk. Words, in fact, must
damned well be shaken out of him. As soon as I saw this I had
a go. I ran upstairs, banged loudly on his door in the manner
customary with us, and pushed in. Fish was sitting at his
writing table. It had the same dismal sort of serge covering as
I remembered adorning the room in which I had discussed

with Stumpe how to start having women—but this was partly obscured beneath a litter of papers scrawled over with mathematical computations. I drew encouragement from the sight; it looked as if Fish was at last managing to do some work for his tutor, or at least obtaining solace or forgetfulness by absorbing himself in his own thing. There was a character in *The Prelude*, I remembered, who, when having a bad time on some desert island, managed to cheer himself up by drawing geometrical figures in the sand. Then I took another look, and saw that the exercises being performed by Fish were concerned with addition, subtraction, multiplication, and division. He was merely assuring himself that he hadn't gone completely mad.

'Martin,' I said, 'quit it. Lay off.'

'Oh, Duncan!' As Fish said this, he looked for a moment startled and abashed. This was quite something, since for days it had been impossible to wring out of him any kind of emotional response at all. 'I was just getting on with a spot of work,' he added, and rapidly shuffled the scattered papers into a pile.

'You were doing nothing of the sort—nothing except doodling. Can't you do something useful for a change? Be a real pal, and make me some coffee. Proper coffee, in that bubbling thing.' Fish's well-appointed rooms ran to a complex percolator.

'Coffee? Yes, of course.' Fish got up obediently, and blundered around. I thought the percolator was going to suffer, but in fact he coped with it competently enough. 'I know I'm being a nuisance,' he said suddenly. 'It's just that I don't seem able to get this straight. What has happened. How it can have happened. I try to see it clearly, but it's behind a kind of cloud. Have you ever lived in absolute darkness? It's just hell. Christ! I don't suppose you even know what I'm talking about.'

'Of course I know what you're talking about. Martine.'

'That's right!' There was an imbecile surprise in Fish's voice which I found daunting. But I saw nothing for it but to charge ahead.

'Listen,' I said. 'If you're not clear about Martine I can put you right at once. She's a girl in your past, and she was a damned bad buy. Or let's be frank, Martin. She was a third-class harlot, but made up for it by being a first-class shit.' I paused on this; it had been a little too elaborate to be quite right. 'Honestly,' I added. 'Honestly, honestly, Martin, she was just no bloody good. Face up to it, man. Take a straight look at her, and you'll see the thing was about as wholesome as trying to get kicks out of a corpse.'

This random vehemence I'd no doubt have disapproved of if I'd been behind my typewriter; it was my idea to get a reaction out of Fish at any cost. If he'd chucked the percolator at my head I'd have done my best to dodge the coffee and the glass, and counted it another scrap of ground won. The young psychologist, that's to say, was thinking in terms of what he'd have called abreaction therapy—meaning, I suppose, the securing of a violent and cathartic emotional discharge. As often with amateur experiments, it failed to work. Fish simply dismantled the percolator, and poured me a cup of coffee with care.

'But I don't see it that way,' he said mildly, and in a tone conveying faint bewilderment rather than strong indignation. Then he did, for a moment, become slightly agitated. 'Oh, God!' he said. 'I know *I'm* no bloody good. I'm making a pest of myself to anybody who knows me. Do believe, Duncan, that I feel awfully bad about it. I feel so miserably guilty. And you're a true cobber, Duncan. Really you are. I see I haven't any sugar. I'm terribly sorry.' He relapsed into mournful passivity.

This was dreadfully embarrassing. As I'd myself, with a hollow gamesomeness, exhorted Fish to be a real pal I couldn't fairly take exception to being acclaimed as the same thing in honest Australian English. But Fish's impulse more or less to apologize for his existence, and the revelation that his kind of depression and defeat could unloose irrational feelings of guilt, were aspects of the situation which took some facing up to.

I had to be firm with myself in sitting down and continuing to talk.

'How much have you got around the Continent?' I asked—thus evidencing at once that I was a good deal under Gavin Mogridge's thumb.

'The Continent?' It appeared that Fish had to run the meaning of the word to earth somewhere deep down in his mind. But he continued with the unfaltering politeness he seldom failed to manage. 'I've never been there at all. Except as a kid. My parents brought me on a trip home before I was old enough to have to go to Geelong, and they traipsed me around quite a bit. I remember hardly anything about it—except seeing a very fast ball-game, rather like what's called pelota, played somewhere in Italy. I think pelota's Spanish, but I'm pretty sure this was in Italy.' Fish paused. He had made a big effort. 'I'm afraid this is awfully dull for you, Duncan,' he added idiotically.

'Why don't we go? In the long vac. That's in no time now, Martin.'

'Go abroad?' Fish stared at me in inert surprise. 'That would be terribly nice,' he added quickly. 'But you see, I'll be having a good deal of work to do in the long vac. Catching up, as a matter of fact. The truth is that I haven't been a hundred-per-cent lately. Not altogether. A little worried. I don't know if you've noticed it.'

It looked like a point at which to give up. But I was getting annoyed with Fish, and this unreasonable reaction in myself made me decide for another round.

'You run a car, don't you?' I demanded.

'A car? Oh, yes—I have a car. Somehow, I don't seem to have been using it much lately.'

'We could go in it. That would be marvellous for me, Martin. Of course, I'd go shares in the petrol, just as in everything else.'

'But there's been this war. We don't really know anything about the conditions.'

'Bugger the conditions. American tourists talk about the conditions. The conditions are quite good enough for you and me. I've been in France, and I know.' I said this with all the air of a travelled man. I had spent a fortnight with a school party in Normandy immediately before my most recent—and alarming—stay at Corry, and we had enjoyed horrifying glimpses of whole landscapes blighted and cities blown to bits. This had been my only experience of travel, although I wouldn't have been in a hurry to admit it. When Ninian and I were quite small, and before the barriers of war had gone up, it had never occurred to our father, deep though his attachment to France was, to take us or despatch us there. Or perhaps it had—since sporadically he was by no means neglectful of us —but he had judged the proper age for it would come when we were not quite children any longer. He would certainly have thought it money poorly spent if all we had been equipped to retain in memory had been, as with Fish, a notably exciting ball-game.

I urged my project for a Grand Tour upon Fish for some time, but he didn't respond. Indeed, after having emerged from himself to the extent of exhibiting a mild play of feeling about this and that, he now seemed to be retreating again into his own misery more deeply than ever. He sat looking at me unrecognizingly, and with a frown creasing his brow. It may fleetingly have struck me that the frown was new, and at least belonged to a man who had started thinking of something. But I went away more discouraged than before, feeling that there was nothing for it but to bring in dons and doctors. Perhaps this was why I hesitated when I ran into the White Rabbit.

It had been one of those odd hesitations which take the form of not knowing on which side to pass the other person. Quite suddenly, and although there is plenty of room for orderly and composed behaviour, one is dodging right and left like a panicked and incompetent rugger player. It is a phenomenon that probably figures in Freud's *Psychopathology of Everyday Life*, a work with which I had no doubt become familiar by that time. But at the moment I was thinking only of being properly apologetic to Tindale, whose entrance to his own rooms I appeared to be obstructing in a spirit of tiresome and disrespectful frolic. I was there at all—down on the ground floor —only because it had come into my head to seek further advice from other of my contemporaries, and notably from Colin Badgery, who had rooms in Howard. Badgery—that John Ruskin Scholar a year ahead of me who had assisted in my frantic hunt for Timbermill—I was inclined at this period to treat as something of a guru. It may have been because my mind was on this quest that the dodging business in front of Tindale overcame me.

'Oh, good evening, Pattullo,' Tindale said. It was the first time he had displayed knowledge of my identity, although this was the third term that we had been on the same staircase. He was a spare middle-aged man, with a florid complexion, a head notably bald and domed, and a fuzz of grey hair over each ear. His eyes had a glitter which a little reminded me of Timbermill —except that they were small, black, bilberry eyes, more suggestive of a plain-clothes detective than of a visionary. For a moment, indeed, his gaze had been bent on me keenly enough for police purposes of the most sinister sort, so that I found myself surprised when his glance suddenly dropped to the neighbourhood of my feet. I'd have been more surprised still had I been able to reflect (as I was to be a long time afterwards) that this was the idiosyncrasy so strikingly exhibited by Cyril Bedworth's shamefast wife, Mabel Bedworth.

'I'm afraid I don't know my neighbours very well,' Tindale said, with a hand on his door-knob. 'Apart from my own pupils, my undergraduate acquaintance seem to come from here and there around the university. At my age, you see, a good many of one's old school friends tend to have sons up at one college or another.' Having offered this explanatory remark, the White Rabbit appeared to feel the way cleared for the next thing. 'Have you a minute or two?' he asked. 'If so, do come in and have a drink.'

I found this very much in order. Buntingford, the tutor so casually confident about the adequacy of my Latin unseen translation, had made fun of my freshman's persuasion that Oxford undergraduates lived in a freely mingling society of learned persons, old and young. We had got it, he once declared, out of inferior Edwardian novels of 'varsity life. But, in fact, the lack of interest in our young lives exhibited by dons at large wasn't absolute. If they tended to know only their own pupils tolerably well, they did occasionally cast a social net a little wider than that. And perhaps most of them acknowledged the staircase principle in some degree. I didn't know whether Tindale had already taken some notice of Bedworth and Mogridge and Tony Mumford. But if he hadn't, he ought to have; and that went for me too. So I accepted his invitation with what I felt to be becoming ease. It was in my mind, of course, that here might be the right senior person to whom to speak about Fish.

'There's much to be said for the ground floor,' Tindale said, ushering me into his sitting-room. 'One gets a window broken rather more often, of course, than if one is upstairs. But the culprits regularly pay up, after all, and it makes honest work for deserving glaziers. Saves a surprising lot of tramping up and down, too, in the course of the day. Foot-pounds, or ergs, or whatever energy is reckoned in. Brandy?'

I approved of brandy. After Fish's coffee, it seemed just right. And it seemed just right, for that matter, after Fish as well. So I accepted quite a tot of the stuff, and looked round the room. There was a typewriter on which it was to be presumed that Tindale's suspect young lady laboured twice a week in the interest of a clearer view of the diplomacy of Pope Zosimus. Apart from this, the place was sparely, even a shade meanly, furnished; it wasn't the room of a man who had been bred up in any tradition of taste. Over the mantelpiece, and thus directly beneath Tony's Roman bagnio, was a large

169

colour-print of the Ansidei Madonna. It was massively framed
—much more massively than was appropriate for a thing so
thin as a colour-print—but it somehow suggested itself as first
cousin to that droopy Corot tree which had adorned the room
in Rattenbury in which I had been lodged during my Scholarship Examination. On another wall there hung the sawn-off
blade of an oar, painted in the college colours and with the
names of some victorious crew or other—all eight of them and
a cox—inscribed in small gold lettering. I wasn't able to make
out, without uncivil peering, whether the cox—or perhaps the
stroke—had been Tindale. It seemed a faintly anomalous
trophy in a don's room: a kind of attestation of something
about a dead self that Tindale didn't want lost sight of.

'Head of the river, as a matter of fact,' the White Rabbit said
casually, noticing my glance. 'Do you smoke?'

I didn't smoke. It seemed a pity, since I vaguely conjectured
that what went with brandy at a donnish level was cigars.
There was a pause, as if Tindale was momentarily at a loss.

'Let me see,' he said, easily enough. 'What was I saying?
Ah, the ground floor. Do you know that I'm a good way in?'

'Sir?' Rather stupidly, I was at a loss myself. 'Oh, I see.
No—I didn't know.'

'A closely guarded secret, perhaps. The Tindale route isn't
given away to freshmen, eh?' My host seemed amused at this.
He glanced at me again, and I had an odd impression that what
he was looking at was my hair. 'Quite an income in it, as a
matter of fact. A toll-gate effect. Come into my bedroom, and
you'll see. Might be useful to you one night. Who knows?'

We went into the bedroom. It was pretty bleak. I felt a
certain awkwardness in the situation. But Tindale was again
quite at ease. He threw open a further door. His set, as I have
mentioned, rambled as the other sets on the staircase did not.

'A kind of dressing-room, I suppose. I really haven't any use
for it. But go and take a look out of the window. I expect you
can still just see.'

'I expect so.' I entered the dressing-room and obeyed my

entertainer's instruction. 'It's what's called the coal-yard, isn't it?'

'Quite right. And that flat roof at the far side is the Dean's motor-shed. Dead easy to get on that from the street, and then there's just this window. They have to come in over the upper sash, because the lower one is chocked up. Kind of jack-knife athletic performance, it has to be. Scatters their small change over the carpet, and they're too scared to stop and pick it up. They bolt through the dining-room, and I collect in the morning. Regular revenue. We'll call it a fine.'

'I see,' I said, and registered adequate amusement.

'But the main thing, Pattullo, is that I keep this door communicating with the bedroom open. They all know that to be my tedious habit. Increases the nervous effect.'

'I suppose it does.'

'And sometimes I give a further turn of the screw.' Tindale led me back to the sitting-room, chuckling softly. 'Seem to stir in my sleep. Or even call out in a smothered manner, as if from a horrid dream. More brandy? But perhaps we'd better not.'

'No thank you, sir.' I judged curious the picture of this elderly character lying in his narrow bed and watching the shadowy forms of these young idiots flitting past. 'Isn't it pretty silly,' I asked, 'keeping up this convention of men having to climb back into college in the small hours? They're coming all the way from Malaya and goodness knows where, some of them.' I paused. 'In a sense,' I added, feeling that Tindale mightn't quite be getting there.

'Ah, but you mustn't deprive me of my *Trinkgeld*!' Tindale indicated comical dismay, although it was clear he wasn't naturally a humorous type. 'Not that you're not quite right,' he went on, with a transition to gravity. 'Another five or ten years, and it will all have vanished. But we adjust slowly to changed conditions in a place like this. Don't you agree? And one has a certain nostalgia for the ancient ways.'

'I don't think I have.' I had abandoned the notion of appealing to this particular don in the matter of Fish's neurosis.

He seemed, somehow, to be a mixed-up type, and moreover I didn't much take to his air of connivance in the irregularities of the young. He got his pay for doing the *in loco parentis* stuff, and he'd do better to play it straight. There was a silence, and I realized he was sensitive to my not being quite on the right beam. 'Thank you very much for the drink,' I said. 'I'll have to be getting along.'

'Ah, always that essay to write!' Tindale produced a small friendly gesture. 'It's a hard life, Pattullo. Do you know an expression I heard the other day? The rat-race. About nails it, I'd say. Good of you to come in, and I hope you'll come again. Sometime.' He moved to the door—entirely the man who could hardly murmur Good-morning or Good-afternoon. 'Good-night,' he said, and made the little gesture a second time over.

I stepped into the quad, wondering whether I had cut this unsatisfactory encounter uncivilly short. If so, it had been partly because, having written off Tindale as a reliable ally, I wanted to resume my plan of seeking out Colin Badgery. It still seemed to me that it was up to us to hand over Fish to the operations of a more adult wisdom than we ourselves presumably possessed. Badgery would know the proper way to go about it.

Hurrying across Surrey, I met Tony. He looked as if he were returning prematurely to his rooms from some disappointing conviviality.

'Come and see Badgery,' I said. 'We must get this Fish business sorted out. It's bad.'

'Oh silver fish that my two hands have taken,' Tony murmured, and had to cast around for something to give this particular Yeats joke any appositeness. 'Do you think the charming Martine chanted that as she grabbed him where she wanted to?'

'I don't care a damn what she did. Just come over to Howard.'

Tony made a resigned gesture and fell into step with me. We found Badgery entertaining one of our own contemporaries, Robert Damian. Being affable and instructive to freshmen was one of Badgery's lines, and he greeted us amiably now.

'Oh, hullo,' he said, 'it's the industrious John Ruskin Junior and his idle hanger-on. There's some beer under the table. It's in those horrible little cans. Please make moderately free with it. We're discussing Behaviourism. It seems it's susceptible— the good Dr Watson's nonsense—of practical applications. Robert says they'll be beneficent. But that's because he still retains the sanguine and guileless outlook of youth. They sound pretty sinister to me. What do you think?'

'We haven't come for a tute,' I said—for Badgery's questions commonly turned into sustained inquisition, conducted on monotonously Socratic lines. 'But I do have a problem.'

'How to gouge a single useful word out of Albert Talbert, I expect. No go, Duncan. I tried myself for a whole year, and it was no bloody go. So I can't help.'

Badgery was still John Ruskin Senior, but he had ceased to read English. With difficulty, and probably on the strength of much hard work, he had persuaded the college to let him change to another School hazardously far on in his undergraduate career. It must have been judged that he had quite a lot of brains.

'Talbert lets one be,' I said defensively. 'He doesn't produce those Five Main Points at the end of your essay, or make lively faces at you to show he's being stimulating and God knows. The appreciation of literature is a delicate business. He refrains from irritating the sensibility.'

'And do you respond to that particular maieutic technique, my child? Does the sensibility burgeon week by week?'

'Not too well.' Badgery's own technique, which was often one of nonsensical badinage, had the unexpected effect of making one grope after a dim honesty. 'I don't do all that for him, as a matter of fact.'

'No matter. Young Pattullo, unlike the frivolous drunkard

Mumford, wins golden opinions from his preceptors, tute by tute. Have you heard of the kiss of life?'

'No, I haven't.'

'It's a newfangled way of resuscitating the moribund. But it's my point that reading English is the kiss of death. Or at least getting a First in it is. Have you ever thought of running through the Class Lists since the racket started?'

'Of course not. It would be a waste of time.'

'Nothing of the sort. It's most illuminating.' Badgery turned to the others. 'Or at least for a literary character like young Pattullo it ought to be. Have you ever heard of anybody becoming a star of the Oxford English School and afterwards a poet or novelist or dramatist of the faintest significance?'

'Aldous Huxley,' Tony said unexpectedly.

'Precisely! He's the exception that proves the rule. The others all become professors of the stuff. Rank upon rank of them. An army of unalterable aridity. It becomes self-perpetuating.'

'For Christ's sake,' Robert Damian said, 'stop talking such stupid shop. Let's have Duncan's problem. I suspect it's this Fish.'

'Oh silver fish——' Tony began, and remembered I'd had this one already. 'Fish it is. Duncan's obsessed with the man.'

'I'm nothing of the kind. But I do seem to be expected to fix Fish, and I've come to wonder whether it can really only be done by doctors and people. So I want to know how to begin. Could I barge in on his tutor—who can't be too bright if he hasn't tumbled to the situation already? I rather thought of putting it to Tindale, as a matter of fact.'

'Tindale?' Tony echoed, and stared at me in surprise. 'But you don't *know* Tindale. Nobody does.'

'Yes, I do. I've just been drinking his brandy.'

'Well, I'm blessed!' Badgery sounded equally astonished. 'Question: why was young Pattullo born so beautiful? Answer: to delight the gods by constraining the elusive Tindale into breaking his rule.'

'What do you mean—his rule?' I demanded crossly.

'Not to pick his young associates from inside his own college. A prudent, a decorous rule.'

'Then that's it!' Tony said rapidly. He regarded it as a duty to snub or short-circuit this particular joke at my expense—partly because he thought Cyril Bedworth to be the sort of person upon whom it was funniest to direct it. 'If this obscure don's tastes lie that way, it releases the typewriter.'

'The typewriter?' Damian queried.

'A nice girl,' I said. It was I who had lately discovered that typists had originally been called typewriters—and, indeed, that Joseph Conrad had bewildered his Polish relations by writing home to announce that he had married one. 'Like the young lady of Barking Creek, she has a date with Tindale twice a week. But Tony's talking nonsense.'

'Not at all.' Tony had already succeeded in opening a second can of Badgery's beer. 'We waylay the pretty creature as she leaves her dull assignment with the inappropriate Tindale, and tell her we have quite a different proposition two floors up. Swiftly striking a bargain as we ascend——'

'Yes, Tony's talking nonsense, all right,' Badgery said, with the air of a mature person suffering the absurdities of the young. 'But perhaps his general idea is on the right lines. Fish must be found another wench. But the notion of simply hiring one and then saying to him, "Look what we've tucked up in your bed" is a shade on the crude side, if you ask me. Duncan, wouldn't you agree?'

'I wish you'd all stop being idiotic. Of course it's true that, if Fish doesn't hang himself or something, time the great healer may weigh in. He'll go back to Australia and make a suitable marriage and have lots of children. But it's not going to happen in a day.'

'Of course not. What a penetrating mind Duncan has.' Badgery paused to drink in a meditative fashion. 'Taking a scientific view, one sees that one has to work in stages. Is Fish still attached to this girl who has ditched him?'

'I don't know,' I said. 'I don't even know that. But I'd suppose so.'

'Then the first thing to arrange is a sort of deconditioning. Does he still see the girl?'

'Almost certainly not. Martine has vanished.'

'Then she must be tracked down, and it must be fixed so that Fish runs into her in an accidental way quite often. And whenever that happens, there must be somebody ready to produce a very loud noise—perhaps by firing a pistol or something—preferably just behind Fish's head.'

'You're dotty,' Damian said.

'Not at all. It's just Behaviourism again. But one also wants Fish—about every second time there's one of these casual sightings of the girl—to experience the sensation of a sudden drop through space. You see, these are the only two things that frighten a baby: being dropped, or being banged at loudly. After that, it's all conditioned reflexes. So that's how we work on Fish.'

'It sounds too easy for words,' Tony said. 'Particularly the dropping him through space. And then what?'

'He's ready to be introduced into new female society. Lots of it, if possible; not just a typewriter delivered at the door. Duncan, what about this old dame you go to tea with in North Oxford?'

'What's that?' Tony interrupted. 'Duncan, you've been hiding something from your very oldest friend. Who is she?'

'She's a Mrs Triplett.' I was surprised to discover that I had, in fact, kept this recent association to myself. 'But all that's totally irrelevant.'

'I'm not at all sure. Everybody has heard of Mrs Triplett. How did you come to achieve the *entrée*?'

'It began with a cow, if you want to know.'

'Duncan began with a cow.' Tony was diverted for a moment to routine impropriety. 'An unassuming, indeed a rustic, taste. And then?'

'She asked me my name and college, rather as if she was the

176

Junior Proctor. Then later it turned out she thought she knew some vague relations of mine, and she started asking me to tea. I don't see the point of talking about Mrs Triplett.'

'The point,' Badgery said with extreme patience, 'is that, at her tea-parties, your Mrs Triplett is said to lay on wenches. Is that right? If it is, the relevance of the fact to the good Fish and his situation ought to be evident.'

'Well, yes—it is right. But not wenches, exactly. I'd say approved young gentlewomen.'

'No matter,' Tony interposed. My report on Mrs Triplett's set-up was interesting him. Later, he would denounce me scathingly for having kept dark about it. 'Fish is quite presentable, despite his obscure colonial origins.'

'The girls are mostly foreigners. The deceased Triplett was Foreign Secretary, or an ambassador, or something of that kind; and when the widow Triplett isn't milking cows she likes to have the old polyglot stir around her.' I caught Badgery's eye, and realized he was taking note of my being not quite easy about these tea-parties. ' "Foreigners" probably isn't quite right,' I said. 'There's a strong bias towards the Empire, or the Commonwealth, or whatever it is.'

'Favourable *milieu* for Fish,' Damian said.

'Well, I'm not sure. Some of them are black——'

'Black?' Tony repeated, surprised.

'Quite, quite black. And others are quite, quite yellow. An acquired taste, I'd suppose, in either case.'

'Unlike cows,' Tony said.

'Oh, shut up!' If I snapped this at Tony, it was because I was conscious of myself becoming sillier and sillier. 'But most of them are brown. Brown girls in all sorts of subtle shades. I like the ones from the Shan States best. They're rather small, and their brown has a hint of gold to it.'

'The Shan States?' Tony was round-eyed before my unwary admission of this exotic interest. 'Does that mean the Road to Mandalay?'

'More or less, I suppose.'

'Where the flying-Fishes play,' Damian said.

There was a moment's silence, nobody thinking highly of this rudimentary joke. The pause was broken by Badgery, who was clanking hospitably among the beer-cans.

'Do we understand,' he asked me, 'that you feel much attracted by these dusky beauties?'

'I'd say I do, rather.'

This was another of the occasions upon which, in the middle of much laboured nonsense, Badgery displayed his power of eliciting a fragment of truth. I had found one or two of the girls we were discussing very exciting. Their appeal lay as much in their miniaturized dimensions as in their complexions; they'd have been, fantasy hinted to me, marvellously handlable. But something deeper was involved. Formative months were passing over me; I was tidying up on a late adolescence; I was more aware of necessities not to be coped with in what Stumpe had called quiet half-hours with sex. These were commonplace circumstances; added to them was the quality of my relationship to the distant, and now elusive, Janet. I had begun to whisper to myself that this had been a boy-and-girl affair; at the same time I was unwilling to think of Janet except in the context of a life-time's fidelity. So Mrs Triplett's Burmese princesses (for I believe they were mostly that) became for me the channel for a tide of feeling which I told myself could run blamelessly in parallel with one both more ideal and more realistic—realistic in the sense of being supported within the embankments of a common culture and shared interests. (Janet Finlay, to put it more simply, was the girl next door.) I was telling myself that East is East and West is West, and that the two can be quite reasonably separated for certain purposes. It was ignoble, this phase of feeling; and I think it made me sometimes see myself as potentially in some not very edifying short story by Colonel Morrison's friend Willie Maugham. But it was to be a situation which, like the majority of situations, never came to anything much. I wasn't—I have to face it—a young man particularly good at forcing the moment to its crisis.

'It seems to me,' Tony was saying, 'that our sly young friend Pattullo here has been behaving in a meanly dog-in-the-mangerish way. And he has told me quite a packet of lies from time to time about his Sunday afternoon toddles.'

'The point is Fish,' I said. 'And I see no solution *du côté de chez Triplett*. The Australians have something called a Colour Bar, after all.'

'But we propose no more than an emergency and salubrious *liaison*,' Badgery said reprovingly. 'And I'm interested, by the way, in this business of brown girls. There's a don somewhere —I think it's at Magdalen—who has written a book about a chap called John. It's one of those pilgrimage fables of an edifying sort. John is rather like Duncan, as a matter of fact. He wants to be serious and truthful, like those boring people in E. M. Forster. He even wants to find God, which is outside the Forsterian terms of reference.'

'Not at all,' Tony said with one of his random admissions of literacy. 'God si Love.'

'God si Balls,' Badgery said robustly. 'That's just a jab at Hindu toshery. The point about this John is that, as he piously journeys, he's continually ambushed by brown girls. That's what they're called: brown girls. They tumble him in the hay. I'm wondering whether they have their origin in Mrs Triplett's *salon*. It might be a fruitful field for literary research. That laborious man Bedworth might do his B.Litt. on it.'

'Isn't it time,' Robert Damian demanded abruptly, 'that we were talking sense about this hapless Fish? He doesn't sound a bit funny to me.'

'The night is yet young,' Badgery said. He glanced at the depleted crate. 'But yes—perhaps you're right. Midnight has come, and the great Christ Church Bell—as your pet poet says. We now listen to Robert. He's the first I call.'

'Very well.' Damian was attractive to me as possessing almost my own disabling juvenility of appearance—a matter of being pink and white—but he owned much self-confidence too.

179

'This talk of an instant replacement for the disgusting Martine is futile. She'd be as useless as instant coffee.'

'Could any of these girls,' Tony asked me, 'be described as coffee-coloured? It sounds less glamorous than brown with a hint of gold.'

'You, Mumford, belt up,' Damian said. 'If you're going to listen, you're going to listen. And, for a start, let me tell you Duncan's right on the bloody ball when he says the man needs a doctor. He's a cot case, if ever I heard of one. Still, his condition's obviously benign.'

'Benign?' I asked.

'Opposite of malignant. Fish is clearly an ordinary virile Australian who happens to be in a mild depression. But it's reactive and not endogenous. So the prognosis is O.K. It's what we nearly always find. Handle the thing vigorously, and Fish can be safely returned from deep misery to ordinary human unhappiness. That's what Freud liked to promise his patients at the end of Interview One. Not, of course, that Freud knew how to go about it. We do.'

' "We",' I said, 'meaning yourself and that equally eminent Behaviourist?' Damian, a freshman reading Physiology as Oxford's regular start to becoming a doctor, commonly used this pronoun to indicate persons working on the furthest frontiers of scientific medicine.

'Well, no—not really.' Damian remained serious. 'I do think it will become possible to tinker with human personality, and control human behaviour, on Pavlovian or Watsonian lines. What they call brain-washing is obviously a crude start on that —which is why Colin here thinks of it as sinister. Perhaps it is. Anyway, it looks like being about as laborious as psycho-analysis. At present, you can just get a bad joke out of it—like that one of confronting Fish with his Martine to the accompani-ment of loud bangs and nasty falls. What we're really working on most hopefully is psychotropic drugs.'

'Giving Fish pills?' I asked. We were being attentive now. I felt that, in a broad way, Robert Damian knew his stuff.

'There are quite a lot of pills, and others are coming along.'

'He'll have to take them three times a day after meals?' I was disliking what I heard. If Damian had recommended that Fish should take to the bottle and drown his sorrows as he might, I'd probably have been slightly revolted. But now I'd been given a vision of Fish fumbling furtively in a little chemist's box for something that would mysteriously take hold of what, whether fallaciously or not, he probably thought of as the core of his being. This wasn't revolting; it was frightening. It was much more frightening then, no doubt, than it would be now.

'More or less that,' Damian said. 'And for weeks and weeks. They're not like narcotics or crude hallucinogens. They get to work rather slowly.'

'Do you know *how* they get to work?' Tony asked.

'No we don't. Different chaps have different theories. But all medicine is surprisingly empirical. People just notice things. As in the penicillin business.'

'But that's not quite the same,' Badgery said. 'You can't just go on mixing recondite drugs in endless permutations and feeding them to loonies to see if anything happens. It would be like the monkeys producing Shakespeare's plays on type-writers.'

'Quite true. But we needn't go into that. Anyway, I don't think they'll give Fish pills. They'll deal with him by other methods. I don't mean asking him if he can remember what happened to him in the wood-shed, or if he ever misinterpreted the behaviour of mum and dad in bed. Other physical methods.'

'Mightn't it be better,' I asked, suddenly turning round on myself, 'if he were just left alone, after all? By doctors and people, that is. Just having us do our best in a companionable way. There is that thing I was being funny about. Time the healer, or whatever I said. These things *must* wear off.'

'Almost certainly, but we can't ever be quite sure. If he has a certain constitutional vulnerability, then this neurotic bout, if left untreated, may just possibly deepen into an untouchable melancholia. No, the only safe thing will be ECT. And the sooner they get cracking the better. In other words, we ought to get cracking ourselves.'

'Just how?' Tony asked.

'Go straight across to the Dean, yank him out of bed, and panic him. Or the Provost himself, for that matter; I'd like to see that bland hauteur with the wind up. But the main thing is to have Fish hospitalized within the next hour or two. So come on.'

Damian had stood up, a simple action which shook the other three of us considerably. I told myself that he was going to be a good doctor, and that in the future he'd save lives by simple decisiveness of this sort. I felt I had to say something, nevertheless.

'Look!' I said. 'Hold hard a minute. Is this ECT thing electric shocks?'

'That's right—although it's an uninformed way to put it.'

'I don't believe it's anything of the kind. And isn't it another of those irrational things, hit on by sheer chance?'

'Oh, quite probably.' Damian didn't hesitate for a moment. 'Like insulin, you know. You pump it in for diabetes, and find it's controlling schizophrenia.'

'Fish is going to be taken away, and be tied up, and have electrodes or whatever they're called——'

'Don't get excited, Duncan. It can be made to sound horrific —and I suppose it really is, in a way. But they have various dodges for toning the drama down. Besides, he won't feel anything at all.'

'Won't he writhe in his bonds, and produce noises commonly heard only by the Gestapo?'

'Oh, stuff it, Duncan! Fish can't be subjected to any treatment without his consent. And it mayn't *be* that treatment. I'm not a doctor.' Damian seemed just to have remembered this. 'I may be quite wrong on what will be thought about him. But he should see someone *now*.'

'Yes,' Badgery said, 'that's true.'

'We ought to wait till tomorrow,' I said, my change of front hardening. 'We ought to sleep on it, before setting so drastic a ball rolling.'

'I don't agree.' Badgery had got up too. 'Come on—all three of you.'

'No.'

It was Tony who had spoken, and we all stared at him. The single monosyllable had come from him with a startling effect of command. It wasn't a turn I recall his ever putting on again during his remaining undergraduate days. We were brought to a halt as abruptly as by a shout on a parade ground.

'We're all concerned about this Fish,' Tony went on. He was entirely relaxed again. 'Half-a-dozen other people are as well. But it's Duncan who has been carrying the can. Think, you two. If you go off to the Dean or somebody now, you'll be gabbling to him about a situation you hardly know about except at second-hand. And that pretty well goes for me too. So if Duncan's instinct has turned against this, I back Duncan. I'm most impressed by what Robert says—and I can see, as I'd expect, that you, Colin, are as well.' Tony paused—it might have been said to radiate a sense that he held the highest opinion of us all. I could once more have reflected, had I not been too anxious about other things, that *homo politicus* in his embryonic form was before us. 'But it just happens to be Duncan who has an intimate sense of the thing, and I think we must leave the responsibility with him for the moment.'

'For twenty-four hours,' I said.

'Something like that.' I could see that Tony disapproved of being unnecessarily specific about one's pledges. 'And now we'd better go to bed.'

This carried the day—or rather the night. Tony and I walked back to Surrey together. It was late; the quads were deserted; only once did we hear revellers conscientiously bawling and breaking things in some distant rooms.

'He's still got his light on,' Tony said quietly.

I took this to be counsel.

'All right,' I said. 'I'll have another go.'

Tony turned into his own quarters, and I continued upstairs. Before I reached Fish's landing I encountered his neighbour, Clive Kettle, coming down. The light was dim. He stopped as soon as he recognized me.

'Pattullo,' he said, 'are you by any chance on your way to see Martin Fish?'

'Yes, I am.' Kettle might have supposed it more probable that I was going on further to call on my own contemporary, Cyril Bedworth.

'I was coming down to see you, as a matter of fact,' Kettle said nervously. 'Because I know you've been trying to help Martin.'

'Well, yes.' Kettle's choice of words embarrassed me. I might have said to Bedworth, 'Cyril, help me with this bloody awful text', but I couldn't possibly have said to Fish, 'Martin, I do want to help you if I can.' I searched for a further reply. 'He does seem to need sorting out.'

'He desperately needs sharing,' Kettle said—thus further revealing that we were of different tribes. 'He's been in deep distress.'

'Girl-trouble can be pretty grim while it lasts. But that's all it has been, as I expect you know.' I produced this coarse-grained remark quite against my own sense of the matter. A kind of instant jealousy was involved. 'Have you turned the chaplain on him?' I asked, more brutally still.

'Yes, of course.'

The manner of Kettle's saying this pulled me up. I hardly knew him at all. Tony and I—and probably Badgery and Damian as well—regarded Christians in the college as harmless eccentrics with whom it wasn't awfully easy to get on. For the moment, however, I felt rebuked.

'I'm sure that's all to the good,' I said. 'It's no doubt the chaplain's thing, in a way. But I feel there's a certain urgency about Martin's case. Medically, one might say.'

'Medically?' Kettle looked blank. 'Well, yes—perhaps.'

184

'Do come down and have a word about it before I see him. I'm glad you thought of me. I have been seeing him quite a lot.'

On this conciliatory note, we went downstairs together. I found myself hoping Tony wouldn't stick his head out and observe this new development. I was certain he wouldn't think much of it.

'What some of us feel,' I said when we had sat down, 'is that it's clinical, really.' I didn't gain much confidence from this vogue word. 'Martin's in a depression—the sort that can take a man into the bin. And he's just not reasonable. Have you met the girl?'

'Oh, no!' The idea of this appeared to alarm Kettle. 'I don't think she can have behaved too well.'

'That's the understatement of the year. Martine's a real horror. After the first nasty shock of being expertly tortured, and if he had any sanity at all, Martin ought to have been damned glad to be shut of her. But you might as well put that point of view to the college cat. I can't make any impression on him. But what about you? I suppose you've known him longer than I have.'

'Yes, I have. And he has always been very friendly. He is still, in a way. That's why I've tried getting him to pray with me.'

'I see.' Again I felt foolish embarrassment. 'And he wouldn't play—pray, I mean?'

'Oh, but yes. He agreed to try.'

'He's always very polite.'

'Polite?' Kettle took this fresh brutality gravely. 'We did pray together. An hour or so ago, as a matter of fact. And I don't think it's been quite in vain. One or two things he said made me feel that. It seemed to me he was coming to a better sense of the matter. And yet I'm puzzled, all the same. That's why I thought I'd come in and have a talk with you. He mentioned you several times.'

'What sort of things did he say?' I was disconcerted to think of Fish offering a word or two about me between bouts of intercessory prayer. Still, if he pulled himself straight by way of the comforts of religion, that was all right by me. If he spent the rest of his undergraduate days scurrying in and out of the chilly college chapel, he'd be in a blessed state indeed compared with his recent experience, and I'd continue to like him quite a lot. I was coming rather to like Kettle, for that matter. His concern was clearly serious and admirable. 'Did he say anything about Martine?' I amplified.

'He didn't mention her specifically. But I'm sure he was thinking about her. I believe he was realizing it had been an unsanctified relationship. Something entirely of the flesh.'

'I'd say it was that, all right.' This time, I had less difficulty with Kettle's vocabulary. 'But the flesh does seem able to take bloody awful swipes at the spirit, doesn't it? I'm not an authority. But it seems to me you go after something you call cunt, or tail, or a free poke—there are any number of care-free words for it—and before you know where you are it's making you shiver in your private parts. Your *real* private parts, right in your ruddy soul.'

'I'm not an authority either,' Kettle said. 'But certainly we are fearfully and wonderfully made.'

'The psalmist says it's something to be thankful for.' I thought I'd show Kettle I'd been properly brought up. 'Sex is coming to seem just one hell of a risk to me.'

'A risk,' Kettle said surprisingly, 'we all must take sooner or later. Unless, of course, one has a vocation for celibacy.'

'I don't suppose Martin has that.' I paused, and saw that we were straying from the point. 'You were going to tell me what he said.'

'He said he had seen the light.'

'Martin said that?' For some reason I felt obscurely uneasy.

'He said that at last he could see. But then—and this is why I'm puzzled—he became agitated. You'd expect calm to follow illumination, wouldn't you?'

'I haven't a clue. Isn't there a lot of ecstatic behaviour mixed up with religion? Even hysteria?'

'Hysteria?' This time, it was Kettle who was uneasy. 'He

has rather been rushing around. And waving. What you might call beating the air. Beating something off.' Kettle seemed concerned to convey with as much precision as possible the disturbing appearances he had been presented with. 'Do you know what I thought of? A chap caught in a searchlight and trying to get away from it. And soon I couldn't make him pay any attention to me. So I thought I'd better leave him for a while. I went back to my own room, and prayed by myself. I was guided to try again. But when I went out on the landing I heard sobbing. I stood outside Martin's door and listened. I hope that wasn't dishonourable.'

'Well?'

'Just that. He was weeping and weeping. It was then that I thought I'd come and consult you.'

'You bloody fool, why didn't you tell me this at the start?' I had jumped to my feet—appalled to think that, but for my own obstinacy, the distraught Fish would by now have been well on the way to being in competent professional hands. 'I'm sorry,' I said. 'I beg your pardon. I'm going straight up again. I'll look in on you later.'

And I left Kettle in my room. He was getting on his knees for more prayer as I had my last glimpse of him and ran upstairs.

There was not much sign of Fish's having so recently been in the state described by Kettle. He answered my knock in a normal manner, and revealed himself as engaged in the commonplace activity of preparing for bed. He greeted me in his pyjamas and carrying a toothbrush; and if he had really been in a paroxysm of tears he had washed all trace of it away. Only he was very pale. Once in bed, his complexion would have matched the sheets.

'Hullo,' I said cautiously. 'I'm afraid it's a bit late to look in. But are you all right, Martin? I thought I'd just like to know.'

This seemed to me fair enough. After what had been passing between us it would be silly to pretend that I didn't have

Fish's condition on my mind. But now for a moment I wondered whether he had it on *his* mind, since he looked as if he didn't know what I was talking about. Perhaps, I thought, after a real brain-storm a protective amnesia sets in, and I was putting my foot in it through not perceiving this. Fish's puzzled expression, however, faded almost as soon as I noticed it; it was as if he was bringing me into focus as a familiar physical object against a background of recent events which it just took a little time to sort out. I concluded that his mind was working slowly, and that he was very reasonably in a condition of extreme fatigue.

'I'm dinkum, Duncan, thank you.'

I didn't know whether to judge this whimsical jingle reassuring; only once or twice before had I heard Fish indulge the affectation of using Australian slang which probably wasn't particularly native to him.

'Then that's fine,' I said, as easily as possible, and wondered whether to go away. Fish looked stabilized at least until the following day, when I could take stock of his state again. This was what, in Badgery's room, I'd suddenly decided to work for; Kettle had panicked me into thinking I'd perhaps been fatally wrong; now I was thinking myself right again.

'Can you stay a minute, Duncan?' It seemed that Fish had detected some slight movement I had made. 'I want to tell you what's happened. Things have cleared up a bit, I think.'

'It all seems less desperate?' I asked—perhaps rashly.

'Well, I don't know.' Fish frowned, as if I had said something obscure or irrelevant. 'It's a matter of finding an objective standpoint, I'd say. Seeing oneself, and being dispassionate about it. I suppose that's what really wise people can do. It's what I'm trying to do. Only, you see, I'm not wise—so ought I to be a bit cautious? Suppose you were an unspeakably hideous old dotard, or some awful sort of abortion. In a country without looking-glasses. And suddenly you were given one. Say you were a king, and nobody could possibly tell you the loathsome truth about yourself. And then an explorer or merchant or somebody made you a gift of a whacking great mirror. If you had sense, you'd begin with no more than a quick peep. That's right, isn't it?'

'I suppose it is.' I found the thought being developed by Martin Fish unnerving. He would never have struck me as a particularly imaginative type, or as having the instinct of the fabulist. But the burden of this concoction was clear enough. He was projecting himself in the image of a man so despicable and repellent that he couldn't stand up to self-scrutiny. And all—for it came down to this—because he had been ditched by a depraved girl, and mocked when caught out as not much liking cold water. That was the cold truth of the matter, and realizing it sent an appropriately chilly shudder down my spine. Fish's grotesque state suggested some travesty of the situation of the Tragic Hero as propounded in my textbooks: a tiny flaw in character or a tiny slip-up in conduct being visited with utterly disproportionate misfortune. And his own sense of proportion had deserted him. The more he looked the humiliating little business in the eye, the less could he bear it.

'Look, Martin,' I said on a reasoning note, 'there's no point in going on about that now. Let's talk about it another time. What you need is a good night's sleep. And I've just remembered. When I was scared about my idiotic Prelim I scurried off to the college doctor and got some sleeping stuff. It's called sodium amytal, and he said it's quite harmless, just in an occasional way. But I didn't use it, after all. I'll go down and get it for you. It's a little bottle of things called capsules.' I paused, and was visited by a moment of sanity. 'I'll bring you up a couple of them. That's a night's dose.'

'It's frightfully kind of you.' Fish had squared himself; his instinct for courtesy was on top; he smiled at me—for the first time in many days. 'But I don't in the least need anything of the sort. I'll tell you what: just see me into bed.'

I performed this nursery ritual, which ought to have been absurd but seemed entirely natural. It was as if I had been fussing in an unnecessary fashion, and Fish had found a light

189

and whimsical way of giving me a sense of being useful to him. Within a couple of minutes I was standing again at the door of his bedroom, managing my own confident smile.

'Good night, Martin. Are you going in to breakfast?'

'Yes, of course, Duncan. I'll call for you. Good night. Pleasant dreams.'


No dreams visited me. But in the small hours I woke up, aware that there was somebody in the room. I didn't know how late it was, and thought at once that a blundering drunk had turned up on me; even—for I was still freshman enough for such alarms—that it was designed to make me the victim of some foolery. In such circumstances boldness is all. I snapped on the bedside lamp.

'Duncan?'

It was Fish—standing strangely in the doorway.

'Good Lord, Martin! You scared me.'

'Duncan—is it you?'

'Yes, of course.' I sat up. 'What is it?'

'The bloody lights have failed. Fused, or something. I was going to the loo.' Fish's voice cracked. 'Duncan, try yours.'

We stared at each other—or rather I stared at Fish—in the clear light of a 60 watt bulb.

'It's on, Duncan?'

'Yes, Martin—it's on.'

'Then that's it. I've had it. I've gone blind.'


I got Tony, and Tony got the night-watchman, and the night-watchman got the Dean. With surprising speed—although it felt like an aeon—the college doctor arrived from somewhere in the town. Habituated to the panics of young men, he was prepared to be tough as well as kind. He examined Fish, and listened to what he had to say. He listened to me. He went to the telephone. I believe I was in a state of considerable shock, but as people were not then removed to hospital on that account Fish presently departed in an ambulance alone.

The doctor gave the Dean a look, and the Dean returned to bed. The doctor packed his bag; he had no appearance of inviting conversation.

'Sir,' I said, 'will Fish have ECT?'

'Have what?'

'Electric shocks.'

'I'd say it was most improbable. Have people been talking about electric shocks?'

'Well, yes.' I pressed on. 'Do you think he's likely to be permanently blind?'

'My dear lad, heaven forbid!' The doctor had moved to the door, but now he paused there. 'Mr Pattullo, does anything else occur to you?'

'Well, this girl——'

'Yes, I think I understand about that. But anything else? Take your time.'

'It does occur to me that Martin—that's Fish—had rather a lot to say about seeing, and not seeing, and not daring to see.'

'Humph!' The doctor appeared to think better of receiving this without comment. 'Does it also occur to you that there's more sense in remembering that than in talking rubbish about ECT?'

'I suppose it does.'

'I expect you'll be able to go and visit him in a few days' time. I'll let you know. Good night.'

Tony had already departed. I was left alone in my bedroom, which had remained the scene of all these activities. I climbed into bed. Shock or no shock, I was asleep again within minutes. But when I woke up I was very anxious about Fish. I had no idea of how to find out where he had been taken, or whether it was more likely to be an eye hospital or an asylum. When at length I received a summons it was to a private nursing home to which he had been transferred—he was to tell me later—on the strength of peremptory cables from his parents in New South Wales. I found him sitting up in bed, reading *Punch*. He was peaked and pale still, but entirely composed.

'Hullo, Duncan!' he said. 'I've been the most awful nuisance to you, and I'm frightfully sorry.' He smiled cheerfully, as one who indicates that his words are to be accepted in a conventional sense. 'But look at this one,' he said. 'Not bad for *Punch*.'

I looked at some meaningless joke, and realized that Fish was a different man—so different that I insanely wondered whether he had been crammed full of electricity after all. I don't think that at this moment I recalled my mother, whose own burdens would sometimes lift and vanish within an hour.

'No, not bad,' I said. Looking up, I saw that Fish had transferred his gaze to a large looking-glass on the wall opposite his bed.

'Funny thing to keep in a place like this,' he said. 'Might turn patients a bit blue, if they weren't exactly feeling in the pink.' He continued to study himself with complacency. 'Do you know? I think I've lost a useful bit of weight. I'd been putting it on, rather. Not enough squash.'

'Or messing about in boats,' I said. Before this transformation, the spirit of experiment was momentarily strong in me.

'Or messing about in boats,' Fish repeated—and if it wasn't indifferently, this was merely because he had recognized the quotation from *The Wind in the Willows*. 'I say, Duncan! About the long vac. That was a good idea of yours. Let's go.'

# IX

Dear Mr Pattullo,

You must certainly dine with us on Thursday! Seven-thirty for eight o'clock. Black tie. The Provost and I are very much looking forward to the occasion.

Yours sincerely,

CAMILLA POCOCKE

I found this note waiting for me when I got back from the nursing-home. It was almost as mysterious as the psychology of Martin Fish, and for the time being banished from my head all consideration of the hazards of foreign travel in Fish's company. I was so conscious of bewilderment that I took the thing straight across the staircase to Tony.

'What do you make of that?' I demanded.

'It's an invitation to dinner. Such civilities are quite common in polite society.'

'It's nothing of the sort. You accept an invitation, or decline it, don't you? I can't do either with this. It's not worded that way. Why should the woman send me a bloody summons, complete with exclamation-mark?'

'I don't think it's a summons, exactly. It's what you might call the vehement expression of a wish. She's conscious of a prospect so enchanting that she expresses it as something that just must happen.'

'Do talk sense. It's very worrying.'

'Worrying?' Tony repeated the word with tolerant amusement. 'Perhaps the lady's conscious of usually comporting herself with excessive formality, just like her better-half. That's what's said of her. Here she's taking a random stab at something else.' Tony read the note a second time. 'No,' he said, 'you're right, in a way. There's an unknown factor at work.'

'That's what I think. But what?'

'She believes you already know something about her jollification, and in fact you don't seem to. The affair's one at which it's so obviously appropriate that you should be present that here's the agreeable way to express herself. She's trying hard. It's my impression that she does try hard.'

'You don't think it has to do with the golf course?'

'Good God, that was ages ago! And how could it? Duncan, you're bonkers. Symptoms of paranoia setting in. A consequence of association with poor old crack-pot Fish.'

'Fish is absolutely okay again, as a matter of fact. Almost euphoric. He'll be back tomorrow.' I saw that the golf course had been a mistake. 'But you must be on the right lines, in a general way. Somebody's going to dinner in the Lodging on Thursday whom I might reasonably be asked to meet. But I just can't think who.'

'Then you'll have to go and see.'

'I suppose so. How do I reply?'

'Pile it on a little. Dear Mrs Pococke, Thank you very much for your kind invitation. It will give me great pleasure to dine with the Provost and yourself on Thursday. Your loving Dunkie.' Tony handed me back the letter. 'I've got it!' he exclaimed. 'She has invited Bedworth, and she knows all about your consuming passion. She must be a very broad-minded woman.'

'What you think to be funny is quite too pitiful. It occurs to me it might be Mrs Triplett.'

'With a leash of brown girls? Have you become a pet of hers?'

'More or less, I suppose.'

'Give it to me again.' Tony took back Mrs Pococke's summons. 'No,' he said. 'It's not Mrs Triplett, even if she has been raving about you—which is improbable. It reads to me as if it must be about a relation. Listen! Have you any relations in Oxford? What about your dear old uncle, the retired brigadier—has he become bursar of Teddy Hall or something?'

'He wasn't ever a brigadier. He sometimes calls himself Captain, which it seems you can do if you were in his sort of regiment. And he certainly hasn't become a college bursar. He couldn't run a chicken farm. He has his hands full, anyway, running a private army.'

'A private army?'

'Oh, never mind.' I realized that this had been a rash confidence. 'I don't have any relations in Oxford.'

'Then one's visiting the place. Have you heard from home lately?'

I stared at Tony, deciding he had said something to the point at last. There came back to me a strong impression that when my father, as he expressed it, entered me at the college he and the Provost had—rather surprisingly—hit it off. And there was always an unpredictable element in my father's conduct. Suddenly I remembered, too, something I had heard at the end of the Easter vac. My father, who was now Lauchlan Pattullo, P.R.S.A., was going to attend a dinner, some time in the near future, given by his opposite number in London. (He had remarked, ungraciously, that he might look up some real painters as well. His attitude to distinction within an Establishment was whimsical and indeed equivocal.)

'I think you may be right,' I said. 'I'll go and ring up now.'

The line to Edinburgh was remarkably clear. Although I was telephoning from the porter's lodge and traffic was roaring past outside, I could hear, behind my father's voice, that of my mother, singing vigorously in the kitchen.

'Dunkie?' my father said. 'Good man! But make it snappy. Taxi's waiting.'

'Where's it taking you?' My suspicion was instantly confirmed.

'The Waverley, of course. I'm going to this old gentleman's dinner on Wednesday. He paints horses. A kind of vet. And I'm coming to Oxford on Thursday, and taking you out to lunch.'

'You haven't told me.'

'Haven't I?' My father's voice was entirely innocent. 'Well, book a table at wherever's best.'

'You'll lunch with me in college.' I was firm about this. 'It's the proper thing. It will be the nice thing as well. What else are you doing?'

'I wrote to your Provost, and said I'd call. It wouldn't be polite not to do that. He has replied I've to stay the night. He wants to show me your pictures. And I'm to dine in the Lodging. I thought it might be your high table.'

'It's because his wife's giving a private dinner party. I'll be there.'

'That's good! And dinna fash yoursel, Dunkie. I ken weel about the spoons and forks.'

This told me two things: that a faint apprehensiveness I had signalled was meeting with a proper rebuke, and that my father had been fortifying himself against his journey with a dram or two. It was chiefly when mildly elevated that he made these random incursions into dialect.

'How are you, Dunkie?'

'I'm fine, thanks.' I hadn't had a word from my father since the beginning of term. But his tone, anxious and therefore suddenly guarded, brought back to me how unhappy—and no doubt tiresome—I had been, only a few weeks before, during the Easter vacation. Oxford—no more, after all, than a second brief eight weeks of it—had lost reality, dissolved like a dream, before my train reached Durham. But Edinburgh had taken on no countervailing solidity; it was a ghost town in which I thought I knew nobody and felt like a tourist. I was astonished at a state of mind that seemed so like affectation, and sought various remedies. One day, for example, I tried visiting my old school. It was a regular thing for boys who had recently gone on to a university to drop in and wander round, and they would usually be invited to stay to lunch, or to witness some match or other judged to be of importance. Plenty of people with whom I had been on more or less equal terms were now putting in a third year in the sixth form. But I got no further than staring at the place from the gates and wondering if it had ever really harboured me. All these feelings of alienation stemmed from the single fact that Janet was at the other end of Scotland, a circumstance perhaps exacerbated by her having formed the bad habit of sending me an occasional picture-postcard. The island of Skye didn't appear to run to anything very attractive of that sort. The messages were mostly brief accountings of what she had read, as if she was reporting to a tutor at a correspondence college while herself inhabiting a region in which real things happened. This was the facet of our developing—or attenuating—relationship which I distrusted most of all.

My father had to head off my mother from pouring sympathetic remarks and romantic laments over my dejected head, and he himself said nothing. But I found that I was spending more and more time in his studio, and this without any awareness that I was being coaxed into doing so. I would be squaring up a canvas for him, or doing the numerous cleaning and tidying jobs such a place requires, and which prosperous painters retain semi-skilled assistants to perform. He talked as he worked—rather, I thought, as a surgeon must do while he operates: wholly absorbed in his task, yet with an equal care to maintain in his pupils an unflagging attention to the work of his hands. That I wasn't a painter myself seemed irrelevant; he was telling me where, in a general way, I belonged, and that for an artist there is no comfort except in the sweat and frustration and elusive triumph of making what it is in him to make. It was this stern message that was being carried in my father's low-toned technical talk. He was perhaps looking forward to what time would falsify: my becoming something other than one of the competent entertainers of my day. Yet I knew I shouldn't stand or fall in his regard according to any eventual revelation of my quality. It is part of nature's general wastefulness that in art, too, only a few of the called are chosen. My father respected all the called alike, and appeared to have no difficulty in reconciling an affection for indifferent performers with a strong dislike of indifferent performances.

Thinking of all this as I hung up the telephone, I was ashamed of my uneasiness at the thought of my father let loose in the Lodging. It is an odd fact that when schoolboys transform themselves into undergraduates they scarcely shed at all their alarmed sense of parents, uncles, aunts and sisters (but not brothers) as fatally inclined to social solecism. I remember our Captain of Rugger at school—an almost god-like figure, with international caps most certainly ahead of him—as reduced to a state of nervous near-prostration by the liability of his father (an athlete with a Soccer background) to shout from the touch-line the wrong thing at the wrong time. These states of apprehensiveness are very little connected with social disparities or insufficiency. They may be remarked in the eye of young noblemen leading old noblemen around. Nothing better instances the edginess of lingering adolescence.

But I was to have a further anxiety about Mrs Pococke's dinner-party. It cropped up as soon as I returned to Tony and told him the state of the case.

'You'd better have your hair cut,' he said. 'And washed. It's rather fetching, as a matter of fact, when floppy. It represents, incidentally, your best chance with Bedworth, if you ask me.'

'I don't think Bedworth notices carnal things.' Except when irritable, I suffered Tony's recurrent reference to this supposed passion of mine patiently. 'But perhaps Mrs Pococke does.'

'Certainly she does. An honest female animal lurks in your honoured hostess. I intend to essay the wench. Oh, by the way, don't forget to wear a gown.'

'Of course not.' I looked at Tony stonily, supposing that this was a malicious attempt to have me make a fool of myself.

'Seriously. You must put on your gown. At least it will match quite well with the natty d–j outfit.'

'Don't be a bloody fool. I don't put on a gown to go to tea with the Talberts in Headington. Why should it be different dining with the Pocockes in the Lodging?'

198

'Because, my child, our Provost has just started his spell as Vice-Chancellor of the university. Don't you know that?'

'Yes, I do.'

'Very well. Gowns are *always* worn in the presence of the Vice-Chancellor. Repeat, *always*. If your Mrs Triplett sent you a card for a sherry party, it might say, *The Vice-Chancellor will be present*, and that means gowns. Until Pococke ceases being V-C, it's the same drill even for the merest social binge in the Lodging. My father explained it all to me, as a matter of fact.'

'I see. Well, thank you very much.' I was appalled to think how easily I might have committed what would clearly be the staggering floater of appearing gownless as a guest bidden to Mrs Pococke's feast. The advantages of having a father who had been a member of the college before one seemed for the moment enormous. Quite soon, however, doubts set in. They were to the credit, if not of my intelligence, at least of my canny nature. I tackled Tony again. 'Look here,' I said, '— about that gown-business. Don't you think it may apply only to senior members?'

'No, I don't.'

'But look!' Tony's reply had been confident, but I thought I had spotted it as coming after a moment's hesitation. 'Listen!' I said urgently—for this crisis was getting me down. 'Last term I went to dinner with my old headmaster in Keble. He's some sort of honorary don there, and turns up on them from time to time. He was moved to give me a square meal, along with an obscure man from Trinity who was the top physics egg-head of my school. Conversation didn't exactly flow.'

'Be relevant,' Tony said.

'But at least it was a slap-up high table affair, with no nonsense about post-war rationing. And floods of port and brandy in common room afterwards. The cigars came from Havana.'

'Well, well!' Almost for the first time, I had succeeded in impressing Tony.

'Finally, there was a stuff called Mar. You pronounce it that way. But you spell it M-a-r-c.'

'At *Keble*?' It was evident that Tony was bewildered. 'I thought Keble was just a place full of suckling black beetles.'

'So it is. But of Marc, as well. These places have their ways. Like Campion Hall.'

'*Campion Hall*? Duncan, you've been in there *too*?' Never before had I quite got Tony down like this.

'Oh, yes. The Jesuits are after me, you know. It's perfectly natural. You're an ordinary commonplace papist, who doesn't much interest them. I had Catholic ancestors about two hundred years ago. Naturally, these people over the road have designs on me.'

'Ancestors on that classy distaff side?' With this, Tony rallied slightly. 'And they have Marc at Campion Hall?'

'Oh, no—and their cigars come from Jamaica. It's an austere set-up, the Society of Jesus. But they do have the most marvellous malt whisky. From Islay. I'll bet the Pocockes don't have that.'

'I suppose not.' Tony seemed almost crushed by this idiotic display of what was soon to be called one-upmanship. 'Duncan, what are we talking about?'

'Wearing gowns. If a don goes to dine with a don at high table in another college, he wears a gown. But if an undergraduate goes to dine at a high table he doesn't. That's what we were told in advance about Keble, and it held for Campion Hall, too. If a high table dresses for dinner, your host tells you so, and you do, too. But you don't go in a gown. I think the rule may apply to this Vice-Chancellor business.'

'It does seem possible.' Tony, acknowledging the sober gravity of the issue, had turned serious. 'I'll tell you what, Duncan. You ought to ask your tutor. Yes—ask Talbert. I'm told he's very keen on the correct thing. It's common among those of the learned late risen from the people.'

'So it is.' With a readiness unbecoming in a crofter's grandson, I concurred in this blandly snobbish observation. 'Talbert told me I mustn't sign letters to him *Yours faithfully*. I'd never written a letter to him in my life.'

'That's what Robert Damian calls prophylaxis. Yes, I think you should ask Talbert. An answer straight from the donkey's mouth.'

'Albert Talbert is one of the most eminent scholars in the university—and the only don in this effete college who isn't totally and absolutely obscure.' It was our habit to reserve exclusively to ourselves the right of exhibiting our several tutors in any ludicrous light; aspersions by others we snubbed at once. 'But that's a good idea. Talbert will put me in the picture, right away.'

Having now begun to read for my Honour School, I was in the enjoyment of two full-dress tutorials weekly. Each of them was a tête-à-tête. At that time, although commoners were frequently taught 'doubled up', and thus had the support of a companion in masking their ignorance and idleness, scholars and exhibitioners (who might be equally idle and ignorant) were obliged to go it alone. This class distinction was later to be loosened up, and indeed progressive tutors were already ignoring it, and isolating or assorting pupils as their instinct (or their own idleness) prompted. Talbert, however, was scarcely progressive. As for Timbermill out in Linton Road, he appeared to occupy a perplexing position as a kind of gentleman or amateur tutor, and he told me that he had never had two undergraduates together in his room in his life.

At least I enjoyed variety, for they were a contrasting couple. Timbermill's enormous room, for example, harboured much more than several thousand books. Most prominent was what I for long took to be the debris of an air-raid, oddly transported to the attic floor of the villa. It consisted mostly of heaps of broken pottery, mixed up with chunks of rusty or corroded metal here and there. Later I discovered that in one of the shadowy bays or open-ended subsidiary chambers into which the room on all sides dissolved a start had been made on arranging bits and pieces of this detritus on shelves. It had all, it seemed, been dug out of the rubbish dumps of Saxons and Angles round about what I thought of as Beowulf's time, and Timbermill knew more about these vestiges of a heroic age than anybody else in the world. And he wasn't only cataloguing them; he was piecing them together with seccotine. It was clearly a job requiring two or three expert assistants at the least, but it seemed that Timbermill wouldn't let anybody else in on it. Oddly enough, I was myself going to be the first person in whose favour he breached this rule. But that wasn't to be for some time yet. I simply thought of him as a near-manic character who taught me once a week. But who *really* taught me. I was mad keen on being taught by Timbermill, even when he was only insisting that I learn how to make Anglo-Saxon noises and sort out Anglo-Saxon verbs. This wasn't exactly going to last a lifetime. But I was never to have a similar intellectual experience again.

Talbert was equally learned in his own line—and that two such men should have found themselves closeted *solus* for an hour a week with a raw youth indisposed to think about anything except how to write plays exemplifies the curiously prodigal character of what is called the Oxford tutorial system. But Talbert, unlike Timbermill, was incapable of putting his learning across; his tutorials, regarded other than in a spirit of comedy, could only be termed scandalous nullities. My sole real contact with him was during those rare and perplexing moments in which—commonly for the most tenuous or elusive of reasons—he manifested symptoms of suppressed but inordinate mirth or glee. And if the man himself didn't do much communicating, neither did that room in which he no doubt thought of himself as conscientiously discharging his tutorial function. I have recorded that it was very small—smaller even than the rooms in his modest domestic abode in Old Road—and furnished with a square table, two upright chairs, and an empty bookcase. From an electric light depending from the ceiling there further depended one of those long strips of thickly sticky paper which represented in that era civilization's only means of liquidating flies. If, having read my essay, I was prompted to catch Talbert's eye and endeavour to elicit from him the divine gift of articulate speech, I had to edge my head either to the right or left of this feebly lethal object. I used to long for Talbert to produce a pipe—having read of some great Victorian, perhaps Tennyson or Carlyle, as accustomed to brood in comfortable taciturnity behind clouds of smoke from one. But all Talbert smoked was a succession of small cheap cigarettes, Woodbines or 'gaspers', to which he probably regarded his honourable poverty as confining him. He invariably held these miserable objects between a finger and thumb in a manner somehow suggesting that he had never manipulated a cigarette before. The silence preserved between us was in these circumstances peculiarly trying.

But on the occasion upon which I presented Talbert with my problem he had proved in quite a conversable mood. I had not, it is true, had much success in interesting him in my views on John Lyly's *Euphues, the Anatomy of Wit* or even in its stirring sequel, *Euphues and his England*; indeed, I had merely been instructed to write an essay on Sir Philip Sidney's *The Countess of Pembroke's Arcadia* for the following week. But then, after no more than five or six meditative minutes, Talbert communicated to me an anecdote, literary in flavour, which appeared to concern a dispute which had once arisen between Swinburne and Jowett on the substitution of a choriamb for an iambic metron somewhere in Aeschylus. This, although not directly relevant to *Euphues*, could be received with respect as interesting in itself, and I managed this so well that Talbert went on to describe a quarrel between Swinburne and Rossetti. (Talbert never said simply 'Rossetti' but always 'the fat rogue Rossetti'—and this invariably with his intimation of deep mirth.) So I plucked up courage and spoke out.

'Sir, I have to go to dinner in the Lodging on Thursday. And I'm wondering——' I broke off in confusion at this point, because Talbert's amusement had in some indefinable manner switched from Rossetti to myself. What seemed a boring hour with Talbert could have the unexpected effect—again indefinable—of sharpening one's wits, and I realized that he was extracting remote entertainment from a form of words betraying my sense that I was facing a chore. I then saw that this was encouraging. My tutor, although so unfathomably deep a scholar, was at least listening to me—something it would have been optimistic to predicate of him when I had been expressing opinions on the role of Euphues's tiresome friend Philautus. 'It's about what to wear,' I went on hopefully. 'Mrs Pococke has said a black tie——'

'Good heavens!' Talbert was much shocked. 'Has there been a death in the Royal Family?'

'Sir?'

'Has somebody fallen out of an aeroplane? Aeroplanes have become extremely hazardous since ceasing to be biplanar. You must certainly wear a black tie. All members of this college are expected to do so until after the state funeral.'

'No, sir—that's not it. A black evening tie.'

'That is another matter. You don't always make yourself clear, Monboddo.'

'Pattullo.'

'Pattullo.' Talbert, who was now speaking with profound gravity, admitted the correction with his customary reluctance. 'But you do very well to consult me. With a black tie of that description you must wear the shorter formal jacket. There is your answer.'

'Yes, sir. Thank you.' I wondered whether to give up, and decided to persevere. 'But there's the question of whether I ought to wear a gown.'

'A gown?' Talbert stared at me blankly. Although I was wearing my gown at that moment, and he himself wore his half-a-dozen times a week, he might never have heard of such a garment in relation to a male person. It was almost as if I had been making some flippant proposal to appear at the Lodging in drag.

'*This*,' I said desperately, and momentarily assumed a bat-like posture on my hard chair. 'Do I wear *this* on top of my dinner-jacket?'

'Dear me, no.' Talbert was now being entirely patient; he appreciated being appealed to as an authority on a matter of social form. 'The gown would, of course, be proper were you summoned before the Provost formally. But on a social occasion, no. How wise of you to ask me, Pattullo. The *Arcadia*. You will find Feuillerat's edition adequate to your purpose, although I am sorry to say it is gravely defective in many ways. I pointed this out—charitably, I hope—in the *Review of English Studies* some years ago.'

'I'll look you up, sir. But the point is that the Provost has just become Vice-Chancellor. So people say there's a different sort of drill.'

'Dear me! You are perfectly right. Yes. I think you will eventually perform creditably in the Schools.'

'Thank you very much.' I was childishly overjoyed at this irrelevant remark. 'And I do wear my gown?'

'Ah, that is an interesting question.' Talbert's deliberative manner would now not have disgraced the Judicial Committee of the Privy Council. 'In the case of a senior member the position is entirely clear. We always wear gowns in the presence —other than purely fortuitously in the presence—of a Vice-Chancellor. But the correct thing for an undergraduate who is going to dine with one is harder to determine. Reflection is required, and inquiry may be possible.'

'Surely there must be a rule?'

'Precedent, yes, Monboddo—but a rule, no.'

'*Pattullo!*'

'Pattullo. It is a matter of courtesy rather than prescription. But I will let you have my opinion next week. The *Arcadia*.'

'But the dinner's on Thursday,' I said despairingly. 'It looks as if I'll just have to guess.'

'Or you might use your common sense.' Talbert produced this suddenly pungent remark without any change of tone. 'What would that suggest to you?'

'Erring on the formal side, I suppose.'

'You appear to be a perfectly clear-headed young man.' Talbert announced this conclusion much as if he had first set eyes on me fifty-five minutes before. 'Don't fail to consult Brunhuber.'

'Sir?'

'*Sir Philip Sidneys Arcadia und ihre Nachläufer*. A most commendable monograph—published, I think, in Nürnberg in 1903.'

'Thank you very much.' I made an unconvincing show of jotting down this reference in the margin of my dreary remarks on *Euphues*. One more Talbert tute was over.

There were two ways in which I could entertain my father to lunch. I could take him into hall, in which case his surroundings would be magnificent and anybody I planted him down beside polite if not talkative. But he was not a man indifferent to what he ate, and as it was well on the cards that the meal provided would be appallingly bad he might be constrained to rise from it without any comment of a gastronomic sort. This would be unsatisfactory, and I decided for the alternative possibility. I'd give a luncheon party in my rooms.

I have already chronicled that such a manner of entertaining had ceased to happen at all freely; it was insisted upon only by the most obstinately privileged; and permission had always to be obtained against a good deal of resistance from the Domestic Bursar. This college officer (as was prescriptive with us) was a retired rear-admiral, although being diminutive and jumpy he suggested what used to be called a powder-monkey rather than one dominating a quarter-deck (if that is what rear-admirals dominate). His appearance, however, was declared to be deceptive. In particular, he was accounted to command a great deal of guile in circumventing the desires and devices of undergraduates. It seemed to me, however, that I was in a strong position, especially if I began by masking my batteries. So I presented myself in his office.

'My name's Pattullo,' I said. 'I'd very much like, please, to give a luncheon party on Thursday. Quite a small one. I think for six.'

'Ah, yes—Pattullo.' The Bursar spoke as if he had heard a good deal about Pattullo, and all to so favourable an effect that he had been much looking forward to encountering him. 'What staircase are you on?'

'Surrey Four, sir.'

'Oh, dear!' The Bursar was dismayed. 'That *is* rather tricky. Yes, as dodgy as anywhere in college, I'm afraid. A faithful old fellow, Jefkins, but getting on. One has to be considerate.'

'Yes, of course.' Jefkins was my scout, and his decrepitude was incontestable. 'But I'm only one up.'

'That's a point, I agree.' The Bursar didn't seem to find it a composing one, however, since he had jumped to his feet, whipped off his spectacles, and started walking rapidly round his office in circles. This gyratory effect he enhanced by elevating the spectacles in air and rapidly rotating them in the manner of a child's windmill. 'And, of course, you are perfectly entitled to give a luncheon party—perfectly entitled.' The Bursar enunciated this with great emphasis, and in a manner suggesting one member of an officer-class vindicating the rights of another. 'Every day of the week—in theory. I just have to make sure, you know, that a man isn't outrunning his means. Piling up a bill that won't be too welcome at home. That sort of thing. Definitely told it was part of my job.' He paused by a table at the far end of the room. There, apparently in much absence of mind, he flicked over the pages of a college roll. He was discovering what school I came from.

'I think I can stand it—just once in the term.' I managed both to hint awareness of his manœuvre and to appear entirely unhuffed by it. 'So will it be all right?'

'Probably, probably. See the chef, anyway, to be going on with. But I still can't promise, you know; I can't promise at all. Anything may turn up. I believe Jefkins is subject to lumbago. In fact I'm sure he is.' The Bursar had resumed his agitated pedestrianism. 'So I may have to ask you to take your guests into hall. The common meal, of course. Yes, I'm afraid it just may happen that way. I hope you understand, Pattullo. I *do* hope you understand.'

'Yes, of course. And I'm sure my father would enjoy lunching in hall very much. Only, he'd have less opportunity of meeting my friends. One likes to arrange for that sort of occasion in a civilized way.'

'Exactly, exactly!' The Bursar waved his spectacles violently. I didn't think his vehemence really indicated his being impressed by a father's thus being brought on parade. It must happen a good deal. 'I'll let you know. Good morning.'

'Good morning, sir. And thank you.' I moved to the door, and there contrived the appearance of one struck by an afterthought. 'I suppose a dinner-party might be easier,' I said. 'There are those extra men who come in to relieve the scouts a bit in the evening. But it wouldn't be any good on Thursday. My father's engaged to dine in the Lodging. He'll be spending the night there.'

'Ah, yes.' The Bursar spoke as one distinctly not interested. But I caught his glance, and detected in it a glint of amusement that momentarily reminded me of Albert Talbert. 'See the chef, anyway. And tell him to finish off with his crème brûlée. Morning to you, young Pattullo.'

I departed—with my sense of triumph mitigated by this further evidence of the wide currency of my sobriquet. I wondered whether I really looked years younger than anybody else in college.

My father, myself, Tony, Mogridge, Bedworth, and Fish newly restored to us from his nursing home. I had decided it was to be a staircase affair, partly on the calculation that Jefkins would be more likely to behave well if gaining merit with a number of his charges simultaneously. It looked like being a successful party, my father proving to be both in good humour and on his best behaviour—conditions which by no means invariably coincided in him. Strangely enough, I'd have been quite as happy if he'd been mildly outrageous. For what troubled both Ninian's and my own relations with him was his well-founded belief that as children he had hardly noticed us; being a model of propriety was somehow his way of coping with an intermittent sense of guilt about this. It was a phase of family history which I never succeeded in analysing. He was an abundantly affectionate man, and must have been so all through our childhood. He had, of course, had my mother's burdens to shoulder, and perhaps he had come to think more of us when we were old enough to help him there. It must also have been a matter of his work; of a sustained effort of creation so concentrated that it had drained him of the ability to turn away to anything more taxing than convivial meetings with his fellow-artists. But one consequence of this was that we now, as a family, existed for the most part in a state of relaxed luxury, a sense that everything had come right. Not that we weren't normal enough—by which I mean that we were all four of us capable of flares of mysterious resentment and hostility between ourselves. Comparing notes in objective and dispassionate moments, for example, Ninian and I discovered that we both rehearsed a good many more injurious speeches for delivery within our family context than we ever actually uttered. And I have no doubt that there continued to be times when our father resented us as chronic nuisances who refused to go away. We were an affectionate family, nevertheless. And we all adored my erratic mother.

A son's first formal entertainment of his father is obviously a milestone of note. If as a result of this I indulged in such reflections as are here set down, I also gave much thought to the party itself—an activity serving usefully to distract my mind from anything problematical in the contrasting feast with which the day was to close. I wondered whether I ought to have somebody of my father's own age to keep him in countenance among what it would be natural for him to regard as a pack of children. I even had the thought of inviting Talbert, but decided that the notice was too short to be polite in the case of one's tutor. What I had in mind was that deep in Talbert as the learned world knew him there lurked another Talbert, intimated only by that strange sporadic glee, and that my father was the man to liberate him—even perhaps to establish a second daylight Talbert, periodically eruptive and in full control, after the fashion of those agreeably bizarre dissociated personalities of whom I had read in the course of my psychological inquiries. This shows that one ought not to arrange luncheon parties on fanciful grounds; had Talbert been present it is probable that gravity and decorum would have held sway throughout the meal.

We did start off that way. There is no deference more unflawed than that accorded by young men to a friend's parent on a first meeting, and my father was exposed to it stiffly even before we sat down. I'd foreseen this a little uneasily, feeling that he might become restive if confronted with too much English public-school stuff. Cyril Bedworth had been a kind of calculated hope here; if he ran to any awkwardness suggesting an odd-man-out my father would kindle to him at once. But Bedworth was unobtrusively respectful in the most orthodox way, differing from Tony and Mogridge, perhaps, only in being more aware of the eminent painter and less of the ordinary elder person as what should determine his attitude. And in this shallow matter of social responses Martin Fish as a contrasting note was no good at all. He was more royalist than the king. Nevertheless Fish attracted my father's attention at once. This was because Fish was just back from the dead. Lazarus, I imagine, must for a time have found absolute wonder in the simplest sensuous qualities of the phenomenal world—been capable, as it were, of seeing a sherry glass as a chalice and a tablecloth as the garment of God. This is to exaggerate; I doubt whether, even with my knowledge of his recent adventure, I'd have divined Fish's state if I hadn't caught it telepathically from my father, who was himself intuitively aware of shades of feeling in this region. Certainly I saw that he was liking Fish—and as a result Fish shot up in my own regard. He was liking Fish rather more than he was liking Tony. I had told him on our drive from the station that my summer plans were changed, and that it wasn't with Tony Mumford but with a man called Fish that I was going to Italy. Now, and as soon as he gathered which of these young men Fish was, he started talking about the Vatican. He had heard, whether correctly or not, that the galleries of the Vatican were already under siege by floods of post-war tourists, and he was insistent upon the importance of getting Fish and myself into those alarming proliferations out of hours. He knew just how to manage that. Fish took the information commendably in his stride. Bedworth was obviously impressed.

It emerged from this that Fish liked painting. He asked whether my father knew the work of Hans Heysen. My father said he did, and that he judged it, on the whole, even better than that of his own old friend D. Y. Cameron. Fish didn't pretend to have heard of D. Y. Cameron (as Tony would have been liable to do). But he said he had a Heysen in his rooms upstairs, and it would be nice if my father had time to go and look at it after lunch. My father agreed at once.

'I have another painting, as a matter of fact,' Fish said, 'which perhaps you'd like to see too. Just as being thoroughly Australian. I don't expect you'll have heard of the painter. His name's Sidney Nolan.'

'Man!' My father had stiffened abruptly. 'Is it a dead sheep?'

'Yes, it is.' Fish was surprised. 'Awfully dead, I'm afraid.'

'I haven't seen one of them. No, I haven't.' My father was distinguishably in a moment of crisis. His fellow-guests must have found this perplexing, but I knew at once that Nolan was a power in the land. My father was an extremely conservative painter; Monet had remained his master—and Monet had died, almost as old as Titian, a couple of years before I was born. When my father heard rumour of some new thing—of some new and potent thing—he was accustomed to hold serious debate as to whether he should expose himself to it. 'I'll see it,' he now said with resolution. He might have been deciding to accept major surgery. 'Yes, I'll see it. After Duncan's good meal.'

'Luncheon is served!'

Jefkins, who had been dozing on his feet in a corner of the room, was alerted by my father's proviso, and now bawled out these words at the top of his voice. We sat down, and the conversation moved elsewhere. This was a relief. I had been afraid that Tony, who didn't quite like Fish's even so modestly holding the field, might assert his own status as a connoisseur and require my father to inspect his Roman bawdy-house across the landing. It was improbable that my father would behave himself before that triumph of Victorian kitsch. But this didn't happen, and as the meal went on his contentment increased. His London trip had clearly gone well. ('The man's no Stubbs, but he knows his claret,' he confided to the respectful Mogridge seated beside him—the reference being clearly to his host of the evening before, Sir Alfred Munnings.) He had particularly enjoyed what he called mysteriously 'a grand crack with Jack about Will', and had heard a number of good stories. He recounted the two or three of these which were likely to be intelligible to us.

Long before the crème brûlée, my father had established himself with my companions. I knew this when they all started asking him questions, since a quick-fire effect of that sort is a sure token of undergraduate approval. (It can also be exploited with hostile intent, but this never happens unless the adversary, too, is judged somebody to reckon with.) My father was good in this situation. He noticed small things, like their forgetting to keep on calling him 'sir', and took satisfaction in them. He seemed very open when they wanted to be told about his career.

'Does a lot depend on having a good dealer?' Tony asked. 'Like Vollard when the Post-Impressionists were getting going?'

This question, although it betrayed Tony in a naïve light (he had plainly been doing home-work), was benignly answered. My father explained that his own early work had been successfully handled by a school-fellow, happily established in a small greengrocery business in Kirkcaldy, who had taken the canvasses round in his cart. I had never heard this reminiscence before, and suspected it of being made up on the spot. The circumstance made me look round warily in the direction of Jefkins, who was standing by in charge of the wine. I was hoping there wasn't too much of it still to come. It was only too likely that I had overestimated the needs of this part of the entertainment.

At least this anecdote particularly pleased Bedworth; it answered to some private mythos of his own.

'Many of the greatest artists,' Bedworth said on his familiar didactic note (hitherto happily in abeyance), 'have had a terrible struggle at first. In some cases, indeed, for many years. There was, for instance, the late Vincent van Gogh.'

'He had a brother called Theo,' Tony struck in rapidly. This time, I believe it was his laudable aim to prevent my father from betraying amusement at being thus informed that van Gogh was dead: something he might, or might not, have done. 'Theo tried to flog Vincent's stuff, but I don't think he had much luck. And Vincent went potty, didn't he?'

'Yes, he did.' My father may have been conscious of saying this curtly, for he quickly added, gently and more seriously than he had yet spoken, that Theo had been a stout fellow, and that Tony might do worse than read Vincent's letters to him.

'Is it always desperately hard at first?' Mogridge asked.

This time, my father didn't answer at once. I saw that he realized a different issue was being put to him.

'I mean'—Mogridge, never slow to feel he had been insufficiently explicit, amplified his thought—'I mean that it must be difficult if it's desperately hard for too long. Not getting much of a green light from anyone, and yet carrying on. A man could come to wonder about himself. And it could be hard, having to go on wondering about oneself after a time. Would there have been great painters who took years to get going—rather at the rudiments, I mean?'

As Mogridge put this specific question, I almost felt myself to be hearing ghostly strains, ditties of no tone, seeping up through the floor-boards. What was much more remarkable, I felt that my father, who knew nothing whatever about Mogridge and his unfortunate 'cello, was hearing them too.

'There may have been,' my father said. 'Probably there have been. I can't remember off hand. But certainly it hasn't been common. A man may take years to find out even things that are radical and deep inside himself: whether his feeling is linear or *malerisch*, for example. But if I understand what you mean by the rudiments: no—not.' My father gave this reply without any assumption of authority, but while looking seriously at Mogridge. 'One's on one's own,' he said. 'That's where the answers have to come from in the end. But blocked artists are often rather far from being ineffective in life. I've known some who have more than made their mark in the world.'

'Hitler,' Tony said.

'I never claimed that wee blackguard's acquaintance, Mr Mumford. But your naming him is no doubt fair enough.'

I again had a dim feeling that Tony and my father would never get along too well—and within seconds this was almost dramatically confirmed. The small *contretemps* took place, unhappily, only because Tony—civilly enough—ignored the faint snub he had received.

'I'm sorry,' he said, '—but you know what I mean. If one has started as an artist, I'm sure the world of action must be a second best. Hitler failed to produce any nurslings of immortality, and set about slaughtering whole armies instead. Much easier, really. By the way, sir, Dunkie tells us he has an uncle who runs a private army. Is that true?'

I was conscious of my father as glancing at me swiftly. He would himself have had no impulse positively to conceal the mild lunacy of his brother-in-law the Glencorry, but he was surprised that I appeared to have been gossiping about it.

And I think he also resented Tony's command of my pet name.

'Laddie,' he said, 'ye maunna spier anent your host's veracity o' anither o' his guests.'

I was furious with my father, who had in this freakish way drawn attention to a minute breach of manners. Tony, despite his father the week-end country gent and his own assured upper-class air, was not among those miraculous youths (of whom there were a number around the place) who had been so made that they couldn't put a foot wrong. Shoving in a question on a family matter he knew nothing about had at least, so to speak, landed his toe in the water. But it was outrageous in my father so deftly to catch at an ankle and tumble him in head-over-heels. And now I saw that Cyril Bedworth was studying this ducking in a teacup attentively. Had I been able to think of him, clairvoyantly, as the future author of *Proust and Powell*, I might have guessed that he was reflecting upon the extent to which a whole social hinterland can be revealed in a dozen words. There was a second's silence in which I could see Mogridge giving thought to a suitable change of subject. Fish cracked his crème brûlée, and exclaimed arrestingly at the result. Fish was one of the miraculous youths.

This awkward moment was ended by my father himself—which was only proper, considering that he had occasioned it, and considering too the responsibility of his years.

'But I'm a havering body,' my father said amiably, and raised his glass in front of him. 'Tony, will you take wine with me?'

This eighteenth-century gesture was a great success. Tony, who had turned rather pale, grabbed his glass cheerfully. It came to me that I could recall no occasion upon which my father had proved unable to extricate himself from an awkward moment. And the wine-bottles, fortunately, were empty. Throughout the final stages of the party, and while inspecting Fish's pictures, Lachlan Pattullo talked what was still at that time called the King's English.

There remained, however, the Provost's dinner-party to face.

And whether to wear a gown or not was an anxiety no longer finding room in my head.

I walked my father round Long Field, and was conscious that we were again very content with each other. If he was a hazard as a parent he was seldom other than a distinguished one. He owned, for a start, a satisfactory physical presence. Informed people, glancing at him, would conjecture him to be somebody of note. I found myself taking the simplest small boy's pride in this.

'It seems your friends keep cars, Dunkie.'

'Not all of them. Not Bedworth or Mogridge. But Tony Mumford and Martin Fish run cars.' I remembered that, early on during our meal, these two had engaged in a short technical discussion in their character as motorists. It was this that had attracted my father's attention. 'I sometimes go out with Tony. I think I've mentioned it in letters.'

'I mind that now. It's something your professors allow?'

'Well, Fish's car is legal, because he's in his second year. Tony keeps his on the quiet. I don't think the dons would much bother about it.'

'You'll be in your second year yourself soon.'

'So I shall. If they don't turn me out.'

'Dunkie, they wouldn't do that?' My father, whose knowledge of Oxford remained sketchy, was alarmed.

'No, of course not. I'm all right with them. I'm being silly.' I guessed where this conversation was leading. I felt uneasy about it.

'Dunkie, I'll get you a wee car. In time for next term.'

'Oh, but I don't happen to want a car, thank you.' I knew at once that this had been the wrong thing to say, or at least the wrong way to say it. For one thing, it wasn't quite true. Owning a car had never entered my head, but the idea was instantly attractive to me. I'd have liked a car very much. And my father infallibly knew when either Ninian or I was prevaricating. I had taken the first step on an ungracious course.

'You could get between Edinburgh and Oxford in a day easy, Dunkie. You could do it that way every holidays. It would save an awful lot of money in the end.'

This was transparent nonsense, but it was also my father's customary tactic when he was prompted to do a generous thing. It had needed to be when we were really poor. We were that no longer. By his own simple standards, my father had quite recently become affluent So here was a false issue. And I was handling the thing wretchedly because of feelings pretty deeply buried in my mind. I groped dully for my father's motives. He was the crofter's son who had prospered, and it was part of his pride to have his boys up with others. That was why I was at Oxford at all; he had been determined not to see me, as he conceived it, distanced by the son of a professor he'd taken a dislike to. If the Dreich's boy was going there, I was going too.

Suddenly and shockingly, I found myself walking beside my father in a state of senseless resentment. Why should he give me a car now when for years he'd ignored the fact that I lacked a tooth-brush? Ninian was in the same case; there was to be nothing that was too good for him. We'd both been ugly ducklings, and we'd both of us—late in the day—turned out clever. Ninian was very clever indeed. We both counted with my father now simply because we had become appendages he could be conceited about.

I heard myself say—but it was only one of those rehearsed speeches that remain mercifully mute—'Bugger your car!' The phantom words terrified me. And then—it had happened before—another voice came to my rescue. It was Ninian's voice. Ninian was a passionate man in ways I was not. But, for me, his voice was the voice of intellect and reason. 'Of course Daddy feels guilty,' Ninian's voice said to me half-way across Long Field. 'Didn't we walk to school with holes in our breeks? But we'll have guilt enough on our own hands, Dunkie, by the time we're his age. Or like enough we shall.'

'I mean I'm not all that keen,' I said to my father awkwardly.

'Just Oxford's a marvellous thing to have happened to me. Daddy, it's almost indecent. I've utterly everything I want.'

'Not quite everything, Dunkie.' My father said this without embarrassing meaningfulness. But I knew what he was thinking of, and all my bad feeling was swept away by love. I even knew what to say.

'Bugger your car!' I said cheerfully, so that the words transformed themselves. 'Not yet, anyway. I'd be wasting my time in it when I should be at my play. Next year. And if you're wanting to give me something meanwhile, Lachlan Pattullo, give me another picture.'

'We'll make it that, then.' My father spoke composedly, and all was well. Or almost. It was a stiff assignment, I told myself, having a parent who could peer inside your head when it was misbehaving.

There was a great deal of activity on the Isis, since Eights Week was drawing near. One was never out of the chock and plash of oars. Their painted blades glinted in the sun, dribbled diamonds, dipped into water, scooped, rose. Young bodies, bowed galley-slaves, heaved at them; from the tow-path and through megaphones muffled men bellowed, pedalled bicycles, bellowed again; coxes echoed or interpreted their exhortations on a shriller note. My father approved, but began to talk about the Seine at Marly. He wanted gentlemen combining straw hats with high collars, ladies with sunshades, full-fleshed attendant females bearing bocks. I myself was remembering telling Janet I was going to row, was remembering her saying it was a poor thing at my age to be going off to boarding-school. Not bearing long to think of her, I thought of Glencorry instead; thought of the absurd pepper-boxes and crenellations, snow-white like a cottage on a Christmas cake, of Corry Hall.

'The folk at Corry,' I said. 'What's happening there? Has Ninian had his invitation yet?' Our annual Highland holidays had never become formally prescriptive; every year a carefully worded summons would come from Aunt Charlotte: one to Ninian, and a week or two later one to me.

'That he has not—and now we don't think it's like to come. Nor to you either, Dunkie.'

'There hasn't been a row?' I was more curious than apprehensive.

'No, no—why should there be? They're decent people enough.'

'Nothing about Anna? That's still all right?'

'It's to be called that. They're lucky—or they think they are —that he was from the gentry.'

Uncle Rory's instinct had been vindicated over the identity of my cousin's seducer. Young Petrie of Garth had almost immediately owned up; it seemed necessary to conclude that Anna had been creating pretty well for the hell of it. A perfectly normal wedding had taken place—at which I'd have been present as an usher in hired morning dress if I hadn't disingenuously pleaded an inescapable examination. Ninian had represented the obscure Pattullo relatives.

'It seems they're having a wee bit of trouble with the other one,' my father said. He affected obstinate vagueness about the Glencorry connection.

'Ruth, you mean?'

'Aye. All that blatherskite you told us of must have unsettled her.'

I was silent, rather hoping that if Aunt Charlotte's invitation did belatedly arrive it would prove to be for the time I was fixed to be abroad with Martin Fish. I recalled my rash promise myself to invite Ruth to Oxford, there to introduce her to abundant escorts elligibly back from the wars. As it had turned out, I hardly numbered one such among my acquaintance. Fish, it was true, seemed older than I was. But I didn't think I wanted to give Fish to Ruth. She might ditch him if she found her own pukka laird. And he might then put on his turn again.

'Yon uncle of yours is a much-tried man,' my father said. 'It's on none of mine I'd wish a frigid wife. There was small promise in all that slam-banging of wee bit tennis balls.'

219

I was startled, for my father had never before said anything like this to me. He may have been anxious to acknowledge me as grown up and ripe for the world's warnings. Or he may merely have still been a little flown with my wine. He had let the Doric—in the muted form I liked—creep back into his speech.

# X

WHEN I ARRIVED at the door of the Lodging that evening I was wearing my gown. My uneasiness about it had surfaced again; it felt as if at any moment it might turn into the pyjama-jacket or whatever it was of Hercules when Deianira had treated it with the nasty dope provided by Nessus. This recondite thought, although it would have been appropriate in a young scholar, was not, of course, really present to my consciousness. I was just thinking that the Provost's butler was eyeing me morosely. But this was said to be his normal manner.

In a superior kind of Gents (it was lined with photographs of former college fellows of the obscurer sort) I bumped into Buntingford. He was scrambling into his own gown, which he must have brought with him over his arm. It came to me at once that it was Buntingford and not the learnedly pre-occupied Talbert whom I ought to have consulted.

'Oh, hullo!' Buntingford said amiably. 'Been reading any more Tacitus lately?'

'Of course not.'

'Or composing in one of the ancient languages? I see you're a writer. You might have a go at the Chancellor's Prize for Greek Verse.'

'Please don't be silly.' I felt that, on a social occasion, one spoke slightly differently to young dons. 'And look here—ought I to be wearing this damned thing?'

'Quite probably not. No, hold hard!' (I had been about to get rid of the gown at once.) 'It's probably a very good idea. You will be well received. The praeposital self-consequence will be gratified. And it will please your father too—which provides a worthier motive for wearing it. Delighted I'm going to meet him. Come on. We start off in that Pre-Raphaelite mausoleum.'

'Oh, very well.' I let the gown be, although I didn't feel that I'd been exactly encouraged about it. 'I say, do you think this is going to be a frightfully senior gathering?'

'Not a doubt of it, young Duncan. May I call you Duncan? Mrs P., poor soul, hasn't a clue about who to ask with whom. You'll have to hand in the Principal of St Hugh's, or some such desiccated vestal. You'll see.'

'Oh, Lord!' This was more depressing still. 'I wish I hadn't come,' I said childishly.

'Copy, Duncan, copy! You can write it up for *Isis*. I read you in *Isis* last week. Promising. Callow, of course—but promising. A shade humourless, perhaps.'

'I could wring your neck,' I said, and felt better at once. We were conducted to the enormous chamber known as the Provost's Day-room, already familiar to me since I had there attended a promiscuous sherry-drinking by as many of my freshman year as had been sufficiently civil to turn up. It fully deserved the title Buntingford had given it, because the spirit of William Morris (although an Exeter man) brooded everywhere over its *décor*.

'You'll have one playmate of your own age,' Buntingford breathed cheerfully in my ear. He was unoffended by my improper remark. 'Madox Brown's loony girl.'

I remembered that the Day-room contained three pictures—the only pictures in the entire Lodging not to represent deceased episcopal personages. The first was a heavy-jowled stunner by Rossetti; the second was one of Burne-Jones's indigestive women, slumbering after having been oddly roped into what would later be called a see-through night-gown; the third was Madox Brown's 'Ophelia Singing'. I wondered whether my father would presently be making inappropriate remarks before these masterpieces. He had behaved well when being shown Fish's pictures, chiefly because Nolan's dead sheep had momentarily induced a subdued mood. But in

222

general he hated being 'shown' works of art, and was inclined to signalize the fact through irresponsible commentary. Looking at the college pictures, I was sure, was going to be the tricky part of the evening.

My father, as a house-guest, was already in the room. Sure enough, he was being shown Ophelia by the Provost—whose fine hands were gesturing sensitively in front of the canvas much as if he had been Roger Fry, Clive Bell, Herbert Read, or another of the higher aesthetic pundits of that period. This was an alarming spectacle, but my father was nodding composedly and keeping quiet. He had a feeling for things perfectly fabricated, and was probably satisfying it quite as fully before the Provost as before Madox Brown's canvas. The Provost's wife was meanwhile receiving newcomers. Buntingford she seemed to treat a shade coolly, so that I wondered whether he was *persona non grata* in the Lodging, and his presence an indication that this was among its inferior feasts. But at least I myself came off much better; it was hard to believe (what must be true) that Mrs Pococke was recognizing in Mr Pattullo's undergraduate son one associated with a disgraceful attack upon her husband on a golf course. Being as yet unfamiliar with some of the received commonplaces of social behaviour, I fondly supposed that I was really being distinguished by special favour. This pleased me, since I thought I rather liked Mrs Pococke. In the way of comportment it was as if a good deal of her husband had temporarily rubbed off on her, so that (as Tony was to assert) with a scrub down she would be a different woman. Perhaps this was really a later perception or persuasion. It is true that I fairly rapidly came to stand quite well with Mrs Pococke—although of my year it was to be Tony himself who, in a blameless way, was to make a conquest of her.

'Now, who do you know?' Mrs Pococke asked me—as if there were the slightest possibility of my knowing anybody. She was all competence, and I felt she ought to be gesturing with a fan as adeptly as her husband was doing with his fingers.

223

'Miss Basket? Cecilia, this is Mr Pattullo's son, Duncan. Mr Pattullo, Mr Buntingford is taking Miss Basket down, so you must be very entertaining with her now.' Whereupon Mrs Pococke turned away to greet fresh arrivals, and I was left to be very entertaining. Not unnaturally, I glanced at Miss Basket warily. She wasn't all that older than I was; in fact she was about the same age as Buntingford. But, so far as my immediate impression went, she might have been as old as the rocks amid which she didn't sit. I suppose because of her name (although I was unconscious of this), I thought of her at once as a Sibyl—the one who was hung up in a cage or a bottle and who kept on saying she wanted to die. Miss Basket was pale and emaciated, and plainly capable, if not of prophesy, at least of conversation of the most awesomely intellectual order. I told myself not to be unnerved, and that here was nothing more out-of-the-way than a top schoolgirl on the classical side, now, half a dozen years on, become a Fellow of Somerville or something of that sort.

'What are you reading?' Miss Basket asked in a papery voice. There had been a bit of a pause.

'The *Arcadia*,' I said—and amplified, even more idiotically, '*The Countess of Pembroke's Arcadia*.' My answer, of course, ought to have been 'English'. I had vaguely supposed Miss Basket's gambit to have been of the 'Have you read any good books lately?' sort. 'Together,' I added (feeling it was now all or nothing), 'with Brunhuber's commentary. Nürnberg 1903.' I observed Miss Basket to be producing a thin pained smile. 'I *was* told to be entertaining,' I concluded pleadingly.

In face of this desperate smartness, Miss Basket—entirely justifiably—looked round the room for help. She couldn't have said more plainly, 'Young man, you've made a rotten start.' It was, of course, true. A few of my most sophisticated contemporaries liked to maintain that female dons were much better fun than male ones; you only had to poke them up a bit, and they could be quite astonishing. I wondered whether Miss Basket was like that. I was about to say, 'I was only trying to poke you up a bit,' but fortunately reflected in time that these words might be indelicate.

'I've never read the *Arcadia*,' Miss Basket said, bringing her eyes manfully back to me. 'But then I'm a chemist.'

'I don't think I could recommend it just as a book at bed-time. Except, of course, that it is a novel. The *Arcadia*'s supposed to be an early attempt at a novel. It would take your mind off chemistry. There's no chemistry in the *Arcadia*.' I felt I was beginning to talk like Gavin Mogridge. 'At least I haven't come on any so far,' I added, perhaps in an attempt to enliven matters. There was a pause. One topic was undeniably exhausted. 'Do you like this room?' I asked.

'It's very remarkable.' Miss Basket looked conscientiously at the room, as if to be quite sure of this. 'It must hold great interest for your father.'

'Yes, I suppose so.' I was aware that what held great interest for my father was the spectacle of his son floundering in polite conversation. At this very moment, in fact, he gave me a scandalous wink across the room. I believe it conveyed his condolences that Miss Basket was so plainly not drawing any very exciting secretions into my blood-stream.

'I haven't spoken to the Provost yet,' Miss Basket said, a little too much with an effect of inspiration. 'I think I must go across.'

I was tempted to say, 'I haven't either, so I'll come too.' But diffidence or my better nature prevailed, and I stayed put. I offered Miss Basket a little bob as she walked away. It made me feel like a shopwalker. At this self-conscious moment a young man whom I'd have taken for an undergraduate if he hadn't been wearing a white jacket offered me a glass of sherry on a tray. I needed it badly. The young man gave me a shy, cheeky conspiratorial grin. I was grateful for it. He was the only person of my age in the room.

The morose butler had almost ceased announcing people. The Day-room couldn't have been called crowded; it was said to be the largest private chamber in Oxford, and a platoon might have marched and wheeled in it. But there were certainly a great many guests, so that the occasion answered to my preconceived idea of a banquet rather than a dinner-party. They seemed nearly all already known to each other (*All know the man their neighbour knows,* I would report to Tony), but nevertheless Mrs Pococke was kept fairly busy at brisk introductions —particularly of, or to, my father. With me she didn't bother further.

For a young man to be left to his own resources in such a situation can be an awkward thing. I had to check myself from employing my sherry-glass as a kind of vertically operating metronome, and from shifting ridiculously from one foot to the other. It was in vain that I told myself I was a detached spectator much at his ease, enjoying the exercise of the superior penetration that was naturally his. It was miles worse than those rare occasions at Corry when my uncle and aunt entertained the local monarchs of the glens, for at them there was commonly some stringy soldier or weather-beaten lady who would advance and put me through my paces whether they supposed themselves to be acquainted with me or not. Academic life—I told myself with desperate condescension—is bourgeois in tone. At this squalid moment I became aware of the White Rabbit.

Tindale was at the far end of the room, talking to a dumpy woman who was certainly another don. He was probably giving her the latest news of Pope Zosimus—which was something she looked as if she might well be all agog for. But although Tindale was talking to this scholarly person he was contemplating me. Or rather he had been, for now he was looking at the floor. Of this, however, he seemed instantly to think better, for he raised his eyes, smiled, and gave me an informal wave which I took to have the character of a summons as well. I don't know that at that time I entirely objected to being contemplated; it was just one of the occasional facts of life. Anyway, any port in a storm. I advanced across the room.

'A young neighbour of mine in Surrey,' Tindale said. 'Mr Pattullo. Professor Babcock.'

I thought 'young neighbour' avuncular and impolite, but that cheerfulness was intended. I made my bob at Professor Babcock. I was at least again doing what everybody else in the room was doing: attempting communion with somebody else.

'A large do,' Professor Babcock said, glancing round. 'But when you become Vice-Chancellor you no doubt have to step it up. Still, it has a pre-war flavour. Can it last?'

'A pertinent question,' Tindale said. 'The Pocockes have entertained most generously from the start. Some feel they have departed splendours in mind. One fears it is against the tide. The butler will transfer his favours to a millionaire in New York. The pantry boys, showing themselves as what is now called delinquent, will depart with the spoons.'

I resented this on behalf of the pantry boy who had brought me sherry. I even resented it on behalf of Mrs Pococke, who had at least invited me to dine in my father's company. And I was, of course, unused to the sub-acid as a conversational mode.

'I think,' I said, 'it's pretty stout of the Provost and Mrs Pococke to try to keep things going. I suppose it's what the whole place is about, in a way.'

'Exactly,' Tindale replied amiably. 'The idea of a university, and so on. Out of the mouths of babes and——'

'Dr Tindale, Mrs Rumsey is casting imploring glances at you.' Professor Babcock made this interruption with splendid brusqueness. I didn't know who Mrs Rumsey was, and much doubted whether she had been casting glances at all. But the White Rabbit departed obediently. 'A charming man,' Professor Babcock said. 'Undistinguished as a scholar. Extremely witty.'

I was to come to know this sort of three-tier remark as called the Oxford sandwich. The first and third parts can be chosen at random; it is the middle one that counts. Being at present ignorant of this, I was perplexed and said nothing.

'I know something about you,' Professor Babcock said briskly. 'The theme of distinction in scholarship brings it to my mind. You are a schoolfellow of Ranald McKechnie's.'

'Yes.' I felt no occasion to go beyond this monosyllable, and was thankful my father was out of earshot. Heaven knew what he would come out with if he thus heard his son being, as it were, trailed in the dusty rear of that supposed rival of mine whom he had dubbed Wee Dreichie.

'Mr McKechnie has become my pupil—just for this term. He is a great joy.'

'Yes,' I repeated stupidly—and added, more stupidly still, 'How nice! I expect he reads Tacitus.'

'Reads Tacitus?' Naturally enough, Professor Babcock was perplexed. 'He comes to me for Greek verses. I am inclined to judge him the ablest pupil I have taught at Oxford. Do you see much of each other?'

'Well, no.' I was abased at having to confess my virtual non-association with this paragon. 'I think McKechnie's very shy. I mean, we're both very shy.'

'*He* is, certainly.' I saw that Professor Babcock was amused. 'But I don't at all know about you, Mr Pattullo. Couldn't you bring him forward? A favourite expression of our hostess's, that.'

'Bring McKechnie forward?' This conception astonished me. 'I could as soon bring forward the Forth Bridge. McKechnie's the sort of man who would walk round the block rather than meet his oldest friend face to face. Heaven knows what will happen when he crosses the Bar.'

This sounded to me, even as I uttered it, a shocking example of a conceited young man putting his best quip forward; it was something becoming a habit with me as a result of having to keep my end up at the scholars' table and in other gifted circles. But Professor Babcock's reaction was quite cordial. In fact it was surprising. She leant forward and nudged me. I wasn't even quite clear with *what* she nudged me. I had misjudged her in thinking of her as dumpy. 'Well-developed' would have been more correct, and it really felt as if what had nudged me was her corsage. She must be one of those female dons who, when stimulated, could be quite astonishing. If she hadn't been as old as my mother she'd have alarmed me. As it was, I just felt that her gesture (if it was to be called that) acknowledged the fact that McKechnie needn't be thought of as having it all his own way. I hoped that I'd be taking Professor Babcock in to dinner. But this was negatived at once.

'I do hope,' Professor Babcock said, 'that Camilla—Mrs Pococke—has a nice girl for you to hand down.' She glanced round the room. 'But it doesn't look like it. Ah! Perhaps it will be our good little Miss Basket.'

'Oh, no!' Perhaps I said this with uncivil promptitude. 'A man called Buntingford is booked for that. Mrs Pococke told me.'

'Then, Mr Pattullo, I sadly fear—— But stay!'

The door of the Day-room had opened, and the butler (not yet having absconded to the United States) stood within it.

'Mrs Triplett and Miss Triplett,' he said. He was announcing the latest arrived of the guests.

This was to prove an important and indeed fatal moment in my life, but I can remember my first thought as being that Penny Triplett—for this must be Penny—might be just right for Fish. Fish was still very much on my mind. I had little notion of the extent to which the conversion hysterias are, or are not, common phenomena. But at least the dramatic means he had involuntarily taken to break the spell of Martine seemed to belong to a world of demoniacal possession and desperate self-exorcism alarmingly remote from any that one would wish so nice a man to inhabit. He had perfectly provided support for the thesis that being in love—or at least being 'madly' in love—is a form of insanity, of irrational concentration upon another person whose supposed objectively-existing attributes may be almost totally the creation of one's own disordered imagination. Nor had his abruptly redeemed state as revealed earlier that day been reassuring. What he had exhibited could be viewed as a chamber swept and garnished, impressively gleaming in a new-pin and virtually pre-lapsarian fashion, into which goodness knew what might at any moment erupt. What this nice man urgently needed was a congruously nice girl.

This therapeutic theory had been proposed in a crude way by some of my friends. It had chanced to be thus proposed (and the terrifying sway of chance may already have been noted as prominent in my youthful philosophy) within the context of old Mrs Triplett's establishment at the end of Linton Road. We had talked rubbish about finding Fish one of Mrs Triplett's brown girls—allurements by whom my own fancy had been not untouched. Mrs Triplett's young relative (of whom I had merely heard rumour) was not a brown girl. I was being introduced to her by my hostess now, and she was extremely fair.

It would be idle to attempt further description of Penny. Her character must later appear, but her person eludes the pen. She shared with the brown girls, at least, the quality of being rather small, and also of that sort of perfection which suggests an exquisite smoothness to the hand and is not readily separable from an answering perfection of turn-out. There wasn't a hair wrong or a crease where no crease should be. Nothing of all this gave rational occasion for supposing her to be the replacement Fish should be provided with. If I hadn't happened during the previous week to seek Colin Badgery's counsel on Fish's behalf, or if a conversation hadn't then taken the turn it did, the notion might never have entered my head. I should still have been suddenly and extremely interested in Penny. But no muddled intentions would have been blowing around.

Going in to dinner involved descending an imposing stair-case, and was rather a formal affair. Mrs Pococke, or perhaps it was the Provost, liked it that way. The gentlemen offered and the ladies accepted arms—not quite with the appearance of being habituated to such a ritual, and in some cases rather as if humorously accepting the preliminary dispositions required for a harmless party game. I was still wondering whether I could possibly offer my arm to Penny Triplett when I found that she had composedly taken it, that we were half-way downstairs, and that she was asking me if I played much tennis.

I said I was fearfully keen on tennis. This first assertion of mine to Penny was, no doubt symbolically, not wholly true. I did no more than quite like tennis, perhaps because Ninian was very much better at it than I was. But I supposed that, as she had raised the subject thus early, tennis was a major interest with her—in which case it would be unenterprising to be tepid about it myself. And Fish must certainly be enthusiastic about tennis. All Australians were.

I imagine I must have talked during dinner with the woman on my other side. Penny was so correct that she kept an eye on Mrs Pococke at the head of the table, and when Mrs Pococke turned was herself alert to turn at the slightest hint too. But I have no memory of this neighbour, or of almost anything concerning the meal. An impression did come to me of being the object, along with Penny, of occasional glances of benevolent regard now from one and now from another of our fellow-guests. Unless one was to count Buntingford and Miss Basket, we were the only young people in the room, and as we were thoroughly pleased with one another we probably presented a spectacle agreeable and even affecting to elderly persons under the gentle influence of a glass or two of wine.

Penny was perhaps a little younger than I was—which wouldn't make her too young for Fish. I learnt that she had just come out, and that the manœuvres of her first season were being conducted by an aunt, since her parents were at present sustaining some diplomatic role in South America. She had arrived in Oxford on a visit to her elderly kinswoman only the day before, and was going to stay for a fortnight.

'We've been hoping it was going to be longer,' I said.

'Mr Pattullo, don't be absurd! You can't ever have heard of me.'

'Oh, but I have. Mrs Triplett has mentioned you. I listened at once. A bevy of beautiful Burmese maidens were dancing on the lawn, but I had only ears.'

'I think you must be a *very* absurd person.'

Penny may well have been right. But I don't think I produced more twaddle like this than was tolerable, and indeed she seemed quite to like it. Perhaps she thought of me as something new and odd. Her own conversation ran on simple lines, and I had the wit to submit my own tone to it for a good part of the time. Not getting much change out of the theme of acquaintances and occasions in common, Penny listed plays seen and books read or heard of. Plays in particular took us some way, although they did seem a little to exist for her for the purpose of being ticked off. She had other conversational resources as well—endless ones, it was possible to feel. She touched lightly on this subject and that, like an exquisite small yacht, all snow-white sails and burnished metal, making a round of the islands in a compendious archipelago. One could say she had been no end 'finished'. It occurred to me to wonder whether my beautiful mother had been like this when my father first encountered her in the Sistine Chapel.

Penny knew nothing about Oxford, and exploited her ignorance in the interest of pretty appeals for information. Her mother had been at Somerville—a circumstance to which she could be felt to attach a sense of slight oddity—but she was vague about the possibility that she might come up to the university herself. If she did, could she arrange to be taught only by men? If she delayed her arrival by a few years was it quite certain that she could have me for a tutor? From sallies like this, which I found headier than the Provost's hock, she would retreat upon more demurely conventional remarks. With deep cunning, I induced her to inquire about my friends. (Muddle was now going strong.) One of my best friends, I said, was a man called Martin Fish, an Australian owning millions of sheep—most of them alive, but one or two dead and painted by Sidney Nolan. Nolan's was the first name to floor Penny.

She professed earnest interest. She loved painting. My most urgent after-dinner task must be to introduce her to my father.

Suddenly I was astounded to see Penny on her feet, and had a mad scramble to contrive any suggestion of having anticipated her. I remembered to sprint for the door, which at least earned me a good mark with Mrs Pococke. The ladies vanished, Penny vanished. I was overwhelmed with the sense of all the vital questions about herself I'd failed to ask. One—only dimly in my head—was why, early in a 'season' about which I'd been hearing a good deal, she was putting in a fortnight in a provincial city with an aged female relative.

The Provost was concentrating his male guests at the foot of the table. He made a gesture—hospitable, but with a sub-suggestion of ecclesiastical benediction such as became his cloth—indicating that I should take my place beside him. It was the proper thing (quite certainly, the Provost never did other than the proper thing), but normally I'd have been horrified. As it was, I didn't care a hoot; I was as confident as a favourite archangel summoned to colloquy with a benign deity. The problem of my father's comportment had evaporated in my mind. Had he at that moment been proposing to perform a Highland reel on the table I would have been approving but not specially attentive. (He was in fact conversing gravely with the President of Magdalen, who was an eminent art-historian.) I took my place with modest ease, and almost—for I was my father's son—gave Buntingford a wink as I did so.

'Have you been getting in much golf lately, Pattullo?' The question, which a little recalled Penny's opening shot at me, was humorously intended, but this didn't prevent the Provost from advancing it with his customary air of considered amenity. 'I have kept an eye out for you—shall I say a wary eye?— on the two or three rounds I have managed myself.'

'I've only been out once, sir. Since we met, I mean. With Tony Mumford again.'

'Mumford? Ah, yes—we have a Mumford in residence once

more.' The Provost didn't seem peculiarly gratified by this thought. 'And Mumford would have been that one of your two companions gifted with the more confident address?'

'Yes, Provost.' (I had been told that one might apostrophize the Provost in this way, just as if one were a don or a don's wife, and I'd thought I'd try it out. The 'Sir' business, which all polite youths employed freely, could get very boring.)

'And who was the man who actually scored the hit with which Mumford vaingloriously thought to credit himself?' The Provost, I was finding, could talk in this ponderous way without marked absurdity except to a cavilling ear, of which there were probably plenty around him. I rather liked it, since I was in a phase of literary development favouring mannered prose. I told myself I must just be careful not to respond with anything mannered myself. It would be insufferably impudent.

'That was another man on my staircase. His name's Cyril Bedworth.'

'Ah, so that is Bedworth?' This time, the Provost sounded interested. 'I must make his better acquaintance. Your friend Mumford was perhaps being a shade officious. Bedworth could very well have looked after himself.'

'Yes, sir. I think he could.'

'You are at one with me in this, Pattullo?' The Provost looked at me curiously as he asked this question. It struck me that he was perhaps more interested in undergraduates than was commonly supposed.

'Yes, I am.' I almost added a qualifying remark, designed to exhibit my own refined perception of Bedworth's staunchness of character and limited command of the social graces. But I was surprisingly sober, and thought better of this. (The butler at this moment was bringing round brandy. It was in observably small tots, and I accepted one with confidence. Being—again—my father's son, I was already coming to drink rather freely from time to time. But I seemed to have an adequate head for it, and used to tell myself there was nothing to worry about.)

'Your father is getting on very well with the President,' the Provost said. 'At our first meeting, when he came to talk to me about you, I discovered him to be decidedly a *Kunstgeschichtler*. It is a kind of learning with which not every practising artist of high distinction troubles himself, I am told.' The Provost paused on this accolade. The effect was rather that of Penny (my mind kept straying to Penny) ticking off plays seen and disposed of. There were no doubt a dozen poeple at the dinner-party to whom some specific civility of this sort had to be offered. 'So we must consider,' he went on, 'the question of showing him our own paintings. My idea is to form a small group later, without breaking up the company. Would that be right?'

'Yes, Provost. I'm sure my father will enjoy it very much.'

'I am only sorry we don't possess one of your father's own works. But it is true that most of the college's pictures came to us rather a long time ago.'

'I have something of my father's in my own rooms as a matter of fact, sir.' This was my first incautious remark. 'It's only a small water-colour,' I added hastily. 'But it's a sketch for quite a well-known picture.' The fame of *Young Picts* was something dear to me.

'That is most interesting, Pattullo. Perhaps you will be so hospitable as to take us over there later. Some of my guests would be quite delighted.'

'Yes, of course.' This was appalling. The notion of the Provost's inviting himself into an undergraduate's rooms seemed to me quite unheard of. I hadn't even bothered to notice whether Jefkins had very effectively tidied up the debris of my own modest repast. And the thought of my father standing by while a gaggle of dons and their wives goggled at Ninian and myself bottom-up in whins intimidated me.

'We have a few more minutes here,' the Provost said, 'before joining the ladies. Perhaps we should move around. Do you go and talk to Dr Tindale.'

I obeyed this command—a reasonable one, since Tindale had

a vacant chair beside him. He gave me a casual nod as I sat down, and it appeared that I had to open the bowling.

'Has turn-over been brisk recently?' I asked. 'Through that window, I mean.'

'A most accurate word for it. But no. Traffic has been rather sluggish, I am sorry to say. It almost looks as if some other route is becoming fashionable. By the way, am I right in thinking that one of the men up above me has been ill?'

'I suppose you mean Fish. He's all right again now.'

'Yes, Fish—the Australian. I'm afraid I scarcely know him. But I heard some murmur about a disastrous affair of the heart. Was it really that?'

'Something went wrong with his eyesight. Perhaps he'll have to wear spectacles.' I didn't intend to have any conversation with the White Rabbit about Fish's misfortune.

'He's a friend of yours?'

'I've got to know him quite well recently. We're going abroad together, as a matter of fact, at the beginning of the vac. To Italy.'

'Splendid! Where are you making for?'

'We've no particular plan yet.' It didn't seem to me that Tindale had any real occasion to pursue these inquiries; and I saw no attractiveness whatever in the boring elderly men round about me. I hoped the Provost had spoken literally when he had said we should join the ladies in a few minutes. My impatience to return to Penny was suddenly extreme. This, I told myself, was because of Fish's name cropping up. I was now quite convinced I was destining Penny for Fish. 'We're going in Fish's car,' I went on, finding that something further had to be said. 'So I expect we'll get at least as far as Naples.'

'Oh, dear! You did say the beginning of the vac?'

'Yes. Isn't that a good time for Naples?'

'Ah, it's not that at all.' Tindale was registering unaccountable distress. 'It just happens that at Amalfi, which isn't all that far south of Naples, I happen to own a very modest villa. I'd have been delighted to lend it to your friend and yourself.

Most unfortunately, I've already promised it at that time to a very old companion of mine.'

'That would have been extremely kind of you,' I said, and hoped I'd got my tenses right. It didn't seem to me there had been much point in Tindale's trotting out a benevolent impulse of this promptly frustrated sort.

'But I hope you will go to Amalfi, all the same. It's where Webster's duchess came from, of course. I see you've been writing about plays in *Isis*.'

'Yes, I have.' I probably said this ungraciously. It was the evening's second reference to my current literary activities. Buntingford had already made fun of me on the score of them. It seemed to me unfair that dons should peer into our lispings in *Isis*.

'Are you thinking of going on the stage, by any chance? You might do quite well.'

'No, I'm not.'

'If you change your mind you must let me know. I happen to enjoy the acquaintance of several actors quite at the top of that tree. They could be useful.'

'Thank you very much.' I went about Oxford, it occurred to me, uttering these words without particularly meaning them. And it struck me as odd that a reclusive authority on Pope Zosimus, one giving the effect of having to break an unnatural amount of ice before beginning to say 'Good afternoon', should frequent theatrical society. But then I knew nothing about such society; the world of the theatre still existed for me only behind a proscenium arch. At the moment I felt myself to be sitting through a tedious interval. 'Do we stay down here for long?' I asked. 'The Provost seemed to say something about joining the ladies almost at once.'

'Ah, you're bored, Pattullo!' Tindale's bilberry eyes met mine for a moment to signal amusement. He might very well have been offended at a demand which hadn't exactly been polite, but I felt the amusement to be genuine. He was probably attracted by the blundering minds of young men, just as he was by their blundering bodies somersaulting through a window. 'I don't blame you,' he added easily. 'Academic labour—although you'll hardly believe it—is utterly absorbing. I lose myself in my wicked old popes. But academic society is another matter. Not that all these worthies *are* academic. There's your father, for instance. He talked to me before dinner, and I found him delightful. And, of course, there's Lord Mountclandon. Have you met him?'

I followed Tindale's glance, and said I hadn't met Lord Mountclandon. I was considerably impressed, since it had never fallen to my lot before to be in the same room with a former prime minister. It was curious I hadn't spotted him. He looked to be by some way the oldest person present: a thin worn abraded man, silver-haired and distinguished. He was being talked to by a don youngish as dons go, vaguely familiar to me although he didn't belong to the college, with what I thought of as dignified obsequiousness. No doubt that was the correct bearing in encounters with eminent statesmen.

'Mountclandon is an old member, as you know,' Tindale said. 'He has just presented us with some very important papers. Come along.' Much before I had collected myself, Tindale was getting me to my feet and marching me round the table. Lord Mountclandon shook hands. He half rose from his chair to do so. Like the Bursar when I had presented myself to arrange my luncheon party, his manner was that of a man who had been expecting to make my acquaintance for some time. He then paused, however, to be given bearings. Tindale explained that I was Mr Pattullo's son. I wasn't confident that this conveyed much, and I had the impression that Tindale's degree of acquaintanceship with Lord Mountclandon didn't quite justify what he had done. Tindale was showing off to a young man he was concerned to cultivate. This was scarcely pleasing. Lord Mountclandon, as if he understood the whole thing, was careful to be particularly courteous to me. As for the youngish don, who had a smooth expressionless face and oddly combined abundant black hair with cold blue eyes and a fair complexion, he simply stared at me with frozen hostility. I felt he was entitled to. He had been interrupted in a cultivation job of his own.

'I suppose you are in Surrey,' Lord Mountclandon remarked. He might have been saying, 'Didn't we meet at Balmoral?' or 'I think I've seen you in White's.' In his time, I supposed, college rooms had been allocated on strictly segregationist principles. But Lord Mountclandon at once disposed of this idea. 'I had rooms in Surrey myself,' he said, 'because it was convenient for the library. I did most of my work there. People couldn't confoundedly interrupt. If a fellow did come up to me with some useless chatter—and some did—I had an arrangement with a pleasant library clerk whose business was to be in the place all the time. He'd call out, "Silence, gentlemen, in the reading-room". That did the trick. I got through quite a number of books.'

'Which is what got you your Double First,' Tindale struck in promptly.

'I don't remember much about the examinations. Probably they passed off tolerably enough.' Lord Mountclandon couldn't fairly have been said to be administering a snub. 'I'd like to have a look at the library again. And the Provost speaks of going over there later.'

The college pictures were at that time housed in the library, so I knew this was the same expedition on which my father was to be conducted. I wondered whether Lord Mountclandon too would be told that I was prepared to put *Young Picts* on exhibition. 'That's me,' I heard myself idiotically saying, 'and that's my brother Ninian.' Tony, jealous of my incursion into high life, would affect to find the episode extremely comical. It might actually turn out that way.

Meanwhile, my only hope lay in the Provost. In pitching me at this top guest of the evening Tindale seemed to have exhausted his social resources, and I couldn't very well take the initiative by jumping up, making my bob, and bolting for Buntingford or my father, who were the only other men I knew. Lord Mountclandon, on his part, appeared determined not to dismiss an innocent youth who had been willynilly thrust upon him, and he continued to converse. I wasn't—not under my father's eye—going to flounder with a prime minister as I had floundered with the female chemist Miss Basket, and I did my best to use any wits left to me. (Penny Triplett appeared to have carried off most of them.) It felt as if this was going on for an hour, although it was probably no more than three or four minutes by the clock. Then the Provost really did move; there was a short interlude in, or hanging around, the superior Gents; finally we went upstairs again to the Day-room.

## XI

I DECIDED THAT, having sat beside Penny at dinner, it wouldn't do to make a bee-line for her again now. This was nonsense; had I done so, nobody taking notice of the fact would have been other than benevolently amused. But I was still much more in a foreign land than I'd have admitted even to Tony, and apt to be a good deal concerned with notions of correct behaviour.

What I could do—and it struck me as an immensely guileful move on Fish's behalf—was to present myself at once to Penny's guardian—which was what I took Mrs Triplett more or less to be. Although I didn't know her very well (for I had simply been one of a crush at three or four of her tea-parties) I did know her rather better than I knew anybody else in the room. So here was the entirely natural thing to do.

Mrs Triplett was sitting on a settle, which had no doubt been carpentered and decorated by William Morris himself. Everything in the Day-room had that sort of provenance, since Mrs Pococke inflexibly preserved it as the notable museum piece it was. One could have argued whether the general stiffness of effect—for everything was pitched on the perpendicular and there wasn't a cushion or upholstered surface to be seen—served to accent the stiffness of the Pocockes themselves or to render it a less obtrusive feature of the scene. The settles, although beautiful, were as uncomfortable as anything on view, but Mrs Triplett was clearly not incommoded by hers. Since she never permitted her back to touch anything (except, presumably, in bed) the irrational rectangularity of the object was in no way detrimental to her ease. The height of the seat was such, and her own stature so diminutive, that her heels hung in air—like those of a child who might be expected at any moment to drum them noisily on the box-like structure that the base of a settle is. But Mrs Triplett's heels, like her hands, were composed; it was only with her head that she indicated I was to take a seat beside her. I sat down on the settle, and thoughtlessly tried to tuck my heels under me. The settle at once responded like a sounding-box, and as the surface I had thus clownishly hacked at was a delicate predella-like affair of angels blowing trumpets and clashing cymbals I was a good deal confused. I was quite sure, however, of its being boldness that was required of me.

'I think Penny is absolutely beautiful,' I said. 'So, please, may I come to tea on Sunday?'

My credit with Mrs Triplett was a matter of the Glencorry connection; she held a vague relationship with the family, and the barbarous name of Pattullo had stuck in her head as denoting something regrettable that had happened to them. It had given me the entrée, nevertheless, to her enormous North Oxford dwelling, and I believed myself to have built up with her a small fund of good will which had generated itself out of my vigorous if unpractised efforts in the matter of the errant cow. And as I now thought the ingenuousness of my comment and request a masterpiece of diplomatic manœuvre I was surprised that the aged cow-wife's response was something less than enthusiastic.

'Yes,' she said, 'you may certainly come to tea. And it appears that my present ward is at least extremely pretty. I had better tell you at once that a number of young men have lately been taking that view of her. She has come to Oxford to benefit, Mr Pattullo, from a vacation from that kind of thing.'

'What a very odd place to come to for that!' I smiled cheerfully at Mrs Triplett, having resolved to be unaffected candour all over. 'Far more young men to the square mile here than in Mayfair, or wherever Penny lives. I hope'—I added anxiously —'it isn't cheek to call her Penny?'

Mrs Triplett, who was incredibly old, eyed me with rather more approval than a few moments earlier. Perhaps I had got the right wave-length in making muted and respectful fun of her.

'Are you reliable?' she asked. 'Or shall I have to send Penny out to tea elsewhere? I don't mean deeply reliable. No young man ought to be asked to answer for that. But superficially reliable—which is almost as important.'

'Oh, yes—I think so.' I had a sense of gaining merit in thus getting on well with Mrs Triplett. I knew that, ages ago, she had married what Tony called some Foreign Office type. But I also knew that, ages before that again, she had emerged from one of the great English aristocracies of the nineteenth century. Arnolds, Darwins, Huxleys, Stracheys, Trevelyans, Greens were names much more glamorous to me than any number of Argylls and Atholls and Buccleuchs. (A literary education has this effect for a while.) Mrs Triplett's house was full of portraits and engravings of these worthies: Darwin holding a skull, Huxley pointing at a microscope. And Mrs Triplett had heady artistic connections too. Incredibly but unaffectedly, she would refer to the artist from whose handiwork I was now nervously averting my heels as 'Topsy'. Burne-Jones was 'poor Ned', and others named with a similar reminiscent familiarity would probably have been equally impressive if I could have identified them. Talking to Mrs Triplett was thus like talking to a legendary personage; she might have been George Eliot, or one of the Misses Pater, or Mrs Humphry Ward. I was convinced she was a brilliant survivor from a more spacious age. 'Oh, yes—absolutely,' I said. 'I can promise not to kiss Penny among your raspberry canes. And may I stop and help milk the cows? I haven't told you, but I *can* milk cows.'

'At least you may pass round the sandwiches, while Penny pours the tea.' Mrs Triplett glanced at me appraisingly, and for a moment she might have been Penny herself. She enjoyed eliciting a mild madness from a young man.

'And I wonder,' I asked, 'whether you'd allow me to bring a friend?'

'A friend?' Mrs Triplett's look of appraisal sharpened; she

was probably accustomed to her young men making this request. 'Who *will* serve among the raspberry canes?'

'Oh, no—it's not a girl. Just a man on my staircase. He's called Martin Fish. He's an Australian, as a matter of fact.' I knew this to be a strong card. Mrs Triplett was prominent among those Oxford great ladies who encouraged wandering children of the Empire—as well as princesses from the Shan States—to feel countenanced and at home. 'The Fishes are good people out there.' (I had this expression from the novels of Ford Maddox Ford—who was probably known to Mrs Triplett as 'Fordie'.) 'They have a tremendous number of sheep. And Martin probably knows a bit about cows as well.'

'Mr Pattullo, go away and talk to somebody else. To Penny again, if you can rescue her from that Mr Buttertub.'

'Buntingford.'

'Very well—Buntingford. And you may certainly bring Mr Fish to tea. I shall be delighted to receive him.'

I got to my feet, and prepared to cut in on my late guide to Latin syntax. My sense of guile burgeoned. And I judged 'receive' to be a very grand word.


Penny Triplett, however, was to be beyond my further reach that evening. The Provost, with motions evoking some choreographic activity, was assembling his little party of art-lovers. In addition to my father and myself there was to be Lord Mountclandon, with a glimpse of whose family papers it now appeared we were also to be favoured. There were to be included in the party, too, the frozen-faced don who had been sucking up to him, and Buntingford (whom I believed to be completely Philistine), and a plump untidy don called Penwarden who was the college's librarian, and Professor Babcock, and an anonymous woman who moved amid much glinting and clinking of tinny ornaments, like a small perambulating pagoda. As we went downstairs my father came over to me in what I thought of as his conspiratorial manner. This was unpropitious. I knew that he would much rather have walked round the college's pictures either by himself or under my sole guidance; he had, indeed, expressed himself to that effect earlier in the day. But it turned out not to be the pictures that were on his mind now.

'Dunkie,' he demanded (and he spoke with unnecessary caution, as if we were in the midst of a press of hostile natives), 'who's that girl you're after?'

'She's called Penny Triplett. Her guardian—the tiny old woman I was talking to—claims to be some relation of the Glencorrys. I told you about that in a letter.'

'That you did—but not about the lassie.'

'This is the first time I've ever met the lassie. She's just in Oxford for a short visit.'

'You're not letting the grass grow under your feet.'

'You've got it entirely wrong. I'm not after Penny, as you call it.' My father's tone had surprised me. In general it was his instinct to approve of most evidences of the power of sexual attraction. So far as Ninian or I could tell, he had always been completely faithful to our mother, and he was moreover carrying through life with him at least substantial traces of the restrictive morality within which he had been brought up. But his deepest impulse was to acknowledge the holiness of the heart's affections, as had been perfectly clear in his attitude (which later would have been called 'permissive') to Ninian's precocious affairs with girls. In my own case I knew that he took, for some reason, a far from sanguine view of my chances with Janet, and I'd have expected him to be alert to further any movement of my fancy elsewhere. Penny, moreover, ought surely to delight his eye. I expressed this sense of the matter now. 'I'm not after her,' I repeated. 'But anybody might be. She's absolutely lovely, don't you think?'

'Aye. She'd do fine on a packet of rock.'

'Oh, come off it, Daddy!' 'A packet of rock' was my father's equivalent for a chocolate-box, and I was surprised and even indignant at so unjust and atrabilious a remark. 'What I'm thinking is that Penny would be just right for Martin.'

245

'Martin?'

'Martin Fish. The man I'm going to Italy with. You met him at lunch.'

'That I did. I liked Martin. Dunkie, what is this you're blethering about?'

'I'm not blethering. Martin has had an awful crash with an utterly ghastly girl, and I think Penny Triplett would be just right for him. I'm planning it that way.'

'Duncan Pattullo!' This exclamation came from my father in a decently low voice, but he had halted ostentatiously at the foot of the staircase and was gazing at me fixedly as he spoke. Such a hint of drama alarmed me; I was afraid that in a moment the Provost's other guests would come to suppose some family *contretemps* in progress. 'Are you for telling me,' my father went on, 'that you first set eyes on this girl not two hours ago, and think her absolutely lovely, and are managing to believe foreby that there's nothing in your heid but acting as a wee pimp for your friend Fish? The guid God forgie me for having begotten a daftie!'

'Daddy, for Christ's sake move on.' My father's words had shaken me a good deal. Their deepening plunge into the accents of his youth must betoken, as usual, that a Bacchic mood was in the ascendant with him. This being so, his wilful misinterpretation (as I conceived it) of my admittedly sudden interest in Penny was particularly inopportune. At the moment —and for whatever reason—he was merely cross. He was quite liable to turn outrageous as well. Ahead, moreover, I thought I saw one flash-point of particular hazard. 'And listen!' I said —having resolved to take this bull by the horns. 'After Cuyp and Caravaggio and all that, there's to be something different. I've told the Provost about my *Young Picts*, and he says we've got to go and look at that. Just stick to being on your best behaviour, will you? Remember I like it very much.'

This avowal—the first I had ever made, since I had certainly accepted the gift in the first place with an affectation of casual grace—was decidedly a gambler's throw. It might have incited my father to any mischief. And his immediate response (although we were at least now walking soberly on) could have been taken as ominous, since it was marked by a return to his conspiratorial vein.

'Dunkie,' my father said, 'ye'll no mind your doup? Ye dinna think it may affront the ladies?'

'And stop being Harry Lauder, will you?' It was always best to stand up to my father. 'It's a braw brave doup, as he'd no doubt call it. But *you* needn't say so.'

This reference was to one of the felicities of the finished picture, already shadowed in my sketch. My father's historical sense (as Timbermill had once hinted to me) was casual. He had attired his Pictish children (Ninian and myself) in kilts. We were lurking in the whins with a stiff wind blowing from behind us. The whole atmospherics of the picture depended on this; it controlled what the spindrift was doing to the vision of Columba's craft coming heroically through the breakers to the bay. The achievement was, to my mind, quite beyond Monet's wishy-washy scope, and the key to it was what had happened to my own kilt, which had blown clean up from my prone bottom. The bottom itself (at least in the finished picture) was a triumph: ahead—again to my own mind—of any of Renoir's dealings with that part of a human anatomy. But my father was capable of ribaldry before the most consummate passages in his own work—a psychological idiosyncrasy which I was only too conscious might disconcert persons like Professor Babcock and the pagoda lady.

'Dinna fash yoursel, laddie. Do not be apprehensive, my dear boy.'

I felt a large childish relief, for it was apparent from this joke that my father's good-humour was restored. I saw, too, that he judged it entirely in order that the company should be led from the contemplation of Cuyp and Caravaggio into the presence of his water-colour. And had I been capable of further thought on the matter at this moment I would have realized that his response indicated a significant change in him.

It was the year in which his reputation was not so much enlarging itself as soaring. More than I had yet tumbled to, he was no longer a Fiddes Watt or a D. Y. Cameron or any other locally esteemed Scottish Academician. He had become a European painter. He was to prove not averse to the consequences of this, whether for good or evil so far as his art was concerned. I have indicated that he was a handsome man, well equipped to carry himself *en prince* when an occasion required it. He had a European sense of these matters. As a young man he had observed from afar the manner in which the grandees of French culture are expected to conduct themselves.

But now the Provost's little expedition had run up against a hitch. We had left the Lodging by a side-door giving directly on Surrey. The library, imposing even in flank, was before us. And it had suddenly transpired that the library's custodian, the plump Penwarden, was not merely untidy but inefficient into the bargain. He had failed to transfer to a pocket of his evening garments the key that could alone admit us to the promised splendours within.

In this situation I was the company's obvious resource. The Provost had only to say to me, 'Pattullo, cut along to the gate, will you, and get the master-key from the porter.' And in effect the Provost did this, although with a polished elaboration which would have been not inappropriate had he suddenly taken it into his head to despatch Lord Mountclandon himself on this useful boy's office. I departed into the darkness of the Great Quadrangle at a run—with such goodwill, indeed, that I almost knocked down Robert Damian. Damian, as was frequently the case when one encountered any contemporary at this hour, had demonstrably been at a party.

'In God's name, you bloody young Pattullo, you!' Damian was clearly feeling friendly. 'And what's this in aid of, anyway?'

'Go home, Robert. I'm getting a key for the Provost. We've got to go and look at a lot of junk in the library.'

'Oh, your grand party! Was the gown all right?' Damian

must have heard of my doubts in this matter. 'And were you the only undergraduate?'

'Yes, I was. I still am. Piss off, Robert, for Jesus' sake.' Damian was amusing himself by playing the infantile game of skipping into my path as I tried to dodge him. 'I've got quite enough on my plate without your buffoonery. We've got to go on and look at my blessed Picts. And there's something about a lot of political papers as well.'

'A feast of learning and art and culture generally. I do think Mrs P. might have asked some circumspect youth to support you. Tony, perhaps. He could have whispered to you about the right spoons and forks.'

'Tony has gone to a funeral. At least that's what he's told his tutor. I damn well wish it was yours.' I had now managed to elude Damian, so this was a parting shot.

'Look for me at breakfast, Duncan.' Damian bellowed this after me in a voice that might well have reached our seniors waiting by the library door. 'We'll want the whole uproarious tale.'

The library, as soon as entered, struck a perceptible chill over our expedition. This was chiefly a physical matter. The building had been unheated during the day, and we were now experiencing the kind of May night that rapidly turns from cool to cold. Moreover, Oxford colleges and similar prosperous proprietors of art collections of modest interest had not yet been sold the notion that such things fade, decay and fall apart unless housed amid conditions approximating to those obtaining in an intensive care unit of a great hospital. So the picture gallery was still innocent of air-conditioning, thermostats, humidity control or anything of the sort, and our cautious progress across its slippery marble floor suggested not only the uncertain poise of unpractised skaters on a rink but the slow freezing of their toes as well. I detected Professor Babcock and the pagoda lady exchanging glances to the accompaniment of those slightly raised shoulders by which women cautiously signal to each other an acknowledgement of such discomfort. I wondered whether the correct-behaviour business required that I should volunteer to undertake another dash through darkness in the interest of fetching their coats or cloaks from the Lodging. I decided that this would be officious, and interpretable as a reproach to the Provost, who might have considered the exigency himself. Besides, I didn't quite want to leave my father even for a brief period to his own devices. He had the appearance of being all decorum. But one never knew.

The state of the thermometers was not quite all; there was in addition a sense, perhaps intensified even by that brief wait before a closed door, that our cultural foray was a shade *voulu*. The Provost was an efficient *cicerone*; he would certainly remember how, at their first meeting, he and my father had talked about Dürer; and would equally certainly show him the Süss von Kulmbach and the little Schäuffelein as a result. So there would be a small success there. But did anybody really want, at this time of night, to trail right round the place? We weren't in the presence of a small private collection, miscellaneous perhaps, but in some degree brought together through reflecting the taste of an individual collector, or at least of an age. Still less were we in a large public gallery, with its vistas of great paintings significantly juxtaposed. Here one was just bumped about—the more perceptibly so since the viewers were as haphazard a bunch as the objects they were to survey. Total strangers are quite undistracting when one is trying to look at pictures, but I saw that with my present companions I'd fail to manage it at all. They had broken up into twos and threes and were wandering at random from exhibit to exhibit. I couldn't decide to whom to latch on, and yet I knew I mustn't for more than a minute or two stalk about by myself. I very much wished that I was out of the whole stupid affair.

'Well, Mr Pattullo, at least you had a good innings at dinner. So you mustn't look so bored now.'

It was Professor Babcock who had remarked my state, and

separated herself from Penwarden to take benevolent if also astringent notice of me.

'Yes, I did,' I said. 'She was an awfully nice girl. And I'm sorry if I'm looking bored. I thought I was just managing proper unobtrusiveness and diffidence. Please, who is the man who goes on making himself so agreeable to Lord Mountclandon?'

'Your question suggests disapprobation. But it does appear, I agree, that Lord Mountclandon is being a little courted. His assiduous interlocutor is Christopher Cressy, known as the brilliant young historian. You can't have been in Oxford for a year without being aware of *him*.'

'I've seen him in the streets, I think. Do you know? There are about a dozen men in Oxford who walk around as if acknowledging themselves to be in the small class of the inescapably identifiable. I can't quite work out how it's done. Perhaps they just turn out their toes or something. This Mr Cressy is one of them. And why's he here, anyway? It's he who's dead bored, not me. Look how he's looking at the pictures. He might have strayed into the wrong class of shop, and be turning down samples of wallpaper that are too cheap and nasty for him.'

'Then it's nice that he judges the spectacle of Lord Mountclandon so agreeable.'

Professor Babcock and I found ourselves glancing at one another with momentary caution, perhaps as feeling some impropriety in this chirpy conversation carried out across the chasm of our years. But if I myself had no business to be thus smart and impatient, my description of the brilliant Cressy had been fair enough. It wasn't clear to me that Lord Mountclandon was any more interested in the pictures than his companion, but he was moving about among them with engaged glances and murmured appreciative words—much as he would do, I imagined, if called upon to inspect the labours of the blind or the handiwork of Boy Scouts. Cressy saw no need to expend this sort of courtesy upon the treasures of his hosts, perhaps because everything he possessed of that order he was concerned to lavish upon Lord Mountclandon himself. What seemed interesting about this effort was its success. One would have supposed that a man who had held the highest offices of the state must long since have ceased to feel gratified at being made the recipient of even the most deftly deferential address. And this would hold even in greater degree—again one would imagine—of Lord Mountclandon, whose forbears had held like offices for generations. Yet such was not the spectacle presented to Professor Babcock and myself. Cressy, whose efforts had already been so discernible when Tindale ineptly interrupted them after dinner, was now enjoying marked success. Lord Mountclandon was judging him more worth attending to than Hugo van der Goes or Bartolomeo Passarotti. I was to learn later that snobbery, far from being confined to the lower and middling reaches of society, can obsess persons of the most unassailably lofty station; it is equally true that flattery, if expertly cooked and served, continues to please the palate of those who have for long been able to command it at will. Lord Mountclandon was being regaled after that fashion.

At this point Buntingford joined us. His approach was made with care, as if he was no more sober than the company of ladies requires. It may have been only the slippery floor that produced the impression. Reflecting that he had suffered my Latin unseens and that Professor Babcock had enjoyed Ranald McKechnie's Greek verses, I guessed that these two must operate in the same territory. This conjecture was supported by a faint sense of confrontation which I now received. Buntingford addressed Professor Babcock as 'Professor'— which I'd have supposed to be eminently correct if I hadn't observed it to make the lady thus addressed bristle. I made a note to communicate this observation to Cyril Bedworth in aid of his studies in English idiom. In Edinburgh McKechnie's father was certainly addressed as 'Professor'; it was evident that at Oxford such a title, divorced from a surname, could be uttered only with some facetious or ironical implication.

'And what do you make of Duncan?' Buntingford asked easily. 'Has he told you he's a pillar of *Isis*?'

Here was more about English usage, for now I was a little disposed to bristle myself. It was true that Buntingford had asked, 'May I call you Duncan?' But he hadn't paused for a reply, and as to what his own Christian name might be I hadn't a clue. Timbermill by this time called me 'Duncan', and even Talbert had got as far as calling me 'Donald' or 'David' from time to time, and it wouldn't have occurred to me that in their case the familiarity ought to be on a reciprocal basis. But then they were old enough (or so I imagined) to be my grandfathers.

'Mr Pattullo and I,' Professor Babcock said crisply, 'have been exchanging, not at all properly, observations on our fellow-guests.'

'Including me?' Buntingford rashly asked.

'Not so far. I will not say that your obscurity spares you. But you are not in the van.'

'Duncan's father is that.' Buntingford had to make no effort to be good-humoured. 'And, I suppose, old Blobs Blunderville.'

'Ah! We are not of the magic circle, Mr Pattullo and I. We have heard from afar that Lord Mountclandon is so termed by his intimates. But we do not feel—do we, Mr Pattullo?—that we are ourselves in that galley.'

I backed Professor Babcock up as required, and wondered why she should make me uneasy. If she liked to talk as if she were somebody in a book, why shouldn't she? Perhaps, being an absorbed and serious scholar, she didn't often go out to dinner parties, and believed that a certain artificial vivacity was required on such occasions. For that matter, I seemed to be believing this myself.

'Mr Cressy doesn't quite get top marks,' I said. 'He ought to be torn between the charm of the pictures and the fascination of Lord Mountclandon's conversation—and Lord Mount- clandon ought to win. As it is, he's just treating the pictures as out of the running from the start.'

'We don't seem to be goggling at them ourselves,' Bunting-ford said.

'Perhaps they are too familiar to him.' Professor Babcock offered this charitably. 'Wasn't Mr Cressy a member of your college in the first place?'

'Oh, yes—and he was a lecturer here for some years before gaining a fellowship elsewhere. He's a member of our common room still, and exercises his dining rights from time to time. He entertains us with ludicrous portraits of his new colleagues. We aren't wholly gratified, since we suspect that, when dining elsewhere, his old ones are also in his repertory. But he's un-deniably witty. And you can get away with murder if you're witty enough. Duncan here has already grasped this great human truth—and has examined it in a serious essay, illustrated from Shakespeare's *Richard the Third*, for his tutor, the learned Albert Talbert.'

'You wouldn't get away with petty theft on the strength of *that*,' I said viciously.

'Very true, Duncan. I was being funny, not witty. Cressy, incidentally, must be rather regretting his move to another college. I suspect he'd quite like a go at the Blunderville Papers himself.'

'Is that so?' Professor Babcock, to whom the last remark had been addressed, was immediately interested. 'I believe we are to be permitted a glimpse of them presently. Perhaps the Pro-vost designs to afford us a reading from them. In his Holy Writ voice, which is always an impressive experience. Not, I suppose, that the Papers are exactly Scripture.'

'They're said to be everything under the sun. Mountclandon has simply turned them in on us for our historians to examine and classify and what-not—and make suggestions about what it might be discreet to publish. It's all very august and hush-hush. State papers and personal papers all muddled up over several generations. Our chaps will have the whale of a time. Better them than me.'

'But surely *we* shan't have to mull over them now?' I asked in some dismay—this chiefly because I didn't much fancy the *Young Picts* ordeal being deferred any longer.

'I'd hope not, certainly. I imagine his lordship is simply to be gratified by a glimpse of how they're cherished. How tight the security, and how shiny the fireproof boxes in which they're accommodated.' Buntingford turned once more to Professor Babcock. 'That's why our librarian, Tommy Penwarden, is so fidgety. Do you notice how he keeps on scratching himself? The pictures, you know, are the Provost's thing. Everybody realizes the Provost is no-end aesthetic. But the Papers are Tommy's stamping-ground, and he feels it's time his turn had come.'

'So it is.' Professor Babcock had glanced down at her watch, which she wore in the manner of a medal far out on her bosom. 'But the aesthetic front, I see, is to detain us for a few moments longer. And we are being remiss. I observe a general movement in the direction of some cows. We must join it.'

We hastened across the gallery in the wake of the other visitors. The cows, of course, were by Cuyp, and the canvas was a very large one. There were three cows, disposed in a triangle, and a voluminously skirted woman (whom I thought of as Mrs Triplett) was approaching them, carrying a pail and stool, so that one had a very fair idea of what was going on. Behind this lay a canal with a boat on it, and behind that stretched a sky borrowed from beyond the Alps. It was a charming picture, well deserving the manifest sensibility with which the Provost's right hand was restrainedly gesturing in front of it. My father was standing beside him, quite still, and with his hands in his pockets. For no distinguishable reason at all, I felt suddenly apprehensive.

The Provost concluded his exposition. My father brought his own right hand out of his pocket, and raised it very slightly. I have remarked that he had the quality known as presence, and he exhibited it now. A pronouncement was to be made; there was a respectful hush; my father's index finger came forward and pointed at one of the cows.

'She's well in milk, that one,' my father said approvingly.

This performance, only mildly mischievous by my father's standards, brought to a close the visit to the picture gallery. What had taken place would have been describable a decade later as a send-up. The Provost was far too intelligent not to understand it in that sense, but he hadn't seemed offended. This was to his credit, and perhaps a little to my father's as well. It illustrated something I was fully to understand in Edward Pococke only many years later. Any fool could have told at sight that he was a vain and sensitive man, swiftly aware of mockery. But a strong intellect had murmured to him— almost, one imagined, in his cradle—the saving admonition *nosce teipsum*, with the consequence that, in his maturity, he got along with his own frailties comfortably enough.

We trooped upstairs to the library proper. The Provost, being slightly the younger man, took my father's arm to ensure him against a tumble. Was this a counter-stroke, a suggestion that a second brandy had been a brandy too many? The thought would have delighted his guest, but would, I believe, have been fallacious. The marble treads were even more slippery than the floor of the picture gallery, and the Provost was a solicitous host. We paused to admire the wrought-iron balustrade; there was a further unlocking of doors, this time with keys Penwarden did possess; the great library was before us, and the spectacle necessitated a pause for admiring remarks. It was a place having nothing to do with the life of undergraduates, and I had never entered it before. I wondered whether anybody ever took a book from these towering shelves, whether even the unfathomable erudition of Albert Talbert would be up to tackling the obscurity they obviously enshrined, whether it would be physically possible for a single man to manipulate some of them. Surely there were areas where they grew six feet high? These were like tomes painted on the backcloth of a necromancer's cell when some illusion of cosiness has to be created on the huge stage of an opera house. At this moment the college's great bell, of which all other

256

Oxford bells are but miniaturized epigones, began banging out the hour. The vast chamber trembled; from the shelves I heard, or thought I heard, slumbering folios faintly stir, creak in their ancient joints like a door breathed upon by the ghost of a wind and shifting on a rusty hinge. From the shelves I saw, or thought I saw, rise a pale miasma, a quintessence of dust, which eddied, rose, sifted itself through the chandeliers to lose itself against the pale rose and blue of the ceiling, and then sank, wheeled, drifted, and returned whence it came. But when I think I remember this perhaps I am remembering something I was to see in Martin Fish's company some weeks later: the pigeons of St Mark's Square in Venice, also moving under the impulsion of a bell.

At least the pagoda lady responded to the deep vibration from without; her costume jewellery rang faint but clear, like tinkling harness audible across the stillness of Russian snows. She hadn't in my hearing produced any other sound, and as I was now advancing across the library beside her I tried to think of some feasible brief utterance. Unexpectedly, she produced one herself.

'Say!' the pagoda lady said. 'Isn't Mr Penwarden cute?'

A few years later it would have surprised me thus to discover the speaker's nationality, since I should have come to know that American women don't commonly disguise themselves as trinket-shops. Now, however, my surprise was concentrated upon Penwarden himself. He didn't strike me as particularly cute, but he did look like a man gone demented. Having hurried ahead of the rest of us, he had dropped first on his hands and knees, and now actually on his belly. In this posture he was snaking his way forward in a manner suggesting Cowboys and Indians. Perhaps it was under the persuasion that he was actually proposing a *divertissement* of that sort to the company at large that the pagoda lady had advanced her question.

'If you wouldn't mind standing still,' Penwarden said to us collectively from the floor. His voice (as seemed reasonable in the circumstances) was embarrassed as well as smothered. 'The system has been changed, and I'm not too clear about the switch. The ray is of the thermal type, which we are assured is more sensitive than the previous sonic affair. It's not a rustle or a creak it picks up. It's body temperature—really a remarkable thing.'

'The security,' the Provost said in the clear tones of one who allays alarm. 'Harmless, we are assured. But it would be humiliating were the police to arrive and take us all into custody. Dear lady, have a care.' This injunction was addressed to Professor Babcock, whom he judged in danger of advancing the forward part of her person into some line of fire. 'Ah, the Librarian has been successful.' There had been a faint click. 'The way to the Blunderville Papers is clear.'

Penwarden had got to his feet, and was again holding in his hand a common-or-garden key. We all relaxed. Lord Mountclandon, who might have been expected to find an element of the ridiculous in these excessive precautions, appeared, on the contrary, gratified. I saw that Cressy had now removed himself from Mountclandon's elbow, as one who feels modestly that he has enjoyed his due share of the countenance of the great. With engaging humility, he was offering his conversation to my father. My father, once more on his best behaviour, listened to him attentively.

'Stop grinning, young Pattullo.' Buntingford breathed this in my ear. 'Of course it's all lunacy, sure enough. You could bone the Cuyp or the Caravaggio downstairs more easily than the junk this old donkey has unloaded on us. But mind your manners.'

'Belt up,' I said—for I had finally resolved to treat Buntingford as if no vast five-years gap existed between us. 'My manners are in working order, thank you. And at least I'm not a bloody drunk.'

'Good man, Duncan. You're coming on.' And Buntingford outrageously patted me on the head. He must really have been rather tight, whereas I was myself as sober as I had resolved to remain from the start of the evening. *Young Picts* was before me still.

It was no doubt because of this preoccupation that I was only intermittently attentive to what was presently going on around me, and there were aspects of what I did notice the implications of which I didn't grasp. The micro-rays, or whatever they were, which Penwarden had courageously contrived to throw out of operation might, indeed, have suggested drama of the gangster variety to a fanciful mind: hold-up and robbery on a large scale. But academic life (as I believe Dr Johnson remarked) puts one little in the way of extraordinary casualties, and as this night represented my first substantial immersion in that life I might well have expected unflawed decorum all through. Almost everything in the general atmosphere suggested this. My father was apparently subdued to the element in which, for the occasion, he had agreed to swim. The suavity of the Provost perfectly matched that of Lord Mountclandon, and the suavity of Cressy exceeded that of either. About Cressy's features in repose there was, as I have mentioned, something fixed and glassy; one would not have expected from him, under any circumstances, a warm flow of human sympathy. He could, however, radiate a mild and seemingly benign intelligence, together with the unobtruded diffidence of one naturally well-mannered. He was doing so now. This was the posture of things as Penwarden embarked upon an account of how the college was coping with the Blunderville Papers.

Penwarden was at once revealed as a conscientious man, who had given proper thought to the occasion. Of the shiny fireproof boxes there were a great many, and in addition the walls of the medium-sized room to which we had been admitted were lined with formidable-looking steel filing-cabinets. It wasn't to be supposed that we were going to rifle these. But on various tables a number of particularly choice exhibits had been laid out for inspection: diaries, engravings, miniatures, genealogies, decorations, swords, cocked hats, letters from exalted persons, and similar family lumber which it had presumably occurred to Lord Mountclandon as proper to lump in with the documents of severer historical interest. About the whole loan—or bequest or whatever it was—Penwarden had prepared a speech, but one carefully pitched to an informal and colloquial note. Perhaps he overdid this a little, so that the general effect was more mumbling and bumbling than it need have been, but it was well-adapted to the occasion, nevertheless. I ought to have listened more attentively than I did; I was in fact calculating that the dinner-party would almost certainly break up as soon as we returned to the Lodging, so that I should have no opportunity of telling Penny how much I looked forward to bringing my friend Martin Fish to tea with Mrs Triplett on Sunday. But at least I should be able to say good-night to her. It wasn't indeed clear how this could greatly advance Fish's suit (as I now almost thought of it), but I was impatient for the opportunity, nevertheless. So all I gathered about the Papers was that they were being worked on by Penwarden himself and two of his colleagues in the college; that the operation must be highly confidential until it was known what was what; and that the mere sorting and calendaring would in itself be a formidable task. I was ignorant enough to think it odd that even a grandee like Lord Mountclandon could have such a chore performed for him, probably for free, by a trio of high-powered dons. It seemed as if the stuff that had silted up in the cupboards of the Blundervilles over the generations or centuries must afford the raw material for the making of a good many learned reputations. Yes, it must be something like that.

Lord Mountclandon himself obviously felt he was being done quite proud by his old college. He made approving remarks, and to Professor Babcock and the pagoda lady he even offered explanations (not, I suspected, always too well informed) of various documents, and in particular of various pieces of knick-knackery, which had been singled out for exhibition. He picked up an ambassadorial-looking hat smothered in feathers, and invited my father to put it on. My father declined this (and quite right too) but avoided any appearance of displeasure by placing it gently on my own head instead. There was general merriment. The occasion was proving a mild success.

Christopher Cressy was wandering around on his own. I noticed for the first time that he had a small sharp nose which, if not impressive, somehow suggested an organ likely to be useful on a scent. Like Professor Babcock's pectoral region, it firmly took the van. He was now led by it into a corner of the room, and when he returned to us he was carrying delicately in both hands—for it was a bulky affair—a battered leather-bound volume. He walked up to Lord Mountclandon with an air of gracefully amused discovery. Lord Mountclandon, as it happened, had moved over to me for the purpose of delivering whimsical congratulations on the fit of the hat; he was determined to show proper attention to the well-conducted schoolboy (as he may have thought of me) who was with a slight mysteriousness a member of the party. This trivial circumstance, curiously enough, was going to complicate my life for a time more than twenty years later. Oxford memories are tenacious and long.

'A letter-book of the fourth marquis,' Cressy said—and with a casualness which was yet wholly polite. 'And I believe—for I've ventured just to peep—covering some rather significant years. Interesting, don't you think?'

'Undoubtedly—yes, very interesting indeed.' Lord Mountclandon's ready smile indicated how effectively he had been softened up. At the same time he scarcely looked very convincingly 'with it'. Like so many Blundervilles before him, he had been a practical politician all his days. He probably had a brother or a cousin to whom he relegated the business of being clued up in family history, and anybody as remote as the fourth marquis didn't mean all that to him. He had been—he doubtless believed himself still to be—a much burdened man.

'With probably a good many pages it would be amusing to turn over,' Cressy said. 'But not without your permission, of course. You wouldn't mind?' Cressy continued to speak lightly—and certainly as of an activity which would transact itself within minutes. Nevertheless I was aware of Penwarden as taking a couple of rapid steps towards us. The guardian of these treasures was alert to anything that was going on.

'Yes, of course. By all means, my dear fellow. Entirely at your leisure, pray.' Lord Mountclandon's graciousness was now seignorial. 'It's entirely yours.'

'Thank you very much.' Cressy articulated this expression much in the manner in which I was accustomed to offer it to Talbert or our jumpy Domestic Bursar. As he spoke, he tucked the volume nonchalantly under an arm and promptly appeared to forget about it. Considerable muscular effort must have been required to maintain it there, nevertheless.

I was conscious that something distressing was happening to Penwarden's breathing. He took a further but indecisive step forward, and then turned away and hurried from the room. He was back within a minute, carrying a slip of paper I recognized at once; it was the small form which had to be filled in and signed when we borrowed a book from the 'working' library in another part of the building. Silently—for he was clearly beyond speech—he handed the form to Cressy. Cressy took it in his free hand, glanced at it, and then looked up at Penwarden with a glare as icy as could have been achieved by a refrigerated basilisk. Having thus expressed himself about this busybody pitifully intruding upon a transaction between gentlemen, he slowly crumpled the borrowing-slip and let it fall to the floor. A moment later, he was talking with courtly ease to the pagoda lady.

The incident had attracted no general notice, and I am sure that I myself made less of it than this account, coloured as it is by hindsight, may suggest. I felt vaguely that there had been some small rumpus between dons and that Cressy had got away with something, and I may even have told myself it was un-surprising that so freezing a character had failed to activate the thermal security system. Penwarden, certainly, had lost out on that brief eyeball to eyeball confrontation. The Provost would have done better, had he been aware of what was happening.

I certainly saw it all as insignificant, and within a couple of minutes it had gone from my head. For our homage to the Blunderville Papers was over, and we were leaving the library.

It was high time to return to the Lodging, where some of the guests must already be wondering whether they could civilly take their leave of Mrs Pococke while she was still unsupported by her wandering husband. But the Provost was not a man readily to be deflected from his purpose, and we hadn't gained the near-darkness of Surrey before he was explaining to Professor Babcock the curious interest of what next lay before us. He had a genuine knowledge of painting—even of contemporary painting—and since first interviewing my father not much more than a year before had gained an actual acquaintance with his work. During the previous winter, and at my father's first retrospective exhibition in London, he had seen *Young Picts watching the arrival of Saint Columba*, and it was a matter of interest to him that an *esquisse* for this now celebrated work hung in the rooms of the artist's son. Having conversed on the matter with Professor Babcock (and not failed to do so with the pagoda lady, who was a woman guest of lesser account), he advanced upon me and laid a fatherly hand on my elbow.

'And now, my dear Pattullo,' he said, 'we shall be most deeply grateful.'

I didn't then know that the Provost was as lavishly given to this assurance as I was to 'Thank you very much', and its disproportion to our present small occasion unnerved me. Moreover at that time—although I didn't realize the fact—I was possessed by a plurality of loves; my rooms in Surrey were among them; I resented the notion of all these people crowding in uninvited (as it essentially was). So I had to tell myself that it was my own fault; that in the vanity of my heart I had divulged my proprietorship of *Young Picts* to the Provost; and that the present dicey situation was only what I deserved.

But at least we were quit of Cressy; he had faded unobtrusively into the night—returning to the Lodging, I suppose, to take due leave of his hostess before making off in triumph with his booty. This relieved me a good deal. Had he remained for this odd private view, and then treated *Young Picts* to that icy stare, I might well have felt obliged to turn him out of the room—when I imagine that the Provost's deep gratitude to me would have faded sharply. As things were, it was probable that all would go well. I realized that only a certain confusion of mind could have blinded me to the fact that my father wasn't going to behave other than impeccably when once more a guest in his son's quarters.

At this hour the only light in Surrey came from a few uncurtained windows, since the college porters had displayed their usual zeal in rendering nocturnal perambulation hazardous by switching off anything they could put a hand to. When we reached the foot of the staircase it occurred to me that I ought from this point to constitute myself Professor Babcock's escort, and I got some satisfaction out of abandoning the Provost in the interest of this further piece of correct behaviour. I don't know whether Professor Babcock was gratified by my punctilio. But she was certainly amused, and as I was now feeling confident and in good humour I thought the better of her for it. Since Tony had departed immediately after my luncheon party, for the supposed obsequies of an aunt, and had declared his intention of making the funeral baked meats spin out over a long week-end, there was no risk of ribald observation from that quarter. We climbed the worn treads at a pace proper to our post-prandial condition. I opened my door, switched on the light, and ushered Professor Babcock within. I then decided (the same anxious considerations still being uppermost in my young mind) that I should let the rest of the company precede me too, and I stood back for this purpose. So when I myself entered everybody was already at gaze with the picture over the chimney-piece. But the picture wasn't *Young Picts watching the arrival of Saint Columba*. It was Tony's atrocious Roman bawdy-house.

Through long seconds nobody uttered a word. I looked wildly round. It seemed only possible to suppose that I was very far from sober after all, and that on the landing I had bemusedly turned right when I ought to have turned left. But this, at least, wasn't true. The room was my own room. My own darling room—as the poet Tennyson somewhere says.

'I don't recall conceiving the subject quite in that way.' My father gave us this information mildly and with complete composure.

'One would decidedly suppose not.' The Provost (because he was not yet the nobly bearded man he was to become) could have been observed as having turned pale around the mouth. 'Our proposed pleasure must be deferred,' he said. His voice wasn't quite steady, and as he was a man to whom a fiasco of this sort must appear an outrage I supposed the *tremolo* effect to be a consequence of blind fury. He turned and looked at me fixedly, and I didn't imagine for a moment that he wasn't judging me to be the perpetrator of this extravagant episode. I told myself my Oxford days were over. Not even Bedworth when he had contrived that luckless swipe with his brassy could have been more confounded. 'My dear Pattullo,' the Provost said quietly, 'we must conclude that you number some lively minds among your acquaintance. Perhaps we might all return to the Lodging?'

We did so—to the accompaniment of what composing remarks by the other members of the expedition I don't remotely recall. Although relieved (and impressed) by the Provost's swift perception of the facts of the case, I was still sufficiently upset to be asking myself whether I had a reasonable chance of worsting Robert Damian in a stand-up fight, and rather concluding I had not.

'Dunkie,' my father asked cautiously, 'your picture will be all right? They'll gie it back to ye the morn?'

'Yes, of course, Daddy. It's as safe as houses.' I knew this to be true. 'Morie-morning, back it will come.'

'Then that's fine.' My father laughed softly. 'Gin ye ever produce the laddie did it, we'll hae a bottle of champagne between the three of us.'

'All right,' I said. 'If I haven't murdered him first.' But I no longer wanted to murder Damian, for I felt entirely happy. I ought to have known (I told myself) that my father would judge the scandalous joke entirely to its inventor's credit.

'Or we might ask your Provost too'—this came reflectively from my father a moment or two later—'and make it a magnum.'

'All right, a magnum. But don't suggest it to him quite yet —not for two or three years in fact. I'm coming to see you on your train in the morning. And I'll breathe more freely after that, Lachlan Pattullo.'

There were still half a dozen cars in front of the Lodging, and the only one with a chauffeur I recognized as Mrs Triplett's. *Young Picts* vanished from my mind. I was certainly going to have that chance to say good-night to Penny. I might even be able to tell her what an unusually nice person Martin Fish was.

The party in the Day-room remained a large one. Indeed, it had been augmented in an after-dinner way by guests who were either of inferior consideration or in the enjoyment, contrastingly, of crowded engagement books. The departure and return of the Provost's small expeditionary force was as a result not much remarked. But one or two people must have been keeping a look-out for their host with the thought of going off to bed in their minds, and this impulse now disseminated itself through the room. I saw that Mrs Triplett was proposing to act upon it with particular briskness—no doubt as having been brought up not to keep the coachman and his horses waiting beyond an appointed hour. The lamentable consequence was that I had only some thirty seconds with Penny. She said good-night with no appearance of judging the allowance inadequate —or not, at least, until what might be termed the final tick of the watch, which she devoted to the ghost of a suggestion of a lingering glance. And at this accomplished performance (as it was) my head swam wildly. Mrs Pococke, who developed one of those long Oxford memories, was to assure me at a future date that I had taken my leave of her in decent form. But I

266

myself can remember nothing more until I was out in the quad.

I walked back to Surrey with Penny Triplett's face hovering in the darkness before me; it faded only when I reached my staircase, the foot of which happened to be illuminated through Gavin Mogridge's open door. I noticed that there was something waiting for me in my letter-rack: only a sliver of coloured pasteboard was visible, and I must have failed to remark it earlier in the day. I picked it up automatically and without glancing at it, and went upstairs to my room. The first thing to do was to cope with Tony's picture. I got it down from the chimney-piece—it was uncommonly heavy—and perched it back to front against the wall. Then I looked at what I had brought up with me and tossed on a table.

It was one of Janet's picture-postcards. It came, as now so often, from Skye. As usual, it depicted an uninspiring scene: a little harbour crowded with the hulls and jumbled masts of fishing vessels. I turned it over, and found the customary uncoloured account of reading achieved. Janet had read, among other things, a book about Emily Brontë and a novel, just published, called *The Moonlight*. Added apparently as an afterthought, however, was a fragment of information on a personal level. *I've marked with a cross*—Janet had written—*my cousin Calum's boat.*

I'd never heard of this particular cousin of Janet's—or indeed by name of any other of her relations in Skye, although it was obvious they commanded her affections and imagination a great deal. I turned the card over again and looked at Calum's boat. It struck me as rather a frail craft to go tumbling around the Western Islands in. I looked at it for quite a long time, and it may well have been with a sombre intuition that Janet was dropping out of my life. But this, if so formulated, would have been a facile phrase; it would have been truer to say that she could only withdraw into the depths of it.

I perched the card above the fireplace where *Young Picts* ought to have been, and went to bed.

267

# XII

People commonly wake up, I suppose, in a more or less neutral state of mind. What is happening is nothing if not customary. Here one is again. One performs such initial actions—making tea, raising a blind—as habit dictates, while vaguely rehearsing yesterday's undramatic events now stacked up by sleep in the shadowy filing-cabinet of memory, or hazily anticipating equally undramatic hours briefly to be called today. Occasionally, however, one awakens to the consciousness of a strong feeling-tone at first possessing no identity. Is it of sorrow or joy, pleasurable anticipation or dread? A fraction of time may pass before one knows even this, and a further fraction before the impalpable answer takes on the body of a specific occasion.

On this particular morning, Friday morning, my mind on surfacing questioned itself and decided that the new medium of its operation was a genial one. The snail was on the thorn, the lark on the wing, the morning at seven, and the hill-side dew-pearled. These Pippa-like impressions appeared to proceed from the fact that Friday was the day of my tute with Timbermill, and a moment or two passed before it struck me that there was anything odd about this. I enjoyed going to Timbermill. Unlike Talbert, he was a conscientious tutor, and I have recorded that he got quite a lot of work out of me. This held all the charm of novelty, since I had hitherto got along on nothing worthier than a disposition to much desultory reading when I wasn't idly chattering. Timbermill took it for granted that I possessed that sort of intellectual maturity (McKechnie's, I thought of it as being) which rejoices in mastering arid disciplines for their own sake; and by a force of will which I didn't understand (for he never exactly bullied me) he had created in me for the time something tolerably like the real thing; after cheerful rubbishing days with Tony and others I would turn up the lamp as resolutely as Cyril Bedworth himself and plunge into the rudiments of Germanic philology. It was natural that I should respect the man who could make me do this; but Timbermill had, in fact, his place among my love-objects as well.

Of course he had his other dimension: that hint of the pre-ternatural I had sensed in him from the start, and which made me refer to him (partly as a matter of mere Oxford topography) as the Wizard of the North. It was during this first Summer Term that evidence of odd matters stirring in him began to appear on paper. I was required to send in my essays in advance —which is not a common Oxford requirement—and when Timbermill handed them back to me for reading aloud they had not been annotated (since that would have been, in a manner, to anticipate my own better thoughts in discussion) but they had been quite extensively doodled on. I soon taught myself to leave wide margins as I typed out the fair-copies to be posted to him, with the result that what I carried back to college with me week by week presented the appearance of leaves abstracted from the Lindisfarne Gospels or the Book of Kells. Long afterwards I was to chance to display some of these *keimelia* (as Talbert would have learnedly termed them) to a wandering American professor, and to receive within days a cable from his university offering to buy them for a large sum of money. It is a curious thought that the moderately successful scribbling of drawing-room comedies had put me in a position to decline the offer. But curious, too, in those May and June days, were the forms, the creatures, beginning to peer out from amid all that intricacy of foliage and arabesque in the margins of my essays on *The Battle of Maldon* or *The Dream of the Rood*. I was witnessing the birth, or the first dim movement in the night of their forebeing, of the presences one day to haunt *The Magic Quest*.

Nothing of all this explains the fact that I was excited by the knowledge of having to be in Linton Road by eleven o'clock. But before that I had to take my father to the railway station, and I saw that I had better tumble out of bed. I was shaving (and wondering, as I frequently did, whether it would be both physiologically possible and socially acceptable to grow a moustache) when I heard a knock on my outer door. I gave a shout, went belathered into the sitting-room, and found I was being visited by Clive Kettle. He was holding *Young Picts* very carefully in both hands.

'Good morning, Pattullo,' he said. 'Will it be all right if I give you back your picture now?'

'It certainly will.' I glared indignantly at Kettle—but also in some surprise. I wouldn't have expected so serious and pious a man to have been involved in the previous night's idiotic joke. 'And what the bloody hell have you been doing with it, anyway?'

'Oh, I'm extremely sorry!' Kettle's principles didn't permit him to be offended at this rude challenge. 'It was Robert Damian, you see.'

'I know it was—the God-forsaken young bastard.'

'Oh, I don't think one ought to say that, Pattullo. In fact, I've seen Damian in chapel once or twice this term already. I believe his mind may be beginning to open.'

'All right—just the young bastard. Why did he unload my picture on you?'

'He was concerned to help. He'd heard of some foolish men, he said, who were talking about raiding your rooms and carrying off this picture as a joke or a rag or simply to make themselves unpleasant. It's sad to think of such darkness of mind.'

'So it is. But go on.'

'Damian didn't want simply to sport your oak, in case you hadn't your key and it turned out awkward for you. And he didn't think he ought to carry the picture across the quads to his own rooms. There were some drunks around, he said. As there too often are.'

'Too bloody often by a long way.'

'Well, yes.' It was hesitantly that Kettle accepted this intensified view of the matter. 'So he asked me to look after it for you and bring it back this morning. So I agreed to. I knew it would be quite safe, because I didn't mean to leave my rooms.'

'Then thank you very much.' I was again furious with Damian for gratuitously involving this blameless Christian in his imbecile exploit, and equally cross with myself for being causelessly uncivil. 'Damian was having you on, as a matter of fact. But it's too long a story to bother about.' Explaining matters, it had occurred to me, would involve introducing Kettle to Tony's picture too—which he had probably never seen and would certainly regard as opprobrious. 'I wouldn't have liked my picture to be mucked about,' I added. 'It's by my father, as a matter of fact.'

'How very interesting!' Kettle held *Young Picts* out at arm's length the better to admire it. 'It must be a very jolly hobby to have—and healthy, too, taking one so much out of doors. I do think your father's pretty skilful. He must go in for it quite a lot.'

'He is. He does.'

'How funny he hasn't noticed there's something wrong with the smaller boy's kilt. Who are they supposed to be?'

'Young Picts.'

'Oh, I see. Stone Age people.' Kettle appeared to feel that this went some way to excuse the impropriety of my attire in the picture. 'Are they rabbiting?'

'They're watching the arrival of Saint Columba. He's coming to the mainland of Scotland from Iona. If you look carefully, you can see his boat.'

'So I can. Oh, Pattullo, what a splendid subject!' Kettle's voice had taken on a solemnity which I tried, and failed, to think of as comical. 'One ought to have a picture with some sort of religious significance in one's room. I'm so glad you have. It's a kind of witness, wouldn't you say? I've got an etching by Rembrandt. It's Our Lord breaking the bread at Emmaus. Nothing but a copy, of course. But I find it very moving. I'd so like you to see it some time.'

'I'd like to very much.' I oughtn't to have said this as awkwardly as I did, since with Kettle I was now, in a sense, forewarned. He subscribed to what I and most of my contemporaries judged to be a tissue of absurdities: Christ risen from the Dead, and things of that sort. There was no reason why he shouldn't. He shared these beliefs, after all, with plenty of people much cleverer than I was, including the Provost and (presumably) the Archbishop of Canterbury. But, unlike these more experienced wayfarers in an infidel world, he was simply unable to accept the fact that anybody he knew could be without some vital spark of faith deep in his soul. The idea was too terrible to contemplate. This was either imbecility or a passionate purity of heart, according as to how one cared to look at it. Rather liking Kettle, all I could do was to shuffle—which was entirely wrong. When he left me now, I was a young man indicting himself of enslavement to ephemeral concerns: my father's acceptability at a dinner party, my own gratifying success in *Isis* or as a rising college personality, even Penny Triplett's face. I returned to my bedroom to finish shaving, and cut myself rather badly on an entirely hairless area below my left ear.

On the railway platform, and after looking round in a nervous manner not habitual with him, my father handed me a couple of five-pound notes—which at that time were still of the large and milk-white kind. Somewhere or other he must have gathered that something of the sort was customary upon visiting a son at any educational establishment of the 'boarding' variety. I might have represented to him that our existing financial arrangement, although random and fluctuating, was on balance very much on the generous side. But it seemed more graceful to accept the present without fuss, and on the strength of it I took a taxi back to college. There I got on my bike and made haste to Linton Road, so that I arrived at the near end of it with ten minutes to spare. I dismounted and went forward, rather slowly, on foot. Anybody might have supposed (I told myself) that the misfortune of a puncture had overtaken me again.

Linton Road was disappointingly empty. The hop-scotch-playing children (mysterious beings, since they could have only great-grandparents among the adult residents) had departed; the ancient with the Anthony Eden hat might by now (as was statistically probable) have sunk into the grave; not a cow was to be seen in the distance on Mrs Triplett's drive, let alone Mrs Triplett (or Mrs Triplett's ward) herself. This shattered a kind of supernatural conviction which I had been entertaining throughout the morning. As I made my way down Linton Road Penny was to appear. I had no good reason to suppose that Mrs Triplett's celebrated herd ran to a freely-roving bull; indeed, any scanty knowledge I had of such matters inclined me to suppose it wouldn't. Still, there *might* be a bull—and if there was it *might* be chasing Penny rather than Penny it. And in such a situation I could cope with any number of bulls.

There was nothing particularly strange in the childishness of these imaginings, but it was perhaps odd that they didn't speak to me of the condition I was in. I still very honestly had the supposed sexual needs of Martin Fish in my head. I dawdled down the void of Linton Road. In addition to being thus unnaturally empty it had telescoped itself in a fashion equally unnatural; its linear perspectives had gone wrong and I'd be at the end of it in no time; the effect was of having walked into a townscape of Chirico's or something equally surrealistic and eerily dead. I racked my brains in search of some pretext for presenting myself briefly at Mrs Triplett's door. Nothing emerged. I made my familiar turn into Timbermill's gate.

At least I could arrive early on my tutor without rebuke. Timbermill took no more than four or five pupils all told, and he appeared to scatter them over the week. My private hour with him (elderly dons still called tutorials private hours) turned into an hour and three-quarters more often than not. My essay on the Christian element in *Beowulf* (a subject which Clive Kettle would have handled much better than I could) must already have been read and doodled on; I'd find Timbermill at his accustomed and unflagging pursuit of sticking bits of pot together with seccotine. I climbed his narrow staircase, banged on his door, and went in. Timbermill waved to me—a reasonable gesture, since he was still twenty yards away. I advanced upon him and saw that he had changed his occupation for the time; he was engaged in examining a tray of coins.

'What do you know about Offa?' Timbermill demanded. This kind of opening gambit was common form with him, so I wasn't disconcerted.

'He built a dike,' I said.

'And what, Duncan, is a dike?'

'It's a wall. Offa, like Balbus, built a wall.'

'Nothing of the kind. He dug a ditch. You've been misled by Bosworth-Toller. If I haven't warned you against Bosworth-Toller I apologize. A dike is a wall in your part of the world—and commonly a dry-stane one. It's because in Scotland you have more stone lying around than you know what to do with. In England the early existence of this sense of the word is entirely doubtful.'

'I'll remember,' I said. In Timbermill's company this took the place of my 'Thank you very much'. 'Did Offa do anything else?'

'That's the point.' Timbermill said this as if my question had been singularly acute. 'There can be no doubt that Offa interested himself in monetary reform. For example, he introduced the *mancus*. And here it is. A beautiful thing.'

'So it is.' I had been handed a worn gold coin. 'Nice to go shopping with.'

'No doubt. The obverse is quite remarkable. But look at the reverse, please. What do you see there?'

'Squiggles.'

'Don't be frivolous, Duncan, or I shall turn you out. People

274

don't put squiggles on coins, although I admit it sometimes looks as if they do. Try again.'

'Runes,' I said hopefully.

'Better—but a wildly unhistorical conjecture, all the same. The answer is Arabic.'

'I don't see why there should be Arabic on an English coin.'

'Perfectly simple. There was Arabic on the *mancus* Offa had taken a fancy to. His moneyer faithfully copied it, and it passed into English currency. It can't have escaped you that there is a great deal of history in coins, although shopping is no doubt what we chiefly prize them for.'

'Yes, of course. May I take it over to the window, please, and look at it there?'

'Certainly. And I'll fossick out something else. There is an effort by the Dobunni which might interest you.'

Timbermill's being, as I have recorded, a somewhat crepuscular room, my request had been reasonable. I moved to the window and studied the *mancus* again. Timbermill was rummaging, so for some seconds I could safely survey the outer world. It included a corner of Mrs Triplett's tennis-court, but Penny (who was keen on tennis) wasn't on view. It included, too, a range of Mrs Triplett's upper windows, but Penny was at none of these. I continued to stare. The *mancus* had gone out of my head.

'It isn't raining, is it?'

'No, sir, it's not.' I turned round in confusion. Timbermill had enunciated his question with a certain dryness which alarmed me. 'I think it's going to be a lovely afternoon.'

'Then you might do worse than employ it in making an expedition to the White Horse of Uffington. You take a bus to Wantage and walk.'

'I've been there, as a matter of fact.'

'Excellent! And what do you know about the White Horse?'

'It's not awfully like a horse. And it has something to do with King Alfred.' I saw that this remark was not being

favourably received. 'Because there was a battle at Ashdown,'
I added on my recurrent hopeful note.

'Absolute rubbish, Duncan. I'm ashamed of you.' Timbermill—who, although a leisure-time tutor, possessed the skills
of the craft in a high degree—said this as if I was one of the few
young men in Oxford worth talking to. 'Alfred had too much
on his plate to fool around digging White Horses out of un-
offending downs. The Dobunni did it.'

'The Dobunni?' I echoed, blankly and stupidly.

'I did happen to mention them a minute ago. The point is
that you wouldn't expect them to have a coinage, would you?'

'I'd have no expectations about them at all.' It was necessary
at times to rally when Timbermill was like this, and truth had
to be one's watchword. 'I've never heard of them, I'm afraid.'

'Excellent! They were an obscure crowd who came over
from Brittany in the first century. Of course they had no
business to have a coinage—no business at all. But they had.
And here it is.' I found that I was looking at another coin: this
time, it appeared to be a silver one. 'What does it suggest to
you?'

'Squiggles.'

'Capital! You're absolutely right. But does it suggest
*anything* to you—anything at all?'

'Well—just conceivably—that White Horse.'

'Praise the Lord!' Timbermill was genuinely and deeply
delighted. 'My dim hope in you is restored. The horse was
their emblem or totem or whatever you care to call it, and they
dug it out on the down. But they'd ceased knowing they had
it on their coins.'

'I don't understand.'

'Yes you do—or almost. That coin goes back. You can trace
it across Europe, back and back from west to east. Through
the centuries a coinage travels as stories do—with the sun.
What you would finally get back to here is a very recognizable
horse indeed, and it's on the coins of Philip of Macedon. If
you're an imaginative type—which you are, God help you,

276

Duncan—you can tell yourself that the squiggle on this coin, and the near-squiggle on that Berkshire hillside, is the descendant of the Bucephalus of Alexander the Great. Which makes my point that there's a certain amount of history in coins. If you think of becoming a scholar—which I don't recommend—you might do worse than become a numismatist.'

'A numismatist?' I was utterly blank again. The word might have been unknown to me.

'Duncan Pattullo son of Lachlan, go back to that window and go on with your gaping. And the sooner your Sunday's tea-party is behind you the better.'

This time, I did my gaping at the Wizard of the North himself. I was in the Cave of the Magician, and I didn't like it.

'I don't quite see,' I said with weak dignity, 'what you can know about that.'

'I am intrusive, and I apologize. It comes of having to fetch the milk.' Timbermill was enjoying himself. 'Is all now clear?'

'Unclear, I'm afraid.'

'A detestable neologism. Do you know what's meant by T.T. milk?'

'I haven't a clue.'

'A capital neologism, that. And T.T. is Tuberculin Tested. The admirable Mrs Triplett is pioneering T.T. milk. Yes, pioneering it. An interesting new transitive use of the verb. And we all have to play. I take my little pitcher every morning before breakfast.'

'And this morning she actually told you——?'

'It shows it's on her mind. She regards you—and a friend of yours whose name escapes me—as a heaven-sent distraction. So have a care.'

'I really don't see——'

'You'd better try. And now we'll have *Beowulf*. I must tell you in advance that you take inadequate account of Miss Whitelock. An admirable scholar.' Timbermill was suddenly magistral and implacable. 'It is not to be supposed that a Christian poet writing for a Christian society would plug the point for the benefit of young men reading his poem in the twentieth century. Not that your essay isn't written with your customary *aplomb*. Here it is. Read it, please, and we'll get to work.'

I wanted to quarrel with Timbermill. Albert Talbert, I told myself, would never have charged into my life like this. But Timbermill, at least, was interested in me, which Talbert was not. I read my essay without sulking, and did my best to defend it afterwards. By the time Timbermill had taken my ideas to pieces and put them together again it was one o'clock.

# XIII

Saturday morning brought a note from Mrs Triplett intimating that Fish and I were to turn up on Sunday in a fit state to play tennis. When I passed on this news to Fish he received it with satisfaction. Like Penny (and this seemed a good omen) he was keen on tennis. Since I understood Australians to divide their time between tennis and aquatic pursuits, and since Fish had so strong a disinclination to the latter, I took it for granted that at the former he would perform very potently indeed. Certainly he became better disposed to our expedition upon hearing of the game's being in prospect. He had received my announcement of Sunday's outing with reasonable surprise, there being little apparent occasion for my carrying him off to the rigours of a North Oxford tea with total strangers. It was true that, since contracted on the strength of only a slight acquaintance to make the Grand Tour together, we ought to be taking all obvious opportunities of getting to know one another better. But we could most readily have done that by gossiping in each other's rooms at midnight.

It did come to me that I knew rather little about Fish. He was much less an identifiable personality to me than was Tony Mumford or Gavin Mogridge or Cyril Bedworth. Yet I had encountered him, as I had encountered none of these, intimately and in a state of vivid sensation. In theory, as it were, Martin Fish's soul ought to have lain bare to me. But in fact it is amid events levelled with the common surfaces of life that one comes to a feeling, perhaps delusive, of knowing people for what they are. Major emotional stresses and all mental aberrations are insulating and mystery-making, and from an actual mad-house one would clearly come away with the conviction that people make no sense at all. Later, I was sometimes to reflect that in a play I'd get nowhere with Fish; the connective tissue between Fish on one day and Fish on another would elude me.

He may have felt he knew as little about me. Certainly he had no notion as yet of my amatory—and even, conceivably, marital—designs for him: a fact excusable in the light of the confused and even spurious overtones which had accompanied these designs almost from the word Go. As we walked down Linton Road together in snowy flannels at Mrs Triplett's appointed hour I was busy being prospectively jealous of Fish, since I was imagining his dazzling performance (as it would be) on the tennis court as carrying everything before it in Penny's regard. It was increasingly a high old muddle, all in all. Timbermill, indeed—and simply because he didn't want a promising pupil mucked around—had illuminated it as with a flash of lightning. But lightning-flashes pass, and commonly leave no very clear vision behind them. I was still as bemused as I had been from the first moment of Penny's appearing before me.

Prelusively swinging my racket (heavy in its press and swathed in its waterproof cover), I tried to review what I *did* know about Fish. I was confident that, at least in any normal situation, he would be much my idea of a friend, would answer to it better than would a number of people higher in the league-table which the undergraduates of any generation so swiftly establish among themselves prestige-wise and as objects of emulation. If I felt that this was important it was perhaps because a certain racial hard-headedness enabled me to achieve, if only intermittently, a disenchanted view of the up-and-coming image I was putting a good deal of energy into cultivating. Not that the hard-headed in general would have condemned this legacy from a scruffy childhood which prompted me to showing off. I was to observe later in life that the pecking-order established in the Oxford nursery remained a durable strand in what journalists were going to call the Old-Boy Network. Men were to become (as Tony became) Cabinet Ministers because somebody recalled them as dominant in their nonage: brilliant in dining clubs or debating societies, famous for senseless agitations and amusing outrages and wild weekends in indulgent great houses. This isn't an observation that I record in order to deplore. On the whole it is qualities like Tony's that public life, and no doubt the upper regions of industry and commerce, appear to require. And septuagenarians remain prominent in the arts as the result of having been quick off the mark when exhibitionists newly liberated from school.

But these were not my reflections now. What puzzled and almost offended me about Fish was his resilience. It seemed no time ago that I had witnessed his being carted off in a van—blind as a bat, and a hysterical bat at that. Now here he was, sauntering down Linton Road, composed, radiant with health, and very obviously capable of keeping his eye on the ball; relaxed, unassuming, and with quiet manners which left me standing at the post; the heir of at least as many ages as the antipodes run to. I told myself his riddle wasn't all that hard to read. Like Conrad's Kurtz (I was mad on Conrad that term) Fish had simply had bad luck; a bit too much on his plate; a ducking which had been both a trauma laid up for him mysteriously at birth and a humiliation contrived by that awful girl when his will had been concentrated on refusing to see her as awful in the least. All that: I had been over it before. But it seemed to have been the very depth of his vulnerability, it seemed to be the extreme oddness of being prone to transmute distress of mind into an equivalent gross disorder of the senses, that had enabled Fish to bob up again a good deal more rapidly than expectation would have allowed. Nature is never generous, but very occasionally she is just. Fish must live in the uncomfortable consciousness that strange things could happen to him again at any time. But in compensation there appeared to be this uncanny recuperative virtue built into his disability. That bizarre turn had owned a cathartic operation.

'Duncan, about this girl you won't stop talking about——'

'What on earth do you mean?' The enigma of Fish vanished from my mind; I stared at him in bewilderment.

'Well, ever since you met her on Thursday. I don't want to shove in. But are you sure she's all right?'

'Of course Penny's all right, you ass. She's beautiful and in every way marvellous. You'll like her quite a lot, Martin. But it's nonsense that I've been jabbering about her.'

'Jabbering wasn't what I said.' Fish swung his own racket lazily, but with a final flick of the wrist confirming my view he'd be pretty good. 'Did you rather invite us?'

'To tea? Well, yes—I did. I think Mrs Triplett quite took to the idea. She probably felt Penny might be finding North Oxford a bit dull.'

'Would you say she much dislikes being a bit dull?'

'Of course she does. Anybody does—or does at our age. I can't imagine what you're getting at, Martin.'

'Oh, nothing—not really. I just hope she's your sort. She sounds a kind of London girl to me.'

'Why shouldn't she be a London girl, for Christ's sake? Do you want all your girls to come from Sydney or Dimboola or Dismal Swamp? I think this is a stupid conversation.'

'Yes, it is.' Fish's agreement was cheerful and immediate. 'Anyway, I suppose there will be lots of other people there.'

'Sure to be. There always have been before. Brown girls, if you prefer it that way.'

But my prediction proved wrong—and of course I might have reflected that one doesn't hold tennis parties for mobs of people. There were no brown girls at all. There were only Mrs Triplett and Penny, and a muscular girl who was decidedly pinko-grey, and a man who was clearly of the tiresome Buntingford species of very young don, and a young woman attached to this young man and probably his wife. I judged the disposition of things, although unexpected, propitious on the whole—although to just what it was propitious I wasn't very clear in my head. Then, only a couple of minutes after our arrival, a car drove up and the Provost and Mrs Pococke emerged from it. They were dressed for tennis like ourselves, and this for some reason startled me. Fish took it entirely in his stride. He hadn't, as I had, disconcerting recollections of events on a golf course.

Nothing could be more tedious than a blow-by-blow account of a tennis party, and I am glad to think that the athletic side of this one scarcely needs reporting. Whether surprisingly or not, the Provost (whom I thought of as an elderly man) proved the best player, with Fish not far behind him. My own tennis has to be described as stylish and ineffective: ineffective because I am by nature not much good at games, and stylish because through successive summers at Corry Hall Aunt Charlotte's sense of family responsibility had obliged her to the effort of making something of my appearance on a court. I don't doubt that an expert would have judged me pitiful and pretentious, but in a friendly company I got by. Through one set Mrs Pococke made me an admirable partner. I imagine that, comparatively early in her occupancy of the Lodging, she was finding that in undergraduates there is a great deal to be amused at, and that she cultivated this sense because she didn't want too much to cultivate a similar sense about her husband. Of the form displayed by the muscular girl, or by the deutero-Buntingford and his wife, I remember nothing. As for Penny (who had so rapidly inquired about my interest in tennis), she was either hopeless or very much off her game. At one point, when Fish and I were both sitting out (if that is a correct expression), my friend confided to me—and with an obscure meaningfulness I didn't take to—his sense that there had been a row.

It was true that Mrs Triplett appeared better pleased with Fish and myself than with her young visitor; at the same time, she was unobtrusively concerned to recommend us both to Penny's good graces. I was quite without the social experience to glimpse in this the dowager's eye for the uses of totally ineligible and also in other regards harmless young men, and I simply felt it was amiable in her thus to preside over an advancing relationship.

'What do you mean, a row?' I asked.

'Oh, nothing much, I'm sure.' Fish had an instinct for moderate statement. 'It just strikes me that your girl-friend——'

'Don't be so idiotic, Martin. How can she be my girl-friend? I never set eyes on her before Thursday.'

'Yes, I know—but she *is* quite something to set eyes on. I give you that. Penny's rather pretty.' Fish glanced round circumspectly, and satisfied himself that we were quite isolated for the moment. 'I just feel she's browned off about something, and has been letting the old lady know it.'

'Why should she be browned off? I think you're browned off yourself. You're taking a jaundiced view of things.'

'Then I'd be yellowed, not browned. It was your own idea that the girl might be finding life a bit dull. Well, I'm not certain she feels that you and I import an absolutely transforming liveliness into the situation. Perhaps it's not an uncertainty that would occur to your robust Caledonian mind.'

'Joke,' I said, sarcastically. In fact this mild thrust by Fish rather pleased me. 'And you're talking nonsense, anyhow. Penny's being very nice to both of us. In fact she's on the job at this moment.' I added this because Penny was advancing on us across the lawn, carrying three soft drinks on a tray.

'She's the perfect little hostess, of course. She's nothing if not nicely brought up.'

These words were unremarkable in themselves, but the tone in which Fish uttered them disconcerted me. For I seemed suddenly to realize—and with a disturbing mixture of feelings —that my benevolent plan for Fish hadn't a chance of success. He had decided not to like Penny Triplett one little bit. I thought it extremely perverse of him, and I even vaguely understood that it summoned me to honesty about myself. What I didn't yet understand was the extreme crudity of my own thinking, which had its origin in that fatuous conversation in Colin Badgery's rooms. We had talked about handing Tindale's typewriter to Fish, and heaven knew what else. Whereas, of course, Fish's only sane and healthy reaction after his crash with Martine would be into a phase—if perhaps only a brief phase—of uncompromising misogyny. A man bruised as he had been might conceivably hurl himself upon hard liquor and harlots, but not upon anything that could be called falling in love.

'You both looked to be rather puffing and panting,' Penny said in a tone of friendly mockery. 'Dr Pococke's a bit out of our class, isn't he? A Wimbledon man in his time, it seems. So I thought I'd bring over these.'

'That's awfully kind of you.' Fish had got to his feet with less of a scramble than I contrived, and was pulling forward a chair in a manner more suggestive of Kensington (as we used then to express it) than of Dimboola or Dismal Swamp. 'Do you like being in Oxford, Miss Triplett?'

It is difficult to be confident about shades of usage over a long period of time, but I believe that, even at that date and upon so short an acquaintance, Fish's 'Miss Triplett' was inadmissably on the formal side. Until he could manage 'Penny' he ought to have got along on nothing at all. And between 'being in Oxford' and 'Oxford' there was certainly a shade of difference; the exiled Ovid might have been asked if he liked being in Tomis. Fish had got the hang of Penny's sojourn with Mrs Triplett much more clearly than I had; he had somehow collected it out of the air. Nothing of this occurred to me at the time. That Fish possessed a nice verbal sense would have appeared to me a proposition altogether implausible. It was self-evident that as a mathematician and a colonial he was doubly debarred from anything of the kind. Weeks were to pass before I discovered that he was usually worth listening to rather closely.

'Oh, I absolutely adore it,' Penny said. Her tone combined artless spontaneity with an absence of anything that could be called gush. But she looked only briefly at Fish, and then her glance strayed away beyond the tennis court and a stretch of garden to the drive. It was a long drive, and disappeared upon a gentle curve towards Linton Road. Except for that glimpse from Timbermill's attic window, Mrs Triplett's dwelling enjoyed complete seclusion; its air was more that of a large country house than I had encountered south of the border so far. The drive was empty. I thought it improbable that any more guests were expected. For tennis our numbers were just right as they stood, and it was for that number that tea-things had been set out on the terrace before the house. 'I think you're tremendously lucky to be at Oxford,' Penny went on, returning her attention to Fish. 'How did you come to hear of it?'

'By what we call bush telegraph,' Fish said easily. He was smiling as if Penny had simply said something amusing, but at the same time I thought he flushed slightly. I myself had to admit the cogency of the view that Penny was not in too good a mood. But Fish, I told myself, if he hadn't been exactly hostile first, had certainly been lacking in any token of the admiration a girl like Penny had a right to expect. Moreover my heart was suddenly pounding, and I knew why. Penny had shifted fractionally on her deck-chair, fractionally towards me and away from Fish, and as she did so had given me the look I remembered at our parting after Mrs Pococke's dinner party. It wasn't a look that could be called vulgarly meaningful; it was simply that it seemed modestly to acknowledge to itself that it had lasted fractionally longer than it should. Penny followed this up (although I wouldn't have expressed the thing at all in that way) by a certain amount of conventional small-talk offered impartially to each of us, and I was thus able to decide that she was being very nice to Fish after all. Her nature was clearly such that she couldn't for more than a moment be anything other than that to anyone. Fish's response was unenthusiastic but decently responsive. I had an obscure sense that he was thinking something out, and not burning his boats meanwhile. This was to explain itself rather notably before the day ended.

A tiny sound, like the papery tap of withered leaves against a bough, came from the far side of the tennis court. Mrs

Triplett was applauding the conclusion of a set. It looked as if the time for tea might have come, but this proved not to be so. Penny, who had undertaken the organizing of the athletic side of things on Mrs Triplett's behalf, collected our glasses and stood up.

'Time, gentlemen, please,' Penny said. And she handed me the tray and smoothed down her skirt.

It was in this moment, I believe, that I had my first significant experience not of wandering concupiscence but of the incomparably fiercer drive of a specific and exclusive physical desire. I had glimpsed the operation of the dark power in my brother Ninian and lately in Fish—and sufficiently clearly to judge it (as I still do) the most senseless of Nature's whims. For what can it matter to Nature that Martin should or should not possess Martine, or that I should marry Penny Triplett and not some almost identical girl encountered only with a complete unregardingness elsewhere? Is sex, is procreation, so frightening or disagreeable an activity, so sluggish a machine, that this tremendous battery is required to start it into life? I was one day to observe a generation which believed itself to have tamed the thing, seeing in it (as *Isis* was to explain) a companionable and civilized indoor exercise. But it was a generation in no danger of going further on this reductive path, and giving over, turning celibate or even sterile. The human species would get along, would interbreed with a genetically desirable variousness, at the pressing of some button much less liable to release distraction and catastrophe. So why these fireworks, why such brouhaha? It is apparent that this particular liability we carry has no special power of building into sexual conjunctions that sort of stability and permanence biologically useful in a race so slow to reach maturition and independence as ours. Contrariwise, if anything. Hard-wearing marriages emerge, on the whole, from a different context. The whole set-up is a puzzle, perhaps explicable only as occasioning laughter among unfriendly gods.

'My turn again!' Penny said with an assumption of dismay.

'And I made such a fool of myself partnered with you, Mr Fish. Duncan, your turn too.'

These two names, this ruthless and malicious distinction, finally pitched me into the condition of Penny Triplett's lover.

It was not Penny's way to hold a stance for long. Half-way through tea—and with a precision recalling her turn from left to right when Mrs Pococke executed the same manœuvre at dinner—Fish was on and I was off. I wasn't staggered by this in itself. Stuffed with literary persuasions far more than with cucumber sandwiches and cream-cakes, I summoned up thoughts of the duel of sex and of *femina* as in general *varium et mutabile semper*. It seemed something merely adorable in Penny that she should turn on this immemorial courtship convention. And I certainly didn't at all remember the late Martine's cruder exhibition of approximately the same technique.

What did hit me hard and to a point of bewilderment was Fish's reaction. To Penny's first hints of interest of a new order Fish was so unresponsive as to be almost rude; he might have been telling her that she wasn't his sort of girl and might as well lay off. But for the second time I had that curious sense of him as thinking something out. Then, all at once, I was seeing him rise from this austere entrenchment and go right over the top. He had become another man, and a remarkably attractive one for the business on hand. Penny, losing her poise, became slightly outrageous herself.

The rest of the company can't have seen anything particularly out of the way in this sudden sharp engagement. Tennis parties are sometimes virtually designed, after all, for the purpose of promoting harmless flirtation. The Provost may have betrayed a sense that well conducted young people ought not to get all that quickly off the mark; although unexpectedly brisk at the net, he favoured a *largo* effect in social intercourse at large. Mrs Triplett, on the other hand, appeared not disapproving; she might have been feeling that two admirers for Penny were better than one—and that four or six would be better still. My own confusion was extreme. Here—out of the blue and at an eleventh hour—my original design was unexpectedly fulfilling itself, and Fish was giving every appearance of falling head over heels in love with a girl he hadn't set eyes on a couple of hours before. I felt this to be utterly indecent, and moreover a monstrous perfidy on Fish's part. My totally illogical jealousy was now naked and unashamed. It seemed to me incredible that I had been entertaining the thought of spending a large part of the coming vacation in the company of a man who could undertake with such celerity a traitor's part.

This was the state of affairs at Mrs Triplett's little party when the blast of a powerful motor-horn made itself heard on her drive. Everybody was startled—but Penny, I thought, turned a little pale as well. I told myself (for my perceptions were as acute as my thoughts were muddled) that this particular cacophony was familiar to her. Then the car appeared, travelling much too fast. It was an open Bentley of gigantic size and of what was probably a choice vintage antiquity. The figure at the wheel wore goggles and gauntlets, and with one of the gauntlets he offered us a familiar wave before addressing himself to the business of bringing his monster to a halt. He achieved this with notable skill, although with a rapid braking which didn't leave quite unscathed the well-raked gravel on Mrs Triplett's drive. His bonnet, however, was neatly beneath Mrs Triplett's nose. He whipped off his goggles and smiled up at us: a handsome young man, fresh-complexioned and with a little military moustache. I seemed to know at once that some sort of fashionable soldiering was his line.

'Fifty-seven minutes from Buckingham Gate,' he called out to us with satisfaction. 'And the devil of a snarl-up in Henley.' He swung himself out of the car. 'Hullo, Mrs Triplett. Hullo, Penny. Just in time for tea.'

If Penny had indeed paled a little at the sound or signal from that horn, the fact was evident no longer. She was flushed now. It was my first impression that she was angry—but, if so, it was anger of an ambiguous sort. There was nothing ambiguous, however, about Mrs Triplett, who was distinguishably far from accepting as appropriate her new visitor's confident address. She had stood up to receive him—and this, paradoxically, had the effect of almost not receiving him at all, particularly as her stance was that of a small but serviceable ramrod. Since her action had, moreover, the effect of bringing the assembled males to their feet as well, the notion of a favoured youth to be familiarly greeted went west in a moment. She performed introductions, however, without a pause—and while they went on I suppose I eyed the young man (whose name was Symington) very hard indeed. My immediate impression was of utter unfamiliarity. Edinburgh didn't produce such a type, nor Glencorry, nor Oxford—although in my own college, perhaps, he might have been thought of as having first cousins a shade more intellectually endowed. What I was exhibiting could, I suppose, have been described as territorial behaviour. I was as stiff with hostility as Mrs Triplett was, but for different reasons. I judged wholly intrusive upon what was now my familiar academic stamping ground the irruption of this cub from the Blues or the Household Division or whatever it was called.

I am certain that the feeling was entire in me before I caught a glimpse of either of two small definitive things that then happened. The first was Mrs Triplett's elderly but alert parlourmaid advancing along the terrace with a fresh cup and saucer. When still some yards away she stopped, hesitated, turned and withdrew. The message she had received from her mistress was conceivably telepathic; more probably, Mrs Triplett had achieved some minute signal with her head. This was the minor phenomenon, and I think Fish also remarked it: certainly it was thus I interpreted a quick glance he gave me as he stood waiting to sit down again. The major phenomenon was itself a matter of a glance—one I caught passing with swift stealth between Symington and Penny. I don't find it easy to describe. In the circumstances, one might have expected it to

be, on Symington's part, no more than a comical acknowledgement that in old Mrs Triplett he had caught a Tartar, had
bitten off more than he could chew. And Penny, correspond-
ingly, might have been indicating either mischievousness and
admiration or a displeased sense that he had been unacceptably
indiscreet. But their exchange was, in fact, not at all like that;
had it been, it would not have affected me as it did. What
passed between Penny and this intrusive young man in that
moment of time declared a mutual consciousness of intrigue,
of complicity, of high excitement that chilled my blood and
numbed my mind by its remoteness from anything I had ever
experienced or imagined.

This sounds extravagant, but at least I am recounting something which, however absurd must seem an infatuation not
four days old, spoke loudly to me of disaster and despair. I
have to be a little more specific here. I didn't in that moment
believe—what an after-day was to confirm to me it would have
been erroneous to believe—that Penny and this young man
were lovers. It may well have been his intention that they
should be, but he hadn't got there yet. Penny had been breaking
all the rules that then still largely governed the behaviour of
young women and their escorts, and had been getting a great
deal of change out of it. It seemed probable that, with a sound
instinct for safety, she had started off doing this with any
number of young men at once. But now she had nothing except
this chap Symington in her head. She had been packed off
to an aged relative in Oxford to cool down, and now in
Oxford her pursuer had impudently turned up. As for either
Fish or myself—and here lay the nub of the matter—we had
existed for Penny only as so much material to file her claws
on.

This larger contour of the affair was lucid to me at once,
although it wasn't entirely to remain so. And I can have spent
very little time thinking it out, since we were still on our feet,
and with the tea ritual suspended, when I heard Mrs Triplett
addressing her unwelcome guest in unemotional tones.

'But you must see that immediately, Mr Symington. Come with me now. Penny, please look after things.'

In this fashion was the martial Symington led away. What 'that' was, I have no idea. Perhaps it was a new milking-parlour. Certainly Mrs Triplett must have made it a topic of conversation with remarkable speed, thus expeditiously to remove Penny's follower from our society. I didn't feel he would return, and I don't think Penny did either. Her kins-woman had received from her a swift, hard glare which might well have heralded rebellion. But in a moment Penny was 'looking after things' as required. She handed me a cherry cake to take round; was attentive to empty cups; in her temporary role as hostess talked to the Provost first, as the person of principal consideration present. As a result of this, and even in the midst of my state of relegation and dismay, my feeling for Penny took on a fresh dimension, a new attribute. In addition to fascination, carnal commotion, love or infatu-ation, admiration marched in. I admired her self-control, her precocious command—as assured as her formidable chaperone's was—of the social aspect of a dodgy situation. This was to prove the longest-lasting of my positive responses to Penny Triplett.

With the exception of Fish and the Provost (a man who regularly noticed small things to an extent surprising in one who noticed himself so much), I doubt whether anybody was immediately aware of an interesting manœuvre as having taken place. The exploring couple didn't remain invisible all that long, and meanwhile conversation flowed sedately forward. When they did appear again it was from an unexpected direction, walking across a stretch of lawn on the far side of Symington's car. Mrs Triplett was conversing, although sparingly; what was chiefly evident in Symington was a dis-position to look rather fixedly ahead of him. They reached the car, and Symington climbed in. The engine started into life with a deep purr, Symington made Mrs Triplett a kind of bow, clashed his gears (something which, in a Bentley, is presumably not easy to achieve), and shot off round the building. What house agents call an imposing sweep made this a feasible escape route to adopt. The sound of the engine faded, and was briefly succeeded by an angry hoot signalling the car's turning into Linton Road. Mrs Triplett paused briefly—not to compose herself but to pick up an untidy twig from the drive. Then she climbed to the terrace and retrieved her tea-cup.

'Mr Symington,' she said, clearly but without emphasis, 'was unable to stay longer.'

It was the Provost who produced a murmur of civil regret. Penny got to her feet and offered the old lady the cake.

Fish and I were driven back to college in the Pocockes' car. The Pocockes made a few suitable remarks about the pleasures of the afternoon. Fish found his own points of gratification to express. Although all I wanted to do was to weep like a child I believe I managed something of the same sort, but when we got out in front of the Lodging I just managed my 'Thank you very much, sir' before walking away. Surrey was deserted and sleepy. Even Provost Harbage on his pedestal, although he normally managed a hard, stony glare as one went by, seemed drowsy and inattentive. At the foot of the staircase the White Rabbit, dodging out of his rooms with a batch of letters, gave me a curious glance, so I supposed I was looking, as well as feeling, not too good.

It must have been after eleven that night when there was a knock on my door and Fish entered.

'Too late to barge in?' he asked.

'No.'

'It's just that it has occurred to me we ought to be fixing things up.'

'I suppose so.'

'Booking the car across, and so on. The Continent's all the go, and there may be a bit of a crush.'

'Yes.'

'It's my idea we ought to be off bang at the end of term.

Unless you're thinking of going to any Commem Balls or things in the ninth week.'

'I'm not. Bugger Commem Balls.'

'That's better—a bit.' Fish sat down—uninvited and decently diffident. 'I don't want to be a nuisance,' he said. 'But, Duncan, are you all right?'

'What do you mean?' I stared angrily at Fish. 'And why the hell did you do that?'

'Do what, Duncan?'

'You bloody well know. Of course it's utterly irrelevant and pointless now. Penny's interested in nothing but that awful little shit——'

'I don't know that I'd call him that. I didn't like him very much. But he may be a decent enough type really.'

'Well, it's not the point, anyway.' This speech had made me furious. 'Why did you suddenly start being all over Penny? You didn't seem to like her in the least. I don't believe you do now. Why did you get playing up to her like that?'

'Didn't you want me to?'

The question bemused me—reminding me of an imbecile proposal cherished in what appeared an infinitely remote past, and telling me, moreover, that Fish must after all have tumbled to some sense of its existence.

'It doesn't matter what I wanted,' I said stupidly.

'I just thought a spot of diversion might be a useful thing. So that you could see the girl's volatile, to say the least. I hope that Symington punched the point home.'

'I don't want your damned hopes—or your damned nannying around either. Frig off, Martin.'

'Duncan, are you really going to be all right? You won't mind my saying I'm a bit worried about you? I'm glad we're getting off to Italy together. A change of scene will do you good.'

Fish's explanation of his abrupt and brief playing ball with Penny had amazed me—but only, as it were, dimly, since I was in a state capable of grasping singularly little. For example, the fact that he and I had switched roles with the precision of artificial comedy didn't at this point occur to me. I did remember, although again dimly, that there had been a scene or scenes like this between us before, and that they had decidedly not been accompanied by Fish's swearing at me. As this memory swam up in my mind I seized upon it as explaining something altogether more novel to me than it ought to have been: the sense of myself as a sinful creature. I didn't like the feeling at all, and in particular I didn't like an intuitive knowledge that it was going to grow.

'Martin,' I mumbled, 'I'm fearfully sorry. I didn't mean to be rude. I'm being a fearful nuisance to you.'

'That's rubbish.' Fish was looking at me in real alarm. He was no doubt recognizing a symptom. 'I say, Duncan—have you any of that stuff left that your doctor gave you? If so, I'd have a go at it, if I were you.'

'Oh, all right. It's in that cupboard beside you.'

'And Duncan—do you know? I think if you don't mind I'll just hang around till you're in bed.'

Despite the sodium amytal (which it was pretty feeble to have agreed to swallow: Fish hadn't), I woke up in the small hours. My mind groped to discover anything it could be said to be thinking of. For minutes or through aeons nothing came. Then, instead of anything of a conceptual order, there floated into my consciousness an image of Janet's picture-postcard, with its cross over Calum's boat. That cleared me, I told myself. Janet had Calum and I didn't have Penny, so I had even less reason to feel guilt than she had.

Nevertheless, and in addition to being harmlessly miserable, I was to experience this guilt-feeling, intermittently and like a toothache, for quite a long time: in the following weeks Fish was to have to cope with it as he could. This first night of my dejection, however, was to end in a stranger echo of Fish's own late condition. As I lay in what was still a pitch-black room there suddenly came upon me the impression of a crisis, a moment of truth, directly ahead. Still mildly drugged, I puzzled over it, and eventually knew what I had to do. I closed my eyes very tight, buried my head under the bed-clothes, and groped for the switch of my bedside lamp. I found it and turned it. After that I think I prayed. Then I stuck my head out and commanded my eyelids to open. They obeyed. The bed-room was bathed in a flood of light.

I turned the switch again and went to sleep.

Humdrum resumed its sway. I was wretched, but these odd experiences had been contracted, after all, within a short span of days. I was young, and they hadn't engraved themselves. I remembered to write a note to Mrs Pococke, thanking her for her dinner party. I managed to do the same thing by Mrs Triplett, whom I suspected of knowing as much as Fish did. My work for Talbert went to pieces, but he didn't notice. For Timbermill, because I loved him, I performed heroically; he said that on *The Seafarer* and *The Dream of the Rood* he hadn't read anything less inconsiderable than my essays for quite some time. (I had to work out these reduplicated negatives.) I pored over maps with Fish, bought guidebooks, operated on a bank balance a good deal healthier than its owner. I had very black spells indeed. But I listened to the vacation plans of my companions, which were all full of enterprise and hope. Bedworth had gained a ticket for the Reading Room of the British Museum, and felt that his learned career was assured. Tony was bound for Washington; he had a cousin in the Embassy, so everything was going to be laid on. Kettle was to absorb himself in an ambitious project for the moral regener-ation of the nation through multi-confessional coffee parties. Mogridge proposed hastening to Paris. He had heard of a marvellous 'cellist, quite young, called Paul Tortellier, who was with the *Société des Concerts du Conservatoire*, and who had already been launched (Mogridge earnestly explained) on a solo career in Amsterdam.

And thus my first Oxford Summer Term came to an end like a day.

# XIV

At Ravello, as in Surrey Quad, Fish and I had our staircase. This one was cut in rock, and pursued a devious course from the plateau on which the little town perches to the Gulf of Salerno a thousand feet below. There were places at which you could turn left for Minori or right for Atrani and Amalfi. The principal wayfarers on this Dantesque *scala* were mules. They perambulated the whole surrounding countryside in the same fashion, such staircases being the main feature of the region. It was only when they came to level ground that the brutes found it necessary to give their minds to the job, and pick their steps on the less familiar terrain with care.

As far as one could look along the sharply indented coast the land tumbled steeply through stony but wooded or terraced slopes to final cliff-like bastions too sheer for anything to cling to. It was only where these natural fortifications broke down in some deep ravine that human habitation was possible at anything like sea-level, and the little concentrated clusters of dwellings, humble and ancient, white-washed and roofed in rusty red, showed in them like the compacted nesting-places of neighbourly-minded birds. Fish had bought a number of postcards portraying these picturesque localities. One of them was described as *Angolo suggestivo*, *Suggestiv Ort* and (for our own instruction) *Fascinating noow*. We extracted a number of indecent meanings from these harmless expressions, and Fish suggested that I should send the card to Janet, marking the position of our hotel with a cross.

It will thus be seen that Fish was by now a good deal in my confidence. He was much more in my confidence than I was in his. Although in general the frankest of companions, he had never once opened up again about the Martine affair. I respected this reticence as indicating that, as between the two of us, his had been the deeper wound. It wasn't quite evident why this should be so. I hadn't, it was true, been ditched amid circumstances impugning my physical courage, and I hadn't been carried off, more or less *coram populo*, to what had been bruited abroad as the bin. On the other hand, Fish hadn't, so far as I knew, been implicated in what I saw in myself as a shameful infidelity, deserting the girl next door (which is what Fish firmly called Janet) almost at the very first glimpse of Penny Triplett.

In general it may be said of Fish and myself that, if we came during this holiday to understand each other very well, it wasn't in the main on any basis of talking things out. We'd had experiences that overlapped. They didn't overlap very much —but they did so sufficiently for the generating of a mute communion. Nothing in my relationship with Janet (which might be viable still, or might not) could have told me anything about Fish's experience. But my brief brainstorm over Penny gave me a genuine understanding of it. Penny and Martine had little more in common than the appearance (delusive, it might conceivably be) of belonging wholly to our respective shattered pasts, but they had left us with a similar revelation of how disruptive sexual excitement can be. We had now retreated—for the earlier part of this long vacation—upon the dumb decent comfort of a reliable asexual relationship. There was a kind of luxury in this which could almost be felt as a sexual thing in itself.

Thus conscious of each other's burdens as we conceived them, we had taken them very seriously at the start of our trip —each warily solicitous for the other, much as if we had been a couple of precocious and mutually considerate valetudinarians travelling for our health. If Fish was less communicative about himself than I was, he was also much more conscious of the social duty of decent cheerfulness. I doubt whether I gave him much credit for this, attributing it to that peculiarity of his constitution which had enabled him to regain composure so notably soon after his disaster. But he was responsible for the fact that I put in progressively less time being low-spirited as our wanderings continued.

They were wanderings conditioned by an unsophisticated notion of the proper way to 'do' Italy, which we supposed to consist in moving rapidly from one large city—always understood to be an 'art' city—to another. The main occurrences in some of these places were not always of a kind foreshadowed in Blue Guides and Baedekers. In Milan, for example, we acted properly by the Cathedral and the Brera, but the really notable happening—notable because of its consequences—was Fish's contriving to buy a copy of *Lady Chatterley's Lover*. It was the first and limited edition of the novel published in Florence in 1928. If Fish's attitude to his find was not that of a bibliophil neither could it have been called in any degree lubricious. He quickly convinced himself that it was an uproariously funny book, and was soon insisting on reading selected passages to me every night before we went to sleep. The appeal of the performance lay, I think, in the support it lent to a role naturally congenial to us at the time: that of experienced and disillusioned young men inclined to a ludicrous and harshly reductive view of sex. This was no doubt perverse and wrongheaded in us, since Lawrence's intentions had clearly been of a high-minded sort not inclining that way. But if Lawrence hadn't been in our heads we wouldn't, in Naples, have made the decision we did.

Naples was just one art city too many: a vast crowded noisy place, set in a tremendous natural theatre by man made variously vile. We sat in a pavement café and surveyed the spectacle discontentedly.

'What does one see here, anyway?' I demanded.

'There's an aquarium.'

'Don't be silly.'

'It's a very celebrated aquarium. The book says it's in the middle of the Zoological Centre for research into the habits of marine fauna and flora. And it's got a star.'

'Are you kidding? Come again.'

'The real thing is the National Museum. It's housed in a vast palace.'

'I'll bet it is.' I stared darkly at my black coffee. I was being difficult.

'It has mosaics and paintings from Pompeii, including the dirty ones.'

'What do you mean—the dirty ones?'

'They're from a brothel. It doesn't say that in this book. It just says, "Certain Rooms: small gratuity".'

'Stupid.'

'Mellors might have been interested. Or even poor Connie herself.' Fish plainly judged my lack of interest in erotic paintings unwholesome rather than virtuous.

'It might give Tony a tip,' I said, thawing a little. 'He could charge a bob for a dekko at that vulgar affair over his mantelpiece. How dirty are these things?'

'Dirt's in one's own eye, I suppose. I think the technical name for them is the postures.'

'How boring. It can't even be called multiplying variety in a wilderness of mirrors.'

'What do you mean—multiplying variety in a wilderness of mirrors?'

'It's something in a poem.' I looked gloomily at Fish, while Naples roared and screeched around us. It was a pandemonium of a place. 'No,' I said, suddenly seeing what I took to be a serious topic before us. 'Painting obscene pictures is obscene.'

'What about inside your own head, Duncan? Doesn't it go on there sometimes? It does with me.'

'Yes, of course. My imaginations are as foul as Vulcan's stithy.'

'I wouldn't say quite that.'

'Well, no. One mustn't dramatize oneself.' I said this in a judicious tone. 'Inventive, though—and even a bit sadistic at times. But the point is that it's one's own affair. But painting an obscene picture is a squalid and demeaning thing to do.'

'What about blue movies?'

'I've never seen a blue movie. One just hasn't come my way.'

'But you'd be quite willing to pay your bob for that?'

'Oh, yes. A good blue movie would be quite different. Only, it would probably be a lot more than a bob, so the simple question of value for money would arise. For me, I mean. It wouldn't be operative with you, Martin. You're rolling.' It was because I saw myself in a weak argumentative position that I introduced this blatant irrelevance. It didn't, however, side-track the discussion. We followed up our coffees with carafes of what we supposed to be Chianti, and went on talking for an hour. As was inevitable, the subject of our recent bed-time studies turned up.

'What about books?' Fish demanded. 'What about all that fucking in *Lady Chatterley*? Was it squalid and demeaning to write that?'

'No, of course not.'

'But isn't it obscene?'

'No.'

'Isn't it indecent?'

'No.'

'Not even when Mellors treats her as a boy?'

'I don't know that he does.' I took this evasive action swiftly. 'I thought the bit you read was rather ambiguous or equivocal. You have to remember that Lawrence came from a simple class of society. They're very straightforward in their fucking, the English proletariat. Anything not of the most jejune and frontal order would seem tremendously dark and perverse to them.' I paused with considerable pride on this piece of sociological nonsense. 'That's all that Connie had to contend with.'

We continued with Connie to our considerable satisfaction for some time—I suppose with a healthy impulse to command a subject the real mysteries of which had lately had both of us badly at sea. But we were still two undergraduates at a loose end in Naples, commanding hardly a score of Italian words between us, and each of us as a consequence the other's sole resource. We did, from time to time, edge towards irritation. But Fish was good at sensing this and heading it off.

'These galleries and things,' he said suddenly. 'We've about had them for a bit.'

'You're telling me.'

'I vote we garage the car and go over to Capri.'

'Frightfully vulgar.'

'There's something called the Blue Grotto. It's best from 11 to 2.' Fish was consulting his guidebook again. 'The sun rays entering through the water fill the cave with a magical blue light.'

'They ought to have blue movies there. But what utter blue balls.'

'Well then, there's Ischia. It's larger, Duncan, and would perhaps answer your notions of refinement better. It has radio-active mineral waters and an important thermal bathing establishment.'

'Full of poxy old men making eyes at you. Quit being so ludicrous, Martin.'

'Making eyes at *you*, not *me*,' Fish said mildly, and took a glance at me, scowling at the empty carafe. 'You see that travel agency across the square?' he said. 'I think I'll go over and cash a cheque there. What about you?'

'No, I shan't do that again until we do our right-about turn. I think that ought to be at Paestum. We should go down the coast as far as that, and make it our terminus. There's terrific straight Greek stuff. Enormous temples. My father has told me.'

'We could do my vulgar Capri first, and your austere Paestum afterwards.'

'Oh, shut up, Martin. Stuff it, for Christ's sake. It's calling things vulgar that's dead vulgar.'

'I shan't be ten minutes.' Fish had got to his feet, and now chucked a packet of cigarettes in front of me as one might chuck a bun at a bear in the zoo. He was always extremely deft

302

with his affectionate gestures. 'Dear Old Sunshine Dunkie,' he said mockingly, and plunged into the traffic.

I smoked a cigarette distastedly, and wished in a glum manner that I was as nice a person as Fish. Then I brooded on other matters—and in so deep an abstraction that Fish had to shout at me when he came back to our table.

'Duncan,' he said, 'an extraordinary thing! He's turned up on us.'

'Who has turned up on us?' I had visions of some bizarre and calamitous Oxford collision: the appearance of Stumpe, or of Killiecrankie, or of the Provost.

'Lawrence.'

'Lawrence died in 1930, you imbecile.'

'Lawrence—and Connie as well. It's incredible. Look!'

This time, what Fish tossed in front of me was a brightly-coloured hotel leaflet. I stared at it incomprehendingly.

'Come again,' I said. I was going through a bad spell, at that time, of what were supposed to be up to date colloquial expressions.

'It's about a pub at a place called Ravello. Have you ever heard of it?'

'Max Beerbohm lives there.'

'That's Rapallo.' Just occasionally, and when genuinely excited, Fish would betray familiarity with matters supposed to be exclusively my province. 'Ravello's about 65 kilometres south of us, near Amalfi.'

'Oh, Amalfi.' The name rang some faint bell with me.

'This blurb-thing says that Lawrence stayed there while cooking up *Lady Chatterley's Lover*. The pub inspired him to it, the Italian says. It's rather uncanny.'

'What awful nonsense! How could an albergo, or whatever it is, in Campania inspire a chap to write about a Priapic game-keeper and a sterile upper-class hide-out in some God-forsaken stretch of industrial England?'

'Well, that's what it says. And there's a poem by him, too.'

'A poem by Lawrence?'

'Yes. Listen.' Laboriously, Fish plunged into the Italian tongue. '*Pensiero di D. H. Lawrence, poeta e romanziere inglese, ospite dell'Albergo nel 1926.* What would you say a *pensiero* was, Duncan?'

'A beautiful and musing thought.'

'You're dead right.'

'Is it in English?'

'Yes.'

'Then read it, Martin. You read verse beautifully. At least, I expect you do. So far, you've only entertained me with the other harmony of prose. John Dryden.'

'No. You've got to read it yourself.' Fish handed me the leaflet. 'Because of how it's printed.'

I took the thing and read:

> «*Lost to a world in which—I—grave no part*
> *I sit alone and commune whith my heart*
> *Pleased whith my little corner of the earth*
> *Glad that I came not sorry to depart.*»

'It's a *pensiero*, all right,' I said cautiously.

'A *pensiero di D. H. Lawrence, poeta e romanziere inglese*?'

'He might have written it in a hotel register or something —or in the manager's wife's birthday-book. Rather with his tongue in his cheek.'

'It's not exactly the familiar voice of D.H.L.?'

'No.' I felt rather like a candidate who suspects some low-down trick on the part of his examiners. 'I suppose one could find out if he was really in this Ravello place in 1926.'

'In fact, we'd better start researching into the problem now? It might be more amusing than either Capri or Paestum. And an addition to knowledge, Duncan. Your first contribution to *The Review of English Studies*. Just your niche, that organ of criticism and research. I've seen it in the college library.'

'We'll set off straight away, Martin.' I played up to this at once. 'There's not a moment to lose. Harvard and Princeton may already be on the trail. Are you more or less sober?'

'Of course I'm sober.'

'Then you can drive like mad.'

It was thus, in a spirit of pure foolery, that we set off for Ravello, of which neither of us had ever heard. Fish, by his remarkable feat of serendipity in the travel agency, had rescued us from childish bickering over our plans. He celebrated this success by driving rather fast along a route cut hair-raisingly *en corniche* across tremendous cliffs, and offering the further hazard of stretches once vigorously bombed and as yet only tentatively shored up. I made the curious observation that Fish's fear of death by water was inoperative as long as the destructive element lay hundreds of feet below him, even when his wheels appeared to be within inches of an unprotected verge. Half a dozen times I was very frightened indeed.

I find it difficult to write of Ravello as it first appeared to me, since it so happened that I was to live there, off and on, over a long period of years. No glimpse of this hovered as we drove into the town. I hadn't in the remotest degree that sense, sometimes reported by imaginative persons in a similar situation, of immediate familiarity, of a mysterious presence whispering, 'Here you are; you're home; you've been here before'. The road up from Amalfi (we had hugged the coast, and so unnecessarily prolonged our route) was daunting even to Fish's car—a handleable little affair of an unobtrusively powerful sort. I was to see this track replaced by a splendidly engineered corkscrew highway equally hazardous only when taken at speed by motor-coaches the length of cruisers. In the little town itself builders and repairers were in various ways at work. It was observable that they weren't much interested in the *duomo*, which dominated one side of a sleepy square in that state of extreme but miraculously suspended dilapidation characteristic of Italian churches in general. Three *albergi* including our own, however, were being banged about at a great rate. There weren't any tourists, but *turismo* was already in the hopeful air. It was later going to come to something in

Ravello but not too disastrously much: just enough for an agreeable touch of imported prosperity and bustle. One may account among the few blessings of our age the fact that the new itinerant classes are so wedded to stepping straight from their hotels into the sea. That what they call the Med is no longer a wholly salubrious fluid in which to immerse oneself doesn't deter them in the slightest.

Fish and I, if incapable of elderly and atrabilious thoughts of this kind, were at least glad to get away from uproar suffered in the cause of art. Our hotel would have been quiet but for the workmen building an annex of hutch-like chambers in the garden; we ourselves had an ancient and enormous room the windows of which surveyed, across a deep ravine, a straggling small town demonstrably even less in the mainstream of life than Ravello itself. This was Scala, and it appeared to be by *scale* alone that these two places could communicate with one another except in some fashion unacceptably devious. We engaged in this odd sort of staircase mountaineering at once, and during the next few days pursued it obsessively all over the surrounding countryside. Aesthetic inquiry (although the pursuit of it through galleries is exhausting even to the young) had left a good many of our muscles unstretched.

It was literary inquiry that had brought us to Ravello, but here our researches for some time hung fire. A faded photograph of Lawrence, looking as if it had been clipped from a newspaper, was on display in the hall of the hotel; framed along with it was a scrap of typescript reiterating the reference to *Lady Chatterley's Lover*; the *pensiero*, on the other hand, didn't again appear.

However it may have been with Fish, I was myself quite impressed by this Lawrence business. It seemed to me beautifully strange that in the very room we now occupied Lawrence and Frieda might have slept at a time when all those fiery thoughts about Connie and her gamekeeper were beginning to stir in the novelist's head. For the first time in my young academic life I missed the Bodleian Library, in which an hour's rummaging would tell me whether there was anything in print about Lawrence staying in Ravello. But this thirst for know-ledge didn't make me pertinacious in personal inquiry, and Fish wasn't much good at it either. We'd have regarded it as very impertinent, for example, to ask to see the hotel register for 1926; and such parleyings as we did have with the manager (referred to impressively by Fish as the *albergatore*) were un-satisfactory. It was his daughter, it seemed, who coped with the English language, and his daughter was away from home. Having discovered that we were students, he assumed, very properly, that Italian ought not to be wholly beyond us; and when he discoursed on Lawrence it was in this flattering faith. We shamefully pretended to understand much more than we did, a phenomenon not uncommon among educated English-men abroad. He was clearly claiming to remember Lawrence vividly, which was colourable in view of the fact that Lawrence was so very rememberable a man. His other point seemed to be that the unrivalled scenic splendours commanded from the hotel, together perhaps with the perfection of its cuisine, had conduced to Lawrence's behaving in the manner of a *poeta inglese* of the most approved sort. At this point, indeed, words failed the *albergatore*, and he was constrained to mime the inspired bearing of his celebrated guest in a manner which might have been thought of as belonging to opera. Fish and I were much embarrassed by such extravagance, and offended by the extremely innocent commercial motive prompting it. Our investigation, therefore, came to a halt. Fish suggested that we should call on the *parroco*, as presumably the man of learning in Ravello, and beg his assistance. I objected that the author of *Lady Chatterley's Lover* was almost certainly ill-regarded by the clergy, and that our application might therefore be offensive to this simple and pious man. Fish (who carried an Italian dictionary) then substituted the *maestro di scuola* as a possible resource. We both knew perfectly well that these were impracticable notions, and that our range of personal acquaintance in Italy was not to extend beyond beggars, policemen, and waiters.

I am attached to Ravello and don't want to write a guide-book about it, but must here record that the environs run to two properties of superior consequence. The first, the Palazzo Rufolo, is one of the oldest houses of its kind still inhabited in Italy, and finds mention in *The Decameron* as the dwelling of a wealthy merchant of the region. Its garden, which is extremely beautiful to this day, is alleged in a local history to have prompted Wagner to write the music of Klingsor's Magic Garden in *Parsifal*. Lawrence is thus not the first genius who may be said to have drawn inspiration from this quite obscure little town.

The other big house, the Villa Cimbrone, isn't ancient at all, although it looks as ancient as a great deal of ingeniously incorporated mediaeval stonework and general knick-knackery can contrive. It is a folly built in the early years of the present century, with a standard eccentric nobleman, Lord Grimthorpe, at the bottom of it. Both houses have been in English, Scottish or American occupancy more often than not over a substantial period of time: a state of affairs obtaining in a notable number of such places throughout much of Italy. The gardens of both are furnished with stupendous views, and serve as pleasure-grounds for anybody prepared to pay a modest fee at the gate. Courting couples of the more substantial sort have frequent recourse to them.

Fish and I, although in fact remaining remarkably pleased with each other, had evolved without discussion a number of rules and conventions governing us as travelling companions. Now at one time of the day and now at another, we regularly parted for an hour or two and went our several ways. On our fifth evening in Ravello, which we had decided to make our last, this custom had taken me into the garden of the Rufolo and Fish into that of the Cimbrone—which is by much the larger of the two. I had found a niche still in sunshine (something which Ravello is rather short of at that time of day) and was more or less snoozing like a lizard when I heard a shout from without and looked up to find Fish gesturing at me through a wrought-iron railing. He seemed to have something of importance to communicate, but was indisposed to pay out a further 200 lire to join me.

'I've found it!' Fish shouted. 'You must go and look.'

'Found what?' I got reluctantly to my feet, and went over to stare at him as if he were an animal in a cage.

'The *pensiero*. It's carved on a stone seat in the Cimbrone, close to that Belvedere thing. We ought to have spotted it before. Come on out.'

I did as I was told, and we walked down a narrow lane which ran past our hotel.

'The place will be shutting up fairly soon,' Fish said. 'But you have plenty of time. Go straight through the garden and turn right.'

'Aren't you coming too?'

'Certainly not.' This was again a matter of 200 lire. Fish, like many people born to affluence, was chary of trifling disbursements. 'I'm going in to get a drink. Take a good look at the affair. Estimate its antiquity. Bill Stumps, his mark.'

Meditating this Pickwickian clue, I went on my way alone, clattered a bell at the entrance to the Cimbrone, and entered the garden. Here there was more sunshine than at the Rufolo, since the place is planted at the highest point of Ravello. Great shafts of light lay across the lawns in alternation with dark bars of shadow cast by ranked cypress trees, and here and there on these warmer spaces lovers lay entwined, star-scattered on the grass. I passed them briskly by, having a learned and improving occasion before me. The unsurprising formal garden, dotted with its prescriptive statuary and mildly terraced into a succession of level parterres elevated or depressed by a few feet each from the other, stretches interminably ahead and then vanishes abruptly into air; a few steps more, and one is on the brink of an appalling precipice, with nothing but the blank Mediterranean a thousand feet below. If one's head doesn't too hopelessly swim one may sometimes distinguish, twenty-five miles away, those temples at Paestum which had been commended to me by my father.

There is, it is true, a parapet of sorts, broad enough for the foolhardy to sit or lie on. At one point, moreover, a little set back from the verge, stands a classical structure of some elegance, within which one can rest less hazardously on a curved marble bench, while supporting one's back, if one is disposed, on the chilly shaft of one or another Ionic column. Here also there were lovers, I noticed in passing, since just visible between two pillars I had glimpsed on the bench two hands affectionately clasped. One seemed to be rather an elderly hand—but then in Italy quite mature couples will engage publicly in modest shows of affection. I walked on, and within a minute discovered the seat to which Fish had directed me. This was a simple affair in a rustic taste, and embellished with a verse inscription in a manner which I believe first became fashionable in the eighteenth century. The lettering wasn't as old as that, but old enough to be in several places barely legible. I read the familiar lines:

> *Lost to a world in which I crave no part,*
> *I sit alone and commune with my heart:*
> *Pleased with my little corner of the earth,*
> *Glad that I came, not sorry to depart.*

Fish had certainly advanced our inquiry—but in a fashion opening up a wide field for conjecture. Had Lord Grimthorpe's own Muse dictated these affecting lines? Or had he caused them to be transcribed out of some birthday album or keepsake book? Or were they really and truly by Lawrence, so that the hotel's mendacious-seeming blurb was entirely justified? Alternatively, what about that '*di*'? Foreign languages are profoundly treacherous, particularly when it comes to prepositions. Might *pensiero di D. H. Lawrence* mean something like 'a thought about D. H. Lawrence' or 'a poem which aptly comes to mind when the life and temperament of D. H. Lawrence are reflected upon'? I was much puzzled—and would have been more puzzled still had I then known that Lawrence, whether or not he had stayed at our hotel in 1926, certainly stayed in the

Cimbrone itself in the following year, when the villa was in the occupancy of some wandering Americans of his acquaintance.

But I wasn't, as it happened, further to bother my head with the problem of the lapidary poem—lapidary in the technical if not exactly the stylistic sense. Beginning to retrace my steps, it occurred to me to round the little temple-affair, and sit down for a moment to plumb the abyss and scan the sea. The affectionately disposed hands had vanished, so their owners, although they could scarcely have departed without my noticing the fact, were presumably not so passionately engaged as to resent intrusion. I obeyed my impulse, and was immediately confronted with an effect of the sort commonly compassed only within the cabinets of stage illusionists. The mature Italian married couple of my imagining had been spirited away. In their place sat Colonel Morrison and Mountjoy.

## XV

Recognitions and discoveries represent, according to Aristotle, mechanisms crucial in the fabricating of a successful drama, and I was one day to give a good deal of professional attention to them myself. But if it was recognition and discovery that were with some abruptness before me now, I was far from exercising the slightest command over them. I knew whom I was recognizing, indeed, but had no notion at all of what I was discovering.

There could be not a moment's doubt that some circumstance very extraordinary indeed was required to account for these two persons being thus revealed in close association in this remote locality. Although much has been written on the ties binding gentle and simple within the blood-kinship of the clan, it can scarcely be averred that social life in the Highlands of Scotland is organized upon strikingly democratic principles. Colonel Morrison was a laird, although not even a middling-grand one like Uncle Rory, and Mountjoy was Uncle Rory's servant, who couldn't possibly (for instance) address me as other than 'Mr Duncan'.

Clear about this, I was only for a moment otherwise at sea, after all. Or so I thought. I recalled—as I stood there, and the others still sat, poised crazily above the Gulf of Salerno—certain naïve yet surely basically shrewd speculations which I had entertained about the mysterious Mountjoy long ago. I had provided him with a most romantic illegitimacy—even tracing in his features the impress of that English monarch who had so merrily scattered his Maker's image o'er the land. This had been an absurdity, as had been the simpler notion that Mountjoy might be a Glencorry, and thus in some remote degree a kinsman of my own. (I remembered invoking this theory to account for the fact that he seemed to find me rather attractive.) My guesses had been within the target area, all the same. Mountjoy—those clasped hands proved it—was in Ravello with a father who was unable publicly to acknowledge his existence. I had concluded so much when Colonel Morrison broke our silence to utter, huskily but firmly, amazing words.

'Duncan, I need hardly say that this is deeply painful to me. I had no idea you might be in Ravello, and that I should thus offend you. It happens that I am attached to the place—and I believe Alec is becoming fond of it too.'

'It's awfully nice,' I mumbled. Revelation had come to me. 'I've never been here before.' Alec, I realized, must be Mountjoy; I had somehow failed ever to think of him as owning a Christian name. 'And it's awfully nice to run into you,' I said. 'Both.'

'My dear lad!' The husky voice of Colonel Morrison faltered. 'The fact is simply that we have been lent a house in Amalfi. By a very old friend. He might be known to you.'

'Dr Tindale,' I said quickly. 'As a matter of fact, I'm on his staircase.' I reflected that here was why the name of Amalfi had rung a bell in my head. At the same time I tried desperately to think of further words, for it seemed to me that Colonel Morrison was about to break down, and that this would make our embarrassing situation worse. But, for some moments, Colonel Morrison merely rambled.

'I always come up to Ravello. There's the view. And I think of dear Morgan. He adores the place.'

'Dear Morgan' meant nothing to me. I had at that time no knowledge that this was the right way in which to refer to E. M. Forster. I simply remembered the Colonel's foible for speaking of eminent literary persons in terms of familiar address, and guessed that here must be something like that.

'One of his first short stories was written and set in Ravello. It's called "The Story of a Panic".'

'Yes, of course.' Forster was one of the possessions of my generation, and I recalled the story at once. Its title might have fitted my own case at the moment. 'Lawrence was here too,' I said confusedly. 'I've just been looking into it.'

'I never met him.' Colonel Morrison had stood up. Alec Mountjoy remained seated, silent and staring out darkly over the Mediterranean. He was inscrutable. He might have been feeling that here was a major crisis. Or he might simply have been in a foul temper. Colonel Morrison I was admiring immensely. Without prevarication, he had come straight out with the thing, and he had maintained his dignity. I felt it was up to me to be forthright too.

'Sir,' I said, 'I'm perfectly reliable. I've been a bit thick. But I'm that.'

'You rather showed it during Anna's trouble.' Mountjoy broke in with this, rather to my surprise. The words had come from him with his intermittent gentleman's air, and he stood up as he uttered them. 'Look, Arthur,' he said, 'I'm going to get this bus. You'll want to talk to Duncan. And there's another bus down at eight.'

'Perhaps that will be best, Alec.' Not very steadily, Colonel Morrison put out a hand, and for a moment two hands again touched. I hadn't got over this—for I found it very moving—when I realized that Alec Mountjoy had gone, striding away between the cypresses in the direction of Lord Grimthorpe's idiotic folly and the town.

'Sit down, Duncan,' Colonel Morrison said. He was once more, and to my immense relief, the kindly older man.

'Does it mean that it's more or less over in Glencorry?' I asked presently. I was still keyed up to bear myself properly. It seemed the only wish of my life. But in face of this strange and somehow touching situation I was beginning to feel curiosity as well.

'More or less. In fact, yes.' Colonel Morrison spoke sadly but without self-pity. He held out his hands in front of him, palms downward, in an odd gesture. They were almost an old man's hands. 'And a meeting like this sets a thing in a clearer light. It shows me the future, really. You see, this isn't—well, simply an affair.'

'No, of course not.' I paused awkwardly. 'I did just hear from my father that matters weren't too good at Corry. And Ninian and I haven't been invited there this summer. That's why I'm in Italy, in a way.'

'Anna is quite all right, you know.' Colonel Morrison said this anxiously. 'Of course young Petrie jumped the gun, and all that. But he's a perfectly decent lad. However, the affair upset Ruth. And that upset things generally.' The Colonel appeared to struggle for some succinct expression. 'There was a changed situation.'

'I see.' I wasn't very sure I did see. But I remembered how these two men—lovers then, it was to be supposed—had obscurely panicked before the unsettled courses of my cousins. Their reasons had been nonsensical, but perhaps their instinct had been sound. It looked as if Ruth, without much under- standing of what she was about, had found a release from frustration in mucking something up. I wanted to elucidate this. 'Just how did it take Ruth?' I asked.

'I suppose she looked around, and felt there was only Alec. So she threw herself at his head, you might say. Awkward. Made things untenable. There were discoveries, disclosures.'

'She thought she was in love with him?' I stared at Colonel Morrison round-eyed.

'We mustn't say it *wasn't* love.' The Colonel was smiling at me. 'It was a great pity, you know, that Ruth could never get away from the place.'

'It was certainly that.' Ruth, I felt, had behaved idiotically, but it was still a shame that she had set her cap at so hopeless a mark. It remained this, whatever further and obscure promptings had conduced to the whole small catastrophe. I remembered guiltily my undertaking to invite her to Oxford and submerge her in the society of returned warriors. But there had scarcely been time for anything of the kind. 'The whole thing got out of hand?'

'Not sensationally.' Colonel Morrison smiled again. 'Alec

had his month's holiday coming along, and of course it's known that I travel a little from time to time. So it was possible to ease ourselves out unobtrusively. I discussed it all with your uncle.'

'You discussed it with Uncle Rory?' This thought dumb-founded me. 'And with Aunt Charlotte too?'

'Not with your aunt, Duncan. One can't quite take up these matters with ladies. Man-to-man is different. Your uncle was fortunately quite all right at the time. A bit at odds with the duke, but not on about that unfortunate standing army. It has been a most regrettable aberration, that.'

'Yes, it has.' The notion of that man-to-man talk took me utterly out of my depth. I held the common belief of my generation that the very existence of sexual deviations had never been revealed to our innocent forbears. 'So you and Uncle Rory quietly worked something out?'

'That expresses it very well. A cover story, as they now say. Of course, it's exile that it comes to. One can't blink that. But do you know, Duncan? It seemed almost simple at the time. A sense of relief, too. Things becoming less covert, I suppose. Naturally there are certain problems. There must be. I see that now. Alec sees it. It's true that money happens not to be a difficulty. If one owns property one can always have a little money follow one around. But we all know that money isn't everything. It isn't everything, by a long way. There's the business of any sort of place in the world. And Alec likes a little society—particularly young fellows of his own age.'

'I suppose he does,' I said. 'Or younger.'

'Yes, yes—you understand what I mean. But he and I are very solid, absolutely together. Still, one has to think a little. One has to try to think ahead. A sudden meeting like ours now —which has been delightful in a way that's utterly due to your way of taking it, my dear boy—somehow a little brings it home.' Colonel Morrison paused, as if this last word had reverberated in his mind. 'I'm rather fond of Scotland,' he said. 'I expect you are too.'

Fish, hungry for dinner, was sprawled on his bed next to mine, once more idly turning over the pages of *Lady Chatterley's Lover*.

'Christ, you've been the hell of a time,' he said. 'We'd better get down to that eternal vitello. Have you solved the problem?'

'Solved the problem?' I stared at Fish blankly. 'Oh, that! No.'

'Then forget it. I say! There's an absurd bit here. Mellors blows his top to Connie about all the ghastly things that have happened to him in bed. He says that pretty well all women are Lesbians. And Connie says, "You do seem to have had awful experiences of women." And Mellors——'

'Martin,' I said, 'do you mind? Just belt up.'

'And why the hell should I belt up?' For a moment Fish was indignant—and fairly enough. Then he gave me a quick look. 'Oh, all right,' he said. And he tossed our bedtime reading into his suitcase.